No Doubt in My Mind

Sheila Solomon Shotwell

Monday, Monday Words and Music by John Phillips Copyright ©1966 UNIVERSAL MUSIC CORP. Copyright Renewed. All Rights Reserved. Used by permission. *Reprinted by Permission of Hal Leonard LLC.*

Petals, and **I Can't Believe in Love Anymore** by The SoulBenders, 1967-68. Used by permission of Aris Hampers.

Wild Orphan from *Howl and Other Poems*, by Allen Ginsberg Copyright ©1956 Copyright Renewed. All Rights Reserved. *Reprinted by permission of Harper Collins.*

Carnival of Souls (1962) is in the Public Domain.

No Doubt in my Mind
Sheila Solomon Shotwell
ISBN 978-0-9994225-3-3
©2018 Sheila Solomon Shotwell. All Rights Reserved.

Visit the authors website at www.sheilasolomonshotwell.com or find her on Facebook.

For Gerald Michael Driscoll (1946 – 2004)
and for all the gay men who enrich our lives, families, and world.

The way in, is the way out.

Chapter One

"Maureen, I have to warn you," I said. "You might be bored half the time we're there. We'll have to eat at my grandma's and go shopping with Aunt Dorothy, and I know my dad will drag me to Wally's Pharmacy, so he can show him my psoriasis." I twirled the phone cord around my index finger, even though Renee yelled at me almost every day for doing it. Ruff, my Siamese cat, was washing his face next to me on the window seat and his brother, Reddy, was sprawled in the window, trying to catch a breeze.

"Bored? Are you kidding, Ruth Ann? I can't wait to go. No matter what, we'll have fun. Especially since we get to find out if your dad's been pulling your leg all this time. Oops, no pun intended."

"You're too funny. Hey, I gotta go. My mom and Renee will be home from work soon and I haven't done half of what I was supposed to do. I'll call you later." I hung up the phone and headed out the back door to get the laundry off the line. Cathy and her mom were just pulling into their driveway.

"Hey there, Ruth Ann," Mrs. Cicerelli called over to me. "Did you get your packing done?"

"Not all of it. I was waiting for some of this stuff to get dry." I pulled the clothespins off my shorts and folded them into the basket. If it wasn't too hot in Saginaw, maybe I'd wear them with tights. I hadn't worn them since the day of the tornado alert. The day I saw my boyfriend, Tom, kissing evil Leta at the park.

Cathy walked over to the fence between our yards. She was holding a bag of groceries with a bunch of celery sticking out of the top.

"Hi," she said. "You really didn't pack yet? Aren't you leaving in the morning?" The main thing that still bugged me about Cathy was all the questions she asked. In some ways, it seemed like she'd gotten more mature. But in other ways, she was just the same.

"Are you really gonna be able to see it?" She looked over her shoulder at her mom, who was closing the trunk.

"Get over here and help me, Cathy."

"Okay, Mom. Just a minute."

"See what?" I asked, even though I knew exactly what she was talking about.

For some reason, Cathy had a way of bringing out the brat in me.

"The leg! What else?"

"Oh yeah, I guess so. If there really *is* a leg."

"Your dad always said so, didn't he?"

"Caterina! I won't ask you again!"

Cathy marched right over to the car. That was Mrs. Cicerelli's "point the butcher knife at you" voice. She didn't use it very often, but when she did, everyone paid attention. I heard her say once that her temper was worse when Aunt Florence came every month. It took me a whole year after we moved to the neighborhood to figure out that Aunt Florence was her period.

No Doubt in my Mind

I carried the laundry basket into the house and thought about the leg.
What if it wasn't true? My dad was pretty famous for his practical jokes.
He loved to do stuff like put fake barf on the floor when he knew
somebody with a weak stomach was coming over. Ever since fourth grade,
I'd been telling my friends there was a woman's leg in my dad's
basement.

*"Jiminy Christmas, Sport, you won't believe it when I tell you what I
found in the basement."*

"What'd you find, Daddy?"

*"I was reachin' up on the rafters in the workroom 'cause I needed
some sandpaper. I'd seen a box of it up there a couple months ago. Old
Doc Warner stores all kinds of stuff down there and I didn't think he'd
care if I borrowed a little sandpaper."*

"Is Doc Warner the guy whose office is under your apartment?"

*"Yeah, he's a nice enough guy, keeps to himself mostly. Well, anyway,
here I am, Sport, reachin' around over my head. Next thing I know I grab
hold of somethin' that just gives me the willies. So, I dragged a stool over,
climbed up and took a look. I thought I was seeing things, especially
'cause the light's not so good in that room. I took hold of it, brought it
down and set it on the work table. And for cryin' out loud, if it wasn't a
woman's leg. A fresh woman's leg, no kidding."*

*"Uh-uh Daddy, you're telling a fib. There was not a woman's leg.
This is another joke like the rubber dog poop you put in Aunt Dorothy's*

bed."

> *"Sport, I am telling you the God's honest truth."*
> *"If it's true, where did it come from?"*
> *"You got me. I figure the doc had to put it up there. Who else?"*

Now that I was going into high school, my mom had finally given in. Instead of staying at my grandma's house like I'd always done when I went to Saginaw, I would be staying at my dad's apartment over the doctor's office. The best part was that Maureen was going with me, and my friend Mimi, who lives in Saginaw, would be coming back with us to Grand Rapids to stay for ten days.

Looking forward to visiting my dad had helped me to get through July. June had been such a bad month that I wanted to erase it from my memory forever. I didn't go to the park for three days after I saw Tom kissing Leta. I stayed home and took sun baths in the back yard to try and help my psoriasis. After being cooped up for ten days on the St. Anthony's pediatric floor, it felt good to be in the fresh air. I finished reading *Margorie Morningstar* when I sunbathed by myself, and when Maureen was over, we talked and listened to the radio.

At least I got back at Tom a little bit because a boy from South High started liking me the first day I went back to the park. I had finished my chores, then decided to head over to the cement block by Garfield Pool to meet up with the other Tandem Riders. We were kind of an unofficial club that formed in the beginning of eighth grade, and that summer, the giant cement block was our unofficial hangout place. We climbed up on it and sat for hours but didn't even know what it was for. Angela said the pipes for the pool were inside it. Her dad's an engineer, so she's always gave us facts that we believed, no matter what.

Two boys from South High came by with their tennis rackets. They stopped to talk to us and it was so cool because we'd been watching them. They stood around talking about all kinds of stuff, and then they said good-bye. After they walked away, Donnie, the cutest one, turned back to us.

"You are so pretty. What's your name again?"

It seemed like he was looking at me, but I knew that wasn't possible, so I looked to my right at Mary Lou and to Peg on the left. Peg elbowed me in the ribs and then he walked back toward us.

"Her name is Ruth Ann," Peg said.

"Well, Ruth Ann," he said, "I don't think you know how pretty you are and that makes you prettier. Are you coming back to the park tonight?"

"I think so."

Peg elbowed me again, and somebody jabbed my back with a finger. I felt like I was dreaming, and somebody was trying to wake me up.

"She'll be back tonight," Maureen piped up.

Donnie smiled and his dimples almost caved right into his tanned face. He and his friend walked away and as soon as they were out of earshot, the girls started squealing. All the girls except Mary Lou. She was looking at me as if she had never seen me before. I knew she was thinking about the terrible psoriasis under my clothes, my unruly hair that caused me so much grief, and the jeans and blouse that I practically lived in, so I could hide my skin. I was thinking about all the same bad parts of myself. Then I wondered if it was a trick. Somebody must have put him up to it.

When I went to the park that night, Donnie and I sat on the steps of the community center and talked for two hours. He told me all about his big family and the sports he played, but he asked me lots of questions, too. When it got dark we lay down on the grass and looked at the stars. He pointed out the Big Dipper and the Little Dipper.

"If we had a small telescope, or even binoculars," he said, "We might be able to see Draco, the dragon. I think it's only visible in July."

I turned onto my side and started pulling grass out of the ground. I wondered why he didn't kiss me and that made me want him to. Tom would have been trying to unbutton my blouse by now. Maybe it was because I was two years younger than him or maybe he had looked at me a lot closer and realized that he had been crazy to say I was pretty.

Donnie eventually kissed me a few days later, and he acted like I was his girlfriend for two weeks, holding my hand and telling me I was pretty, even though I ran around in my kooky cover-up clothes, while the other girls wore sleeveless shells and matching print shorts.

Cathy swooned whenever I mentioned him, and she always compared it to *A Summer Song* by Chad and Jeremy. Of course, she would think that, since it was one of the only records she'd ever bought. I didn't have the heart to tell her the real reason we broke up. The two hippie girls from

Burton School told me that Donnie's girlfriend, Jolene, was coming back
from camping in Montana and was most likely "going to kick my ass."

As it turned out, I got some dirty looks from Jolene and her friends,
but that was it. I saw Donnie with his arm around her a couple of days
after she got back, and I didn't even feel bad. It was like Cinderella going
back to wearing rags, but like Cinderella, at least I'd been picked. Even if
it was just for a short time.

It was a different story with Tom. We'd had the romance of the year
all through eighth grade. And now, we hadn't talked once since the day of
our graduation party. Every time I thought about that damn party, I wanted
to die. Whenever I heard the song, *Hurts So Bad*, I felt like I could have
written it.

But at least Maureen and the other Tandem Riders still liked me. In
fact, ever since Donnie had paid two weeks of attention to me, even Mary
Lou seemed to like me. She sat by me on purpose on the cement block,
asked me what my favorite songs were this summer, and wanted to know
if she could borrow *Marjorie Morningstar*. It was hard to believe since
she'd been so mean for most of eighth grade. I think her brother dying in
Vietnam had changed her too. Even with a picket fence and perfect
ponytail, something bad can happen to you.

"Getting out of town is just what I need," I said to myself while I
stuffed my days of the week underwear into the pouch of my paisley
suitcase. It was the underwear I'd gotten for Christmas along with the
guitar I didn't want, which turned out to be a good thing. If I hadn't

received the guitar, I never would have met my guitar teacher, Pete, who was one of the nicest guys I'd ever known. I got a lump in my throat when I thought of him visiting me in the hospital. He was the only person with psoriasis that I'd met since I got it myself, last fall. Maybe I'd go back to Pete for a few more lessons when I got back from Saginaw.

"Ruth Ann, turn that music down!"

I turned around to see my mom standing in the doorway. I guess the music was loud, because I didn't even know she was home from work.

"What'd you do all day, go on that beep-line? The dishes aren't put away, the front porch isn't swept, and your stuff is everywhere. It's a good thing Renee isn't home yet."

Chapter Two

"You really didn't see who was driving?" Maureen asked. I shook my head.

"Well, whoever it was, he didn't drive down your street by accident. Tom must have told him to. Maybe it wasn't the first time. You're not always out sweeping the steps."

We were ten minutes from Lansing, where our bus was headed next. The bus to Saginaw wouldn't be leaving for over an hour, so we decided to eat lunch and look around near the station.

It was a very hot day, even for late July. Maureen was wearing a blue flowered baby-doll dress and sandals. I was wearing a sleeveless top with jeans. The psoriasis on my arms wasn't gone, but the patches were smaller than they had been a month ago, so I figured I'd be brave and go without sleeves.

We exited the bus station and stood on the corner looking around. There was a cafe across the street and a couple of small shops.

"Hey, girls, want a ride?" A teen-age boy hollered out the window of a car as he drove past us.

"How 'bout that? Maureen said. "Boys in Lansing are bigger flirts than boys in Grand Rapids."

"I think your mini-dress would bring the flirts out in any town," I said as I elbowed Maureen's side.

We walked a few blocks before picking out a lunch spot. Rounding a corner, we spotted a gorgeous department store called Knapp's, and couldn't resist going in. It was great fun roaming around in a strange store in a strange city. Maureen bought a pair of yellow and white striped sunglasses. I was tempted to buy several things but forced myself to hold out since I didn't have much spending money. Babysitting jobs had been scarce so far this summer.

"Oh no. We're gonna miss our bus," Maureen said as she pointed to the clock by the elevator.

We realized that we'd have to skip lunch, so we grabbed bags of potato chips at the bus station snack counter and boarded the bus just in time.

"I love hanging out with you, 'cause you're always up for an adventure," Maureen said as she opened her potato chip bag with her teeth.

I guess she thought shopping in Lansing was an adventure.

"Just think of this as an adventure, Ruth Ann. You've got your Tiny Tears doll and I packed a couple of your favorite books. C'mon now, let's get in the car."

"What about my bed, Mama? Don't we need to bring my bed?"

"No, honey. There's a bed in the apartment. You and Renee will share it. She's coming there right after school."

"Why aren't we telling Daddy? Can't he come to the apartment? Is it because he has a girlfriend? I heard Renee say he has a girlfriend."

I saw my dad as soon as we pulled into the Saginaw bus station. He was holding a cigar between his fingers and talking to a cab driver. The cab driver threw his head back laughing at something my dad said.

"Good old Dad," I said to Maureen. "I swear he knows almost everyone in this city and it's bigger than you'd think."

"Is that because of his car lot?" Maureen asked.

"He also had a TV repair and pawn shop when I was younger and was the only white guy around there, so he has tons of black friends too."

"That is so cool. Get me out there to meet him." My dad lifted me off the ground when he hugged me. Then he messed my hair up with the hand that wasn't holding the cigar.

"Nice to finally meet you, Marlene," he said.

"Maureen, Dad. Not Marlene."

"Okay sure, *Maureen*," he said. "Dorothy and Grandma can't wait to see you, so we're going there first."

He put our suitcases into the trunk of a copper colored Mercury and waved at the cab driver. "Take 'er easy, now, Leroy."

We pulled up to the big Victorian house on Tuscola Street and Grandma was already on the front porch in a flowered house dress and apron. She was smiling and waving at the car as she opened up the front door and hollered inside. Aunt Dorothy came out with her hair up in pin-curls. She was wearing a hot pink house coat and matching slippers with pon-pons. Aunt Dorothy never gets dressed unless she's going somewhere. But when she goes somewhere, even to her secretary job, she always wears a girdle, high heels and lots of perfume.

We all went into the kitchen, and Grandma offered us chopped liver and Tam Tam crackers. There was pickled herring in a dish and bagels.

"Eat, eat," Grandma said. "It's a long trip all the way from Grand Rapids. Danny, get the girls a cold Vernors from the ice box."

They liked Maureen right away because she tried everything. Even the herring. I couldn't tell if she was just being nice, or if she really liked it. Since we'd missed lunch, we were both starved.

"Your girlfriend, she has a good appetite," Grandma said. "This one used to eat like a bird," she said pointing at me "Now, she's bigger, she eats better." When I was a little kid, Grandma told everyone I ate like a bird. The main reason was that I always hit the candy dish on the coffee table as soon as I got to her house. I'd be too full of M&Ms to eat her roast chicken and kugel.

We sat with Grandma on the porch swing, while my dad fixed a leaky faucet and replaced a light bulb on the kitchen ceiling. Then we headed over to my dad's apartment and parked in the doctor's office parking lot, since my dad's place was upstairs. Wilma, my dad's wife, was talking on the telephone when we walked into the living room. She was tapping her cigarette ash into a chartreuse boomerang ashtray on the coffee table.

"I have to go, Fern," she said. "Danny just walked in with his daughter and her friend. I'll call you tomorrow."

Wilma walked over to me and gave me a kiss on the cheek. She was wearing very short shorts, and an orange blouse that was tied at her waist.

"Marlene, it's so good to meet you," she said.

I didn't bother to correct her. I just looked at Maureen and shrugged.

"Danny, be a doll and make me a martini. I'll show the girls to their room."

We followed her into the guest room that overlooked two busy streets. The building was on a corner and there was lots of traffic outside. We put our stuff in the drawers and turned the turquoise clock radio on to the cool local station. Maureen flopped down on the bed with her arms over her head.

"This is my favorite song lately," she said.

I flopped down next to her and together, we sang every word of *I Love You* by the band, People. When we opened our eyes, I saw my dad standing in the door with a giant grin on his face.

"If you crooners are done, I've got the shoestring potatoes in the french fryer. Come on out to the kitchen and keep me company."

We followed my dad into the kitchen where grease was crackling. There was a salad on the table and a basket of fried shrimp. Wilma was dropping an olive into her martini, and my dad walked over to the sink to drain the corn on the cob.

"Wow, this looks great," Maureen said. "How can we help?"

I figured Maureen would be a fun person to bring to Saginaw, but I hadn't thought about how she'd act around the adults. I could tell everybody liked her, so I was even more glad that I'd brought her. The food was delicious. I'd been thinking about my dad's homemade french fries for months. As usual, Wilma barely ate a thing. She smoked and sipped her martini. "Hey Dad, when are you going to show us the leg? *Remember, you promised.*"

"Oh Danny," Wilma said. "You are not dragging that thing up here again, hear me?"

"I'll take you and Marlene to the basement tomorrow, Sport. Doc never shows up here on Sundays."

"For real, Dad? You brought it up *here*?"

"Yeah, I had a poker party here in the kitchen a few months back when Wilma was out with her sister. McNalley bet me fifty bucks there was no leg for me to show, so I brought the damn thing up here. Went to bed and left it in the middle of the table, then woke up to Wilma screamin' at two o'clock in the morning."

"Eww, Dad! This table?" Maureen and I both slid our chairs back.

"Don't worry, I had it on a bunch of newspapers."

"Well, I made him get right out of bed and take it back down to the basement," Wilma said.

After dinner, we watched *The Dating Game,* and *The Newlyweds.* My dad made so many crazy comments through both shows that we were weak from laughter. I thought about how I hardly ever laugh at home, and then I sat up from leaning against Maureen.

"Oh no. I forgot to call my mom," I said. "She wanted me to call her as soon as I got here."

"Well, go ahead and call her right now," my dad said, handing me the receiver.

"She's gonna kill me. We've been here for hours. I can't believe I forgot."

I dialed my house in Grand Rapids. It only rang once, and Renee picked up.

"Well, if it isn't her highness," Renee said. "How very kind of you to remember that your mother might possibly be worried sick."

"Just put Mom on the phone, Renee."

"I guess she's still alive, after all," Renee called to my mom.

"Thanks a lot for thinking of me, Ruth Ann," she said. I could tell my mom was furious that I'd forgotten to call her because she was only sarcastic when she was mad. Then Renee picked up the upstairs extension phone. "Oh, by the way, I thought you might be interested to know that creepy boyfriend called you."

"What creepy boyfriend?"

"That kid who gave you Ambush cologne for Christmas. Whatever his name was."

"You mean Tom? He called? What did you tell him?"

"What do you think I told him? I said you weren't here.

Chapter Three

"He's trying to get back with you. I know he is," Maureen whispered.

"I don't know. Maybe Renee was making it up."

"Yeah, I might think that too, if he hadn't driven by your house yesterday."

We were in bed with our heads right under the window. The traffic outside was quieter than before, but still pretty steady. My dad had put a fan on the dresser and we had my transistor radio propped in the window. The song, *You Keep Me Hangin' On* by Vanilla Fudge was playing.

"Boy if that ain't the truth," I said.

I turned over on my stomach and looked out the window as a convertible sped by.

"I don't know Maureen, maybe I should just forget about him. What do you think?"

"I wish I knew the right answer, sweetie. He used to be so nice."

"Or so we thought," I said and flopped over on my back.

My dad made silver dollar pancakes for breakfast. Wilma kept the newspaper in front of her face, unless she took a drink from her coffee cup.

"So wadda ya say, crooners? How 'bout we take the boat out and have a picnic on Ojibway Island today? We'll get Ma to pack us a picnic and maybe she and Dot will come with us." He pulled down on the top of Wilma's newspaper. "Sound good, Willie?"

"Danny, it's too early for chit-chat. Give me a few, would you?"

"Dad, we have prior plans, remember?" I asked.

"Prior plans?" My dad fluttered his eyelashes.

"The leg, Dad. The leg! Come on, don't act like you've forgotten."

"You crooners really wanna see that damn thing?"

"Yes!" we both answered at the same time.

My dad dried his hands on the dish towel he had draped over his shoulder.

"Well, let's go down there right now. We'll clean this up after. I need a screw driver from down there anyway. Last time I took the boat out, the door on the cupboard was loose."

We followed my dad down the stairs from his apartment, through a door in the foyer, and down some other stairs that led to the basement.

"Now where the hell is that light switch?" my dad asked. "I can never find it. You girls wait here while I get a flashlight." We heard him walk away and a shiver ran up my spine.

"Cut that out, Dad! Don't you dare leave us here."

I could hear him snickering. He flicked on a switch and the room lit up. It looked like an ordinary basement. Emptier than most, and very clean. The floor was painted gray and there were green striped curtains covering the windows. I had expected it to look more like a dungeon.

"Follow me," my dad said as he walked toward a wide door made of rough wood. He turned the knob and then I heard him pull on a chain. A florescent light flickered on over a large work table in the middle of the room. The table was made of the same rough wood as the door. My dad climbed on a metal stool and reached up to some rafters on the ceiling.

"You know, this doesn't look anything like it did when I first found it. What was that, five years ago? Back then, it was as fresh and pink as a baby's leg."

He slid his hands under something wrapped in brown paper. Then he climbed back down and set the bundle on the table.

"Okay, you crooners, have at it. I'm gonna look for that screwdriver in the other room."

Maureen's eyebrows were two inches higher than usual. "Should we just unwrap it?"

"Oh, for cryin' out loud." My dad rolled his cigar from one side of his mouth to the other, as he pulled open the brown paper.

And there it was. A withered, leathery column with a human foot, ankle, and knobby bone sticking right out of the top.

"Holy cow! It looks like a giant, dried up chicken leg," I said.

"You're right," Maureen said. "It does. It looks ancient. Almost like a mummy's leg. But where do you think it came from, Mr. Bloomfield? Mr. Bloomfield?" She turned her head toward the door. "Ruth Ann, where'd your dad go?"

I walked to the door and looked into the other room, and then I noticed a small desk by the furnace. Next thing I knew, I was shoving the desk against the closed door to block Maureen from coming out. I knew it was a sneaky trick to play on my friend, but for some reason, I couldn't stop myself.

"Ruth Ann Bloomfield, don't you dare lock me in here with this thing! Open this door! Right now!" She pounded on the door four times. "Do you hear me? Open this damn door!"

"Boy oh boy," my dad said, as he came out of a corner room with a screwdriver. "If you aren't a chip off the old block, I don't who is."

I shoved the desk back and opened the door. Maureen's face was bright red. "You little brat, what were you trying to pull?"

In spite of her words, she was laughing as hard as I was.

"You just wait. I'll get you back for that one!"

"You were in there less than a minute," I said. "Maybe thirty seconds. But it was just too tempting. I couldn't resist."

We were breathless from laughing by the time my dad had the leg wrapped in the brown paper. He chuckled.

"You sure you don't wanna take this on our picnic today? We could get all kinds of mileage with it. I bet we could even get your Aunt Dot to run in her high heels, Sport."

Maureen and I headed toward the stairs while my dad turned out the lights. When we passed the door to the doctor's office, Maureen whispered, "Why in the world would this doctor have that leg, anyway?"

"Who knows? Like I said, my dad has lots of friends, but my mom says most of them are shady characters."

"Well, you sure were right about him being funny. I haven't laughed this much all summer."

We were cruising down the Saginaw River on my dad's boat, less than two hours later.

"What a perfect day for a boat ride," Maureen said. "I'm so glad your dad thought of this."

"I know. And I'm really glad my grandma and aunt decided to come," I said as I turned around and waved at Aunt Dorothy who was sitting on a deck chair. She was wearing a flowered sundress and matching sandals with wedge heels. Her hair was covered with a chiffon scarf that matched her turquoise sunglasses. Grandma was inside the cabin because she said the deck was too breezy.

"How'd your dad come up with naming the boat, *The Whole Megillah*, anyway?"

"I guess it's some Jewish holiday thing," I said. "I don't know. But wait until you see Ojibway Island. It's the park we always went to when I was a little kid. Back when I lived here, they put in a new playground that was really cool. The climbing toys all looked like spaceships and rockets. I'll show you when we get there."

"Does your stepmother ever do stuff with your grandma and aunt?"

"Stepmother? You mean Wilma? Oh gee, I guess she is my stepmother. I never thought of her that way."

"I can see why you don't," Maureen said. "She's not very motherly, that's for sure."

"You know, I don't think I *have* ever seen her around Grandma or Aunt Dorothy now that you mention it."

My dad pulled the boat up to a dock at Ojibway Island and we set our picnic up on a table right on the river bank. Aunt Dorothy put newspapers on the benches for us to sit on, which Maureen thought was pretty funny.

"This is the best fried chicken I've ever had, Mrs. Bloomfield," Maureen said as she took a second drumstick.

"Danny, give her another pickle," Grandma said.

That was my grandma's way of saying thank you.

Right after we ate, my dad wanted everyone to get back on the boat. I figured he was worried Wilma wouldn't like it if we stayed away too long. I talked him into letting me and Maureen check out the playground first. We ran over to the other side of the narrow park and I was relieved that the space-age toys were still there. The closer we got to it, I could see it looked kind of shabby. The paint on the flying saucer had chipped and faded, and the space capsule was much smaller than I remembered. We climbed inside of it and shared a Winston. Maureen blew smoke rings that almost made it out of the top.

"I still can't believe I finally saw the leg," I said as we walked back.

"Yeah, that was so creepy, it felt like a dream."

"What should we do tomorrow? We'll have the whole apartment all to ourselves."

"I don't know. What do you want to do?"

"We could walk downtown and check out the stores."

"Okay, that sounds fun. Let me ask you something. Has your dad ever asked you to come live here?"

"He's mentioned it once or twice. I doubt it would fly with Wilma, though."

"Hmm. That's too bad. Would you consider it, otherwise?"

"No, I couldn't do that to my mom. She's practically sacrificed her whole life for me."

"Hey, you crooners," my dad shouted. "Get a move on. Your grandma's been on the boat for fifteen minutes already."

On the way back, we hung out on the double bed in the boat's little knotty-pine bedroom.

"It's so cozy in here," Maureen said." The way the walls just wrap around the bed."

"This whole thing used to be a trailer. My dad put it on the pontoons."

"Wow, that is so cool."

I switched on my transistor radio and the song, *Time Has Come Today* was playing.

We both stretched our legs over our heads, so our toes touched the wall behind the bed.

"What do you think this song really means?" Maureen asked.

"I'm not sure. Maybe they're talking about kids like us getting older."

"It's kind of scary, isn't it?"

"You mean getting older?" I asked, thinking about us smoking at my old playground, which had felt kind of strange to me, but I didn't want Maureen to know.

"Yeah, I guess I mean that. You know, high school and stuff. And the world is pretty messed up right now."

I lowered my legs and looked at the knotty-pine ceiling.

"Things *are* pretty messed up *and* scary. *And* confusing. I bet that is what the song is trying to say."

Maureen sat up on the edge of the bed. "Hey, I know what I want to do tomorrow."

"What?"

"Summer Blonde. You know, that stuff that's always on commercials. It's exactly what I need. I need to be a summer blonde."

Chapter Four

"Just in case you ever wake up, here's some orange juice."

I opened my eyes and saw a Flintstones glass filled with juice, on the nightstand. I sat up and stretched my arms over my head. Maureen was looking out the window.

"There's a drug store on the other side of the parking lot. Do you think they have Summer Blonde there?"

I drank the juice before answering. "I don't know. Maybe. Let's go over and check. How long have you been up? I didn't mean to sleep so late."

"It's okay. They have different reruns here. I just watched *My Little Margie*. Remember that show? Hey, there's blueberry Pop-Tarts. Want one?"

We walked around the corner and Maureen bought Summer Blonde and the back-to-school issue of *Seventeen Magazine*. I wasn't in the mood for thinking about school yet. We were barely into August. When we got back to the apartment building, patients were entering the door ahead of us to see Dr. Warner.

"Boy, oh boy," Maureen said. "I wonder what they'd all say if we gave them a tour of the basement."

"No kidding. They'd be peeling out of this parking lot in no time."

I read the Summer Blonde directions out loud while Maureen smoked a Winston.

"This'll be easy," she said. "After all, it's just a hint of blonde. Like the commercial says. It's just supposed to look like you go to the beach all the time."

We followed the directions exactly like it said on the box. While we waited for the color to take we looked through the magazine.

"Wow, these knit sweater-dress things are really in," Maureen said. "I'm not sure if I love 'em or hate 'em."

"All I know is that they look hot as hell today. It's time to rinse your hair. Come on."

Instead of looking like she went to the beach, Maureen's hair looked like the rusty nails we had in a coffee can in the garage. I could tell she was close to tears.

"Oh my God, Ruth Ann, what was I thinking? You have to go back and get brown dye to fix it."

"By myself? I don't have a clue what color to pick out. Can't you wear a scarf and come with me?"

The sign above the hair color section said, "Does She or Doesn't She?" Nobody would have to ask that question if they'd looked under Maureen's scarf. We picked up every shade of brown three times before settling on Coco Loco. Maureen was a definite brunette when we got done. A darker brunette than she had been, but at least there was no hint of orange.

"I guess I'll never find out if blondes have more fun," she said into the mirror. "Uh-oh. Look at this towel. What should we do?"

The beige bath towel closest to the sink, had three dark stains on it.

"I think we should get rid of it," I said. "I doubt my dad would say anything to my mom, but if he did, she wouldn't let me stay here again. In fact, she'd probably blame Wilma for your hair. We better not mention anything about this."

"Won't they notice that my hair is way darker?"

I shook my head. "Let's hope not."

"Give me the towel and the boxes," Maureen said. "I'll find a trash can outside."

She wrapped the boxes into the towel and left. I cleaned the sink with Ajax and blotted the walls with a sponge. Maureen came back a few minutes later.

"What took you so long?"

"I couldn't find a trash can."

"Where's the stuff?"

"I walked down the alley and threw it over the fence. And you know what? I think your idea was better."

"What idea?"

"To go downtown today. My Summer Blonde idea was really dumb."

"Oh well, let's just think of it as an experiment. And we can still go downtown."

"Hey, yeah," Maureen said. "We could have entered my head in the eighth-grade science fair. Thank God, we're done with that. Okay, let's go downtown, but I'm changing clothes 'cause it's even hotter outside than before."

I got my shorts out and put them on with the tights. I felt a lump in my throat when I looked at Maureen in her baby-doll mini dress. I sat on the edge of the bed and let the fan blow right on me.

"What's the matter?"

I peeled off my shorts and tights. The psoriasis on my legs was way better than before I went in the hospital, but it was still pretty bad.

"Would you be mortified if I didn't wear these tights?"

"Me mortified? Of course not. I think you'd be crazy to wear those tights today. First of all, it's hotter than hell out there. Like you said. And second of all, your legs are much better than they were."

We crossed the bridge from the west side of the river toward downtown with my bare legs right out in the open.

"Maybe it is better that I try this here, before I do it at home," I said as I looked down at my legs.

A carload of boys hollered out the window to us.

"There goes that baby-doll dress again," I said.

It was fun to show the Saginaw department stores to Maureen. We tried on summer clearance at Winkelman's and a couple of new fall fashions at Heavenrich's. We had lunch at the Woolworth's lunch counter and decided the grilled cheese sandwiches were much better in Grand Rapids. I bought mascara and white eye shadow, figuring that if I wore a little more make-up, maybe it would be a distraction from my arms and legs.

When we got home there was a note from Wilma on the coffee table, which said my dad was going to be late, and we should walk around the corner to meet her at the Tip A Few Tavern.

I shrugged at Maureen. "I guess we have no choice. I'll tell you what, though. My mom would be furious if she heard this."

We splashed cold water on our faces, we applied blush and lip-gloss, then made our way to the bar. After being in the sunshine, it was hard to see when we walked in. There was a xylophone and drum set in one corner and a juke box in the other. *A Taste of Honey* was playing. The one my mom liked, not the one by the Beatles. Wilma was smoking a cigarette and reading *True Confessions Magazine*. She folded it when we walked up.

"Hi, girls, have a seat. I hope you don't mind, but when Danny called and said he'd be late, I decided we needed to get ourselves into some air-conditioning." She took a sip of her martini. "I ordered you each a toasted ham salad sandwich." She hollered to the bartender, "Chet, make a couple of Scarlett O'Haras for the girls, would ya?"

"Sure thing, Wilma," Chet called out.

"I need to powder my nose, girls. I'll be right back."

"What's a Scarlett O'Hara?" Maureen asked me.

"I don't know, it's probably like a Shirley Temple. I've never heard of them before."

The waitress set down two goblets of red liquid and two sandwiches. I lifted the skimpy toasted triangles to see if there was anything inside. Maureen took a sip from the drink and puffed her cheeks out like she wasn't sure she should swallow.

"How do you like that?" Wilma asked as she slid back into the booth.

"What's in it?" Maureen asked, blinking hard several times.

"Cranberry juice and Southern Comfort."

I picked up my glass and tasted it. My mom would call the cops if she got wind of this one.

"So," Wilma said. "How was your day? Get in any trouble?"

We set our glasses down and both said at the same time, "No. We went downtown."

I kept watching Wilma's eyes to see if she noticed Maureen's hair color. She looked right at her when she was eating the olive from her drink, but she didn't say a word. We drank most of our Scarlett Oharas and when we stood up to leave my legs felt kind of rubbery. We giggled all the way back to the apartment. Especially when we passed the drugstore and saw the display of Summer Blonde in the window.

Chapter Five

My dad called after breakfast and said that Mimi's mom had called him at the car lot and invited us to go for lunch and a swim at their country club

The last thing I felt like doing was wearing a bathing suit in public. Even though my psoriasis was a little better, I'd purposely left my checkered two-piece at home. Every time I looked at it, I thought of the graduation party at Delaney's cottage. My skin was monstrous looking, and Tom and I had disappeared in a row boat for hours. It still made me feel sick to think about it. Maureen's beach blanket had been a great cover-up all day, but Tom insisted on peeling it off me. When we got back to the cottage everyone acted like we were going straight to hell. Especially me. My mom and Renee threatened to put me in Villa Maria, a place for bad girls.

"I can't, Dad. I don't have my bathing suit with me."

"For cryin' out loud, Sport, why not? In case you haven't noticed, it's ninety degrees already. And if I remember right, swimming used to be your favorite thing."

"Well, Dad, in case *you* haven't noticed, I look like the creature from the black lagoon, and I don't need the snobs at Saginaw Country Club gawking at me. Those girls stared at me when I had *good* skin."

"Listen here, Sport. Don and June are good friends. Not just my good friends, but your mother's. You and Marlene get ready and I'll pick you up at ten. There's an Arlan's on the way. We'll stop and pick up a suit. I gotta go. There's a customer lookin' at that Pontiac."

"Arlan's?" I yelled into the phone, even though he'd hung up. I took the Winston Maureen was offering and slammed the receiver down. "My dad is out of his mind if he thinks I'm buying a bathing suit at Arlan's!"

As usual, Mimi ordered a club sandwich and a glass of milk at the country club. I had never met another kid who ordered milk when their parents weren't even there. Maureen and I ordered cheeseburgers and Cokes. The muzak seemed louder than I remembered and the baby blue carpet thicker. I always felt like such a klutz in this place.

"I can't believe I'm sitting here with the real Mimi," Maureen said as she placed her linen napkin on her lap. "Ruth Ann has talked about you so much and you're just like she described."

Mimi gave me a cautious look and I felt kind of bad. I had warned Maureen that Mimi still liked the Monkees and that she was practically blind without her glasses. But I'd also told her about all the fun we'd had as little kids. And there was still no way around it, Mimi laughed at stuff I said more than anybody I'd ever known. I'm always funnier than usual around her so I can crack her up and see her eyes crinkle behind her glasses.

The summer after third grade, Mimi spent a whole month with us. We even pricked our fingers with a big safety pin and licked each other's blood, so we would be blood sisters forever. That was a great summer, partly because Renee was so much nicer to me when Mimi was there. But it was Renee's fault that Mimi had to leave four days earlier than we'd planned. I clearly remember the night we whispered in the dark after waking up to voices in the kitchen.

"Is that your dad?"

"It sounds like him. I wonder what he's doing here."

"He sounds mad. What'd he just say?"

"He told Renee he'd sit here all night till she tells him the truth. Shh...he's talking again. Listen."

We slipped into the locker-room cubicles to change into our swim suits. I had talked my dad out of going to Arlan's by telling him that their clothes fell apart when you put them in the washer and that my mom even said so. And what would happen when I got in the chlorine pool? I convinced him that the suit might disintegrate, so he took me to the Yankee Store which was almost as bad as Arlan's. I'd actually found a mint-green two-piece that wasn't hideous. When I tied Wilma's beach towel around my waist, my legs were mostly covered. Mimi loaned us bathing caps since they were required by the country club. Mine was covered with pink flower petals and Maureen's had lime-green daisies all over it. I'd always hated bathing caps because they looked ridiculous, but now I had an itchy scalp to think about.

"We have to wait an hour and fifteen minutes before we can go in the water," Mimi said, pointing to the locker-room clock.

"Why?" Maureen asked. I already knew the answer.

"Because we just ate. You have to wait an hour and a half, so you don't get cramps."

"I wasn't planning on swimming laps," Maureen said. "Can we at least dangle our feet in the water?"

I was happy to put off swimming. It would give me more time to stay wrapped up.

We found three empty chaise lounge chairs. The nice kind with wheels and cushions. We were surrounded by ladies sipping drinks under umbrellas, and others sunning while they smoked and chatted.

"Wow, look at that high-dive!" Maureen said. "It's way higher than ours."

By "ours," I knew she meant the one at Garfield Park, because that was the only pool we ever used.

As soon as we settled into our chairs, three girls stopped by Mimi to chat. They all had great tans and were wearing Villager brand bathing suits. She introduced us and I recognized two of their names from Mimi's letters.

"What's all over your arms? Poison ivy?" one of them asked me.

"She has psoriasis and was even in the hospital for it," Mimi said, squinting up at them.

"You're not going in the pool, are you?" the girl with the nautical bathing suit asked, taking three steps backwards.

They all looked at me with such disgust, I thought they might start gagging. And here I thought I looked so much better.

"Is it on other places besides your arms? Don't they have stuff to put on it?"

I could almost hear Maureen's blood boiling next to me and I knew she felt like shoving all of them into the pool as much as I did.

"No, they don't have anything to put on it, and yes, I'm almost completely covered with it," I answered.

"And you know what the doctor said?" Maureen asked them. They shook their heads. "He told her to drink vodka and smoke Salems. It's the only thing that helps."

I looked at Maureen with the most serious face I could put on. "Well, except for the Scarlett O'Haras he prescribed that one time. Remember?"

"Oh yeah, that's right. I almost forgot."

"Scarlett O'Haras?" the blonde named Kimmy asked.

"Cranberry juice and Southern Comfort. It cleanses your whole system before you start the vodka/Salem treatments."

"Let's go, Kimmy," the other girl said. "I have to practice my butterfly stroke."

Maureen and I nearly busted open from holding back laughing.

Mimi's parents invited us to stay for a cook-out on their patio. They also invited my dad, but not Wilma. My mom thought Mimi's mother, June, was the greatest friend on earth, because she refused to acknowledge that Wilma even existed. Our parents had all been friends way before we were born. There were pictures of us in a playpen together right next to the card table where they played Canasta.

We were sitting on the floor in Mimi's bedroom, listening to records. Maureen was being very nice about Mimi's choices in music. Her favorite bands were the ones that I would switch off on the radio. It was hard to believe we'd had Beatlemania together only a few years ago. For my tenth birthday, she had sent me a Beatles wallet with their pictures on the front and a plastic coin holder inside.

"Hey Mimi, do you have any lotion I can borrow? My skin's killing me from the chlorine today. I have some at my dad's, but I didn't think to bring it."

She gave me her Jergen's Hand Lotion to use. I applied it to my arms and legs while the girls read album covers. The chlorine in the pool had burned my skin, even though I had only stayed in the water for a few minutes. Instead, I'd watched Maureen and Mimi swim and jump off the high-dive while I flipped through a Look Magazine someone had left behind on one of the umbrella tables.

"Ruth Ann, I'm sorry those girls were mean today," Mimi said as she watched me rubbing the lotion on my skin. Maybe I shouldn't have told them about your psoriasis. "Would you have just said it was poison ivy if I hadn't opened up my big mouth?"

"Maybe. I don't know. It's okay, 'cause I'm sort of used to it. And anyway, it was worth it, just to see their faces when Maureen said vodka and Salems were my treatment."

Even Mimi laughed then. I almost told her about Wilma ordering Scarlet O'Haras for us at the Tip A Few but decided against it. She'd probably tell her mom who would tell my mom, there was no doubt in my mind.

The next day was so hot that we just sat in front of the fans and watched TV.

"I can't believe we only have three days left here," Maureen hollered from the kitchen. "Time has gone by so fast. Hey look, there's Wilma's gin. Want to try it?"

I was lying on the floor with my legs on the coffee table, reading an article about Twiggy in one of Wilma's magazines.

"I guess so," I answered. "Hey, did you love Twiggy back in sixth and seventh grade?" I threw the magazine down and walked into the kitchen. Maureen was holding onto Wilma's fifth of gin.

"Oh boy, I sure did!" She lifted the fifth and took a slug. "Wow! That stuff burns like hell. Here you try it."

She handed it to me and I took a small sip. It made my lips feel like they were on fire. We sat down at the table and each took a couple more sips. My head got woozy and I felt like I needed a tonsillectomy.

"You want to know the truth?" I asked Maureen. "I practically had a crush on Twiggy. But don't worry, I'm not a lesbo or anything. My cousin, Jerry Michael, the one I told you about that likes boys. He said it was normal for a girl my age."

Maureen was thinking hard, I could tell. The phone rang and we both jumped off our chairs like whoever was calling could see the fifth of gin on the table and knew we were talking about lesbians.

I picked up the phone. It was my dad.

"Hey Sport, how would you and Marlene like to go to Daniel's Den tonight? I just sold a car to the guy who owns the place and he gave me two passes when he heard you were in town. I guess they got a band playin' there called some crazy thing. Cherry Rush or Mush or Slush. Hell, I don't know. You wanna go?"

I waved my arm at Maureen and did a little jig in place which made my head feel even woozier.

Daniel's Den was an old movie theatre. The seats had been taken out and the floor was filled with teen-agers, laughing, talking loudly, and shoving each other around. I spotted a few tables on the side.

"How 'bout we sit over there?"

Maureen nodded and followed me. The band was setting up on the stage where they used to show the movies, and in the meantime a jukebox was playing *Incense and Peppermints,* and a few kids were dancing.

"Boy, this place is cool," Maureen said, as she pulled out a chair and sat down. "Did you see that sign in the lobby that said we're supposed to be sixteen to get in here?"

"It said sixteen or tenth grade. My dad probably told the guy we're in tenth grade. That'd be just like him. And anyway, he can never remember what grade I'm in."

"Well, they took those free passes without a question."

"This *is* a pretty cool place," I said.

Maureen reached into her purse and got out her Winstons. I had a feeling she was trying to make us look older. She offered one to me, but I decided not to. I was already thinking about how Renee and my mom would explode if they saw me in this place. They'd have heart failure if cigarettes were added to the picture. Even though my mom was rarely without a Salem in her hand, she and Renee seemed to think I should still be playing Barbies with Cathy.

As soon as Maureen blew out her match, a girl walked up to our table. She was wearing a mini-dress in an orange and yellow print and I couldn't help but notice her long, tanned legs with perfect skin.

"Hi, remember me? Aunt Wilma told me to look for you."

It was Wilma's niece, Paula who I'd met on spring break when Mimi and I went to a dance at the YMCA. The night had ended badly because I'd danced with the boy that her friend had a crush on. The whole thing was ridiculous because I didn't even know he was the boy they'd been talking about. I was actually surprised she was being friendly.

I introduced her to Maureen and was relieved that she didn't seem fazed by her smoking. Not that Wilma would probably care.

"You girls are gonna love Cherry Slush. They're probably the best band in Saginaw. Maybe not as good as bands from your town, but they're really good."

"Well, we sure don't have any places like this," Maureen said.

"I saw a Question Mark and the Mysterians poster in the lobby," I said. "Do they ever play here?"

"They do once in a while. I haven't seen them here, but I plan to," Paula said. "I remember you saying that you always tell your friends they're from Saginaw."

"She tells us all the time," Maureen said, and winked at me.

Paula leaned on our table and lowered her voice a little. "Listen, my friend Bobby, has some hootch on him. If you girls want your cokes livened up, let me know."

"Thanks," Maureen smiled up at her. I swear she can handle anything. There was no doubt in my mind that my mom would find a gun and shoot Wilma if she ever thought her niece offered me alcohol.

"See you on the dance floor," Paula said. She waved at us and walked away.

"I'll take a Winston after all," I said with my hand out.

"Do you like her?" Maureen asked me as soon as she was sure that Paula couldn't hear us.

"To tell you the truth, I'm not sure I trust her."

"Isn't she the one who got all mad about you dancing with 'one of *their* boys'?

"Yup," I nodded. "She's the one. I wondered if you remembered that."

The Doors song, *People Are Strange* began playing, and we both started laughing.

"That's just too perfect," Maureen said.

"Well, if you ask me," I said, "She was just showing off. Telling us that her friend Bobby has hootch on him."

We got up and danced to two songs and had to admit that Paula was right. Cherry Slush was a good band and three out of four of them were really cute. I felt more comfortable at the table, though, watching everybody else dance, because most of the kids looked older than us. If I had known how dark the place was, I might not have bothered to wear tights. Better safe than sorry, I had figured. Nobody on the dance floor seemed to notice my arms. We had worn skirts and sleeveless shells and blended right in. So many times, when I was younger it didn't feel like I blended in. I still didn't have many clothes, but I felt like I was getting better at figuring out what I should wear to different places. It would be so much easier if this damn psoriasis would go away.

"I wish we had a place like this at home," Maureen said, when we got back to our table. "We should try to see the SoulBenders sometime. I hear they're really good and they probably play *somewhere* we could get in."

"We should. I've heard they're the best band in Grand Rapids."

My dad picked us up at eleven. I was afraid he would come inside to ask the owner how he liked his new car, but he didn't.

"So?" he asked. "Did you girls make like the Rockettes, or did you hide in a corner somewhere?"

It was funny. I felt so much older than after the YMCA dance in

April, when he'd asked almost the same question. Was that only four months ago?

"A little of both," Maureen answered. "It's a really cool place, Mr. Bloomfield. Thanks for taking us there."

"You're *welcome,* Marlene. I'm glad you had a good time."

Maureen was so polite and friendly. There was no doubt in my mind, my dad would let me bring her to Saginaw every time I came.

I was watching *Rocky and Bullwinkle* and nibbling all around the edges of a pop-tart, when Maureen walked into the living room, yawning.

"Sorry I slept so late," she said. "Wow, it feels much cooler. What do you feel like doing today?"

A breeze lifted the window shade.

"Maybe we should walk downtown again, since it's not as hot."

The phone rang. It was my dad.

"Listen, Sport. It turns out your sister's coming on the bus and staying at Grandma's for a couple of days. Your mom will be here on Saturday and she'll be giving you a ride home."

"What? Renee's coming *here*? To Saginaw? Why's she coming here? You mean we're not all taking the bus back? Is Mimi still coming back with me?"

"Whoa, hang onto yer saddle, Sport. Yeah, you heard right. Renee will be here this afternoon. And your mother is picking all of you up on Saturday. Including Mimi."

"But why is Renee coming here? That's what I want to know. What about her job?"

"She took a couple days off because she's got something to take care of."

"Like what? Is it about college? Acting?"

"Yeah, something like that. We'll all be having supper tonight at Grandma's. I gotta run, Sport. See you around five."

I hung up the phone and walked into the kitchen, where Maureen was buttering a piece of toast.

"What was that all about?" she asked.

"Boy, you got me. Renee is coming here for some reason, and my mom is picking us up on Saturday, instead of us going home on the bus."

"That seems weird. Did she talk about doing that before you left?"

I shook my head. "No, not even once. She never takes days off from Wurzburg's. And she never visits my dad. They don't even get along. I can't figure out what's going on."

We listened to Maureen's transistor radio while we crossed the bridge on our way downtown and sang along to *Angel in the Morning* so loudly that people stared at us from cars. For some reason, it made me feel better. Ever since I'd heard that Renee was coming, there was a funny feeling in my stomach.

"You're my favorite teacher of my whole life, Mrs. Van Hoose. And I wanted to get Mrs. Tilley for fourth grade next year.

"I'm sorry you're moving, Ruth Ann, but I think you'll like Grand Rapids. My husband grew up there. He said it snowed there once in July!"

"In July? Oh no! Well, we just moved here last summer so my sister could go to college. It's my favorite town, and I don't want to move away."

"Doesn't your mother like it here? Is your sister staying for college?"

"My mom says there's no full-time jobs here, so that's why we have to move. I think Renee's coming with us."

"Well, I want you to promise me that you'll stop in and say hi whenever you come back to Mt. Pleasant, you hear me?"

We practically drooled over the shoes at Jacobson's, and then went to Seitner's and tried on Villager and Ladybug clothes, even though we couldn't afford them.

"I'm gonna try and get more babysitting jobs so I can buy this shirtwaist," I said into the mirror. "I bet they have it back home at Wurzburg's or Beverley's."

"If they have it at Wurzburg's, couldn't you get Renee's discount?"

"Hey, I bet I could. But I'd have to hurry before she goes back to college next month."

I must have had a weird look on my face, because I saw Maureen behind me in the mirror with her hands on her hips.

"What the heck is going on, Ruth Ann? You've been acting funny ever since you heard Renee's on her way here. I know she drives you nuts, but is there more to it?"

My heart started to pound. It was tempting to tell her, but thankfully, I stopped myself. There was no doubt in my mind, Maureen was the most trustworthy friend I would ever have. But some secrets just have to be forever.

Chapter Six

We were a block from the bridge, on our way back to the apartment when a horn started honking. We both assumed it was more flirty boys, so we didn't look until the car pulled up to the curb.

"Hey, you're under arrest, so get in the car."

It was my dad, and Renee. She barely looked at us as we slid into the back seat.

"What the heck? I didn't think we'd see you 'til Grandma's house, Renee."

"Grandma wasn't home, and the spare key wasn't under the marigolds," my dad said. "So, Renee's just gonna keep you girls company for a couple hours."

The way he was checking my reaction in the rear-view mirror, told me that he was a little worried about this arrangement. Renee had never gone to my dad's apartment and had never met Wilma. This was all so strange, that I couldn't think straight.

"Didn't Grandma know you were coming?" I asked.

"Apparently, she forgot," Renee said, as we pulled into the parking lot.

"You don't have to come up, Dad. Just go back to work."

He looked at me reluctantly. "Well, okay. I'm supposed to meet a guy at three o'clock. I'll be back in less than two hours. You can all watch *General Hospital,* right?"

I nodded and took Renee's suitcase from him. Good old Maureen looked a little confused, but she came to the rescue. "Don't worry about us. You just get to your appointment and we'll be ready to go over to Grandma Gertie's when you get back."

My dad pulled the cigar out of his mouth and snickered. "You're a keeper, Marlene."

Renee followed us up the stairs and I unlocked the door.

"So, you have your own key to the place, huh?" Renee said.

"Well, yeah. While I'm here."

"He's just been letting the two of you run willy-nilly wherever you want?"

"Willy- nilly, Renee? What is that supposed to mean? We went downtown and tried on school clothes. And talk about willy-nilly, I don't even know why you came to Saginaw."

Renee stood in the middle of the living room and looked around like she expected giant cockroaches to come out and attack us. Her eyes rested on the two pictures over the TV set. They were flamenco dancers on black velvet.

"Oh God. I remember those hideous things from the pawn shop. I guess her taste is as bad as his."

"Dad lived here a long time before Wilma moved in," I said. "And anyway, they're probably going to buy a house soon."

"By the way," Renee said as she dug through her purse, "The creep called again last night. The creep you went off with in the boat."

Maureen raised her eyebrows. "I'm dying of thirst. Anybody want lemonade?"

I felt like slapping Renee for bringing up Tom and the boat, so I didn't even respond to her about the call.

"Where's the bathroom?" Renee asked. "It has to be cleaner than the one at the bus station."

I pointed to the bathroom and then went to the kitchen.

"Hey, we gotta get Renee to the basement. Think of something quick."

Maureen opened her mouth as wide as possible but didn't make a sound. Then she shook her finger at me. "You have the devil in you, Miss Ruth Ann."

Renee walked into the kitchen and took a glass from the cupboard. She checked it closely, then put it back. She inspected two more before she finally settled on one. She rinsed it out anyway, then took the top off the lemonade pitcher. She looked inside and smelled it before pouring a small amount into her glass.

"Hey, Ruth Ann," Maureen said. "Did you ever figure out how to work the washing machine?"

"No. It's way different than ours."

"You didn't leave the clothes down there, did you?"

"Yeah. Isn't that okay?"

"Oh, for heaven's sake," Renee said. "Are they your clothes?"

I knew Renee wouldn't care about my dad or Wilma's clothes, so I nodded, and she sighed loudly.

"Just show me the machine. You are the most helpless person I've ever known."

"Ruth Ann, get the key," Maureen said. "I'm coming too."

When we passed the doctor's office on the way down, a little boy was screaming outside the door, and his mother was pulling on his arm. I got a little nervous about the doctor being in the building, but I decided the chance was too good to pass up.

Once we were down in the basement, I directed Maureen and Renee to the laundry area, and I headed straight to the room with the leg. I could hear one of them turning the dials on the machine. I climbed on the table as fast as I could and grabbed the paper wrapped package from the rafters.

"But where are the clothes?" I heard Renee ask.

"In here," I hollered.

Jumping off the table almost caused me to lose my balance, but I finished unwrapping the leg just as they walked into the room.

"Here they are," I said, stepping away from the table.

Renee took about three steps toward me. Maureen and I were already holding our stomachs.

Renee's face turned white, her hands flew over her open mouth and she began shaking her head back and forth.

"Oh my God," she said. She turned and ran from the room so fast, it scared me. I heard her feet on the steps.

"Uh-oh," Maureen said. "Maybe this was a bad idea."

"Go up there, would you? I'll put this back."

By the look on Maureen's face, I wondered if she was thinking about heading to the bus station.

"Please? Unless you want to put this back."

Maureen glanced at the leg. "That's okay. I'll go up. But get your ass up there pronto, hear me?"

Getting the leg up was harder than getting it down. My arms were just a little too short. Every time I tried shoving the package, it slipped back down. I started to panic, thinking of Maureen having to deal with Renee all by herself and worrying that someone from the doctor's office might come down.

Sweat was rolling off my face as I tried over and over to get the leg back up on the rafters.

"Shit shit shit! What should I do?"

I stood on the table holding the leg and looked around for somewhere to stash it until my dad got home. I set the package on the table, jumped down, and began running in circles.

"This basement is too damn clean."

I finally decided to stand it up behind the door of the tool closet, figuring if someone went in, they'd probably leave the door open and not see it. I turned off all the lights and made my way upstairs. My heart leaped when I got to the small foyer and a nurse was coming out of the doctor's office. I smiled and said hello, trying to act as natural as possible, realizing as I climbed the apartment steps, that nobody besides the doctor probably knew about the leg. Except us, of course.

"Boy, could I use a Winston," Maureen said when I opened the apartment door.

"Where's Renee?"

"In the bathroom. Barfing."

"She's barfing? Are you kidding?"

"What the hell took you so long?" Maureen actually seemed mad at me.

"I couldn't get that damn thing back up."

"Oh no. But you got it, right?"

"No. I couldn't do it, I'm telling you."

"What? You left it on the table?"

"No. I stashed it in that little tool room. My dad'll have to help me put it back."

"Holy crap, Ruth Ann. Please tell me you're kidding. I mean pulling my leg."

She started laughing, fell back on the couch and put an orange triangle pillow over her face, just as Renee walked in, paler than she'd even been in the basement.

"Wait until Mother hears about this, you evil child."

"I'm sorry, Renee. It was supposed to be a joke. I never dreamed it would make you sick."

"Well, *you* are sick. As sick as your father."

"I knew you never believed the story about the leg."

"Why would I ever believe anything from him?"

She walked into the kitchen and sat in a chair looking out the window. Maureen shrugged at me and shook her head. I turned on the TV and we watched the episode of *Leave It to Beaver* when Beaver uses a voo-doo doll to put a curse on Eddie Haskell for getting him in trouble. It crossed my mind that Renee might be out in the kitchen, making a voo-doo doll out of a pot-holder. Putting a curse on me would be the perfect revenge. And this time, I felt like maybe I deserved it.

We watched TV until my dad came home. Renee stayed in the kitchen, even when *Dark Shadows* came on. I turned the TV up louder, so she could hear it.

"You crooners about ready?" my dad said as soon as he opened the door. "Your grandma feels so bad about missing Renee, she's over there making knishes."

Even though knishes were one of my all-time favorite foods, all I could think of was how mad Renee was, and getting the leg back on the ceiling.

"We have a little problem to take care of first, Dad."

"For cryin' out loud, Sport," my dad said as he hoisted the leg up on the rafters. "I know I'm not one to talk about practical jokes, but go a little easy on your sister right now, would ya?" He jumped off the table and shifted his cigar to the other side of his mouth. "She's goin' through a rough time right now."

"What do you mean? What kind of rough time?"

"Let's just say, she's got a lot on her mind. Now come on. We gotta get out of here. If Wilma sees my car out in the lot, she'll going over to the Tip A Few to avoid your sister."

I had been wondering what would happen if Wilma had walked in with Renee there.

My grandma waddled back and forth between the dining room and kitchen, bringing out more knishes and brisket. She had even made pineapple-upside-down cake, which I hated but Renee loved.

Maureen and I helped clean the kitchen while Aunt Dorothy took Renee upstairs to look at her most recent purchases. After we finished the dishes, we sat on the porch swing waiting for my dad to replace the fan belt on Aunt Dorothy's Riviera. The priest from Mt. Carmel church waved to me from his front step across the street. He was Grandma's landlord and loved the fact that her granddaughters were Catholic.

"Your grandma really hustled in the kitchen," Maureen said. "I didn't think she could move that fast."

"This is a big TV night for her. She wouldn't want to miss *The Flying Nun* or *The Dean Martin Show.*"

"Was your dad mad at us for getting the leg down and scaring Renee?"

"Normally, he would have thought it was funny. But he mostly just talked about Renee having a lot on her mind and stuff."

"What the heck is going on? Do you have any idea?"

I could feel Maureen looking at me more intently than usual. Maybe she suspected that I had an idea, but I swatted at a mosquito and shrugged.

"My grandma always has Neapolitan ice cream. Want some?"

My dad took Friday afternoon off, so he could take us on a boat ride. He told me to invite Mimi, but she was busy getting ready to come back with us to Grand Rapids. I had been asking him to let Maureen and me sleep on the boat one time, but the whole deal with Renee showing up had thrown a wrench in those plans.

"I love this boat," Maureen said, as she handed me the Copper Tone sun lotion.

"Yeah, but too bad we didn't get to sleep on it."

"That's okay. Maybe next time. I know you and Mimi had a blast on Spring break when you did that."

"We did have a good time. I guess Renee showing up here kind of changed everything."

"Too bad Mimi couldn't come with us today."

"Yeah, but at least she'll be with me in G.R. for over a week."

"Hey, my parents will be going to the cottage next weekend. We should all either go with them or stay at my house *without* them."

"Sounds good to me, but I have to remind you Mimi's not as daring as you and me. We have to mind our Ps and Qs around her."

"Yeah, I know. But she is really nice. I like her a lot. She's more like your cousin or something, right?"

"Yeah, I guess she is."

"So, do you have a plan about Tom?"

"What do you mean, a plan?"

"Well, are you planning to talk to him or ignore him?"

"I don't even know if I'll see him."

"Come on. You're going to the park, aren't you? You'll see him there. Plus that, he's driven by your house and he's called twice. Or maybe more."

"I don't know, Maureen. I'm not sure what I'll do."

"Come on now, you must be curious."

She was right. I was curious. It made my stomach feel grabby to think about it. And that meant something, didn't it?

Chapter Seven

"Renee, can you please turn up that song?"

She pretended not to hear me, so my mom turned it up. I noticed her shooting a quick glance at Renee while she did it, probably to do a mood check.

"Thanks, Mom," I said a little louder than necessary.

I was squeezed between Maureen and Mimi in the back seat and we were approaching the little town of Edmore on Highway 46.

"Hey Mom, can we stop for a donut at the Chat 'n' Chew when we get to Edmore?"

"We don't have time, Ruth Ann," Renee piped up. "The girls are counting on me for all the decorations."

"Killjoy," I said under my breath.

My mom shot me a warning look in the rearview mirror.

"It's a little apartment, Ruth Ann. But I think you'll like it. Besides, we aren't going to be there long. I'm planning on buying a house as soon as we get on our feet."

"I wish we didn't even have to leave Mt. Pleasant. Everybody's so nice here. I'll never find friends like Vicki and Barbara. And Daddy says Grand Rapids is way further from him, so I bet he won't come to see me anymore.

"Don't worry, he'll come to see you in Grand Rapids. You didn't

want to leave Saginaw either, and look how much you ended up liking Mt. Pleasant. Hey, look at that cute little place, The Chat N Chew. Why don't we stop there? Does that sound good to you, Renee?

"No. Nothing sounds good to me. You two go in. I'll wait in the car."

The Wurzburgers were giving a bridal shower for someone in the billing department, so as usual, Renee was ruining any fun we might have had on the way home. It was bad enough we didn't get to take the bus like we'd planned. We'd been hoping to go back to the department store in downtown Lansing.

Maureen's mom came out of the house when we pulled into her driveway.

"Did she behave herself?" Mrs. Abraham asked as Maureen and I got out of the car.

"I think my dad wanted to swap daughters, he liked her so much," I said as I pulled Maureen's suitcase out of the trunk.

My mom introduced Renee and Mimi to Maureen's mom and then Mrs. Abraham said they should have lunch one day soon. Maureen waved to us as we backed out of the driveway, and I already missed her. It had been so fun to have her to myself all those days. She made me forget that I usually felt lonely.

Mimi was very excited to see Ruff and Reddy when we got home.

"Do they look any different than last summer?" I asked her.

"I think Ruff's put on some weight. Can we take them to your room?"

We carried the cats up the stairs and I closed the door and turned the radio on. The DJ was announcing that The SoulBenders would be playing at Garfield Park at seven o'clock.

"I can't believe it! I have to call Maureen. We were just talking about seeing that band when we were at Daniel's Den."

Mimi looked a little puzzled when I stepped into the hall to use the phone.

"I was just gonna call you," Maureen said as soon as she heard my voice. "The SoulBenders are...."

"I know, that's why I called."

"You call Peg and make sure she and Irene know, and I'll call Angela to make sure she and Mary Lou know."

I hung up the phone and called Peg. She said they were already planning on it and would meet us there around six-thirty.

"Well, guess what?" I said to Mimi, who was dangling a string over Reddy's head. "You get to meet the Tandem Riders *tonight*."

She didn't look as interested as I thought she should be. Maybe she'd forgotten everything I'd told her about them.

"You know, the new friends I made in the beginning of eighth grade. Of course, you already know Maureen, but hopefully the other four will all be there too."

Mimi looked less than excited. I felt like reminding her about the mean girls at her country club and how I had to put up with them, but I didn't.

"You wanna go, don't you? It'll be really fun, I promise."

My mom called up the stairs for us to come down. A horn was honking outside when we got to the dining room.

"There's Bonnie," Renee said. "Bye, Mimi. I hope Ruth Ann doesn't drive you nuts with all her music and endless chatter."

"Glad she's gone," I said as Renee went out the front door with a shopping bag of streamers and cardboard wedding bells.

"She's so pretty," Mimi said. "I've still never seen eyes so blue as Renee's."

"You don't know what she's really like. She puts on an act for you."

"I hope you girls don't mind tuna salad and watermelon for dinner," my mom called from the kitchen. "Set the table, would you, Ruth Ann?"

"This is like a picnic," Mimi said, after we began eating. "And I really like the carrots in the salad. It adds something."

"Thanks, Mimi," my mom answered. "We're very glad you're here."

She looked and sounded tired. I knew that driving back and forth to Saginaw had worn her out, and that she probably would fall asleep in front of the TV as soon as she sat on the couch. She didn't even fuss or argue when I told her about the music at the park. She just lit a Salem, blew the smoke at the ceiling, and said, "Home by ten, Ruth Ann. Hear me? Come to think of it, I should probably call June and make sure she's okay with Mimi going."

"Oh, I don't think she'd mind," Mimi said. "It's really close-by and everything."

I could have kissed Mimi. She was coming through after all.

"Well," my mom said. "Don't think you're off the hook for that escapade to Daniel's Den. I'm just too tired to talk about it right now. Your father already got a piece of my mind."

I was pretty sure she wouldn't bring it up again. She seemed distracted with whatever was going on with Renee. And since Renee wasn't home to put any fat on the fire, my mom just dropped it. Come to think of it, my dad hadn't mentioned my mom giving him a piece of her mind. Either she hadn't given him a very big piece, or he was distracted too.

We headed out the door as soon as the dishes were done.

"We'll be home on time, right? Your mom seemed worried about us coming here."

"Don't worry, we will. She's still thinking about last summer. You know, the riots. There was a curfew and everything."

"Oh yeah, Saginaw had riots too. But I'm not sure if there was a curfew. Detroit had one. I know that for sure."

"Yeah, the riots weren't very far from here, so my mom expects another one to break out, I guess."

Mimi looked worried, so I gave her a little shove. "It's fine, Mimi. Don't worry. I promise you there will not be a riot."

"Boy, I sure was right about this park being close by," Mimi said as we crossed Burton Street.

"That's the only reason I can swim," I said. "Before we moved here, I took lessons at the Y, and it was terrible because I was already wearing a bra and the other girls were in first grade."

"So, did you just learn how by coming here every day?"

"Once I learned to float, I got it on my own. But my cousin Jerry Michael taught me to float. When he stayed with us a few summers ago. You know, the cousin who likes boys. Renee's friend, Bonnie, calls him queer, but we get mad at her for that. He's definitely my favorite cousin. I wish he lived closer. And he hasn't visited in a long time. We mostly just see him at weddings and family reunions. And then Renee completely dominates all of his time. Oh no, does this sound like endless chatter? Just like Renee said I would? I hate it when she's right."

Mimi laughed. "That's okay. I wish I could meet your cousin. You always tell me about him. Aren't he and Renee pretty close?"

"Yeah, she behaves around him, like she does when you're here. He thinks she's cool 'cause of her acting and stuff."

There was a big stage set up in front of the warming house where we put on our ice skates in the winter. A couple of guys were testing microphones and another guy was sitting behind the drums. People were sitting on blankets in front of the stage and there were rows of benches set up behind them.

"Hey, Ruth Ann. Over here!"

Angela was standing up and waving her arms at us. Mary Lou was sitting on a blanket next to her, wearing just about the cutest sundress I'd ever seen.

I led Mimi over to the blanket and introduced her to the girls. Angela offered her box of pumpkin seeds to us after we sat down. Maureen, Peg, and Irene walked up right away, and Maureen spread her beach blanket on the ground. It was the same blanket I'd covered up with at the cottage party earlier this summer.

"I wasn't sure you'd want to see this again," Maureen whispered. "But, then I thought it might do you good. Your skin is *way* better than it was that day."

I glanced at my arms. She was right, they did look better. My legs were a little better too, but I'd still worn my jeans, because to me, they looked hideous. I thought about how Maureen had brought her blanket for me to cover up with at the party because my psoriasis was so bad. Without thinking, I put my arms around her.

"Thanks for coming to Saginaw with me. It made staying at the apartment so much better."

"Well, thanks for taking me. I had a great time. Hey, I had to fess up to my mom 'cause she noticed my hair was darker right away."

"Was she mad?"

"Not as much about my hair as a couple of other things."

"Uh-oh. What?"

"Don't worry, nothing about Saginaw. She found an ashtray full of butts under my bed and my bill from Mitchell's came. You know, for my baby-doll dress and those print shorts. But she got over it when I told her all about your grandma and your Aunt Dorothy and your dad's houseboat and all the fun we had."

She turned toward Mimi. "And my mom thought it was so nice you took us to your country club. Thanks again."

"Oh, that's okay," Mimi said.

I pulled a loose thread on the blanket and started thinking about all the terrible stuff that happened right at the beginning of the summer. Disappearing with Tom at the cottage party and everybody acting like we'd eloped. The horrible tar treatments I got in the hospital for my psoriasis, and then seeing Tom kiss Leta *right here at this park*.

But here I was now, sitting between the two best friends anyone could ask for. And four very cute guys were about to play music *right here at this park*.

Some older girls were by the stage talking to the drummer and the guy who was behind the portable organ. They had long, straight hair and were wearing bell-bottom jeans. One girl had a flower behind her ear and the other was bare-foot. I wondered if they were the band member's girlfriends.

"You know," Mary Lou said as she leaned over to Mimi, "These guys have had two number one songs here. I'm sure they'll play both songs. And they placed fifth in a national contest."

"It's true," Angela said. "Number five in the national Battle of the Bands."

"They're right," I said to Mimi. "I still have the WLAV chart from when they were number one. I should have shown it to you before we came. They were number one over The Monkees, Lulu, Strawberry Alarm Clock and a bunch of others."

I could tell Mimi was impressed because she sat up a little straighter and looked harder at the musicians who were about to begin. Since she was a huge Monkees fan, I knew that information would interest her. Maureen offered her a hunk of Heath Bar and Irene passed us a bag of red licorice.

Just before the music started, Maureen tucked my hair behind my ear and leaned toward me. "Don't look now, but there is somebody trying very hard to catch your eye."

"Where? Who is it?" I stared straight ahead.

"Way down, on the far right. Guess."

"Tom?"

"Who do you think?"

I wanted to look, but held my breath, and willed myself not to. The music started, and it was so cool to hear the song, *7&7 Is,* live. Somehow, I kept myself from turning my head for the entire song. When they played their second song, *Petals*, I managed to stay focused on the stage and laughed especially hard at something Peg said. I didn't even know what she said, but I wanted to look happy and carefree. Partly because that's how I wanted to feel, but also because I knew I was being watched.

When the third song, *I Can't Believe in Love Anymore*, started, it was impossible not to look at Tom. It sounded so much like The Doors that I could almost feel his arms around me and I could almost smell his Brut cologne. He was staring at me so hard, my stomach turned over. He lifted his hand in a wave, but I looked away quickly without waving back. Like it said in the song, "my brain was in a swirl." I felt my chest tighten over the lyrics, about being "hurt too many times before," and then purposely looked at him again. I was disappointed that he'd turned toward the band with a far-away expression. I wondered if he was thinking about how he'd hurt me or if he was thinking about Leta, who didn't seem to be around and maybe had hurt *him.*

"Is he still there?" I asked Maureen when the concert ended. While we matched up the corners of her blanket, she looked over my shoulder to where Tom had been sitting. "He's walking this way. I'll pretend I didn't notice so he doesn't think we're talking about him."

"Hi Ruth Ann. When did you get back?"

I looked to my right and there was my next-door neighbor Cathy with her brother, Frankie. She was holding a cake pan covered in a dish towel.

"Oh hi, Cathy. We got back this afternoon. How'd you like the music?"

I looked at Maureen to try and get a signal about Tom, but she had a funny look on her face that I couldn't read.

"We only heard the last song. We're just coming from my Aunt Mary's."

I should have known Cathy wouldn't be at the SoulBenders. She probably never even heard of them. I saw her look behind me and then at my face and then behind me again. The scent of Brut hit me, but I still didn't turn around.

"You remember Mimi, right?" I asked Cathy.

Maureen took hold of the situation. "I forgot you two know each other. From other summers, right?"

"Hi."

That's all he said, and I could feel my heart slamming. I turned my head slightly toward him. The first thing I noticed was a shadow of dark hair over his upper lip. Those lips that I had kissed so many times.

"When did you get back from your dad's?"

"Today."

"Did your sister tell you I called? A bunch of times."

Damn. I wish I'd planned this better. Was it better to say yes or no? I did a half shrug, half nod thing, but I didn't smile.

"Did you have a good time?"

"Yeah, I did. Maureen came with me."

"We have to go, Ruth Ann," Cathy said as she stared at Tom. It made me remember all the times through eighth grade that she acted like such a goofball about him.

"Hey, Cathy. How's it goin'?" Tom asked her.

"Oh, hi. I'm fine. Bye. C'mon Frankie." She pulled on Frankie's shirt with her free hand, and they took a few steps before turning around. "Ruth Ann, my mom's making cannoli tomorrow if you and Mimi want to come over. And you can come too, Maureen. That is, if you want. Bye." She and Frankie headed toward Burton Street.

"Good ol' Cathy," Maureen snickered.

"Well, aren't you going to introduce me?" Mimi asked.

Thankfully, Maureen took over again. "Mimi, this is Tom. Tom, this is Mimi."

"Oh, yeah. Ruth Ann's talked about you. How long are you staying?"

"Nine days to be exact," Mimi answered.

"You guys like the music?" he asked.

"Completely outasite," Maureen said. "Sorry Mimi, but they were way better than the band we saw in Saginaw."

Mimi shrugged and shook her head.

"You saw a band in Saginaw?" Tom asked.

"Yeah, the Cherry Slush. We saw them at a club there called Daniel's Den. It was a very cool place. You're supposed to be sixteen to get in, but Ruth Ann's dad knows the owner."

Tom was looking back and forth between the two of us. He looked worried, like he didn't know everything about me anymore. I loved Maureen for saying all of that.

"Hey, are you girls coming or not?" Mary Lou shouted. She was holding a banana popsicle over her other hand and taking a bite from the side. She and the other Tandem Riders had walked over to an ice cream truck.

"We need to catch up with them," I said to Mimi and Maureen.

"I'll see you later then," Tom said as we walked away.

We trailed behind the other Tandem Riders as they headed toward our cement block.

"Well, well, well," Maureen said. "How did that feel?"

I was walking between her and Mimi and they were both staring at me.

"I don't know. Weird, I guess. I'm still so mad at him, you know. But part of me says to just forget it all because he's so damn cute."

"He *is* so damn cute," Mimi said.

"Mimi Robart! I've never heard you swear!"

"I'm just repeating what you said."

It was so obvious that she was trying not to laugh that all three of us started laughing and Maureen farted.

"Oh my God, I didn't mean to do that. Especially not in front of you, Mimi. You're probably thinking, good thing she didn't do that at my country club."

"I did not think that," Mimi said. Then Maureen farted again, and we all busted a gut. Maureen fell on the ground, laughing, and rolled back and forth holding her sides. When she finally stopped laughing, she held her hand out for me to help her up. "Okay, that's it. I need a Winston. Mimi, please tell me you don't care if I smoke."

"Go right ahead. I sure don't want one, but you can smoke all you want. Both of you."

"Yeah, I will take one," I said. "I could also use a Scarlett O'Hara right now."

We leaned against two giant oak trees and smoked.

"Where did the tree fall during the tornado?" Mimi asked me.

"Back the other way. Closer to Burton Street."

"I can't believe you were that close to it."

"Yeah, that was one hell of a day. Sorry Mimi, there I go again."

"Stop saying sorry. I'm in your town now. You *should* be yourself."

"Well, look out then," Maureen said. "'Cuz herself swears, smokes Winstons and drinks Scarlett O'Haras."

"Herself is not as bad as you make her sound," I said.

"I just want to hear about the tornado day," Mimi said.

"Okay, but let's start walking. The girls must think we went home."

"They probably think you headed to Burton Woods with Tom," Maureen said.

"Uh-uh. I wouldn't have gone with him to Burton Woods even when we were hot and heavy."

"What's Burton Woods?" Mimi asked. "And what do you mean, hot and heavy?"

"You girls have a lot of catching up to do," Maureen said. "Good thing you've got nine days."

"Nine days, *to be exact*," I said and poked Mimi in the ribs.

When we rounded the corner of the pool building, Angela, Mary Lou, Peg and Irene burst out singing the Tandem Riders song, *Let's Spend the Night Together.*

"You've got some lively friends," Mimi said to me.

"I know."

No Doubt in my Mind

As I hoisted myself up on the cement block, I realized that I didn't have to fake feeling happy and carefree, because right now, I really did.

"Hey Ruth Ann, are you guys still up?"

It was Cathy, hollering over from Frankie's window to mine. I knelt down in front of the window to talk to her.

"You can see we're up, silly. The lights are on."

I instantly felt bad that I called her silly. It was so Renee-ish of me.

"Where's Mimi?"

"Brushing her teeth."

"Are you and Tom back together?"

"No. Why would you think that?"

"Well, I guess because of the way he was looking at you. Didn't you notice?"

Mrs. Cicerelli yelled something in Italian from another room.

"I gotta go. What Mass are you going to?"

"Probably eleven. Go. Your mom's gonna kill you."

"Okay, good night. Don't forget about the cannoli."

Mimi and I were a lot more crowded in my twin bed this summer, compared to other years.

"Sorry my bed's so small," I said after I turned off the lamp.

"That's okay. We've been sleeping together in this bed for as long as I can remember. But I guess we're a lot bigger. Especially me."

"Yeah, I feel like such a shrimp next to you," I said. "Mind if I turn on the radio for a while?"

The Look of Love was playing. As I listened to the words, two tears rolled down my cheeks, and into my ears. I was glad it was dark, so Mimi wouldn't notice. Seeing Tom had made me realize how much I missed him.

"You're awfully quiet," Mimi said.

"Oh sorry. I was just listening to this song. I really like it."

"I like it too. My mom doesn't even turn the station if it comes on in the car."

"But Mimi, doesn't it make you think about a certain boy?"

"What certain boy?"

"You know, somebody you have a crush on or something."

"I don't have a crush on anybody."

"Okay, maybe not now. But ever? You can't tell me you've never had a crush on any boy *ever*."

"I guess I'll have to think about it. Ask me tomorrow. Meantime, you need to fill me in on that tornado day."

"Oh yeah. I forgot. Well, I was at the park with my friends on the cement block. I had just gotten out of the hospital, in fact."

"I hardly even know about the hospital, either," Mimi said.

"One thing at a time. The weather had been getting funny. It was windy, and the sky was kind of yellowish-green. Anyway, all of a sudden, the siren went off, you know the tornado alert siren. Maureen wanted me to run home with her, 'cause it was closer. But thankfully, I remembered that Cathy was alone and she's terrified of tornadoes and always hides under her bed even when it just storms."

"Yeah, I remember you telling me that."

"Well, I ran to her house and when I got close to Burton Street, a whole tree crashed down and a park bench went flying by me."

"You could have been killed! So, what about Cathy?"

"Sure enough, she was under the bed and I practically had to drag her down to the basement."

"How did you keep her calm? Or did you?"

"I talked her ear off down in the basement."

"What'd you do, tell her jokes or stories about your dad or something?"

"No, I talked about Tom, which was her favorite topic, or obsession, for all of last year."

"Oh, that's right. I remember you telling me that on spring break."

"Yeah well, I hadn't heard from him since before I went in the hospital. Actually, since our graduation party at a cottage, which turned out to be a nightmare. Then I saw him when I was running home."

"You hadn't heard from him? Hmm. And there was no time to stop and talk then, right?"

"No, I didn't stop for lots of reasons. But the main one was that he was kissing another girl."

"Oh no. Boy, Ruth Ann, he's not such a great guy after all, is he?"

Chapter Eight

After Mass, we had pancakes and sausage. My mom did special things when Mimi visited, and like Renee, she stayed in a better mood.

"Where's Renee?" I asked as I reached for the Log Cabin syrup.

My mom blew smoke over her shoulder.

"Laying down. She doesn't feel good."

Maureen called as we were clearing the table and asked if we wanted to lay out in her backyard.

"That's not a bad idea, Ruth Ann," my mom said. "You're supposed to be doing that for your psoriasis, anyway. And by the way, you have an appointment next week with the new dermatologist."

We cut through the park on our way to Maureen's house. The cicadas sang above us in the trees and the Rose of Sharon trees were in full bloom along the path.

"I hope Renee's not sick," Mimi said.

"She probably just has her period. She always carries on like she's the only one in the whole world who has one."

"Hey Ruth Ann!"

I looked toward the playground and Tom was leaning over the monkey bars. A few Burton School kids were hanging around, but I checked and didn't see Leta.

I wasn't sure what to do.

"Do you mind if we stop for a couple minutes?" I asked Mimi.

"I don't mind. Go ahead."

As we approached the playground, Tom walked over to a bench and sat down. Two of the Burton girls were chasing a boy around and laughing. We stopped by the bench.

"Hey girls, where you off to?"

"We're on our way to Maureen's," I answered.

"I can't remember the last time I was on a swing," Mimi said. "I'll be right back."

It was the first time I had been alone with Tom since the day in the boat.

"Well, sit down for a minute." He patted the bench.

Then he put a weird looking, old pipe in his mouth. It was white and had a face carved into it. There was nothing in the pipe, but he sucked on it.

"Help, Tom, help." One of the girls ran by the bench and was laughing over her shoulder at the boy who was chasing her.

"Who are these kids?" I asked. "Do you know them?"

"Yeah, kinda. I don't know. Here, taste this."

He held the pipe toward my mouth and I shook my head.

"Why not? There's nothing in it. Just try it."

"Uh-uh, I don't want your germs," I said as I pulled my face back.

"Oh, come on. Like we haven't swapped germs before."

That did it. I don't know why. All my old feelings came rushing back. I wanted to kiss him so bad right then, that I might have if Mimi wasn't over on the swings. But a little voice in my head told me to hold completely back. I did take a taste of the pipe just for the heck of it. It was kind of bitter.

"What was in this?" I asked.

"What do you think?" He winked at me and I noticed that little mustache-y thing again.

How did he get so much cuter and older looking in only two months? He seemed different in a bunch of ways. I couldn't put my finger on it.

"I've really missed you, Ruth Ann."

"Oh, really? What about Leta?"

"Leta? Are you kidding? That meant nothing. I will always love you. Forever and ever until the end of time. You didn't forget that, did you?"

I just stared at him. A thousand things were on the tip of my tongue, but I couldn't sort out my thoughts or my feelings.

"We have to get going," I said.

He leaned in for a kiss, but I turned to pick up my beach bag and stood up.

"Come on, Mimi. Let's get going."

As Mimi skidded to a stop on the swing, Tom stood, and set the pipe on the bench.

"You can't forget what we had," he said, looking into my eyes. "I know you can't. Can I call you tonight?"

Then he leaned toward me and put his nose by my neck.

"Why aren't you wearing Ambush anymore?"

I felt like saying, because it makes me think of you, but I didn't. The girl who'd been running around like a nut, stopped behind Tom and took hold of his shoulders. She was practically panting, she was so out of breath.

"Tom, you need to drag Joey over that fence and throw him in the pool!"

Then she took off again, as the boy chased her toward the community building.

"Let's go, Mimi," I said. "Maureen'll wonder where we are."

Maureen had three chaise lounges set up in her back yard. Her Pomeranian, Teeney, started yapping as soon as we got there. The radio was playing and there was a bowl of Bugles on a table and a package of Lorna Doones. Mimi and I spread our beach towels on the chairs and plopped down.

"What really matters is how you feel about him," Maureen said, as she unscrewed the lid from a bottle of nail polish. "Who wants Hot House Tomato on their toes? Actually, I don't want it either. I'm sticking with Pearly Gates, so I'll look more tan."

"To be honest," I said, "I still get all fluttery inside when he's close by. But I'll probably never trust him again."

"Seems to me, you could forgive one kiss," Mimi said as she applied suntan lotion to her arms. "I thought he said it didn't mean anything."

"I'm sure it was more than just that one kiss, that I just *happened* to see. There's no doubt in my mind about that."

I picked up a pile of teen magazines that Maureen had brought out.

"Oh, jeez, I read this one in the hospital. What a bad memory!"

Mimi gave me a sympathetic look because, after telling her about the tornado last night, I'd filled her in on all the tar treatments and other stuff that happened at the hospital.

"I still feel bad that I was out of town then," Maureen said.

When Mimi went inside to use the bathroom, Maureen leaned over the arm of her lawn chair, "I get the feeling you haven't told Mimi all the stuff about Tom. Only about seeing him kiss Leta."

"I haven't filled her in on what happened at the cottage party, if that's what you mean," I said as I scratched the top of Teeney's head.

"Did you tell her that he never came to see you in the hospital?"

"I don't think so. I might tell her that, but not about the cottage. She would flip if she knew I ever went past first base."

When we got back home, my mom's on-again, off-again boyfriend, Larry, came around the side of the house, wearing Renee's comedy-tragedy apron and holding a spatula.

"Well, how 'bout that," he said. "I finally get to meet Mimi. I feel like we're long lost friends. I just threw the hot dogs on, girls. Go see who's out there, Ruth Ann."

A huge burst of laughter rang out from the backyard. I knew instantly who it was.

"Look who's here!" My mom's friend, Trudy, came running toward me with open arms. She kissed both of my cheeks and then held them.

"She's the same, Bruce, but much wiser looking. She's still got those cats' eyes though, just like her mother."

I introduced Mimi to my mom's friends, Trudy and Bruce, and wondered why my mom hadn't told me she was having company. I also wondered what Mimi thought of Trudy's outfit. She was wearing a shiny blue party dress with a full skirt and fluffy bedroom slippers she should have thrown out. Her German accent was as strong as her laugh. I knew after she had a couple of beers, we would hear the whole story about when she was captured by the Russians as a girl, and then escaped under a pile of coal on a truck. It was a great story, and I never got tired of hearing it.

We sat in a circle with our paper plates on our laps. My mom apologized that we didn't have a picnic table.

"I guess you forgot to come over."

I turned around and Cathy was standing at the fence with a plate of cannoli.

"Oh, sorry, Cathy. I didn't see you after Mass, and I didn't know if you'd mentioned a time or anything. Maureen asked us to lay out over at her house. Come on over."

"Well, okay, I guess. For a while."

"These are so delicious!" Trudy said to Cathy, as she bit into one of the cannoli. "How does your mother make them?"

"What I'd like to know," Renee said, "Is why you all have to smoke at the same time? I'm going in. The mosquitos are biting too."

I looked over at Mimi who had a cannoli halfway to her mouth. She'd finally gotten a hint of the real Renee.

"That one," Trudy said, after my sister left the yard, "She winds up like a top, every time I see her."

The phone rang while I was making more lemonade. Everyone else was still in the yard. It was Tom. "Did you think about what I said today?"

"About what?"

"About us. About what we had together and how we should keep having it."

"You make it sound like something we should keep having for dinner every night. Like salad or something."

He laughed really hard when I said that, which got to me, because he did have a really good laugh. It made me remember how he used to be, before he was in the band and before he was friends with so many kids from Burton School.

"Well, I'll see you at the park tomorrow," he said. "At least, I hope so."

Mimi and I walked to Alger Heights the next day to have lunch at the Sundae Shoppe with the Tandem Riders. We wandered around in Fenstemacher's Fabric Shop after we ate.

"I wish I could sew," I said.

"Why don't you have Renee teach you?" Mimi asked.

"First of all, she'd kill me before I got the needle threaded, and second of all, she can't sew her way out of a paper bag. You should see the granny dress she made me for Christmas. The sleeves cut off the circulation in my arms."

"At least we can wear anything we want with our uniform skirts this year," Mary Lou said, as we flipped through catalogs of patterns.

"Yeah, we should all burn our uniforms from St. Boner's," Maureen said. "I'm serious, let's have a bonfire some night."

We stopped at Mitchell's Young at Heart to see what was new in the teen department.

"I haven't seen you all summer," the owner said to me. She was always so nice about letting me put things on lay-away.

"We've got some navy blue uniform skirts all ready to go out," she said.

"No offense, Mrs. Roshevsky," Maureen said, "But we're not quite ready to think about that yet."

"I have to go school shopping as soon as I get back," Mimi said.

Mimi went to public school and got a whole new wardrobe every season. It was a good thing I had to wear a uniform, because I would have a real problem with the few clothes I owned.

We stopped in the park after Alger Heights. As we walked toward our cement block, I heard somebody singing and turned around.

"Look, it's Zeke," Peg said.

I turned to Mimi, "The first time I heard Zeke sing was the day of the tornado. You wouldn't believe the voice on that kid. His best song is *I*

Wish It Would Rain."

"And remember?" Angela laughed. "It started pouring right after he sang it."

"Good afternoon, lovely ladies." Zeke bowed to us, and I saw Mimi's nostrils flare, which happens when she's amused.

"Got any songs that aren't about rain?" Irene asked.

"As a matter of fact, I do. You wanna hear my latest?"

We all answered yes at once, while we climbed up on our block. Zeke began singing *Little Bit of Soul.* When he added dance moves, we all clapped and started singing with him. I couldn't help watching Mimi, because it was so nice to see her lighten up. When he was done singing, we all offered him candy from our Alger Variety bags. Then he ran off to play basketball with his friends.

Two boys from our class, Teddy Zukowski and Gerard Waterman, wandered over after Zeke left.

"What're you girls thinkin'?" Teddy asked.

"What do you mean?" Maureen asked him.

"Talkin' to that little spade and having him sing to you. What do you think I mean?'

"Oh my God," I said. "I can't believe you just called him that!"

"Well, that's what he is. What do you want me to call him?"

"How about a kid, a boy, a human being? How 'bout that, Zukowski?"

I was shouting at him. The other girls were all looking at me. A bunch of kids with towels around their necks had stopped walking and were listening. Gerard Waterman was shifting his weight from one foot to another and looking around nervously.

"Well, excuuuse me!" Teddy said in a mocking voice. "I didn't know you were so fond of spades, or I woulda watched my mouth. Maybe since you're a leper that makes you feel sorry for everybody, huh?"

"Shut your fucking mouth, Zukowski," Maureen said, as she jumped off the cement block. "And get the hell away from us."

I jumped off too and stood beside her. I shot a glance at Mimi and she looked like she'd just woke up from a nightmare.

"Okay, spade lovers," Zukowski laughed. "We'll go find us some *real* white girls."

After they walked away, Maureen and I both turned and faced one another and for a minute I thought we were both going to cry. Then we started laughing.

"Wow, you two really told him," Peg said. "That was extraordinarily cool!"

"Yeah, and he's always bugged the hell outa me, anyway," Mary Lou said.

I glanced toward Mimi. "Sorry, Mimi. This kind of stuff hasn't happened before, I promise. And I'm sorry about all the swearing." She gave me a serious nod.

"Enough with all the sorry stuff," Maureen said. "Who the hell has a match?"

Chapter Nine

When we came through the side door, I could hear my mom talking on the phone in the dining room.

"Thanks for listening, Trudy," she said. "You've really been a doll. I can't talk to my sisters about this."

Mimi was getting a drink of water and didn't seem to be paying any attention to my mom. I was dying to know what she was talking about but decided to keep my mouth shut for once.

"Is that you, Ruth Ann?" she hollered in. "I gotta go, Trudy. Can we talk tomorrow? Okay then. Say hi to Bruce."

I walked into the dining room, where my mom was stubbing out a Salem in an ashtray. She seemed nervous. "Did you girls have a nice day? Where've you been?"

"Oh, here and there," I answered.

"Where exactly is here and there?"

"Alger Heights mostly. And the park."

"You're spending way too much time in that park, Ruth Ann. I don't see Cathy traipsing over there every day. She really likes Mimi, you know. I'd like you to stay home tonight and have her over."

"Oh Mom, come on! Cathy's such a bore."

"I think she's really nice," Mimi chimed in.

"See," my mom said. "You give her a call right now while I take Renee a glass of ice water. She had a rough day at work."

I turned around to look at the kitchen clock. "She's home already?"

"Yes, she left a little early. Now, go call Cathy, would you? Then I'm going to make pork chops and Rice-A-Roni. How does that sound?"

"It sounds fine. Hey, how come you were talking to Trudy today, and she just came over yesterday? And, you never even told me they were all coming over here."

"Trudy and I have a lot of catching up to do. I hadn't seen her or Bruce since New Year's Eve. Anyway, aren't I allowed to have company over?"

Her answers made no sense to me, but I decided it wasn't worth the trouble to drag out the conversation.

Cathy came over after dinner and the three of us took the ladder out and climbed up on the garage roof. It's something we had done the past couple of summers. We were in the back, facing the lilac bushes where nobody could see us. It felt so peaceful and private, that I wondered why I only did this with Cathy and Mimi.

"Remember what you told us up here last summer?" Cathy asked.

"No," I said. "What was it?"

"You told us that Mary Lou Bender paid Gerard Waterman a nickel to come over to your house and you sat up here with him."

"Oh yeah, I almost forgot about that. I had a huge crush on him in sixth grade."

"Gerard Waterman?" Mimi asked. "That kid from today?"

I gave her a direct look and shook my head as slightly as possible. I didn't feel like explaining the whole story about Zeke to Cathy.

"Speaking of crushes, Mimi," I said, "you were going to think about who you've ever had a crush on, remember?"

Mimi's nostrils flared, and she turned pinkish. "Okay, I did think about it and you're right. I did have one, at least I think it was a crush."

"You're not even sure?" I asked. "Who was it?"

"Chad. The towel boy at our country club."

"The towel boy? Did we see him when we were there last week?"

"No, he's not there this year."

"I wonder if he could tell you had a crush on him."

"I don't think so. The problem was, I didn't wear my glasses when I went to the towel bar, so I couldn't see him very well."

"Why didn't you wear your glasses?" Cathy asked her.

Mimi hesitated, probably because Cathy's glasses were even thicker than hers.

"I hate to tell you, Cathy," Mimi said." But boys don't really look at girls with glasses."

"Oh, yeah. I guess that's true," Cathy said.

"Cut it out, you two. You both have the prettiest eyes of all my friends. And look over there. Isn't that the prettiest tree you ever saw?"

Both girls turned their heads to the left and looked up.

"Yeah, it is," Mimi said. "What kind is it?"

"It's a Chinese Elm. They're kind of rare, I guess."

I thought about telling them how I looked out my bedroom window and talked to the tree the first couple years we lived here, but decided they'd think I was even more of an "oddball," as my mother liked to say.

"It's very graceful," Mimi said. "I can see why you like it."

Mimi had a respectful look in her eyes when she made that comment. Maybe my tree loving would balance out my recent swearing and smoking.

"What about you, Cathy?" Mimi asked. "Do you have a crush on anyone or do you have a boyfriend?"

"No, not me. But almost every girl in my class had a crush on Tom LaBelle last year. And then the girl I played Barbies with ends up being his girlfriend."

"Well," Mimi said, "I remember the three of us playing Barbies and Ruth Ann's Barbie was always making out with Paul."

"My Barbie did a whole lot more than just make out with Paul," I said. "And it seems to me your Barbie had a few sessions with George."

"Ruth Ann's Barbie had her period all the time too," Cathy added. "Remember how she made Kotex out of her evening gloves?"

"Let's not talk about that," I said. "I have cramps right now. In fact, I'll probably start bleeding any minute."

Neither Mimi or Cathy made any comment, so I checked, and sure enough, they were both practically blushing. It was getting harder and harder to be myself around them.

"Come on you guys. Let's go in and make popcorn. Maybe there's something good on TV."

We ended up watching *How to Marry A Millionaire,* and the three of us sat on the couch with me in the middle, and the popcorn bowl on my lap. When Marilyn Monroe took off her glasses around men, Mimi leaned over me. "See what I mean, Cathy?"

Renee wandered in and sat on the arm of the couch for a few minutes. It felt weird, because she never hung around me and my friends. I guess Cathy and Mimi were different, though.

"Are you feeling better, Renee?" Mimi asked. "Want some popcorn?"

"No thanks," she said quietly. She watched the movie for about fifteen minutes and even laughed with us when the guy on the airplane told Marilyn Monroe she was "quite a strudel." Then she picked up Ruff and said, "Good night, girls. I'm going to bed."

I could tell that both Mimi and Cathy didn't think anything was off with Renee. But I knew something was off. Way, way off.

Mimi and I decided to take the bus downtown the next day. We had just locked the door when I heard the phone ringing inside.

"Hang on, Mimi. It might be my mom."

It was Tom. "Hey there," he said. "I hear you ripped Zukowski to pieces yesterday."

"Not really. It was just what he deserved."

"Yeah, I know that Zeke kid. He's cool as hell, and can really sing."

"Well, I didn't do it just because he can sing."

"Oh sure, I know. Hey, are you and your Saginaw friend going to the park?"

"No, we're actually going somewhere else and if I don't hang up, we'll miss our bus."

"All right," he said. "Maybe I'll catch ya later."

"Was it your mom?" Mimi asked when I came back out.

"No, it was Tom. Come on, let's run or we're gonna miss the ten-thirty-four bus."

"What did he want?" Mimi asked as we sprinted down Beulah Street toward Madison.

"If we were going to the park."

"Wow. He really wants to get back together. Are you playing hard to get?"

"Hard to get?" I laughed. "You got that from Archie and Veronica, didn't you?"

It was fun showing our big department stores to Mimi. We stopped at the candy corner in Steketee's where we bought licorice records. Then we went next door to Fanny Farmer's for French Mint candy bars. The bell on the door chimed when we walked in, and two girls turned around.

"Well, look who the cat dragged in!"

It was Irene's cousin, Denise, who had visited me in the hospital a bunch of times. We hugged immediately.

"Oh my God, I was gonna call you last week. I'm not kidding," she said. "This is my friend, Julie Westover. She'll be in our class."

I introduced Mimi to them and then we all decided to eat lunch together at Muir's Drug Store. After we sat down in a booth, Denise noticed I was wearing the seashell earrings she'd given me in the hospital. I could tell she was pleased.

"Remember Vivian, the tray girl from the hospital you made friends with?" Denise asked. "She's pregnant, but don't worry, they got married and she's going to Park School, you know the school for pregnant girls?"

"Pregnant? Wow. Married? And she's not even sixteen yet!" I said.

"I saw her in the hospital gift shop and she remembered me from visiting you. Of course, nobody ever forgets my fat ass."

Vivian had brought my breakfast and lunch trays every day in the hospital, and we became friendly. Her life at home was rough and she was working at the hospital, too. I couldn't believe things could get any worse.

"I didn't get a chance to say good-bye to her before I left," I said, as I salted my french fries.

"Yeah, you left in a hurry," Denise said. "I came up to see you, but they said you'd been discharged. When I tried to call you a couple times, the line was either busy or nobody answered. Then I got too busy, mostly babysitting. I've barely had time to brush my teeth all summer."

"She really hasn't," Julie said.

Julie had beautiful, silky brown hair that curled over her shoulders. She had braces and wore blue eye shadow with dark blue mascara. She was slightly plump, but nothing like Denise. Denise was the heaviest girl I'd ever known. And the funniest.

"I meant to call you all summer too, Denise," I said. "So you haven't been hanging out in the hospital with your friends much?"

"No, they got summer jobs, anyway. In fact, Charlie got a job at the hospital. Can you believe it?"

Denise was good buddies with three guys who lived in the neighborhood near the hospital. She'd brought them up to visit me a bunch of times because they hung out in the hospital cafeteria. They were funny and smart. Way different than the guys from St. Boner's.

"Are you going to the St. Blaise dance?" Julie asked. "It's for the incoming freshman, so we can all meet each other."

"Some of the older kids go too," Denise added. "It's on August 24th. You should really go."

"I heard something about it from my friend, Angela," I said. "It does sound kind of fun."

"You have to go," Denise said. "I'm pretty sure Michael, Charlie, and Eddie are going. They'd be so stoked to see you."

"Hmm, really?"

"They liked you a lot," Denise said, "and felt bad you left the hospital before they saw you again. Weren't you supposed to stay longer?"

"Yeah, I sort of got kicked out the day after they came last time."

"You're kidding! Kicked out? What for?"

Mimi was looking at me like I was a stranger who had randomly slipped into the booth. Oh well, I thought to myself. *She may as well hear this.*

"Well, it was partly because they thought I wasn't taking the treatment seriously," I said. "But I think that bitchy head nurse wanted me out because of the boys coming up."

"Seriously?" Denise asked. "They never got out of line or anything, did they?"

"Well, actually, Michael swiped a guy's pipe. He'd left it in the ashtray in the visitor's lounge. But he denied the whole thing. It doesn't matter. I needed to get out of there anyway."

Denise shook her head and chuckled. "It helped though, didn't it? Your arms look way better."

"It helped some. I'm also using this special cream and laying out in the sun as much as I can."

"What were you in the hospital for?" Julie asked.

When I explained psoriasis to her, she had such a disgusted look on her face that I thought she was going to lose her lunch. I wasn't sure I liked her after all and was kind of surprised Denise was friends with her.

After we got done eating, we looked at the make-up for a while and then said good-by.

"Listen," Denise said, "I'm calling you next week about the dance. You *are* going, hear me?"

I nodded and gave her a hug. "It's so good to see you again," I said.

"You didn't tell me you got kicked out of the hospital," Mimi said as soon as we sat down in the bus. She sounded kind of hurt.

"Well, it wasn't official or anything, and like I said, I was about to go crazy in there."

"You sure know a lot of troubled boys," Mimi said.

"Troubled? Oh, Michael wasn't troubled. He's a really cool guy. That pipe thing was like a prank. Seriously, he's smart and knows a lot about all sorts of things."

"Oh." She pulled the Top 40 list from her purse. We'd picked them up at Dodds Record Shop. She was pretending to study it, but I knew she was thinking about how different I was from her.

"Isn't Denise nice?" I asked. "She came up to the hospital almost every day, and I'd only met her once before."

"Who's Vivian?" she asked. "You didn't tell me about her, either."

"She's the tray girl from the hospital. We kind of made friends while I was there. I can't believe she's married *and* pregnant! But I'm glad to hear she's still going to school."

"Hey there, Sport. How was your first day of school?"

"Terrible. My teacher is a crabby old nun named Sister Patrice. She never, ever smiles. And she asked me, "What kind of name is Bloomfield?"

"Did you tell her it was Martian? What grade are you in this year?"

"Oh, Daddy, I told you before. I'm in fourth! And what I want to know is why Renee didn't have to go back to school. Nobody around here tells me a thing."

"Well, Sport, your sister needs to take a little time off."

"*Is it because she flunked geology? I bet they kicked her out. I'm a rock collector, you know. I wouldn't have flunked geology.*"

"*It's a few different things, Sport. Don't worry, she'll be outta your hair before you know it. You do a good job in school and maybe I'll buy you that microscope you've been askin' for.*"

"*Telescope, Daddy. But I'll take a microscope too, if you find that first. And guess what? There's a store here called Rozema's Rock Pile. If you ever visit on a Saturday, maybe we could go there.*"

"*Sure, Sport, we'll get you to the rock store. I gotta go now. Grandma's old ringer washing machine is on the fritz again. I promised her I'd come take a look at it.*"

When I woke up the next morning, Mimi had already gone downstairs. She was sitting on the couch with Ruff and Reddy, watching *Channel Three Clubhouse*.

"What is this show?" she asked. "I've never heard of it."

"I think it's only on this side of the state. And they never had *Ding Dong School* over here, like they did in Saginaw. How long have you been up?"

"Not too long."

"I'm starved. Want some cinnamon toast?"

"Sure."

Reddy followed me to the kitchen and jumped up on the counter.

"Oh, no you don't," I said to him as I knocked him down. "Renee would spank you for that."

I set the toast on the coffee table and sat down next to Mimi. Reddy stretched out and came over to my lap.

"Are you having a good time here?" I asked Mimi.

"What do you mean?"

"I don't know. You've been quieter than I ever remember. I know we've been with my friends a lot. I had no idea we'd run into Denise downtown. I kind of meant for us to have yesterday to ourselves."

"They weren't with us that long."

"Well, I hope it's okay. I mean I hope *we're* okay."

Mimi nodded and smiled.

"What do you feel like doing today?"

"Maybe just sticking around here and watching TV. Unless you have another idea."

"No, that's fine. I'm supposed to lay out for my skin, so you can join me if you want."

After we watched reruns of *Bewitched* and *The Lucy Show* in our pajamas, we changed into our bathing suits, and took the transistor radio and several issues of Renee's *Glamour* magazines out to the backyard.

"Renee would kill me for taking these outside, but I don't care. We'll just be extra careful." I flipped through the June issue. "I would give anything to look like Cheryl Tiegs. Just look at how thin her lips are."

"She's very pretty," Mimi agreed. "My mom says she has an all-American look. But I never noticed her lips before."

"That's because you probably don't hate your lips like I hate mine."

"Hey, you guys. Guess what I have in the oven."

I looked up from my magazine to see Cathy at the fence.

"Hmm, let me guess. Cherry chip casserole."

"Very funny. But you're right about the cherry chip part. I'll bring some over after it's frosted."

We ate our lunch of peanut butter on crackers, and peaches, on the blanket in the back yard. The Chinese Elm tree swayed gently in the breeze and there was a sweet scent in the air.

"I love summer," I said to Mimi. "I wish it wasn't almost over."

Maureen called at three o'clock. I filled her in on our trip downtown and how we'd run into Denise.

"She really wants all of us to go to the St. Blaise dance. You know, the one that Angela was talking about."

"Well, let's go then. I wouldn't mind checking out some new guys. We better practice that new dance, though. You know, the one Mary Lou showed us the other day. But listen. The main reason I called, was to be sure you and Mimi are planning to stay here this weekend when my parents go to the cottage."

"I want to, but I'm not sure what to tell my mom," I said.

"Just tell her the truth. Tell her I don't want to go, but I can't stay alone."

"Well, let me see what kind of mood she's in when she gets home. If she's really tired, I'll ask tomorrow. Maybe if we stick around here tonight that'll soften her up."

When I went back outside, Mimi and Cathy were giggling and eating Cherry Chip cake.

"What's so funny?" I asked.

"I found this in your room," Mimi said.

"Oh that. Renee gave it to me for my birthday."

They were pouring over the booklet, *Necking and Petting and How Far to Go.*

"Listen to this," Cathy said. "It says necking turns into petting when feet are off the floor and hands are no longer on deck. What deck? What does that mean?"

"Oh my God, you guys," I said. "Give me that stupid thing, or better yet, Cathy, just take it home. I can't believe you're even reading it."

"Did Renee give you this one too?" Mimi asked. "Look, it's by the American Bandstand guy." She held up a copy of *Your Happiest Years* by Dick Clark.

"That was hers. It's probably from the fifties. Where'd you find it?"

"It was right next to the necking and petting book on your shelf. It says it's a "frank and friendly book for and about young adults."

"Renee must have shoved that in there. Let me see it." I opened to the chapter entitled, *Some Signs of Teen-itis.* "Okay, maybe that's why Renee hates me. She thinks I have teen-itis!"

My mom was talking to Trudy on the phone while we washed the dinner dishes. I was trying to listen because she was talking quietly, and I was still curious about all their recent conversations. Mimi was chattier than she'd been the past few days. Probably because Cathy had been over. I could tell she liked her better than any of the Tandem Riders. Renee leaned over me at the sink with a peach in her hand.

"Let me wash this a minute," she said. "Oh by the way, I just looked in the TV Guide, and there's a Hayley Mills movie on tonight at nine."

"Oh good. Thanks, Renee."

Renee was always nicer to me when I was working.

"Are you doing a good enough job of rinsing?" Renee asked. "You always leave soap residue on the dishes."

"You would think I never did the dishes," I said to Mimi.

Renee stuck her head back in the doorway. "That's because you hardly ever do."

We invited Cathy over to watch *The Chalk Garden*. I practically had a crush on Hayley Mills when I was younger, and I'd never even seen this movie. My mom was so pleased that Cathy was over again that she made her famous caramel corn. The phone rang right when Hayley Mills was figuring out that her governess had "a past." I was hoping that my mom or Renee would answer it upstairs.

"Oh, shoot," I said. "I guess they're sleeping and my hands are all sticky."

I set the popcorn on Cathy's lap and climbed over her legs to get to the phone. It was Tom.

"Hey there," he said. "What are you up to? I haven't seen you at the park. Is your Saginaw friend still here?"

"Yeah, she's here until next Monday. I guess we've been pretty busy."

"Well, I miss you. Do you miss me?"

"Well, like I said, we've been busy."

"Too busy to miss me?"

"I don't know," I said. "Kind of."

"I know you better than that, Ruth Ann. All I can think of is holding you in my arms."

"Your parents are gone, aren't they?"

Tom laughed. That good old laugh that made me miss him again.

"Listen, we're watching a really good movie and I'm missing the best part. Maybe I'll see you tomorrow, okay?"

My heart skipped a beat when I hung up the phone. *Ha ha ha*, I thought to myself. *You go ahead and miss me. How do you think I felt in the hospital and for all those weeks after?*

Irene called the next morning and said she was going crazy because Peg was on vacation. "Since Peg is gone and your friend is still here, how' bout the rest of us rent tandem bikes? Peg won't mind as long as we all do it again before school starts. I'll call Mary Lou and Angela. You call Maureen."

Mimi thought it sounded fun, so we met the girls at Alger Schwinn

Bike Shop after lunch. We pedaled up and down the prettiest streets in Alger Heights. We even went down to Plaster Creek and looked in the giant manhole.

"I heard that Leta was down here last week making out with Rick," Angela said.

"So they're back together?" Maureen asked.

"Yeah, I think her deal with Tom lasted for less than two weeks," Mary Lou added. "I heard it was just to make Rick jealous. So I guess Tom's free again, Ruth Ann. That is, if you're interested."

Maureen gave me one of her knowing looks, and then we all pedaled toward Brookside School, up to Jefferson Drive, past Burton Woods and down the hill into Garfield Park. We circled the wading pool that was filled with little kids, splashing and shouting. I spotted Tom sitting on the top of the slide, slinging wood chips at his next-door neighbor, Marty, who was popping wheelies on a Stingray bike. A few kids from Burton school were sitting on the monkey bars.

We all stopped our tandem bikes and got off. Marty wheeled over and jumped off his bike.

"Hey look, it's the Tandem Riders minus Peg. Where is she?"

Peg and Marty had a brief romance when Tom and I first got together. We had even gone to the movie together once. Peg said Marty was kind of immature and so it hadn't lasted very long.

Tom walked over while we were talking to Marty.

"Hi. How 'bout we take a walk?"

No Doubt in my Mind

I looked over at Mimi who was looking at the monster stickers on Marty's bike. He was explaining his collection. The other girls were headed for the drinking fountain.

"Well, okay, I guess. But just for a minute, 'cause we have to get the bikes back by three."

We walked around the side of the building and I couldn't help but wince when we walked right past the place I'd seen him kissing Leta. He took my hand, which felt strange. I wanted it to feel like it did on the Ferris wheel in the beginning of eighth grade, but it didn't.

"Let's sit over here," he said as he led me to a giant oak tree.

I thought about telling him how I'd seen a giant oak tree fall the day of the tornado. He didn't even know about that. In fact, he hardly knew anything about my entire summer. We used to tell each other every detail of our lives. I felt like I didn't really know him anymore. He traced his finger down the side of my face.

"I've been dreaming about this," he said. And before I knew it, his lips were coming toward mine and I wanted them to. Even though my mind and heart felt confused, I couldn't resist letting him kiss me. At first, it felt like the old Tom and the old grabby feeling started up. Then I thought of him pressing down on me in the boat and how bad my skin hurt and how I wished I was dead that day. I pulled away.

"What's wrong?" he asked. "I could tell you liked it. Don't say you didn't."

"I'm just not ready."

"Not ready? I heard you were plenty ready with Donnie Walker."

"Donnie Walker? Whoa! You should talk. I didn't even know if we had broken up when I saw you kissing Leta. Donnie Walker and I mostly looked at constellations and cloud formations."

"Okay, okay. Settle down. What matters now is that we're back together. Come on, Ruth Ann, you need to let yourself love me again."

Mimi came around the building, walking the tandem bike. "It's quarter to three, we need to leave."

The other girls wheeled up behind her and they all stopped their bikes and stared at me and Tom. My stomach and heart felt like they'd switched places. Maybe Dick Clark and Renee were right, I thought to myself. Maybe I really did have *teen-itis*.

Chapter Ten

I didn't tell Mimi about Tom kissing me at the park. She asked me on the way home if we were back together and I said no.

"That's what he wants, but I'm not sure that's what I want."

I couldn't explain to Mimi how my chest pulled and felt empty when I thought about him, and how it all moved down to my stomach when I was with him.

"I have a feeling there's more to the story than you're telling me," Mimi said as we rounded the corner of Prospect Street. I had taken the long way home from the bicycle shop, so I wouldn't run into Tom again at the park. I considered telling her what had happened at the cottage party, but my neighbor, Mrs. Harris, stopped her car in the middle of the street.

"Hi, Ruth Ann. I've hardly seen you all summer. I'm going to need a sitter in a couple of weeks because I'm going to a wedding. I'll call you, okay?"

"Sure." I waved at David and Steven who were in the back seat.

I babysit for those boys quite a bit," I told Mimi after they pulled away. "Steven walks in his sleep. It's pretty funny."

"Gussie used to do that. Remember?"

I laughed. "Oh yeah, he did, didn't he? I can't believe we used to play Gypsy Rose Lee and force him to be the audience while we did a strip-tease. Do you think he ever told your parents?"

"Not that I know of," Mimi said. "I know they would have said something like, how could you do such a thing to your precious little brother?"

The phone was ringing when we came in the back door. I wondered if it was going to be Tom. It was my mom calling from work.

"I wanted to be sure you girls were back from your bike ride. We're going to Fiesta Cafe for tacos as soon as I get home, so stick around."

"Can't we go to Fables or Kewpies?" I asked. "I doubt if Mimi likes tacos."

"She can get a hamburger at Fiesta. You know that. Renee called me from work because she's dying for tacos. Look, I have a report to type before I leave. Just be ready, okay?"

My mom was shaking her head over a bill when Renee came down the stairs wearing one of the shift dresses she'd made back when we lived in Mt. Pleasant.

"I can't believe you still have that," I said.

"What's that supposed to mean?" Renee asked, as she took her sunglasses out of her purse.

"Nothing. I'm just surprised you still have it, that's all."

"It's comfortable. Not that it's any of your business. I happen to enjoy a rotation in my wardrobe. Unlike you who lives in those jeans and that blouse."

"Well, Renee, *unlike you*, I have a skin disease to cover up and I don't exactly have a wardrobe *to rotate to*."

"I'm fully aware you have a skin disease, dearie. Who do you think vacuumed up all your shedding skin when it was so bad."

"You two cut it out right now," my mom said. "Poor Mimi doesn't want to listen to this. I think we're all hungry. Wait for me in the car. I just want to change into my pedal pushers."

The phone started ringing, and Renee walked over to the window seat and answered it.

"Oh, hi, Jerry Michael!"

"You two get in the car," my mom said, and she gave me a little push toward the door.

"Jerry Michael?" Mimi asked. "Your cousin?"

I turned and nodded to her as she climbed into the back seat behind me.

"I wonder why he's calling," I said.

"Renee's kind of grouchy today," Mimi said.

"I told you before what she's like. For some reason, she's not being as fake around you as she usually is."

My mom got in the car and told us Renee was just about to hang up.

"So how was your bike ride, girls?"

"It was fun," Mimi answered. "I've never rented bikes before."

Renee opened the car door with an actual smile on her face.

"Well, it looks like Jerry Michael will be here for the weekend," she announced. "We'll have to pick him up tomorrow night at the Greyhound station."

"Oh good," my mom said. It seemed like my mom wasn't surprised that he was coming. In fact, she sounded relieved.

Mimi ended up ordering tacos. She said she felt adventurous. Renee was in a much better mood.

"Jerry Michael hasn't been here since the summer before last," she said to my mom.

"Yeah, I dragged him to the pool last time," I said. "And he was the only guy there. He thought it was pretty funny and said it was completely wasted on him."

I looked at Mimi. "You know, 'cause he doesn't really like girls. I mean he likes them. Just not the usual way."

Mimi nodded as though she understood all about these things.

"He's a total blast," I said. "Remember when he wore that lampshade through our entire dinner?"

Renee looked up while she was dousing her tacos with hot sauce. "I'm glad Jerry Michael doesn't mind sleeping on the couch. At least he didn't last time he was here."

That's when inspiration took over. "I have a great idea," I piped up. "Jerry Michael can sleep in my bed, and we can stay over at Maureen's. Her parents are going to the cottage and she doesn't want to stay at home by herself."

"Why is she staying home by herself?" my mom asked with a taco halfway to her mouth.

"She's kind of sick of going there and she has some kind of project, I think."

"Project?" Renee asked with a suspicious tone.

I looked at the plaid material of Renee's old shift dress.

"She's trying to make a skirt for a dance that's coming up. Remember I told you we went to Fenstemacher's Fabrics the other day?"

"I didn't know any of you had a real reason to be in there," my mom said. "I thought you were all just fooling around. And I knew Peg was taking sewing lessons. Anyway, I'm not sure it's a good idea for the three of you to stay alone. Maureen should stay at our house."

"But there's no room," I said. "This way, Jerry Michael can have my bed. I'll even wash the sheets tomorrow. "We'll probably just watch TV over at Maureen's and play records." I looked at Mimi. "Hey, we need to check the TV guide to see what's on Channel 13 Shock Theater tomorrow night."

My mom shook her head and lit a Salem. "I better call Don and June and see how they feel about it."

"Oh, I'm sure they'd go along with whatever you decide," Mimi said. "I think they've already left for their golf outing."

"Oh, that's right. Here it is Thursday, already," my mom said. "Where did this week go? I have the number for the place they're staying up north, but I hate to bother them."

Just then my mom's boyfriend, Larry, walked up to our table. He was wearing a Hawaiian shirt, and his bright red hair seemed extra curly.

"Well, look who's here, the whole gang, including the famous Mimi."

"Oh my gosh," my mom said. "What are you doing here? Want to join us?"

"Sure, but just until Bruce shows up." He pulled up a chair.

"Is Trudy coming too?" I asked.

"No, Bruce is bringing a guy from work who just moved to town and was looking for Mexican food. So, are you two having a fun week?" he asked me.

"I think we are. This is Mimi's introduction to Mexican food. And we're trying to talk my mom into letting us stay at Maureen's for the weekend while her parents are gone."

I couldn't believe my good fortune in having Larry show up. He was the one who had talked my mom into letting all the Tandem Riders sleep over last winter. Renee called him a "free spirit," so I was counting on him to spread his freeness toward us.

"Oh, come on, Marla. You know you can trust these girls," he said. Then he reached into his pocket, pulled out a card, and handed it to me. "Here's my number. If any problems come up, give me a call. If it's a burglar, call the police first."

My mom picked up her iced tea and tried to keep from smiling behind the straw. Good old Larry.

"If I let you stay there," my mom said, "I'm going to call every hour and you still need to go to Mass on Sunday."

"We will," I said.

"And don't be surprised if I stop over once or twice," she added.

"Well, it would be nice to offer a real bed to Jerry Michael," Renee said.

I kicked Mimi's foot under the table because I knew the deal was sealed.

The next day, I washed my sheets and bedspread, straightened my room, and dust mopped under the bed. I even let Mimi play an old Monkees album of mine that I hadn't listened to since seventh grade.

"What's all over this album cover?" she asked.

"Glue. I had to make an art project out of toothpicks and I did it on top of that album."

"Boy, I guess you really did stop liking them," she said.

I felt like saying, I can't believe you *still* like them, but I didn't because no matter what, I would always love Mimi like a sister. A nice sister, that is.

Maureen called around five o'clock. "My parents just backed out of the driveway and I'm ready for you guys to come whenever you can."

"Okay, I said." "We'll be there right after we eat."

We had BLT sandwiches for dinner with corn on the cob. Renee was wearing another old shift. This one was gray with black dots. I decided not to make a comment because she seemed to be in a pretty good mood. I knew she'd be a total charmer when our cousin arrived.

"What time is Jerry Michael getting here?" I asked.

"His bus gets in at eight-thirty-three," Renee said.

"Will he still be here on Sunday?" I hated to miss him altogether.

"I really don't know," Renee said. "He's coming here to see *me* anyway."

I let it drop. A weekend with no adults sounded like heaven right now and my paisley suitcase was packed.

"You can borrow my blue baby-dolls if you want," Renee said. "They're in my lingerie drawer. Just don't mess them up."

"Gee, thanks, Renee."

I couldn't believe it. This was the first time Renee had offered to loan me anything since her daisy earrings for graduation. Either she felt bad about being a snot, or she wanted me to stay away even longer so she could hog Jerry Michael all to herself.

Chapter Eleven

There was already a line for the evening swim when Mimi and I walked by the pool on our way to Maureen's house.

"How come you never go swimming there anymore?" Mimi asked me.

"Teenagers really don't go there," I said.

"Some of those kids are teenagers," Mimi said as she checked out the line.

I glanced over and saw Bernadette Walker and Alice McRory in bathing suits that looked like 1959. I decided not to point that out. Then I wondered if kids at Mimi's school thought of her as a Bernadette Walker. When I looked at her cute shorts and top, I decided they probably didn't. Even though she still listened to the Monkees, and wore glasses, she did like *some* cool music and had good taste in clothes. I felt bad when I looked back again at the girls in line, because unlike Mimi, Bernadette and Alice came from families with tons of kids who always had snotty noses at church.

"Did you ever tell Maureen that I'm adopted?" Mimi asked, as she swatted at an insect.

I couldn't believe my ears. This was something Mimi and I never talked about. Only one time had she ever brought up the subject of her being adopted. We were eight years old and she was visiting me in Mt. Pleasant right after we moved there. She asked me if I knew. I said yes, and we never talked about it again.

"I think I did tell Maureen once. I'm sorry. Is that okay?"

"Just Maureen?" I nodded. "Then I guess it's okay."

It was a white lie. I was pretty sure I'd told Cathy and maybe even Peg and Irene.

"Honestly, I hardly even remember you're adopted."

"Neither do I," Mimi said quietly.

"Adopted? You mean just give it away to somebody else?"

"Ruth Ann, sometimes it's the best choice for everyone. Think of Mimi. She's adopted, and she has a wonderful life. Her parents love her, she has Gussie, and a beautiful home. We have no idea what her life would be like if her real mother had kept her."

When we got to Maureen's back door we could hear her singing along with the radio in her kitchen. It was the song, *It's a Question of Temperature.* I waited for the refrain, then leaned toward the screen and joined in.

"Hot diggity, you're here!" Maureen practically shouted. "Come on in."

We followed her up to her room and put our suitcases on the twin bed we'd be sharing.

"It's so weird without Teeney barking at our heels," I said.

"Yes, Teeney is probably lapping up little waves on our lake right now," Maureen said. "And my parents think I'm at your house lapping up your mom's caramel corn."

I looked over at Mimi to see her reaction. Maureen must have realized right away that she shouldn't have said she was supposed to be at my house, because she jumped to a new subject.

"Hey, did you check to see what scary movie is on tonight?"

"*Carnival of Souls*. I've never heard of it, but it sounded pretty good in the *TV Guide*."

Mimi was reading the back of a Kinks album. Or at least it looked like she was. I had a feeling she wasn't very happy with our deceptive ways. But I knew just how to get to her.

"Maureen, can we raid your pantry for frosting mix?"

One thing I knew for sure about Mimi was that chocolate could distract her from anything.

"Sure, let's go look," she answered.

We followed Maureen down to the basement where there was a pantry and extra refrigerator. I stepped into the laundry room where Tom and I had made out last fall at Maureen's fourteenth birthday party. It was before I had told anyone about my psoriasis, which had just started. Thinking about how scared I was, and how everything felt so out of control, sent a shiver down my spine.

"Ruth Ann, what are you doing?" Maureen called from the other room.

"Thinking about your birthday party," I said as I walked back to them.

"What? My birthday party? Oh look, there's Hostess Sno-Balls in the freezer. Want one? They're even better when they're frozen."

"Did you know Tom and I made out in your laundry room at your party? It was our first time."

Mimi's eyebrows shot up and she bent over and brushed the toe of her shoe.

"I'm honored that you made out in my laundry room," Maureen said. "Anybody want Chicken A La King?"

I opened the pantry and found the boxed chocolate frosting mix.

"This is what I want," I said, reaching for a box. "But the question is, will one box be enough? There *are* three of us this time. And Mimi happens to be a chocolate fiend."

"Bring two boxes up," Maureen said.

I spotted a piece of yellow crepe paper hanging from a corner of the ceiling, and I grabbed hold of it.

"Look at that. I bet it's from your party, Maur."

"Oh yeah, I didn't notice that before. Seems like a long time ago, doesn't it?"

"We hardly knew each other," I said. "In fact, I was surprised you invited me."

Maureen started up the steps and we followed her. "You were the first person on my list. I'm not kidding. And I remember you and Tom dancing to *How Can I Be Sure?*"

"That was my first slow dance ever," I said. "And like I said, my first time making out. We had kissed at the movie, but not like that."

"That reminds me," Maureen said. "There's a quiz about going steady in the new *Tiger Beat* magazine. Let's take it while we eat our frosting."

My mom didn't call every hour, but she did call at eight, ten and eleven o'clock. When I told her about the eleven-thirty movie, she said good-night.

Carnival of Souls turned out to be good and creepy. Mimi fell asleep right after it started, but she woke up twice when we screamed over a ghost face that kept appearing in windows.

After sleeping until ten the next morning, we tried to lay out in the sun. It was eighty-five degrees by eleven-thirty. Terry O'Malley, who lived next door, came over for a while. He and Maureen had been friends for a long time. He was really good at drawing cartoons, so he drew caricatures of each of us. Mimi's mood really seemed better when he was there, and I was glad because she'd been so quiet.

"You girls sure are lucky to be parent-free all weekend," Terry commented as he put his pencils back in their wooden box. "I'm going into my basement where it's cooler. See you later, and hey, don't do anything I wouldn't do."

"He's really nice, Maur," I said after he went back in the house. "Did you really used to play with him when you were little?"

"Everything from pirate ship to space people."

"Mimi and I mostly played *Gypsy* and *West Side Story*, right, Mimi?"

"That's because you always told me every single thing that happened in both movies," Mimi said. "Since I wasn't allowed to see them."

"It could have been worse. They took me to *Psycho* too, you know."

"Terry was right, you guys," Maureen said. "It's too hot out here. Let's go inside."

We sprawled out on her parent's bed because they had a window air conditioner and watched American Bandstand on their portable TV. Then Maureen fell asleep, Mimi read *Seventeen* magazine, and I started *Valley of the Dolls*, which Wilma let me take home because she was done with it. I didn't really like the way it made me feel, but I kept reading it anyway.

At five o'clock, we pooled our money and had a pizza delivered. We dipped our slices into Wishbone Italian dressing, and afterwards Maureen offered us a Winston.

"Want to try a menthol?" I asked them. "I took two of my mom's Salems."

The pizza must have put Mimi in an even better mood, because she did a taste test of each cigarette. After a couple of sputtering coughs, she said, "I guess if I had to pick, it would be the menthol, but really, I don't get smoking at all. I wish my parents would both quit."

Maureen shrugged and lit a new one with her old one. "We need some music, you guys," she said. "Let's play something on my parent's stereo. Any suggestions? Most of my records are upstairs, but that pile on the piano are mine."

"You pick, Mimi," I said.

She flipped through the pile without much expression, and then broke out with a grin.

'Let's see," Maureen said.

Mimi held up the Monkees

"I might have known," Maureen said. "Okay, Ruth Ann, you told her to pick. So here we go."

"All right, one song. And how about we vote on which one?"

It was unanimous, so we cranked up, *(I'm Not) Your Stepping Stone* and we all sang it so loud I'm pretty sure Terry O'Malley could hear us next door. After the song ended, we decided to make a batch of Jiffy-Pop popcorn, but it didn't pop very well, and the kernels that did pop were mostly burnt.

"Why does this stuff always look perfect on TV?" Maureen asked. "It never works in real life."

She headed toward the waste basket.

"Wait," I said. Don't dump it out. I love burnt popcorn."

We stood at the counter nibbling through the kernels.

"Can we make frosting again?" Mimi asked.

"Sure," Maureen answered. "There's more in the basement. But let's put on our PJ's first."

We headed up to her room and I put on Renee's baby-dolls, Maureen, put on her butter yellow baby dolls, and Mimi, her mint and peach striped seersuckers.

"Look at us," Maureen said. "We look like a bowl of after-dinner mints."

I looked in the mirror. "What is going on with my bangs? Can I borrow your hair tape?"

"Must be the weather," she said. "Mine are doing the same thing."

Maureen tore a piece off for herself and then threw the roll to me. We flattened our bangs down with the pink hair tape, then headed to the basement.

After we made the frosting we pulled up to the kitchen counter on stools and dug into the mixing bowl with three spoons. Maureen lit a Winston.

"Hey, we haven't gone on the beep-line in ages," Maureen said. "You guys want to?"

Mimi looked a little baffled.

"Remember, we talked about the beep-line in Saginaw and you said you didn't think Saginaw had it?"

"Oh yeah," Mimi said. "How did you say it worked?"

"You call a phone number that you know is gonna be busy, like a radio station or your own number," I said. "Then you hear kids shouting phone numbers back and forth. You copy one down, yell for them to hang up, and then you call them back and talk."

Maureen was already dialing.

"I still don't get it," Mimi said.

"Angela says it's something about the telephone wires being all mixed up," I said. "Her dad's an engineer."

"Yeah, but I don't understand why you'd want to talk to strangers,"

Mimi said.

"Are you kidding?" Maureen said. "It's a perfect way to meet new boys, possibly gorgeous ones."

"But how do you know if they're gorgeous?" Mimi asked her.

"You can just tell. You have to weed out the duds."

Mimi looked more confused than before.

First, we talked to a guy who said he went to Creston High School, but he sounded twelve. Then we talked to two guys who said they were race-car drivers and could get us free tickets to Berlin Raceway on Sunday and they'd bring a six-pack of Black Label beer.

"*My Three Sons* will be on in a minute," Mimi said, looking up at the clock.

When neither of us answered her, she said, "Mind if I turn on your TV?"

"Oh sure, go ahead," Maureen said.

When we heard the familiar theme song playing in the den, Maureen leaned over the counter and whispered, "Gee, she got bored fast. I know we got some losers, but we're just getting started."

I shrugged and pointed my thumb at the den. "She would never admit it, but she has a huge crush on Chip. She'll be happier if she watches the show. Come on, let's get dialing."

The next guy we called, asked if by any chance we were wearing black bras, so we hung up on him immediately.

"That's why it's always better to get *their* numbers," Maureen said.

"Last thing you want is a pervert calling you back".

Mimi wandered back into the kitchen.

"Is it a commercial?"

She nodded.

"Re-run?"

"Yeah, but it's my favorite episode of the season. It's the one where Chip is in a band, and this guy from Liverpool is visiting his neighbor."

"What's your num-ber?" Maureen yelled into the phone between the busy signal sounds.

Mimi ate a spoonful of frosting and headed back to the den.

We hung up and dialed the number that Maureen had copied down on her mother's pad of pastel paper. She pointed to the ceiling which meant I should go upstairs to her parent's room and get on the other phone. I took the steps two at a time.

"Yeah, all three of us are sixteen," Maureen was saying when I picked up the phone.

The guy she was talking to sounded older, but for once we had someone who didn't sound creepy or dumb. He said he and his friends were in a band, took classes at Junior College, and had jobs. Then his friend got on and asked where we lived, but Maureen just kept laughing and saying she wouldn't tell him. I started talking too and then Mimi came in and flopped down on the chenille bedspread.

"Come on, let us come over," the first guy kept saying.

"We'll call you back in a few minutes," Maureen said.

Maureen came running up the stairs.

"Ruth Ann, what the hell? I love these guys! I wish we could see what they look like."

We followed her into her room where she lit a Winston and blew three perfect smoke rings at herself in the mirror. She jumped back when the ash fell onto her dresser.

"Those guys sound so outa site, I can't stand it," she said. "Can you believe they're in a band?"

"How old are they?" Mimi asked.

"Eighteen," I said.

Maureen stubbed her cigarette out in the ashtray. "I just wish we could get a look at them."

We both peeled the tape from our stiff, now slightly straighter bangs.

"Hey, I've got it, I said. "Why don't we give them the address next door, turn out the lights, and peek out the window to see what they look like."

Maureen scooped her fingers into the jar of Dippity-Do. "That is one completely boss idea."

Mimi was sitting on the edge of Maureen's bed with her hands on her knees. "I don't think it's a good idea, you guys," she said.

"There's no way they'll see us, Mimi. We'll just peek out the window."

"It's really okay, Mimi," Maureen said. "Then we'll stay off the beep-line and watch a movie."

Mimi shrugged her left shoulder, so we called the guys back. We told them they could come over, but only for five minutes. We gave them the O'Malley's address because that was the house we could see best from the upstairs windows. They said it wasn't more than ten minutes away. We turned off the air conditioner and crouched under the open window in Mr. and Mrs. Abraham's window, hiding behind the ruffled crisscross curtains. Whenever a car came down Godwin Street, we gasped and grabbed each other's arms. Mimi seemed relieved every time a car drove past the house.

After about twenty minutes, a car slowly edged along the curb, cut the lights, and stopped right next-door. The passenger door opened, and the guy that got out was wearing a poncho, sandals, and a headband over his chin length hair. When the driver's door opened, Maureen gripped my shoulder. "Hippies," she whispered.

"They're probably on drugs," Mimi whispered back. "And they're old enough to burn their draft cards."

We watched one of the tallest people we'd ever seen emerge. He had shoulder length blond hair. A short guy wearing bell-bottoms got out of the back seat.

"What do you know?" Maureen whispered. "I bet they really are in a band."

"You know our dads would keel over if they saw those guys," Mimi said to me.

They walked up to the O'Malley's front door without the slightest hesitation and rang the doorbell. We heard the door open, and a muffled question. Then in a loud, booming voice, we heard Mr. O'Malley.

"Gee whiz, fellas. You must be looking for the girls next door."

"Oh my God!" Mimi said, as her hands flew up and knocked her glasses sideways. "I Am Not Here!" Then she dove under Mr. and Mrs. Abraham's bed.

Before we could even absorb the fact that Mr. O'Malley had just turned us over to bona-fide hippies, which we'd mostly only seen in *Time* magazine, our doorbell was ringing. We heard Mimi squeal under the bed, and Maureen and I began hopping up down.

"Oh no, what do we do, what we do?"

The bell rang again, and then we heard one of them call through a downstairs window.

"Hey girls, we know you're in there. Open the door."

Another voice said, "Yeah, come on now. We want our five minutes."

We crept down the stairs, to the front door, and stood behind it.

"Let's just stick our heads out," Maureen whispered.

We opened the door a crack and peeked around.

"Hi there," the guy with the headband said.

Maureen and I looked at each other and shrugged. Even though none of them appeared to be ax murderers, I was terrified and excited all at once. They followed us into the kitchen. I ran for the stool behind the counter because it was right by the wall phone, and I could hide my legs. The tall guy leaned against the door to the den, the other two guys jumped up and sat on the countertops by the sink and stove.

"You're taller than my cousin," Maureen said to the tall guy. "And he's six-four. How tall are you?"

"Six-six. Didn't you girls say you were sixteen?" he said with a grin on his face.

"I'm fifteen," Maureen said quickly. "What do you expect from the beep-line?"

They glanced over at me and I wanted to blend into the wall.

"Yeah, I'm fourteen and a half," I said. "But you guys *really are eighteen*, right?"

"What should we do to these girls for lying?" the headband guy tipped the red Pyrex frosting bowl and looked inside.

"Not sure, Billy," the short guy said. "Need a utensil?"

He slid a butcher knife out of the wooden holder and tossed it to Billy, who caught it, dipped the point into the frosting bowl, and licked it.

"Hmm, looks like somebody around here likes chocolate. Where's the cake?"

He tossed the knife back to the short guy on the other counter, and then he tossed it to the tall guy. I thought of how mad Renee would be if I got stabbed in her baby-dolls.

"Wait a minute, didn't you say on the phone there were three of you here?" the short guy said.

The tall guy disappeared into the living room.

"Our friend is too shy to come down," I said, and regretted it immediately. I should have said she left, so they wouldn't look for Mimi after they killed us.

The tall guy reappeared in the door-way with the stack of Maureen's records that were on the piano.

"Not bad, not bad," he said. *"Except for the Monkees."*

"Okay then," Billy ran the knife under the faucet, wiped it on his poncho, and threw it to the other guy, who stuck it back in the knife holder. "Well, it's been real nice meeting you girls, but we gotta hit the road."

He jumped off the counter, headed toward the door, followed first by the short guy, and then the tall one. I was behind him, feeling relieved that we actually might not be found dead in our baby-dolls after all. As soon as they walked out the door, the tall guy turned around and came back in. He put his hands on my waist and lifted me into the air until my face was level with his. Then he closed his eyes and came in for a kiss. I was so shocked I didn't even stop him. His tongue darted into my mouth. I didn't know if it was a joke or an accident or a test. My eyes flew open as he set me on the floor. Then he turned around and left without saying a word. I closed the door to see Maureen sitting at the top of the stairs, her hands over her face and mouth. "Oh my God, you just made out with that giant hippie!"

"Shh. It was *not* making out, and I had no idea he was gonna do that! But you know what he did?"

Maureen shook her head. I had never seen her eyes so big.

"He stuck his tongue in my mouth!"

127

"He did not!" Maureen jumped to her feet.

"Yes, he did. And we *just met*!"

Mimi came out of the master bedroom, looking very rumpled and flushed. "I'm going to bed," she said. Then she stomped into Maureen's bedroom, and slammed the door.

Chapter Twelve

"Wake up you guys, it's after ten already."

I opened my eyes to see Maureen stretching and yawning in front of her open closet.

"What day is it?" I asked.

"Sunday. And we have to get ourselves to eleven o'clock Mass. Remember?"

Mimi threw back the covers, grabbed her toiletry bag, and left the room without saying anything.

"Uh-oh," I said. "I hope she's not still mad."

Mimi barely said a word while we ate cinnamon Pop-Tarts at the kitchen counter. Maureen chatted about everything imaginable, except our adventure the night before. She remained chatty while we cut through the park on our way to church.

"Mimi, when you come next summer, we'll definitely go to my cottage. Have you ever water-tobogganed? I finally got Ruth Ann to try last month. It was a riot, right, Ruth Ann? We fell off and my dad circled the whole lake before he realized that we'd fallen off. We almost drowned from laughing."

I got a little nervous about what else she was going to tell Mimi. Last thing Mimi needed to hear is that when Maureen's parents went to a party across the lake, we ate raw hamburger with onions, shared a can of beer, and went skinny-dipping. But she changed the subject to the upcoming dance and what she was thinking of wearing.

"I'll probably just wear this," she said looking down at her print skirt. "Maybe with a different top. What about you?"

"I'm not sure. But I guess I better start thinking about it, since it's next Saturday."

Mimi made sure that Maureen sat between us in the pew, so she wouldn't have to sit by me. About three minutes after Mass started, we heard shuffling behind us. I glanced over my shoulder and saw Tom, Marty, and Tom's younger brother, Matthew sliding into the pew behind us. Tom smiled at me, and I quickly turned away. I hadn't seen him since our kiss in the park on Thursday. How could I have had two accidental kisses in three days? My heart started racing and my palms got sweaty. Was something wrong with me? I thought about the guy from last night. Six-foot-six, eighteen years old, in a band, and he had kissed *me*? Me with my short legs, big lips, unruly hair, and hideous skin. Standing behind the counter must have helped disguise my short legs and hideous skin. Then it dawned on me that he probably just wanted to show off because I was easy to lift up in the air. Once I was up there, he figured he might as well kiss me while he was at it.

I felt a tug on my skirt. It was Maureen. Everyone was sitting down and I was still kneeling. I had almost forgotten that we were at church. While people came back from communion, Mimi leaned back and started talking to Tom. He looked confused and doubtful. She finally stopped when the priest asked us to rise. I didn't know what to think, since Mimi had barely ever talked to Tom before.

The boys walked with us on the way back to Maureen's house. Tom was pretty quiet, and so was Mimi. Marty and Maureen talked about funny stuff that had happened at St. Boner's, and about the teachers both of their older sisters had in high school. Tom's younger brother ran ahead and joined his friends when we were cutting through the park.

"I'll see ya later, Marty," Tom said when we got to Maureen's driveway. Mimi and Maureen hesitated, and then went inside.

"So, what's your version of the hippie story?" he asked.

"What's that supposed to mean?"

"Well, your Saginaw friend said you let some beep-line guy kiss you last night. What the hell, Ruth Ann? Are you crazy or what?"

"It was no big deal, believe me. And anyway, we aren't together anymore, so I don't really think this concerns you."

"Wait a minute," he said. "I seem to recall that you kissed *me* just a couple days ago. Or was that my imagination?"

"I think *you* were the one that kissed *me*. I never meant for that to happen."

"If I remember correctly, you weren't exactly fighting me off."

"Would that have helped? It didn't help that day in the boat, did it?"

"In the boat? What are you talking about? That was not a one-sided deal, Ruth Ann."

I looked at him like he was crazy because that's how he seemed to me. I had no idea what to say and I didn't want either of us to ever think about the boat incident again. In fact, I was sorry I had even brought it up.

"I need to go in," I said. "I'll see you later."

"Maybe you will, maybe you won't." He turned around and walked away.

When I came in Mimi and Maureen were making sandwiches.

"You guys wanna put on our suits and lay out?" Maureen asked. "It's not as hot as yesterday."

"I'm not sure Mimi wants to do anything with me," I said.

Mimi dangled a piece of honey-loaf over her bread and looked at me. "What do you mean?"

"It's obvious that you're mad at me, and then you went and told Tom about the guy from last night."

"I'm not really mad anymore. I'm just not boy-crazy like you two are. I figure I have plenty of time for that in a few years."

"Gee, Mimi," Maureen said. "What exactly did you tell Tom?"

"I told him that Ruth Ann kissed a six-foot-six guy that she met on the beep-line."

"But, why?" I asked.

"I thought it served him right," she said. "You haven't told me *all* the details, but I kind of figured out that he's a jerk. So why not tell him? Maybe he needs to know there's competition out there."

Maureen's eyebrows were as high on her forehead as they could go, which meant she was holding back from saying anything else. I felt even more confused. I wasn't sure I believed Mimi's motives or not. I wasn't even sure she knew why she was mad before, or why she told Tom about the guy. But when I thought about how long we'd been friends, and how she was leaving the next day, I decided to just let it all go. I was a little worried she might tell my mom or Renee or even her own parents about the beep-line guy, but I put that out of my mind. I needed to trust her, and I wanted to trust her. The phone was ringing, and Maureen answered it.

"Sure, she's right here." She handed me the phone. "It's your mom."

I glanced over at Mimi to try and get a feeling of her loyalty. She was putting the condiments back in the refrigerator.

"I'm glad to hear you made it to eleven o'clock Mass," my mom said. "Mrs. Harris mentioned that she saw you. What time do you plan on coming home?"

My mom gave in right away when I said we wanted to spend the afternoon, so I figured she and Renee wanted Jerry Michael all to themselves. They were probably playing Ray Charles records and dipping their bread into hot Italian peppers from the jar.

All three of us fell asleep in the backyard. I woke up first and Terry O'Malley was sketching us, with our loose straps, open mouths, and tipped-over pop bottle.

"Boy, you don't leave anything out, do you?" I said with a chuckle.

"I'm into realism," Terry said.

"What was your dad into last night when he told those beep-line guys where we lived?" Maureen asked as she set her drink upright.

Terry grinned. "Yeah, he told me about that this morning, but I trust you listened to my last words."

"What last words?" Maureen asked.

"Not to do anything I wouldn't do."

Maureen and Mimi both looked over at me.

We stretched out on Maureen's parents' bed and turned on their TV. Our choices were bowling, golf, and a re-run of *Lassie*. We kept it on *Lassie*, but I went back to *Valley of The Dolls*. Maureen was reading over my shoulder when we heard a loud buzzing.

"I wonder who that is," she said. "It's the back door."

"Terry?" I asked.

"I'll go see," Maureen said.

I was on page twenty-five, where one of the characters was describing how sex and love were two different things for a man, when Maureen came rushing back in. "It's your guy, the hippie guy, from last night. He wants to see you."

"What? You're kidding, right?" I asked.

"No, hurry up. He's at the back door."

Part of me felt like running out the front door, and the other part wanted to see if the guy had even been real. I slipped my cut-offs and blouse on over my bathing suit and made my way toward the back door. When I got there, the tall guy was standing on the top step. Taller than last night, hair longer, and eyes bluer.

"Hi," he grinned. "Can I come in for a minute?"

"Gee, I don't know. My friend's parents could come home anytime."

"I woke up this morning and realized that I never got your name," he said.

I opened the door. "Okay, for just a minute."

He stood very close to me and grabbed hold of my hands. Once he had them, he steered me backward until I bumped into the bench to Mrs. Abraham's sewing machine. He lifted me onto the bench, wrapped his arms around me and then kissed me, tongue and all. I felt like I was being swallowed, but this time, I knew the tongue was on purpose. Then he slid his hands over my rear end and kind of held them there. I wasn't sure if that was an accident, or on purpose.

After the kiss, he lifted me down, and said, "It was nice meeting you." Then he left, and I realized he still didn't know my name and I didn't know his. I wondered if I'd ever see him again. Maureen came up behind me. "Is he gone?' I nodded. "Did he kiss you again?"

"Yup, and you know what else? He grabbed my butt. But *whatever you do,* don't tell Mimi."

Chapter Thirteen

"I'm glad I'll get to meet your cousin," Mimi said as we walked home from Maureen's house. "I don't think I've ever met a homosexual. Except for maybe this waiter at our country club. He might be one."

"Just so you know, you shouldn't say homosexual."

"But I didn't say homo like the kids at school. What should I say? Queer?"

"Gay. You're supposed to call them gay."

"Gay? Like happy gay?"

"Yes, it's the same word. But it doesn't mean happy."

"How did you find that out?"

"Jerry Michael told us. He has friends in New York. It's just a better thing to say than homosexual. Or queer."

Just as I reached for the handle on the side door, I heard Renee in the kitchen. "All things aside, it's going to kill me not to play Elvira in *Blithe Spirit*."

"My dear, my dear, my dear, there *will be another chance*. You have to hold onto that."

I stopped in my tracks. Why wasn't Renee going to play Elvira? That's all she talked about. Then I realized she hadn't mentioned it lately. In fact, maybe not since June. We walked into the kitchen and Renee and Jerry Michael were hugging.

"Well, look who just walked in," Jerry Michael said, breaking out of the hug. "It's my little swimming buddy all grown up and apparently out of her training bra. Look at you!"

I hugged Jerry Michael and laughed at the same time because he was wearing my mom's flowered apron, which looked especially ridiculous with his long legs and goatee. Renee pulled a napkin out of the napkin holder and blew her nose. I pointed my thumb at Mimi.

"This is my best friend since we were babies," I said.

"How do you do, best friend since babies. But you must have another name."

Mimi giggled and told him her name. He kissed her hand, and I could see her mood lift instantly, and boy, was I thankful. What a mistake to think Maureen and I could be our regular selves around her. As if reading my mind, Jerry Michael spoke up, "What kind of mischief did you two get into? I heard there was no parental supervision around this weekend. Hmm?"

"Well, let's see," I said. "We burned the Jiffy Pop and we watched *Carnival of Souls.*"

"I love that movie. I wish I'd known it was on!" Jerry Michael crossed his arms over his chest. "*It's funny. The world is so different in the daylight. In the dark, your fantasies get so out of hand. But in the daylight, everything falls back into place again.*"

"I guess you do love it," I said. "You even know lines from it?"

"I brought a pen the third time I saw it."

Renee had gone back to the counter and was squeezing a lemon over

137

some avocado slices.

"Where's mom?" I asked her.

"She's giving Trudy a ride home. She'll be right back."

"Why was Trudy here?"

Renee gave me a strange look. "Does she need a reason? She's our mother's friend."

"I'm not allowed to be curious in this house," I said to Jerry Michael. "It's a crime to wonder about anything."

"Children should be seen and not heard," Renee said.

"Come on, Mimi. Let's put our stuff upstairs."

"Your sheets are in the dryer," Jerry Michael called to me. "Thanks for letting me use your room."

Ruff and Reddy were on my bed washing each other.

"Oh, that's so cute," Mimi said.

I was glad there was something else to keep her mood lifted.

"They shouldn't be on the bare mattress, though," I said. "But that's cats for ya. The minute anything is slightly different, they have to investigate."

Mimi sat on the bench to my dressing table. "I see what you mean about your cousin. Now I *can* totally picture him eating dinner with a lampshade on his head. I figured you were exaggerating."

"You don't have to exaggerate when it comes to Jerry Michael. Wait here. I need to get the sheets, so I can make my bed."

Just before I entered the kitchen to get to the basement, I heard Jerry

Michael.

"I'm so glad your mother got Trudy's advice. Think about it. Anyone who snuck out of a prison camp under a pile of coal should be able to solve a problem like yours."

I took a few steps back and stopped so I could listen longer.

"There is something about her," Renee said. "She seems a little crazy at times. But mostly when she's been drinking. When she's serious, though, she has a really good head on her shoulders."

"Well, next time I come, I want to see the crazy side of Trudy."

I walked through the kitchen. "What are you guys making, anyway?"

"All kinds of delizioso," Jerry Michael said.

"Have you been hanging around the Cicerelli's?" I asked.

"As a matter of fact, Mrs. C. came over with some homemade bread to go with our, what was it, Renee?'

"Giardiniera."

"Darn it," I said. I knew you guys would have those Italian pepper things while I was gone." I headed down the basement steps. "And I bet you played Ray Charles records while you ate them."

"How'd you guess?' Jerry Michael started singing, *Hit the Road Jack*. "I should be singing *Volare* or something Italian to go with those hot peppers."

As I pulled the sheets from the dryer, I could hear him belting out the whole song and it made me laugh. We hardly ever laughed or sang in this house.

No Doubt in my Mind

I stepped out of the laundry room with my arms full of the clean, warm sheets, and glanced over to the dinette set in the corner where Tom and I pretended to play Yahtzee all last winter when really, we were making out. I felt sad thinking about our romance and how I never expected it to get so messed up. Then I thought about eighth grade at St. Boner's and how fun it was to be in the Tandem Riders. No telling what high school would be like. Except for huge. That much I knew. There were already over four hundred kids enrolled in my class. I probably wouldn't even see any of the Tandem Riders.

I glanced up at the Yahtzee game on the shelf and recalled Tom's kiss at the park last Thursday, and his Crayola midnight blue eyes. There would be at least two hundred new girls in the freshman class to see those eyes. My heart started racing when I thought of him kissing someone else. Another Leta all over again. I set the sheets on the dinette table and took the Yahtzee game down. It was covered in a layer of dust. How could that be? We never had dust anywhere when Renee was living home. What was going on around here? Renee shows up in Saginaw out of nowhere, and now she's not going to be in *Blithe Spirit*. I set the game down, picked up the sheets, and started bawling right into the bundle. In addition to thinking about high school, Tom, the Tandem Riders, and Mimi leaving, I had no idea what the hell was going on around here. It felt like a dam was bursting. I hadn't felt this confused in a long time.

I heard my mom in the kitchen, "Watch that butter so it doesn't burn."

I pulled myself together and walked up the stairs, where my mom was rinsing a pan.

"Hi, honey," she said. "Have you been crying? What's the matter?"

As usual, she looked mad. Sympathy was not available in this house. Whenever I got injured or had hurt feelings, it was an irritation. They always blamed me for causing it somehow.

"No," I lied. "My hay fever is really bad. Did you pick up any Allerest?"

"No, darn it. I forgot. And there's ragweed in the yard behind us. When it gets dark, I'll sneak over there and yank it out."

Dinner almost felt like a party. We showed Mimi how to pull the leaves off the steamed artichoke and dip them in melted butter.

"Like this," my mom demonstrated, scraping the leaf against her teeth.

My mom's cheese soufflé was one of her best ever, and for dessert, Jerry Michael had baked his mother's 7up Cake, which he knew I always loved at family reunions.

Mimi and I cleaned the kitchen while my mom and Jerry Michael chain smoked in the dining room and sipped Drambuie. I think my mom was a little tipsy because she joined right in with Jerry Michael when *I Can't Stop Loving You*, by Ray Charles came on the record. Mimi gave me a wide-eyed look when I handed her a clean plate to dry. It was a side of my mom that we rarely saw.

Renee drove Jerry Michael to the bus station to catch the bus back to

Ann Arbor. He said he'd probably sleep all the way because of the Drambuie. He gave me a long hug before they left, and then lifted my chin and looked into my eyes.

"You're a tough kid, remember that."

I had no idea what he was talking about, but I nodded. "All right. Don't wait for two years to come back, okay?"

As he walked out the door he started singing, *What the World Needs Now Is Love*.

After they left, Cathy came over to watch the Ed Sullivan Show with us. She brought freshly baked anise cookies. I kept looking over at Mimi to try and get a feeling if she was going to tell her parents about the beep-line, and if she suspected I'd been upset earlier. Just like my mom, I had told her my allergies were bothering me. She seemed to be enjoying Cathy and so I felt a little less worried by the time we squeezed into my twin bed. When the lights were out, and all we could hear were crickets, I said, "You'll come back next summer, right?"

A few too many seconds passed before she said, "Of course. Boy, am I tired."

Chapter Fourteen

By the next morning, I didn't have to lie about my red eyes. My pollen allergy or as my mom called it, "hay fever," was awful.

"I've never had it this bad," I told Mimi as I reached for another tissue.

"You always get it this bad. Every single year. I can't believe you don't have any medicine for it."

"I'm surprised we have Kleenex."

"If you don't call your mom, I will. Maybe she could bring you something on her lunch hour."

"I'll call her after you get picked up."

"Promise?"

"I promise."

"If you don't hurry up and take something, you'll start wheezing."

Mimi knew about the asthma attack I'd had in Saginaw last summer. My dad had to get an inhaler from his friend Wally the pharmacist.

Mimi's parents pulled into the driveway at 10:27. Three minutes early. Not just on time, but early. I couldn't imagine how it felt to always know what was going to happen next. Getting new clothes before you outgrew the old ones. Going for check-ups at the doctor when you weren't even sick. Stuff like that. Then I remembered that Mimi didn't even know who her real parents were. At least I had that information.

No Doubt in my Mind

Our hug goodbye seemed less best-friendish than usual, but then I probably wouldn't want to hug somebody with a bright red nose and slits for eyes, either. After they left, I wondered if that was the real reason. There was no doubt in my mind, that the beep-line incident had changed things between us.

I called my mom at work to request some Allerest.

"Ruth Ann, I wasn't even going to take a lunch hour. I have a huge report to type for Mr. Trimble. Don't forget, I'm taking off early on Wednesday, so you can go to the dermatologist. Go next door and ask Francesca for a Dristan or something."

The last thing I wanted was Cathy hanging around right now. If I asked her mom for a pill, they'd both be all over me. I had too much to think about. I hadn't been alone for over two weeks. Since before Maureen and I went to Saginaw.

The phone rang as soon as we hung up. It was Denise calling about Saturday's dance.

"You're going, aren't you?" she asked.

"Oh yeah, all my friends are planning on it."

"You sound terrible. Are you sick?"

"I just have hay fever. I get it every year around August fifteenth."

"My little brother gets that too. Hey, I told Michael and those guys they'd probably see you at the dance and they were stoked."

"Oh, really? That's nice."

We talked a little longer about school uniforms and schedules, and then agreed to talk on Saturday before the dance. I felt weird about seeing Michael. I wondered if he still had the pipe he took from the hospital when I was in there. My stomach felt grabby whenever I thought about it. Not the good kind of grabby like when Tom started liking me. That kind had a sort of flutter with it. This was the kind like I got in fourth grade when the nun took my book called, *"Three's A Crowd,"* and told me I was a "dirty girl."

I went upstairs and splashed cold water on my face over and over. It made my eyes feel a little better. I found two aspirin tablets in a bottle that I knew I should save for period cramps, but I took them anyway. I laid on the couch and watched reruns and soap operas. The phone rang just before five. I had fallen asleep trying to read *Valley of The Dolls.*

"Hey, Ruth Ann, are you finally alone?" Maureen asked me.

I yawned. "Yeah, but I fell asleep. My hay fever's really bad today."

"Well perk up, kiddo. We've got some fun ahead of us."

"You mean the dance?"

"The dance? That's not 'til Saturday. Tonight, there's another band at the park at seven. We're all meeting there. And tomorrow my parents are going to Indiana for the whole day, so I say we take the Dart and go to Grand Haven."

"Take the Dart? Who's gonna drive?"

"Me, silly! Who else?"

"You think you can drive? You don't even have your permit."

"So what? I'm a great driver! My mom's calling me. Come to the park before seven, Bye."

After I hung up the phone, I continued sitting on the window seat. Reddy jumped out of the window where he'd been napping and brushed against my legs. I thought about the beep-line guys and how that could have been a disaster. Renee would force my mom to put me in Villa Maria if she ever found out about it. I needed to convince Maureen that driving her mom's car to Grand Haven was too risky.

While I was helping Renee get the leftovers ready for dinner my mom walked in and handed me a bag from Riordan's Drug store. She had picked up the Allerest along with nasal spray and eye drops.

I kissed her cheek, which I usually only did at bedtime, because it was expected of me. "Thanks, Mom."

"Well, you look terrible."

"Doesn't she?" Renee said, as she pulled leaves off a head of lettuce.

"I picked up the spray and drops because I remember from last year that Allerest wasn't that great."

"I just remember how tired she gets," Renee said. "It's hard to believe she could get any lazier, but she does."

After cleaning the kitchen, I went upstairs and took an inventory of my closet. I pulled out my print skirt and Poor Boy top. They would have to do for the dance. My friends had seen the outfit way too many times, but the new kids I'd be meeting wouldn't know the difference. The medication had started to help, so I decided I'd walk over to the park, after all. I changed into my jeans because my legs would show more if we were all sitting on a blanket.

My mom was sitting on the couch reading the paper. Renee was watching the news and knitting. I hadn't seen her do that since she made a crooked sweater for one of her college boyfriends.

"I'm going over to the park. I'll be back before dark."

My mom put the paper down and reached for her Salems. "I thought you didn't feel good. You shouldn't be out with all that pollen flying around."

"I feel lots better. And there's a band there again. I guess they're doing it every Monday night in August."

"I'd rather you stayed home, Ruth Ann. We wanted to talk to you about something."

"Talk about what?" I asked. "Can't it wait? Maureen and the other girls are expecting me."

My mom's lips disappeared like they always did when she was mad.

"All right, fine. But listen here, I want you home before dark, hear me? Nine o'clock or you're grounded from that park."

When I walked by Cathy's house she was moving the sprinkler. "Are you going over for the music?" she asked. I knew she wanted me to ask her along, but I felt like my mind was in quicksand. I turned around and took a few backward steps.

"I'm just going for a little while. Mostly so I can meet with the Tandem Riders. We have to figure out some plans."

"Plans?"

"Yeah, you know, like about the St. Blaise dance, and some high school stuff."

Cathy nodded with her mouth open. Jeez, had she forgotten I was *in* high school now?

I held up my hand, "See ya.'"

I turned around and headed toward the park. More quicksand. I needed to try and think. Why did my mom and Renee need to talk to me?

"You knew all along? Ruth Ann, why didn't you say anything before?"

"I was waiting for you to tell me."

"Oh, honey, you don't have to cry."

"I always cry about it. You just don't see me."

"We know it's been a rough time for you. But pretty soon it will all be over. And then we can all go back to normal, just like before."

Maureen was sitting on a blanket with Mary Lou, Angela, Peg, Irene, and a really cute older boy with curly dark hair. He was talking to all of them but seemed focused on Mary Lou.

"Hey, Ruth Ann, you made it, hay fever and all," Peg said.

"I took some medicine. Otherwise I'd still be on my couch."

The band looked like they were ready to start. There were two guys with really long hair on guitars, a black guy on drums with an afro, and two girls. One had braids and held a tambourine, the other was behind a small piano.

"Who is this band?" I asked.

"They're from Detroit," Peg said. "They're called Wayward Angels."

I sat on the blanket and the cute boy said, "Hi. I'm Vinnie. Vinnie DiMartino."

Vinnie filled us all in about the St. Blaise dance. He would be a junior at our school, so he'd been to lots of them. I was kind of surprised a junior would even talk to us, but the way he was looking at Mary Lou, I figured that was the reason.

"Your cousin Denise called me today about the dance," I told Irene.

"Denise LaCroix?" Vinnie asked. "I know Denise's whole family. She and my sister are good friends."

It turned out that Vinnie knew lots of people that Denise knew, and I started to feel like maybe high school wouldn't be a sea of total strangers, after all.

Before the last song, the band brought out a huge banner that said, STOP THE WAR. A few people in the audience cheered. Their music was a lot different than The SoulBenders, and the last song was one I loved from the radio, "*Come on People Now, Smile on Your Brother.*"

"Holy shit," Maureen said, turning to me. "Are you sure this isn't the real group?"

We all sang the chorus with them and had our arms around each other. I was sitting next to Mary Lou, and I knew she was thinking about her brother who'd been killed in Vietnam. I leaned my head on her shoulder for a few seconds to let her know that I understood. She turned her face to me and smiled. We sure had come a long way in the past few months. I was glad that I'd decided to come to the park, and I realized that even though I missed Mimi, it was kind of a relief not to worry about her impressions of everything.

"Don't look now," Maureen said as soon as we stood up, "But here comes Tom with Johnny. I didn't think they ever hung out anymore."

Johnny had been Maureen's boyfriend all through eighth grade, but they had broken up after school got out.

"Well, I gotta go home," I said. My mom threatened to ground me if I'm late. Anyway, I can't think straight on this hay fever stuff."

"Okay, but I'm calling you in the morning about Grand Haven."

"You're crazy. We're not driving to Grand Haven."

"Oh, yes, we are," Maureen laughed.

I said goodbye to the other girls and Vinnie, and then turned toward Burton Street. Tom came huffing up alongside of me. "What's the matter? You can't even wait to say hi to me?"

"Hi. I have to get home, that's all. My mom made a huge deal about me getting there by nine or else."

"So, where's your Saginaw friend? Did she leave?"

"This morning. Look, I really have to go."

"Ruth Ann, I miss you so much. I'd do anything to get you back."

I looked into his eyes to try and get a real feeling from him. Part of me wanted to slap him and part of me wanted to kiss him with all my might.

"Tom, I *have* to go."

"Okay. Can I call you?"

"I guess so. Bye."

I broke into a run and made it to the front door exactly one minute before nine. It was eerily quiet when I walked in and saw Renee and my mom sitting at the dining room table. They looked up when I came in, and then looked at each other.

"Hi. I'm not late, am I?"

My mom looked down at her watch. "No, right on time. Come in and sit down. And please shut the front door."

Renee was piling up her game of solitaire when I sat down.

"We need to talk to you," my mom said.

My heart began thumping loudly. I figured Mimi's mom had probably called and reported the whole beep-line story. I was going to Villa Maria for sure this time.

"You might already have guessed," my mom said as she looked at Renee, and then back at me. "Since you figured it out last time."

Last time. It felt like a giant wave hit me in the face as everything started to make sense. I dug my fingers into the seat cushion.

"Oh My God! Please tell me this isn't happening again," I said.

She put her hand on my arm. "Yes, but it's not the same, Ruth Ann."

"The taxi's here. Don't worry, I have plenty of time to get there.

Mother is going to the hospital right after work, and then she'll get you later, after the baby comes. Be a good girl, and just watch TV, okay? Make yourself a sandwich when you get hungry. This could take quite a while. If anyone comes to the door, tell them I'm sleeping."

I looked at Renee and stood up. "How could you do this again? Wasn't it bad enough the first time? What's the matter with you, Renee?" I shouted. "Are you a sex maniac?"

"Ruth Ann Bloomfield!" My mom stood up and raised her right hand to slap my face. I took a step back to avoid her.

"Don't you ever..."

"Well, how can someone be so stupid twice?"

"I'll have you know, you mean little witch," Renee shouted back, "I didn't even know what happened the first time."

"What are you talking about?"

"Your sister has no memory of that night."

I looked at Renee. "Are you saying *he raped you*? Sean? Your boyfriend?"

"I don't remember."

"Is that why Daddy socked him in the face?"

My mom pulled a new pack of cigarettes from her purse and sat down. "You were nine years old. How would you remember that?"

"I was right there in the room! We were roasting marshmallows in the fireplace!"

My mom looked up at the ceiling and closed her eyes. I felt like my head was going to explode.

"So, what the hell happened this time, Renee? You don't even have a boyfriend!"

"Watch your language, young lady," my mom ordered. "And sit down!"

Renee had her hands over face and she was shaking her head back and forth.

"No, she doesn't have a boyfriend, but she has dates. And she did something very careless that should be a lesson to you. All it takes is one time, Ruth Ann."

"One time! She's been pregnant twice!"

My mom pointed her finger at me. "You're probably just as fertile as her, so you better mind your Ps and Qs if you know what's good for you."

"Wait a minute," I said, looking across the table at Renee, "I can't believe you only did it twice and got pregnant both times."

"How dare you doubt me!" Renee stood up this time. "Mother, I told you she'd be awful about this. You have no right to judge *me,* little sister. I wouldn't call you any example of purity. Look what happened with your creepy boyfriend at that cottage. Even the Cicerellis heard about that one. The whole parish probably calls you a slut behind our backs!"

"All right, both of you stop this right now," my mom said.

My stomach began churning and I felt like I might throw up. My mom lit a Salem, blew out the match, and took a long puff.

"We are going to stop all of this blaming right now. Renee had a date with an old boyfriend from high school. She made a mistake, and now we're going to make the best of it."

"What old boyfriend?" I asked. "Timothy Madden?"

"Never mind, Ruth Ann," my mom said. "You wouldn't remember him, anyway."

"Well, then it's not Tim," I said. "Are you giving this one to the same orphanage?"

"There was never any orphanage," Renee answered. "The baby was adopted right away into a wonderful family. Just like Mimi."

"This is what we wanted to tell you, Ruth Ann," my mom said. She had a fake gentle tone that made me want to throw up even more. "We're going to keep the baby and raise it together."

"What? Are you kidding?" I stood up again. "You're just gonna run around as an unwed mother. And you don't think the *whole parish* won't call *you* a slut?"

"Sit down and listen to us," my mom said. "We have a plan. And you are going to go along with this one hundred percent. You are old enough to handle this. And we expect you to handle this."

"You see this ring," Renee said, holding out her left hand. "This is my wedding ring."

My mom's eyes bored into mine, and she looked at me more seriously than I ever remembered. "Here's the story. Renee got secretly married in March and her husband was sent to Vietnam right away. She got pregnant on her honeymoon and he was killed in June. The baby is due in December. Do you think you can handle that?"

"Do you really expect people to believe that?" I asked.

My mom crushed her Salem into the ashtray. "Why not? It's happening all the time now. It's the only way to make this work for us and the baby."

My head was swirling. It all felt like a dream. I walked over to the window seat where the cats were both sleeping. I moved something out of the way to sit down. It was a piece of heavy cardboard with square papers hanging off. Renee got up from her chair and picked it up.

"Want to see the wallpaper I chose?"

I started to imagine the music from *Rosemary's Baby.* She flipped through the samples until she came to a pale green paper sprinkled with daisies. "Isn't this cute? I think it's okay for a boy or a girl, don't you?"

I not only couldn't answer her, I couldn't even get my mouth to close. I ran up the stairs and slammed my bedroom door. After sobbing into my pillow for what felt like an hour, I snuck into the hall and dragged the upstairs phone into my room. Even though it was after ten, I dialed Maureen's number. She answered on the second ring.

"Hey Maur," I said. "What time are we going to Grand Haven tomorrow?

Chapter Fifteen

I stayed in bed until I heard Renee leave for work. Maureen called when I got downstairs.

"I can be ready as soon as you get here," she said.

"Okay. Should I bring beach stuff?"

I looked down at the psoriasis on my legs, hoping she'd say no.

"Sure. Why not? We have the whole day to do whatever we want, except I'm still not sure what to do with Teeney. They left her here for me to watch, and she'll need to go out at least once."

"What about Terry? Would he do it?"

"Great idea. I'll go ask him. Hey, should I just pick you up?"

"Hell, no! My neighbors watch me like a hawk. I'll walk over."

The cicadas were calling to one another as I crossed the park. My head felt so fuzzy that I thought about lying down on the dry, brown grass for a nap. It was partly from my allergy medicine, but also from waking up all night. When I opened my eyes the first time, I thought sure it was only a dream that Renee was pregnant again. When I realized it was true, it felt like I'd swallowed my heart. Before I woke up the second time, I was dreaming about Renee carrying her suitcase to the taxi. Instead of a taxi driver, my dad got out and waved to me. "Don't forget to eat," he called. "And make Wilma a martini, okay?"

Maureen was putting her beach bag in the Dart when I walked up her driveway.

"Terry's gonna let Teeney out a couple of times, so we're all set," she said. "For Pete's sake, what's the matter? If you're worried, forget about it. My parents are going all the way to Shipshewana. They won't be back 'til way after dinner."

"It's not that. Let's just go before I change my mind."

"Yeah, I'm surprised you ended up wanting to go. You were totally against this last night at the park."

I shrugged and got into the car. Maureen knew exactly how to get to the expressway and didn't even flinch when she merged to get on. I was digging my fingernails into the plastic coating on the seats.

"Light me up a Winston, okay?" she asked. "They're in my purse."

She took the cigarette from me and after a puff, transferred it to her left hand. Then she rested her arm on the open window.

"Can you really drive with just one hand?"

"I knew you were worried about my driving. Just relax. My dad has taken me out a thousand times. I'm fine."

"You're more than fine. I can't believe how well you drive. It's not that at all. It's something else."

"Am I your best friend, or what? Is it Tom?"

"I wish that's all it was."

I thought back to last night when Tom had tried to talk to me at the park. Before I knew about Renee. I wanted to turn the clock back and somehow wish it all away.

"Is it your skin? Is your psoriasis worse?"

"No, it's not that either. Listen, Maur, I'll fill you in later. But right now, I need to forget about it for a while if that's okay."

"Of course, it's okay, silly."

"There's a car coming up on your left."

"I can see it in my side view mirror, but thanks," Maureen turned her head toward me and smiled. We listened to the radio. She leaned over and turned the dial a couple of times, which made me nervous.

"I can do that," I offered.

"Would you just relax? I'm fine."

I felt like I would burst if I didn't say something about Renee, but I wanted Maureen to concentrate on the freeway. I kept watch in my side view mirror too.

"Oh my God, Maur, there's a cop behind you."

"So what? I'm not doing anything wrong."

"Except for driving without a license," I said. "And stealing a car."

"I did not steal this car. It belongs to my mom."

"Okay, maybe not stolen. But taken without permission."

A siren began blasting behind us. I bent over and wrapped my arms around my head.

"Oh no! Pull over. Pull over!"

The cop sped past us on the left just as Maureen was aiming toward the right shoulder.

"See, it wasn't us. He's after somebody else."

I unwrapped my arms and looked up to see the cruiser disappear.

"Holy shit! I thought I was having a heart attack."

"Come on, Ruth Ann. I've never seen you like this."

"I'm sorry. You probably should have called Angela or somebody else to go with you."

"Uh-uh. I only wanted to do this with you."

"Thanks, but I think I'm ruining all your fun."

"Hey, it's early. Let's just start all over."

I told her okay, but I knew that would be impossible until I spilled my guts. I decided I'd tell her at least part of the story when we were off the expressway. After she took the exit marked, Grand Haven, I waited a few more minutes before speaking.

"Is this Grand Haven?" I asked.

"No, this is Spring Lake. You go over the drawbridge to get to Grand Haven."

Sometimes Maureen seemed about eighteen. I couldn't believe she was only a few months older than me. I took a deep breath.

"I can't hold this in any longer. Can you pull over somewhere?"

"Okay, sure. I'll pull into that parking lot."

Maureen turned into a parking place in a grocery store lot, turned off the engine, and leaned back against the car door.

"Finally," she said. "What the hell is going on?"

"I found out last night that Renee's pregnant."

"Pregnant! Are you kidding me?" I actually saw spit fly out of Maureen's mouth.

"If only," I said.

"I can't imagine Renee even making out, let alone doing it! Who's the father?"

"She got secretly married. I think it was in March."

"Married? Wow! Did you know all this time?"

"No. They didn't tell me. And the terrible thing is that he got killed in Vietnam."

"Oh, no!" Maureen leaned forward and grabbed my hand. "Ruth Ann, that's unbelievable! How's Renee doing?"

Once she said "unbelievable," I wished I'd never opened my mouth.

"She's tired and even bitchier than usual."

"No," Maureen said. "I mean about her husband getting killed. What was his name?"

My mind flashed to the song that had just played on the radio by Gary Puckett and the Union Gap. One of Mimi's favorite bands.

"Gary. Oh, yeah, she's upset all right. Of course. She hadn't seen him since their honeymoon." I took a deep breath. "Can I have one of your Winstons?"

"Of course. I'll have another one, too."

I lit two at the same time, like I'd seen on *The Man from U.N.C.L.E.* and handed one to Maureen. She took a puff, then blew her smoke at the car ceiling.

"Honeymoon baby, huh? I guess that happens a lot. So, she must be due sometime in the winter?"

I batted at a fly and nodded. "I think in December."

"Did you ever meet Gary?" Maureen asked.

I felt like the biggest jerk when she said the name I'd made up. I wanted to cry, and I hated my mom and sister for putting me in this position. The least they could have done was fill the lie out a little more. A name at least.

"No," I said. "I didn't know anything about him until last night."

"Unreal. Will she live with you and your mom after the baby comes?"

"Probably. I don't know for sure."

I thought about the daisy wallpaper sample that Renee had showed me. I felt nauseous all over again thinking about it.

A mother and two kids rolled their shopping cart up next to my open window.

The boy yanked on his sister's hair and she screamed.

"Hmm, Aunt Ruth Ann," Maureen said. "How 'bout that?"

"Yeah, kinda hard to believe, isn't it?"

I took an extra long look at Maureen. Something told me she wasn't buying the story, and I didn't any feel better than before. In fact, now I felt worse.

"Oh well," I said, stretching my arms over my head. "Let's change the subject. What are we gonna do in Grand Haven?"

"Well, first of all, we have to go to the A &W by the sand dunes. That's the really boss place to go. Then we'll see from there."

"Okay. Sounds good to me. Anything to get my mind off this crap."

Maureen shot me a strange glance, and then turned the key. "I'm ready if you are. Grand Haven, here we come. Aunt Ruth Ann is on her way."

"I guess it's still pretty early for much action," Maureen said as she set her root beer mug on the tray attached to her car window. "This place is usually crawling with cute guys. They do make the best chili dogs here, though. Are you sure you don't want another one?"

"No, thanks. I'm not very hungry."

"You still seem pretty upset. Do you want to talk about Renee some more?"

"That's okay. I'm fine."

We parked the car downtown and walked around looking in windows. We bought peanuts and penny candy at a store called Fortino's, which reminded me of the little grocery stores my uncles owned in Jackson and Saginaw. I felt sad when I thought of those stores. I wanted to be six years old and holding my mom's hand at my Uncle Hal's produce market.

We parked our car on the road and walked into the state park. After spreading our towels on the sand, Maureen propped her radio against my beach bag, and pulled her baby-doll dress over her head. "Do you have your suit on under your clothes?" she asked me.

"I do, but my legs are pretty bad. I'm going to see a new dermatologist tomorrow, in fact. My mom found one downtown, just a couple blocks from school. That way, I can go myself, and she won't have to leave work."

"That was a good idea," Maureen said.

I could tell she was studying my face extra close, like she wasn't sure she even knew me.

We were surrounded by teenagers and families, all wearing bathing suits, laughing, running and acting carefree. Between my skin and my family, I couldn't imagine how they felt.

"I guess I can drape a towel over my legs."

I took my blouse off and then started to pull my jeans down. When they were just to my knees, I closed my eyes and took a deep breath. There was something about showing my legs that made me feel so real and honest. How could I do that and keep up the lie about Renee? I thought about her and my mom and how they tried to make me feel like we were a unified force that had to stick together, no matter what. I took my jeans off and flopped over on my stomach. The back of my legs didn't have as much psoriasis.

Maureen was reading *Tiger Beat* Magazine with her head propped up against her beach bag. The disc jockey on the radio was talking about back-to-school sales. Maureen blew a huge bubble with the sour grape bubble-gum she'd bought at Fortino's. It covered her whole face. She looked at me just before it popped.

"I wish I had my camera right now," I laughed.

"Serves me right for chewing two of them," she said as she peeled the gum off her face and hair.

As soon as we stopped laughing, I started crying. It was so weird, I couldn't believe it.

"Oh my God, Ruth Ann. Are you crying?"

I nodded. "It's no use."

"What's no use?"

"Me lying. To you. You of all people. I just can't do it."

"What do you mean?"

"Renee."

"You mean she's not pregnant?"

I wiped the corners of my eyes with the extra towel.

"She's pregnant, all right. She's just... not married. And never was. They're gonna run around telling the whole world this crazy Vietnam story, and I'm expected to go along with it."

Maureen's jaw was as low as it could get. "Oh man. That's asking a lot from you."

"I can do it. Just not with you. And I know you'll never tell anyone."

"No, of course not," Maureen said.

"I know I can do it, 'cause the truth is, I've had a lot of practice."

"Practice at what? I don't follow."

"This isn't the first time."

"Now I'm really lost. What are you talking about?

We both turned on our sides with our heads on our outstretched arms.

"Renee gave a baby up for adoption when I was in fourth grade. I've never told a living soul, so please promise me you never will."

"Of course, I promise, but I can't believe it."

"Yeah, in fact that's why we moved here from Mt. Pleasant."

"Because she was pregnant?"

"Yup. It was terrible. We lived in this apartment building, and she only left to go to the doctor."

"That sounds *awful*, Ruth Ann."

"Nobody talked to me about it. I guess they hoped I didn't notice."

"I wonder what the neighbors thought. They must have seen her."

"I guess they probably knew but acted like they didn't. I had a stomach ache every night after dinner and I'd cry in the bathtub."

"Did your mom and sister know you cried?"

"Yeah, but they thought it was 'cause I hated my teacher. That mean nun who called me a dirty girl for reading the teen romance."

"Oh yeah. I remember you telling me about that. The first baby's father wasn't the same guy as this time, was it?"

"No, that time it was her college boyfriend. They told me last night that he got her drunk and she doesn't remember what happened. I'm not sure I believe that. But it explains why my dad socked him in the jaw."

"Are you kidding? Were you there?"

"Yeah, my mom yanked me out of the room right after, but I saw my dad hit him at the front door."

"No offense, but your life is like a soap opera."

"Yeah, I guess you could call it *The Secret Storm*."

"My grandma watches that every day of her life. But seriously, I bet you wonder about the baby all the time. Was it a boy or a girl? Did they tell you?"

I sat up and wrapped my arms around my legs, focusing on a ship in the distance.

"It was a boy. The doctor let me see him for a minute. He was only five pounds and had a bunch of silky, black hair."

Maureen sat up. "Renee saw him too, right?"

"She did. She acted kind of weird after he was born. It was sad, but also spooky. The first thing she did when she came home from the hospital was throw her maternity clothes into the incinerator. Then she went back to college for second semester."

"But you knew she was pregnant the whole time, huh?"

"Yeah, the sad thing was that when it was all first happening back in Mt. Pleasant, I thought my mom and dad might get back together."

Maureen lit a cigarette, and offered one to me, but I shook my head.

"It was the best summer of my life. Mimi was supposed to stay for three weeks. We were having a blast catching polliwogs in this pond every day and walking all over the campus by ourselves. I loved living there. Then, all of a sudden, they took Mimi home and my dad was staying overnight. He even slept in my mom's bedroom."

"Well, no wonder you thought they were back together."

"Turns out, he was just waiting for Sean, the boyfriend, to get back to town. Next thing I knew, my dad left, my mom packed us up, and we moved to Grand Rapids."

Maureen put her hand on my shoulder. "You poor thing. Damn! Well, *I'm* sure glad you moved to Grand Rapids."

I wanted to smile but could only nod because I had a lump in my throat. I'd never told this stuff to anybody. Ever. But the last thing I wanted to do was bawl my head off right at the beach, in front of a girl who wasn't even fifteen, but could smoke and drive to Grand Haven all at the same time without even blowing her cool.

Chapter Sixteen

I watched a third trickle of blood roll down my leg. The doctor chased it with a square of gauze.

"How about one more?" he asked. "Then we'll call it quits for the day. Next week we'll do six or seven."

Dr. Boersma was kind and gentle. If he hadn't been, I wasn't sure I could tolerate the pain of the needle gun, that he shot right into my patches of psoriasis. His white hair and constant smile reminded me of Captain Kangaroo. That was a good thing, since I thought the Captain was my best friend back when I was four, and my dad moved in and out of our house every other week.

When we got in the car, my mom lit a Salem before turning the key. "Pay attention to where this building is, so when you come next week on the bus you don't get lost."

"I won't get lost. Holy Rosary's only two blocks from here."

"That's exactly why I picked this doctor. Today is the only time I'm taking off work to bring you here. Remember, once school starts, every Monday at 3:15."

My mom dropped me off and went back to Lowrey Piano to type a report for her boss, Mr. Trimble. Before she drove away, she told me she'd be late, and I should be nice to Renee when she got home from her job at Wurzburg's. "There's some leftover goulash in the fridge. Just remember that Renee is very tired, Ruth Ann. She's going to be grouchy, and that's all there is to it."

"Oh, lovely," I said. "You mean it's going to get worse?"

I sat on the edge of the tub and placed a cold, wet washcloth on my left leg, where the doctor had injected the needles of cortisone. It only gave a little relief. There were large, raised bumps where I'd gotten the shots. The phone began ringing, so I answered it in the hall, while I continued to hold the washcloth on my leg. It was Maureen.

"Guess who I'm meeting at the park tonight?" she asked.

"Hmm, if you're making me guess, it must be Ringo Starr. Or Johnny."

"Ha ha. You guessed it. We just talked on the phone for over an hour."

"No kidding? Are you getting back together?"

"Maybe. We'll see. Please come with me. He's bringing friends, too. Meet me at seven?"

I heard Renee downstairs. The thought of being alone with her sounded awful.

"What are you doing right now?" I asked Maureen.

"We're about to leave for a cook-out at my aunt's house. But I'll be at the park by seven, no problem."

"Okay," I said. "I'll see you then."

I draped the washcloth on the side of the tub and put my jeans back on.

When I came downstairs, Renee was filling the cats' dishes.

"Am I the only one around here who ever gives food and water to these poor cats?" she asked. "Do you ever even look at their dishes?"

"Yes, I do. Quite often, in fact. It so happens that I just got home from the doctor with bloody legs, and I needed to take care of that first."

"Bloody? What are you talking about?"

"He shot a needle gun right into the psoriasis four times. And starting next week, it'll be double that amount."

"Well, I'm glad somebody's finally taking some real action," Renee said. "Maybe I won't have to vacuum your scales every day."

"Nobody ever asked you to vacuum my scales, Renee. In fact, nobody else even notices."

"That's because you're such a pig. When was the last time you cleaned that room you sleep in?"

I headed for the front door. I wasn't sure where I was going, but I knew I needed to get away from her. I had a million mean things to say on the tip of my tongue, but instead, I turned around and shouted back to the kitchen. "For your information, I already knew you were pregnant. I knew all summer."

I walked by Cathy's house as fast as I could. I didn't want her to run out and start yakking away at me. For all I knew, the Cicerellis might have heard me yelling at Renee. Oh well, I thought. It would serve her right. Her and her phony dead husband.

No Doubt in my Mind

I ran across Burton street and into the park, wishing Maureen was home. I glanced over at Angela's house, and considered going there, but decided it would be rude since it was dinnertime. I thought about the slumber party she had when I had first started hanging around with the Tandem Riders. I remembered her dad singing Beatles songs while he made pancakes for us. As soon as Mr. Droski crossed my mind, I started missing my dad. I wondered how he was taking the news about Renee. It was hard for me to think of him as a grandfather.

I followed the path that led to the playground. A few kids were playing on the equipment, so instead of swinging as I'd hoped to do, I sat on a picnic table by the swimming pool fence. It was in a secluded porch area, under an awning, where the kids did crafts in the daytime. I got up to find a sharp stick, and then tried to carve my initials into the table top. I scratched away, and the more I thought about my sister's mess, my dad being clear across the state whenever I needed him, and facing the needle gun every Monday at 3:15, the further I felt from Garfield Park.

"Six months ago, that RB would have had a plus TL under it, right?"

I gasped and looked up to see Tom standing there with Marty and Johnny. He must have shot them a look to get lost, 'cause they both turned and headed around the building.

"Sorry," he said. "I didn't mean to scare you. But I am right. Right?"

"Maybe. Maybe not," I answered.

He sat on the bench of the table. "So, I hear yesterday you helped steal a car, and now today you're vandalizing city property. Turning into quite the juvenile delinquent, aren't you?"

"Shut up," I laughed. "We did not steal a car. And anyway, how'd you hear about that?"

"Johnny. Looks like he and Maureen are back on. Wish I could say the same about us."

I blew the shavings of wood out of my capital B, and then he moved from the bench to the table top, where I was sitting. When I looked up, his face came toward mine for a kiss. I didn't think twice about letting him. I dropped my stick and put my arms around him. I wondered if he'd also heard about the French kiss with the beep-line guy, because he was kissing with his tongue, and that wasn't the way he'd ever kissed me before. It occurred to me that he might have learned it from Leta or some other girl, so I broke the kiss and stared into his dark blue eyes.

"What?" he asked.

"Nothing," I answered. I decided not to think about the other girls. All I knew was that this was making me forget stuff better than anything else. We kissed several more times, and then Maureen and Johnny came around the corner of the building. Maureen was beaming, and I noticed they were holding hands.

"Hey, you two, how's it hangin'?" Maureen asked.

"We're good," Tom answered. He looked over at me. "We're real good."

I gave him a poke in the ribs with my elbow.

"You know who else is real good"? Maureen asked.

I shrugged, figuring she was talking about herself.

"Mary Lou. Remember that guy, Vinnie, we met last week? Well, it looks like they're hitting it off."

I threw my carving stick toward the sandbox. "That guy that's a junior?"

"Yup. He's got a car and everything. Come on. Let's go talk to them."

When I started to slide off the table, Tom pulled my hand and leaned in for a short kiss. I could tell Maureen was surprised when I turned around. We left the boys and walked around to the other side of the community building.

"Well, well, well. Looks like we're both back with our old flames, huh?"

"I don't know about that," I said. "I'm not thinking very far ahead."

"Listen," Maureen said. "My parents are going to the cottage this weekend. Johnny's coming over on Friday. How 'bout you spend the night and ask Tom to come over too?"

"Let me think about it. You're still going to the St. Blaise dance, aren't you?"

"Of course. That's the excuse I gave my parents for not going to the cottage. They think I'm staying at your house."

"You can stay at my house on Saturday," I said.

Mary Lou and Vinnie were sitting on the grass, leaning against a tree. She giggled and gave him a push. He threw back his head laughing. Mary Lou motioned for us to come over.

"Hi," she said. "Guess what? Vinnie says he'll drive us to the St. Blaise dance. We're gonna meet in that parking lot at seven. She pointed to the lot behind us.

"Wow," Maureen said. "That's extremely cool. Thanks, Vinnie."

"Angela's coming too," Mary Lou said. "And Irene. But not Peg. She's going to New York with her family. So, it'll be the Tandem Riders minus one."

"We better get back," Maureen said. "I'll call you on Saturday, Mary Lou."

When we got out of earshot, Maureen whispered, "I bet she gets a whole new outfit for this shindig."

I nodded and laughed. "There's no doubt in my mind."

We walked over by the tennis court to watch Tom and Johnny, who were playing frisbee with Marty, and some boys from Burton School.

"So, you kinda got over being mad at him, huh?

"Sort of. When I'm not with him, I don't feel like I used to. But when he gets near me, I turn into mush. It's weird. I can't really explain it."

"I get it. I'm like that with Johnny too. I guess we're both just hopelessly romantic."

"Or hopelessly stupid."

Maureen's hair was set on giant rollers when she came to the door on Friday.

"I'm so glad you're here," she said. "I was starting to think my parents would never leave."

"Why is there a tent in your back yard?" I asked.

"It's my sister's. She wanted to air it out before she goes camping. There's no yard at her apartment." Maureen pulled the pink tape off her bangs. "Hey, Mary Lou called about the dance, so I asked her to come over. You don't mind, do you?"

I followed Maureen up the stairs to her room. "No, I don't mind. She's way different than she used to be."

"I talked to Johnny around four, and he said he'd try to get Tom to come over with him." She pulled the rollers out and raised her voice while she sprayed Aqua Net on her hair. "Did you tell him you'd be here?"

I parted the curtains and looked out the window. "Yeah, I mentioned it when he called me. Here comes Mary Lou. I'll go let her in."

Mary Lou was at the back door wearing plaid shorts with a matching shell top. Instead of her usual pony tail, her hair was down. She was holding a small flowered suitcase. Maureen hadn't mentioned that she was spending the night.

"You look as cute as ever," I said. "I like your hair down."

"Does it make me look older? I have to think about that, you know. Since I'm dating a junior."

"It does make you look older," Maureen said as she entered the room. "Is Vinnie coming over?"

"Later. He works until eight. Do you have popsicles, by any chance?"

"Probably in our basement freezer. Why?"

175

"Go check, okay?"

Maureen came back with an opened box, peering inside. "Orange. That's it."

"Give 'em here and find me a pitcher." Mary Lou said. She opened the four popsicles, slid them off their sticks, and smashed them in the pitcher with a potato masher.

Maureen stood behind her with her hands on her hips. "What the hell are you doing, Lady Jane?"

Mary Lou reached into her shoulder purse and pulled out a flask.

"I found this in my brother's room," she said as she unscrewed the top.

"Since he won't be needing it, I thought we should make use of it." She emptied it into the pitcher.

"But why the popsicles?"

"I remember one time he and his girlfriend made this. Right before he left for Nam. It was the only way she could stand to drink alcohol. So, get some glasses out so we can drink a toast."

"What is it?" I asked.

"I don't know. Some kind of hooch. Whiskey, maybe."

We raised our juice glasses and clinked them together.

"In memory of Kevin," Maureen said.

We all shivered after we took the first sip.

"Look what I got today," Maureen said. "Winston Super Kings. They last way longer."

All three of us lit up and took more sips from our drinks. We were sitting on the same stools at the counter where we usually ate our frosting. It was less than two weeks ago that we were doing that with Mimi.

"What is the matter with me?" Maureen practically shouted. "We need some music."

She turned the kitchen radio on. "Of course my mother has it set on Wood Radio. Let me find LAV."

You Really Got Me, by the Kinks was playing. The three of us sang along loudly and poured another drink when it ended. I could feel myself letting go of all the worries I'd been hanging onto. I was almost happy, and when I thought about Tom coming over, even happier.

We had one more drink, and my head felt woozy.

Maureen slid off her stool. "I don't know about you guys, but I'm gonna put on my baby- dolls!"

"Great idea," Mary Lou said.

I followed them upstairs, hanging onto the railing a little tighter than usual. I unzipped my paisley suitcase and pulled Renee's baby-dolls out.

"Fantabulous!" Maureen said between hiccups. "Did Renee finally give you those?"

"Are you kidding, Maur? I just took 'em. Hell, she won't be needing them."

"Oh yeah, you're right!" We both fell on the bed laughing.

"What are you two talking about?" Mary Lou asked.

Maureen and I turned our heads toward each other. "Uh-oh, Ruth

Ann, you let the cat outta the bag."

"You guys are totally tipsy," Mary Lou said. "Tell me what cat's out of what bag, right now or I won't give you any more hootch-sicle."

"Hootch-sicle?" I asked. "Is that what we were drinking?"

Then Mary Lou collapsed on the bed laughing, and Maureen got the hiccups.

"It's the doorbell, you guys," Mary Lou said. "Somebody answer the door, hurry."

"I'll-get-it," Maureen said between hiccups. She was wearing her yellow baby-doll top with her jeans.

"So are you and Tom back together?" Mary Lou asked as she brushed her hair in the mirror.

I got up and dropped Renee's baby-dolls into my suitcase and would most likely leave them there for the night. I wouldn't have minded if Maureen saw my messed up legs, but not Mary Lou. "No, not really. We've just started hanging around again. I'm going down. Coming?" I wanted to get away from Mary Lou before she started asking more questions. Renee's pregnancy couldn't stay a secret much longer, but somewhere in the back of my mind, I knew I shouldn't be talking about it after drinking hootch-sicle.

"Yeah, what was I thinking?" Mary Lou asked as she looked at her profile in the mirror. "I'm not wearing baby-dolls with Vinnie coming."

Tom, Marty, and Rick were in the kitchen when I came downstairs. Tom was holding the pitcher up and sniffing it.

"Hi," he said, turning toward me. "What the hell are you girls drinking?"

I could actually feel a silly grin on my face. "I don't know. Something Mary Lou brought. We smashed it up with popsicles."

"Hey, set that down," Mary Lou said, coming up behind me. "You guys can score your own somewhere else. That stuff's sacred. Where's Maureen?"

Tom set the pitcher back on the counter and picked up the Winston Super Kings that Maureen had left on the counter. "She's in the tent with Johnny."

That was quick, I thought to myself. I hoped her hiccups had stopped.

He shook out a cigarette out and lit it. Then he offered the pack to the other boys.

"Oh good, here's Vinnie," Mary Lou skipped to the back door to let him in.

Rick and Marty went into the living room and started messing around on the baby grand piano.

"So, how ya feelin'?" Tom asked. "You girls drink much of that?"

"I'm okay," I answered. "Mary Lou says we're a little tipsy. It's kind of gross."

We were sitting on stools across the counter from each other. Tom's hair was falling over his right eye. I reached over and brushed it back.

"You're gonna have to get a haircut before school. They'll kick you out like that."

"Holy Rosary would kick me out."

"Well, yeah. Holy Rosary."

He tapped his ash into the ashtray. "I might not end up at Holy Rosary."

"What are you talking about?"

"My dad might be getting transferred to Grand Haven. So we'd have to move there."

"Are you kidding?"

Tom shook his head. "He should be finding out in the next couple of weeks."

My chest felt tight, and my thoughts began racing through my fuzzy mind. It almost felt like a dream.

Johnny and Maureen came in the back door, Maureen laughing loudly.

"Somebody make coffee," Johnny shouted. "This girl needs to sober up."

Tom walked around the counter and held his hand out to me. "Come on. The tent's free."

I was more confused than dizzy. I couldn't imagine being at Holy Rosary without Tom. Or Tom living in a different city. As we made our way to the back yard, I tried to imagine Garfield Park without him. He unzipped the tent, and we ducked down and entered. He pulled the zipper back down. It was mostly dark, but a small amount of moon light showed through the side window. Tom flopped down on the sleeping bag with his head on the pillow. I sat on my heels facing him.

"Wow, this is like a dream come true for me," he said. "Come here."

I snuggled into the crook of his arm and let him kiss me. We kissed over and over. Every time I thought of him moving away, I melted a little more. He kissed my neck and throat and that felt so good, I could hardly believe it. It seemed like electricity in places where there used to only be sparks. When Tom slipped his hand into my bra, I didn't stop him. Even when he unhooked it.

"I've missed you so much," he whispered in my ear. I could smell his Brut Cologne and wondered if it was from the same bottle I'd given him for Christmas.

He unzipped his pants and put my hand at the top of his underwear. I was startled by the position of his penis. "Why is it upside down?" I asked.

"Upside down?" Tom laughed so loudly, that I thought Terry O'Malley could probably hear him next door.

Before long, our jeans and shirts were by the door of the tent. I didn't know my body could make me feel that good. Next thing I knew, Tom was trying to take my underpants off.

"No, Tom," I said. "Everything but that."

"It's okay, really. I can pull out. I won't let you get pregnant, I promise."

For some crazy reason, I pictured Renee in the back seat of a car, embracing a mannequin from Wurzburg's. I sat up and dove for my jeans.

"Nope. Not going to happen. I can't do this."

He put his hand on my shoulder. "Come on, Ruth Ann."

I shivered and turned back to him. "I can't do this and I *won't* do this!"

"Okay, but don't leave."

I dressed quickly, unzipped the tent, and ran back into Maureen's house.

Chapter Seventeen

Mary Lou poured a second glass of pineapple juice and drank it down. "Boy, that really hit the spot."

I peeled the wrapper from a Hostess Sno-ball. "You can always count on weird stuff to eat and drink in this house." I bit into the Sno-ball.

"Okay," Mary Lou said. "I'll see you two at the park at seven and don't be late." She picked up her suitcase. "Hey, thanks for inviting me. I had a good time. Hope I didn't cause hangovers or anything like that."

After she left, Maureen shrugged. "You gotta admit, she's a lot nicer than she used to be."

I nodded. "You're right, she is. I need to get home. You wanna come with me or should we meet at the park later?"

"Aren't you gonna fill me in on the Tom story? I didn't want to bring it up with Mary Lou around. I got the feeling things didn't go so well."

"Yeah, I don't know, Maur. He really only has one thing on his mind, and I'm not about to go all the way. For a bunch of reasons. I especially need to watch it, since my sister seems to be a fertility goddess."

"Wow, I'm impressed you figured all that out. Especially last night after that hootch-sicle." We both laughed. "Hey, I'm gonna take a shower and do my nails and stuff, so let's meet up at seven. I'll just leave my overnight crap in Vinnie's car while we're at the dance."

"Okay. Speaking of that, I gotta figure out what to tell my mom about our transportation. Riding in a junior boy's car is a ticket to Villa Maria, for sure."

My mom was standing on a ladder in the kitchen when I came in the side door.

"Oh good, you're just in time," she said. "Here, take this, and give me that light bulb."

She handed me the light fixture from the ceiling. "What'd you do over at Maureen's house?"

"Nothing exciting," I answered. "Remember, Maureen's sleeping here after the dance tonight, 'cause her parents are going to the cottage."

"I forgot about that dance. How are you getting there?"

"Mary Lou. We're all meeting at the park at seven, so they don't have to drive all over."

My mom pointed at the fixture. "Wipe that out with the rag, and hand it back to me. How are you getting home?"

I wiped out the glass globe and held it up to her. "Mary Lou. Oh, gee, I'm supposed to call Denise. Remember Irene's cousin who visited me in the hospital?" I walked out of the kitchen as fast as I could before my mom could dig any further. Renee didn't seem to be around, so I snuck the baby-dolls, which I hadn't even worn, back into her drawer. I closed my bedroom door and flopped on the bed. I felt like I needed to think about a lot of stuff. Especially about last night with Tom. I had felt so different than I did in the boat. It had to be partly from the alcohol, that much I knew. But mostly it was being in the dark. He couldn't really see my skin, and that changed everything. I thought about my mom's Billie Holiday record when she sang about what a little moonlight can do.

"Ruth Ann. Hey, Ruth Ann." It was Cathy, calling over from Frankie's room.

I got up and knelt on the floor in front of my open window. "Hi," I said. "What are you up to?"

"Nothing. I just haven't talked to you in ages. I bet you miss Mimi. Has she written?"

"Of course not," I said. "She just left Monday."

"Oh yeah. Hey, a little bird told me you and Tom are back together. Is it true?"

"A little bird, huh? Named Teresa Sullivan by any chance?"

Cathy laughed. "Maybe, maybe not. Is it true?"

"Maybe. Maybe not. But, listen, Cath, I gotta figure out what to wear to the St. Blaise dance, so I'll talk to you tomorrow, okay?"

"Oh yeah, I forgot all about the dance. Have fun and promise to tell me all about it. Okay? Promise?"

"Okay, sure. I gotta go."

I slipped into my closet, so Cathy would leave the window. I took my print skirt and matching Poor Boy top out and laid them on the bed. Last time I'd worn these was to Daniel's Den in Saginaw. I was so tired of this outfit, but I really had no other choice. Luckily, the bumps on my legs from the shots had gone down, but it didn't seem like those psoriasis spots were any better.

I noticed on the way to the park that the light seemed different. You could tell summer was about to end soon, and that made me feel sad. I stopped and looked down at my legs. At least with summer over I could start wearing tights again. I just hoped the lights were dim at the dance.

"Hey, Ruth Ann. Wait up."

It was Angela crossing Madison Street from her house. I stopped walking and waited for her, glad to see she was wearing a print skirt and matching top too. When we got to the parking lot, Vinnie and Mary Lou were sitting on the hood of his dark blue Falcon. Irene, and Maureen were walking toward the car from the other direction. I noticed that Mary Lou was wearing the new Villager shirtwaist dress that I'd tried on in Saginaw.

"All right, let's go," Vinnie said hopping off the car.

"Who all wants a Winston Super King?" Maureen asked. "Push in your lighter, would you, Vinnie."

Vinnie pushed in the cigarette lighter on the dashboard. After it popped out, he handed it to us in the back seat. "You girls hear 'bout the new Beatles song coming out in a couple days? They're saying it's gonna be huge."

Maureen offered a cigarette to Vinnie. I noticed he didn't take one. And I noticed that he looked sideways at Mary Lou all the way to the dance.

We followed Vinnie down the stairs to the basement of St. Blaise Church.

The room was packed with kids and the song *Pictures of Matchstick*

Men was playing. Unlike the dances in Saginaw, there weren't any strobe lights or psychedelic images projected anywhere. I was relieved that it wasn't bright like a gym, at least.

A boy came up to Vinnie and slapped him on the back. "Hey, DiMartino, how's it hangin'?"

Vinnie introduced us to Andy Schmidt. He had shiny platinum blonde hair. "You girls let this character drive you here?" he asked. "You really took your life in your hands, let me tell ya."

He smiled at us and walked away chuckling, and then he turned back and looked at me again.

"What kinda bull is Schmidt spreadin' around?" I turned toward the voice, and it was Denise.

We hugged immediately, and then she took both my hands.

"Wow, Denise," I said. "You look gorgeous!"

"Listen," she laughed. "When you got a fat ass like mine, you need to spend two hours on your make-up. It's *so damn good to see you*. I was afraid you wouldn't make it."

Next, she hugged her cousin, Irene, and then we introduced her to Angela, Mary Lou, and Maureen. Denise put her hand on Maureen's shoulder. "I have been dying to meet *you*. Ever since I heard about you mailing that daisy earring back to save Ruth Ann's hide."

We all patted Maureen on the back. "It's true, Maur. You did save my hide."

Even Mary Lou was nodding. A few months ago, she would have

tried to embarrass me about losing Renee's earring when I had snuck off in the boat with Tom.

"Look, Ruth Ann," Denise said. "Here comes the Three Musketeers. They can't wait to see you."

Denise's friends, Charlie, Eddie, and Michael were headed toward us, all grinning.

I turned to the girls. "These are Denise's friends that came with her to visit me in the hospital."

"They came without me a couple times too," Denise said.

I knew she was thinking about the time Michael had stolen the guy's pipe.

"Wow, I hardly recognize you without a hospital gown," Michael said.

We all stood around laughing and talking about Michael's addiction to the hospital french fries, who was taking Spanish, and who was taking French, who would be in each other's homerooms, who was going to the beach one more time, and who knew which day the new Beatles song was coming out.

Andy Schmidt walked up to Michael. "You got an Old Gold?" Michael reached into his pocket and handed him one.

"Hey, Andy, this is Ruth Ann, the girl from the hospital." Michael looked at me. "I've had the misfortune of having Andy for a neighbor my whole life."

"You're way behind the eight ball, Fitzpatrick. We already met. You frosh are so slow." "Frosh?" I looked at Denise.

"Freshman. Get used to it. Andy's a sophomore. We'll be teased all year. Hey, let's go have a cig in the girls room."

I followed Denise into the bathroom, watching her large rear-end sway back and forth. I loved how she seemed so comfortable with it, and to me, it seemed as beautiful as her fancy eye-liner. But I wondered if she really hated her weight like I did my psoriasis and wondered if we'd ever be close enough for me to find out how she really felt.

Denise held her match out to light my cigarette. "Tell me everything that's going on with you. I can see your psoriasis is much better."

"It's got a long way to go, but yeah it's a little better. I'll be getting shots every Monday. The doctor's really close to school."

"Oh, no kidding? Hey, I'll go with you if you want."

"Denise, you're just about the damned nicest girl I've ever met."

Mary Lou came bursting through the door with Maureen, Angela, and Irene behind her.

"Guess what?" she asked. "You know that dance we practiced all last week at the park? It's totally out. Not one person out there is doing it."

"Yeah, they're all out there doing something completely different," Angela chimed in.

"Line up, girls," Denise said, putting her cigarette in the corner of her mouth. "I'll show ya the dance."

So, the five of us stood behind Denise and tried to copy her fancy footwork. I glanced sideways at their serious faces, and smiled to myself, because I could tell they didn't give a hoot about her large rear. I felt like kissing every one of their cheeks.

Once we made it out to the dance floor, girls were in lines doing the nameless dance. St. Ursula girls here, Holy Name girls there, Sacred Heart girls by the stage. My feet didn't want to cooperate, and I thought the whole thing was silly. It felt more like cheerleading than dancing. I left the line when I spotted Michael and Eddie leaning on the wall, having a lively conversation. Michael stopped talking when I walked up and turned to me.

"Now here's a girl who likes good music. Let's ask her."

"Ask me what?"

Michael looked over my shoulder with a huge grin. I turned around and saw his neighbor, Andy Schmidt, standing right behind me. He was holding his arms out and mouthing the words to the song that had just started, *Turn Around Look at Me*. It reminded me of something my dad would do.

"Hey, Frosh," he said. "If this song didn't suck, I might ask you to dance."

"Lucky for you, the song sucks," Michael said to me with an extremely serious face. "You won't have to put up with Schmidt's B. S."

"Or his B.O.," Eddie said.

"Sounds like you characters both need wedgies," Andy Schmidt said.

Michael and Eddie turned and ran across the dance floor with Andy close behind. They bumped into several dancing couples, and disappeared down a hallway, leaving me to wonder what they meant by a "wedgie."

"Those guys are nuts," Denise said. She had just walked up with her friend, Julie. "Ruth Ann, you remember Julie, don't you?"

What I mostly remembered was her beautiful hair, and that I wasn't sure I liked her.

"That's right," Julie said. "We ran into you downtown. You had a friend with you from somewhere else. Really quiet girl?"

"Mimi," I said. "She's really not that quiet. That was an off day for her, I guess."

"Oh, yeah," she said, "I also remember you have some sort of skin disease, don't you?" She looked at my arms, then backed up to look down at my legs. Before Julie could say another word, Denise spoke up. "Hey, your friends are cool as hell. I like all of 'em. Maureen totally cracks me up. Julie, you gotta meet Ruth Anne and Irene's friends.

The song, *Love Is All Around,* by the Troggs came on. Vinnie and Mary Lou were dancing, and Maureen was dancing with a guy I'd never seen.

"Look, Michael's dancing with Joanne Rogers," Julie said. "I bet she asked him."

"Did any guys from your school come?" Denise asked.

"No. We told 'em about it, but they weren't interested," I said. "Maureen just got back together with her old boyfriend, but he didn't want to come either."

"I wish it was like the old days, when you could cut in," Julie said, looking at Michael.

Andy walked up and stood in front of me. "Even though the song's half over, at least it doesn't suck. Wanna dance?"

He led me to the dance floor. "Fitzpatrick told me you like good music."

"He did?"

"Yeah. He mentioned it. I play guitar. You'll probably hear my band practice over at Hogan's basement."

"What's Hogan's basement?" I asked.

"It's our hang-out place. You've met Katie Hogan, right?" I shook my head. "She's a frosh, and her brother's a junior. Their ol' lady doesn't care if we hang out in the basement and their ol' man died a long time ago. So that's where the band rehearses."

The song ended. Andy saluted me and walked toward the boys' bathroom. Denise, Julie, Irene, and Angela were talking to a girl who towered over them.

"Hi." She smiled at me. "I'm Katie Hogan. Denise has been wanting us to meet all summer."

"Oh, hi. Andy was just telling me all about your basement."

She laughed. "Oh, yeah. Now that I'm in high school, I'm making my brother share it. You'll be seeing it real soon, I'm sure. You can ask Denise and Julie. It's just a crummy old basement."

"Yeah," Denise said. "But your mom's so cool about everybody hangin' out down there."

"I guess she'd rather have us in the house," Katie said.

"I don't know about you guys." Maureen said as soon as Vinnie turned the key in the ignition, "But I had a great time."

Mary Lou was sitting right next to Vinnie and he had his arm around her shoulder while he drove. They looked so grown-up to me. That made high school feel more real to me than even the schedule of classes I'd gotten in the mail.

"You girls want to stop at Burger Chef or The Hut?" he asked us.

We all told him we had promised to come straight home. He dropped me and Maureen off first since my neighborhood was closer than the other girls. My mom and Larry were playing cards with Bruce and Trudy when we walked in.

"Looky here, Bruce." Trudy said. "The dancing girls are home."

She got up and threw her arms around my neck with her cards in one hand and a cigarette in the other. She smelled like beer. Then she pinched Maureen's cheeks. "This one has chimples, Bruce."

"It's dimples, dear," Bruce said. "And it's your turn."

"But I want to hear about the dancing," she protested.

As soon as we closed the bedroom door, we burst out laughing.

"Chimples? Oh my God, Ruth Ann. She's a riot. And I loved her slippers."

"She always wears her fluffy slippers over here. I'm sure I've told you that."

"Where's she from again?"

"Germany. Remember I told you she got back into West Germany under a pile of coal?"

"Oh yeah. Wow. I do remember now."

I closed my curtains, thinking Cathy might be tempted to holler over.

"Tell me the truth," Maureen said. "Did you have fun tonight?"

"Yeah, pretty much. I loved seeing Denise again, and the boys from the hospital."

Maureen unzipped her print suitcase. "That Michael is cool as hell if you ask me. There's something about him that's different. Does he have a girlfriend?"

"I don't know," I said. "But Denise's friend Julie sure has a thing for him, and there's something about her I'm not sure I like."

"Yeah, he doesn't seem like her type. He's really cute for a guy with glasses."

When I woke up Tuesday morning, my legs felt stiff from the shots I'd gotten the day before. Maureen took the bus with me to the doctor, and then we'd walked downtown after. I turned on the radio just in time to hear the disc jockey say he would be playing *Hey Jude,* the new Beatles song, in fifteen minutes. I hobbled into the hallway and called Maureen to tell her, then I laid back on the bed to listen to it. The song made me feel happy at first. Then I felt sad, and by the ending, my heart felt full and hopeful. Almost overflowing. I wished I could hear it again, so I turned on the radio in the kitchen while I made toast.

The phone rang in the dining room, and it was Tom.

"Hey, haven't talked to you in a few days," he said. "What's new? You go to that dance?"

"I did go," I said.

"We haven't talked since the other night at Maureen's and I wanted you to know I'm not mad or anything."

"Oh? I never thought you were." What I felt like saying was, *Why the hell would you be?* But I looked down at the window seat and noticed a catalog that'd been left open. The top of the page said, "You'll love these casuals!" Somebody had circled numbers four, eight, and ten. A skirt, top, and jumper. Then I spotted a baby in the corner of the page, holding a block with an M on it that began the spelling of maternity. That's when I realized these were maternity clothes.

"So, it could happen sooner than we think," Tom was saying.

"What could?" I asked.

"Grand Haven. Didn't you hear what I said?"

"Sorry. Something distracted me. You're moving sooner than you thought?"

"Yeah, my dad's new job is starting. Look, I gotta go. I just wondered if I'd see you at the park tonight."

"I don't know. Maybe. I gotta go too."

I hung up the phone, and *Hey Jude* was playing on the kitchen radio. I leaned against the window and closed my eyes for the whole song. It felt like there was a message in it for me somewhere.

When the song ended, I looked down at the maternity page and wondered what the hell my dad was thinking about all of this baby and fake marriage stuff. I wondered if he'd like *Hey Jude*. He always told me that the song *Yesterday* made him feel sad. Just for the heck of it, I flipped to the baby section in the catalog. That's when I saw two babies that looked alike, holding up a sign that said, *Twin Insurance. Order any set on this page before your baby is born. We will send you extra free sets if it's twins or more! Send enclosed slip signed by your doctor or minister.* What about your priest or rabbi, I thought. And what *if* Renee had twins! Then I panicked, picked up the phone and dialed Dixie Used Cars in Saginaw. My mom would just have to deal with this long-distance call on the bill. I had a few questions for my dad. Turned out, he didn't seem all that shocked or upset. Not like I expected anyway. He talked more about "those damn hippies in Chicago raising hell at the Democratic convention."

Chapter Eighteen

I held the navy blue skirt up in the mirror. "At least we can wear whatever we want with these. And let's face it, anything's better than those ugly St. Boner's jumpers."

"Any sweater or blouse you want on top, and it's still a uniform?" Cathy asked.

"I guess so. I got a five dollar tip yesterday for babysitting, so I might have enough now for a Villager or Ladybug sweater."

"You deserved a tip since Mrs. Harris was gone so long."

"Well, she went to a wedding in Manistee, but that was fine with me. I need the money. Now I have to figure out what to wear on the first day because we don't have to wear the blue skirts until the second day."

Cathy pointed to a dress hanging on my closet door. "Wear that. It's so cute on you."

"I can't. I wore it to orientation."

It was the same dress I'd worn in the eighth-grade talent show. Aunt Dorothy had bought it for me in Saginaw on spring break. My chest felt tight when I thought of eighth-grade and, just like that, high school sounded terrifying.

"Did orientation help?" Cathy asked, patting the bed so Reddy would jump up.

"Help what?" I didn't mean to sound snappy, but it felt like Cathy knew I was scared.

"You know. Where to find stuff, like the cafeteria and your homeroom."

"I guess so."

The last thing I wanted to tell her was how overwhelmed I'd felt. Nobody'd ever told me there'd be two separate buildings. Not to mention thousands of kids.

I went into my closet to search for other ideas. The wool skirt I'd worn last year to Maureen's birthday party would probably fit, but it was too early for wool. Maybe the corduroy skirt from my suit.

"Hey, Ruth Ann? I was wondering why you haven't talked about the baby."

I stepped out of the closet with the corduroy suit.

"What?"

"My mom told me last night about Renee having a baby and that her husband died. It's *so sad and so terrible.* But aren't you excited about the baby?" Reddy lifted his chin while Cathy scratched his neck. "I guess you didn't know that I knew, huh?"

I hadn't thought about getting tested without a warning. If my mom had tipped me off that she'd told Mrs. Cicerelli, I would have been prepared. I didn't have the slightest idea what to say. I could hear words coming out of my mouth, but they sounded like somebody else's. I sounded like my mom talking on the phone to Trudy or my Aunt Maxine. I was saying something about Renee not being ready for people to know and how she was already in her second trimester, whatever that meant.

Where was this coming from? I stopped myself before I said it was God's plan. That's how my dad said they were explaining it to Grandma Gertie. What a load of B. S.

"Just think," Cathy said. "You'll be an aunt!"

Why did everybody think that was so cool? Even Maureen had said that on the way to Grand Haven.

Cathy ran her fingers down Reddy's tail. "My mom wants to give Renee a baby shower. I said I'd help. You can give us ideas if you want."

I walked back in the closet, gritted my teeth, and hung up the suit.

"Well, I guess I'll go see if my mom needs any help." Cathy said.

"Okay, I'll see ya' soon," I answered from the closet. Too soon, I thought, since the Cicerelli's were having a Labor Day cook-out.

I waited in my room until I was sure she was gone, and then I stormed down the stairs. My sister was on the phone and my mom was dropping melon balls into a fruit salad.

"When were you guys planning on telling me?"

"Telling you what?" my mom asked before she popped a blueberry into her mouth.

"That all the Cicerellis know about the baby! That's what!"

"Well, we had to tell them sometime, Ruth Ann. Renee's beginning to show."

"Okay, but couldn't you have let me in on it? Cathy just blabbed all over about it and I didn't even know what to say!"

"Do you mind?" Renee hollered from the dining room. "I'm on the phone in here."

"Have you guys told the whole world?" I asked.

"What do you mean, the whole world? Don't be ridiculous. And hand me that Saran Wrap. You need to pull yourself together, 'cause it's almost time to go next door."

Renee walked into the kitchen. "What is all this yelling about?"

"It's about you, Renee," I said. "It would be nice if you filled me in on who knows what about your *situation*."

"What's that supposed to mean?"

My mom stretched the cellophane over the bowl of fruit salad. "I forgot to tell her that I told Francesca about the baby. And Cathy just mentioned it upstairs."

"She didn't just mention it. She cornered me about it. About being an aunt and baby showers and all kinds of crap! I don't even know where it's gonna live or what the dead husband's name is or anything."

"It? Did you just refer to the baby as it?" Renee's mouth was hanging open.

"Renee and the baby will live here, of course," my mom said.

"You better face the music, little sister," Renee said. "You are not going to be the center of attention forever."

"Was I ever?"

My mom dried her hands on a dish towel. "And why would you need to know the husband's name?"

"Because people will ask me. I don't know what I'm supposed to say."

Renee and my mom exchanged glances. "We'll let you know," my mom said. "Don't worry about it right now. You've got school starting tomorrow and enough other stuff. Now let's go enjoy ourselves at the cook-out. No one's going to ask you for a name today."

"Let's hope not," I said. "And if they do, I hope they ask you guys, and not me."

"And for your information, Francesca is thrilled," Renee said.

"So I gathered. Cathy's probably baking a cherry chip cake for you right now."

I woke up the next morning with a giant batch of butterflies in my stomach. Nobody had called me to get up and the house seemed too quiet. At first I thought I'd overslept, but it was actually fifteen minutes earlier than I'd planned on getting up. My corduroy skirt and olive green Poor Boy top were draped over the dressing table bench. I'd tried them on when we got home from the Cicerellis' party, and I was surprised how cute they looked without the jacket. It was a decent enough outfit and would just have to do.

My mom was in the kitchen actually cooking breakfast. She was scrambling eggs in one pan and shoving sausages around in another. It was weird getting up early enough to see her. She was always gone by the time I got up for St. Boner's.

"Hungry?" she asked. "I thought you should eat a good breakfast on your first day. Butter that toast, okay?"

Renee walked in with a Wurzburg's bag. "So, I'll look for this in size ten. Mother, you don't have to make breakfast for me every day. You have enough to do in the morning."

"It's important for the baby that you eat right. Get a plate, honey."

So, my mom had been making breakfast for Renee every day. For a minute, I thought it was special for me. I felt bad for wishing that. Then I felt mad for feeling bad. It was all too confusing.

"Why aren't you wearing your cute print dress?" my mom asked as I sat down.

"I wore it to orientation last week. I can't wear it again."

"Oh, for heaven's sake," my mom said. "I wore the same dress all four years of high school."

"What *are* you wearing?" Renee asked, looking up from the newspaper.

"The skirt to my suit. I'm sick of my other print skirt and top. And I just wore those to the dance."

Renee scrunched up her face. "It's too early for corduroy."

"It's going to get pretty hot later," my mom said. "The weather man said at least eighty degrees."

"Well that's just great. What am I supposed to do?"

"It's too bad your father didn't send you some money for school clothes," my mom said as she lit her cigarette. "Or bought you something when you were there."

No Doubt in my Mind

Renee set her juice glass down and headed straight for the stairs without saying a word. She was back down in less than a minute, holding a dress on a hanger. "Why don't you try this on? I know you've always liked it, and I can't wear it now, that's for sure."

I would never wear most of Renee's clothes, but this was one dress I loved. I had actually picked it out when my mom and I visited Aunt Maxine in Hartford, Connecticut, the summer before eighth grade. My mom felt bad that Renee couldn't come, so she bought her gifts. I would have gladly traded the trip for the dress and paisley scarf that I picked out.

"Are you sure?" I asked her.

"Go ahead, try it."

I ran up the stairs before she could change her mind, took off the skirt and top, and slipped the dress over my head. It was a forest green, Empire style, dotted swiss with bell sleeves that came to the elbows. It was a half size too big, but close enough. I could hardly believe Renee had offered it to me. I practically floated out the front door. I hadn't felt this pretty since first grade when I wore a black corduroy skirt with a checkered Scottie dog and matching checkered blouse.

When Vinnie pulled into the parking lot at the park, we were already smoking Winston Super Kings, and *Hey Jude* was playing on the radio. All six of us Tandem Riders piled into the Falcon, and sang with The Beatles, all the way down Division Avenue on our way to Holy Rosary High School.

Chapter Nineteen

"Pass it over here, Bloomfield," Julie said.

I passed the bottle of Boone's Farm Apple wine to Julie and wiped my mouth with the back of my hand.

"Are you sure this is a safe place?" Maureen asked.

Denise took the bottle from Julie. "Don't worry. I've heard that only kids who drink at Fuller Park get busted, but never at Wilcox."

Maureen lit a Winston. "How far is it to Hogan's basement?"

"Just a few blocks," Julie tipped the bottle toward the sky to get the last sip. "Let's start walking. I'm freezing."

It was the second weekend since school had started. The first weekend we'd gone to the football game, and the weather was unseasonably warm. Now I was wishing I'd worn my pea coat. I felt a little tipsy as we passed Orwant's Liquor Store.

"This is where everybody goes to get booze," Denise said.

Maureen wrinkled her forehead. "What do you mean?"

"You stand right here on this side of the building and ask people to buy for you," Julie said. "Usually college kids come through."

"It was nice of your sister to get us the Boone's Farm," I said to Julie.

"It probably won't happen again, Bloomfield. Ha, or should I say, Bloom Farm?"

I'd hoped to warm up to Julie since she was Denise's friend, but so far it hadn't happened. One thing that irritated me was that she never called anyone by their first name.

"*Your* last name sounds so biblical," Julie said to Maureen. "What kind of name is Abraham anyway?"

"It's Lebanese."

"Lebanese? Is that where lesbians come from?" Julie was the only one who laughed.

"That joke got old by sixth grade," I said. "Maureen's dad is Arab and mine's Jewish, so that's why we have to work so hard to get our hair straight, right, Maur?"

Julie looked at my hair and then at Maureen's. "I can always tell who has curly hair even when they try to straighten it. It's not as shiny."

"We should've peed in the woods," Denise said as she did a little jig on the sidewalk. "I gotta go."

"Yeah, let's stop at Rax," Julie said. "Just so you guys know, we can't use the bathroom at Hogan's. There's only one and it's way upstairs. My sister told me that you never leave the basement."

We stopped at Rax Roast Beef and used the bathroom. The guy behind the counter frowned at us.

"I'd buy a pop" Denise whispered, "but I don't wanna drink anymore."

Julie combed her hair as we walked toward Katie's house, better known as Hogan's basement, then she applied a Yardley lip gloss. "I wonder if Michael will be there," she said.

"Do you think Katie's home yet?" Maureen asked.

"The people she sits for are always late," Denise said. "But it doesn't matter. Her brother and everyone else will be there."

"Have you guys ever been there?" Maureen asked Denise and Julie.

"We've been to Katie's, but not officially to Hogan's basement," Denise answered.

It was a large, older house with a big front porch. We entered the notorious hangout through the side door. Music was playing, and the air was filled with smoke as we walked down the stairs. Michael, Eddie, and Charlie were sitting on crates playing cards with Andy Schmidt.

"Setback," Denise said to me over her shoulder. "They're nuts for it."

The basement room was small and had plain old cement walls and floor. There was an oval braided rug in the middle. Mary Lou was sitting on Vinnie's lap in an old, beat up arm chair. She smiled at us, "Here come the winos."

Another couple was making out in a better looking arm chair that was tipped back against the wall. Denise must have seen me looking at them. She whispered over my shoulder. "That's Katie's brother, Dennis, and that's his throne. Nobody else ever sits in it."

"I'm out," Andy said, slapping his cards down. He walked over to us and offered me an Old Gold from his pack. As he lit it, he motioned for us to sit on the floor. Katie Hogan came down the steps just as we sat down. She seemed even taller in this basement. "Hey, the St. Bonaventure girls are here!" she said. "I wasn't sure you'd make it. Sorry I'm late. I've been babysitting for six hours. Anybody got a cigarette I can bum?"

"That's one of the nicest girls you'll ever know," Andy said. "Exact opposite of her brother."

I looked over at her brother and his girlfriend, a pretty blonde. "You don't like him?"

"He's one of my best friends, but he's a royal prick."

Michael got up from the card game and stretched his arms over his head. I noticed Julie sat up a little straighter and coiled the end of her shoulder length flip around her finger. He came over and sat on the floor, facing me and Andy. "So, Ruth Ann, we've survived two weeks of high school. What do you think so far?"

"It's all right, I guess. What about you? And *what* is this music playing?"

"It's cool as hell, isn't it?" Michael said. It's "The band is Love. The album's called *Forever Changes*."

"Is that a stage?" I asked, pointing to a platform next to the stairs that had drums in the back.

"Yeah," Andy said. "For our band. We built that last year from some scrap wood we found." He nodded toward two guys I didn't know. "They're in the band too, and so is Hogan." He pointed at Katie's brother, who was lighting his girlfriend's cigarette.

I noticed Julie staring at us, but the music was loud enough to block her from hearing our conversation. Michael was talking about a book, *Catcher in the Rye*. He had just finished it and said it was probably the best book he would ever read in his entire life. I was only partly listening to him because I was thinking back to when I'd met him at the hospital and thought he was cute. I'd never been attracted to a boy in glasses before. I also noticed his teeth were perfect when he laughed. When Michael scooted over by Vinnie and Mary Lou to talk to them, Andy lit another Old Gold.

"So, where's your boyfriend tonight?" he asked.

"Boyfriend?"

"Yeah, I thought Denise said you'd had a boyfriend for a whole year."

"Not really. Well, kind of. He hasn't actually been my boyfriend lately. He's supposed to be moving to Grand Haven."

Before Andy could respond, a bunch of other tenth-graders came down the stairs. Andy and I moved over to make room, and I was next to Michael again. I could feel Julie staring at us, but I made an effort not to look at her. Andy got up to talk to the newcomers.

Michael leaned toward me. "Crazy down here, isn't it? This place is the best! Schmidt talked about coming here all last year, and I couldn't wait."

Denise was standing by us next. "Hey, move over, you two, so I can fit my fat ass in here." She got down on one knee at a time before she sat down.

"Wait a minute," I said. "Is this Bob Dylan?"

"It's the album, *Blonde on Blonde*, Michael said. "This album is so tits, but it really deserves undivided attention."

"I've never heard the album before, just *Rainy Day Women*" Maureen said as she squeezed in beside us.

hjhhhhhhhjjjjj "I don't know about you guys," Denise said, "but I'm having a riot."

I looked at Denise. "I'm glad you talked us into coming. It's almost made me forget about all the shit going on in my family."

Denise looked concerned. "There's shit going on in your family? Oh, no. Let me guess. Your sister?"

I nodded. "You guessed right. She's pregnant."

"Wow. Is she keeping the baby?"

"She is. And remember when I told you what a bitch she can be?"

"How could I forget?" Denise looked at Michael, who was listening. "You should hear some of the stories."

"Well, try to imagine that same person, only pregnant."

"Oh my God, Ruth Ann. Maybe you should move into *my* house. We've got so many people, nobody would even notice one more."

Michael flashed a smile with his gorgeous teeth and nodded. "That's a fact."

When I looked over his shoulder, I saw Julie glaring at us.

I smeared the ointment on my leg, wrapped it in Saran Wrap, and then wound the ace bandage over that. Then I did the same thing to my other leg. This was going to be a big pain in the butt, and in the back of my mind, I wondered how long I'd really do it.

No Doubt in my Mind

It had been a bad day even before I went to the doctor. As soon as I'd walked into the girls' bathroom, I heard everybody talking about Tom's new girlfriend, Nadine Wilkerson. A baton twirler. I had to admit she was kind of pretty, but if you asked me, it was mostly all the eyeliner she wore. I'd barely talked to Tom since our night in the tent, but for some reason, the idea of him with another girl made me feel sick.

"Ruth Ann, your father's on the telephone," my mom hollered from downstairs.

I picked up the extension phone in the hall. "Hi, Dad."

"Jiminy Christmas, Sport. Why so glum?"

"Sorry. I didn't mean to sound glum. I just had to wrap my legs up in Saran Wrap, and they feel like submarine sandwiches."

"Oh, yeah, I remember Wally said you should do that with the medicine. Did you get the shots too?"

"Yeah, I got the shots and now he wants me to put on all this stuff every night. How come you're calling, anyway?"

"Whadda ya mean, how come I'm calling? Do I need a reason?"

"I guess not, but you usually have one. You're probably checking to see if Renee and I have killed each other yet. Right?"

"Well, I have been thinking about driving over there one of these Sundays. Maybe I could bring Grandma and Aunt Dorothy."

"I heard you told Grandma about Renee. Good thing, she can't hide it much longer."

"Yeah, yeah. We told her the phony baloney soldier story, and she bought it. What else could she do? Listen, Sport, you take 'er easy with those sub sandwiches and put your sister on the phone a minute. You doin' all your schoolwork?"

"Of course. Just a minute, I'll get Renee. Bye, Dad."

I wasn't used to this. My dad usually avoided Renee if he could, and here he was planning a visit out of nowhere. I hung up the phone when Renee got on downstairs and turned on the radio. The song, *Those Were the Days*, was playing. I hadn't paid much attention to the words before, but they hit me when I was picking up my bloody knee socks from the floor. It was about endings. Things that were gone. Times you could never go back to. Like the sweetness of Tom when we first met. The halls of St. Boner's. Renee at college, instead of sitting downstairs when it was almost October. Those clear smooth legs I had the summer before eighth-grade. Next thing I knew, I was sobbing into my pillow. Damn that baton twirling hussy.

"So, what'd Dad say last night?" I asked Renee as I set the Saran Wrap on the counter.

Renee dropped a tuna sandwich into a brown bag. "Saran Wrap's expensive, you know. Be careful not to waste it."

"Don't worry. I won't. Anyway, what'd Dad say?"

"About what?"

"About coming for a visit. He said he might come on a Sunday and bring Grandma and Dorothy."

"Well, it won't be this Sunday, that's for sure. Jerry Michael's coming to help me wallpaper my room."

"That figures," I said. "I'm always the last to know everything around here."

Renee peeled a banana. "Why would we bother telling you? Since you're not the least bit interested in anything that concerns the baby."

"Well, I *like* Jerry Michael, even though you always hog him all to yourself."

The week didn't get much better. It seemed like I saw Tom with the baton twirler every time I turned a corner at school. On Friday, Mary Lou and I got a ride to Wilcox Park from Vinnie and we met Denise and Katie Hogan there. Katie and Denise had scored a bottle of something called Sloe Gin that tasted like cough syrup. We took turns taking swigs from the bottle.

"Do you guys know where the boys are watching those stag movies?" Mary Lou asked.

"Yeah," Katie said. "But they block the windows. We tried spying on them last time."

"Forget the boys for once," I said. "I've about had it with all of 'em."

"Oh, yeah. Sorry about your Tom and that Nadine girl," Katie said.

"Thanks, but he's not *my* Tom. Not anymore anyway."

Denise handed me the bottle. "She's from St. Stanislaus, right?"

"Yeah," Katie said. "Those girls from the Wyoming schools seem pretty cliquish, don't you think?"

"The only good thing Wyoming ever had," I said, "was Roger's Plaza."

Denise opened a new pack of Winstons. "And who needs Roger's Plaza now that we have the new malls?"

"Well, Tom is supposed to be moving to Grand Haven." I took a drink and handed the bottle to Katie. "And all I can say is good riddance." I thought I heard myself slur the word riddance, so I giggled.

"Hey, Ruth Ann," Mary Lou said. "I forgot to tell you that I saw your sister at Alger Variety."

"Oh. Did she look any different?" I asked her.

"Well, yeah."

I took a longer swig when Mary Lou handed me the bottle. "I guess I haven't told that many people. She's pregnant. Due around Christmas."

"Who's the father?"

I hated the fake story about the husband dying in Vietnam, but since it was Mary Lou, and her brother'd been killed there, the lie flew out of my mouth. She put her arms around me. "I am *so* sorry. That's just awful! Poor Renee."

I took another big drink from the bottle and then answered a flood of questions about everything from baby booties to the stupid daisy wallpaper.

"Can you even imagine it, you guys?" Mary Lou asked. "It's bad enough getting tampons in and out. I never want to give birth."

"They say it stretches this big," Katie held her hands several inches apart.

"Well it has to for the baby's head to come out," Denise said.

Mary Lou covered her nose and mouth. "Ewww. Just think how much that hurts."

"Well they give you drugs," Katie said.

Denise tossed the bottle down the embankment toward the creek. "We killed it, so let's head over to Katie's."

When we stood up, my stomach seemed to shift from side to side.

Mary Lou grabbed my sleeve. "I'm not sure I can walk. I think I'm drunk, you guys."

Katie locked arms with her and looked at me. "You girls are so little. It hits you harder."

I took Denise by the arm and started singing, *"Those Were the Days, My Friend."* The other girls joined in and we sang it all the way through the park. We seemed to get to Hogans' basement in no time and made way too much noise going down the stairs.

"Shhh," Mary Lou was giggling and falling back against me and Denise.

The only person in the room was a girl, sitting in Dennis Hogan's throne, reading a book. She looked up and shook her head smiling. "You ladies are toast."

"Hurray!" Katie said. "I was hoping you'd show up. You guys, this is Frannie Murphy. She lives next door and had to work. Otherwise she would've drank with us."

Frannie was tall, with long, straight brown hair, and dark eyes that gave away her mischievous side. I felt myself drawn to her right away.

"Hi," I said. "Where do you work?"

"Right on the corner at Rax Roast Beef," she answered.

"Have I seen you at Holy Rosary?"

"No. I go to Ottawa. But, I've gone to school with these characters since kindergarten. This is my first year away from them." She winked at Katie and Denise.

"I'm glad the boys are gone," Katie said. "I'll sneak upstairs and put a record on the stereo."

"Won't your mom see that you're drunk?" Mary Lou asked.

"She's probably in her room, and besides I'm not drunk. I told you before, us larger gals can hold our liquor." She stopped halfway up the stairs. "Any music requests?"

"Surprise us," Frannie said.

I began hopping up and down because it felt like my bladder was about to burst.

"Oh no," I said. "I really have to pee. Should I go outside?"

Frannie got out of her chair and walked around the room. "See if you can squeeze in here," she said, pointing to the washer and dryer. "There's a drain right between them."

I turned sideways and slid into the crack. "I fit, but I can't bend or get my pants down."

"Well, then here," Frannie said. "Just use this and then dump it down the drain." She set a small, glass ashtray on the floor.

"I doubt if that's big enough," I said. "But it's either that, or I wet my pants."

"Oh my God, Bloomfield." Mary Lou fell over from her sitting position on the rug as I slid my Wrangler jeans down and hovered over the ashtray.

"Sorry girls," I said, "but I can't wait."

The song *I Feel Free*, by Cream began playing from the speakers on the stage. Denise was laughing so hard she staggered and fell into Dennis's throne. I could hear Frannie laughing and gasping, and then even as I concentrated on the stream, I saw her fall to her knees out of the corner of my eye. Katie stopped on the stairs as she returned from putting the record on. "Tell me I'm not seeing what I think I'm seeing," she said.

Denise choked from the chair. "Oh, you're seeing it. You really are."

Frannie walked over to me on her knees. "Perfect aim. This girl can't be drunk. This is too impressive."

The ashtray turned out to be just big enough.

"Now what?" Katie asked as I zipped up.

The other girls all pointed and laughed at the same time. "Right there. Pour it down the drain."

The five of us continued laughing over one story after another. We especially lost it when Frannie acted out an entire scene as a clerk working in a shoe store. She stayed in character the whole time, while trying to fit us with "proper fitting shoes." When Vinnie appeared on the stairs to take us home, we could hardly get our coats on, we were laughing so hard.

"That Frannie's a total riot," I said to Mary Lou from Vinnie's back seat. Mary Lou hiccuped and snuggled up to Vinnie.

"How were the stag movies?"

"Same as last time," he answered. "It's the third time I've seen them."

As we made our way toward our neighborhood, I began to feel nauseous. I thought about having Vinnie pull over. When I closed my eyes, everything was swirling. How would I ever make it past my mom and Renee?

"Are you sure you're all right?" Vinnie asked as he pulled up in front of my house.

"I just need to get upstairs as fast as I can. Thanks for the ride, Vinnie. I'll see ya, Mary Lou."

She hiccuped again. "See ya."

I unlocked the side door and tried to walk quietly through the kitchen, stretching my jaw, and blinking several times, hoping to sober up. I could hear the TV on in the living room. I knew I couldn't just go upstairs without saying something to my mom. I poked my head through the doorway to say hi. Jerry Michael was sitting in front of the television. "Well, look who's home. My little cousin, R. A."

"Hi Jerry," I whispered. "Where's my mom and Renee?"

"They were bushed so I told them to go to bed. And besides, one of my favorite movies is on. *Sunset Boulevard*. Have you ever seen it?" He patted the couch. "Come watch. It's just getting to my favorite part."

I walked as carefully as I could and sat on the edge of the couch, holding onto the arm.

"Holy Mary, mother of God," Jerry Michael said. "You're snockered."

"I'm not snockered," I said, looking straight at him. Then my stomach lurched, and I put my hand over my mouth.

"Oh shit, are you gonna barf?"

I shook my head and then nodded quickly. Jerry Michael jumped to his feet, ran toward the kitchen, and came back with the waste basket just in time for me to lose the entire contents of my stomach. Afterwards, he put a cold washrag on my forehead. "You can't lie down yet. We'll stay down here until you sober up."

We watched the movie together, and by the time Norma Desmond told Mr. DeMille she was ready for her close-up, I was feeling much better. Jerry Michael looked at me after he shut the TV off. "Well, wherever you were, did you at least have fun, I hope?"

I burst out laughing while he was lighting a cigarette.

"Whatever is so funny?" He sat down again. "Do tell, please. Because I had a hellish week and could use a laugh."

"I peed in an ashtray tonight."

"Peed in an ashtray? What kind of an ashtray?"

I made a circle with my fingertips.

"Oh. My. God. I'd trade my Bette Davis autograph to see that!"

Chapter Twenty

I woke up to a terrible smell, a strange sound, and a headache. I'd been dreaming about dyeing Easter eggs with my mom's boyfriend, Larry. He was drawing pictures of the Beatles on them with an ink pen and Tom's new girlfriend was twirling her baton.

When I opened my bedroom door, the smell and sound were even worse.

"What the hell?" I said to nobody as I walked down the short hall to Renee's room. Jerry Michael was standing on a ladder holding a flat metal disc to the wall. He was wearing a flowered babushka on his head. I recognized the steaming machine because my mom had used one in our dining room when we first moved in.

"What is that smell?" I hollered over the hissing sound.

He stepped off the ladder and shut the machine off. "Well good morning to you, too, R.A. How are *you* feeling this lovely morning?"

"Like crap." I turned around to be sure nobody else was around. "Thanks again for last night."

"Don't mention it. Go eat something and take some aspirin. And don't worry, my lips are sealed."

"Thanks." I managed to smile, even though it made my headache worse. "But what is that smell?"

"Vinegar. It helps the wallpaper come off easier."

"Oh. Maybe that's why I was dreaming about Easter eggs."

I passed Renee on the stairs. She was also wearing a babushka. "Well, what do you know?" she said. "Her majesty has awakened."

I was relieved that my mom wasn't around when I got downstairs. I was nibbling on toast when somebody knocked on the back door. I thought about ignoring it, since I was in no shape to face anybody, but they continued knocking. When I opened the door, Cathy was standing there with a small plate and some scrapers.

"Hi. Your mom wanted to borrow these," she said. "And here's some anise cookies too." I must have looked confused, because she went on. "They're for the wallpaper. To scrape the wallpaper."

I really wanted to take the stuff and shut the door, but I knew that would be rude. "Oh yeah. Thanks, Cath. You wanna come in? I'm just getting something to eat."

She sat across from me at the dining room table while I sipped on Carnation Instant Breakfast.

"It's so keen that Renee's changing the wallpaper for the baby," she said.

I had never met anyone who actually said keen. I'd only heard it on TV. Poor Cathy. Always trying so hard. I did have to admit that she was looking more mature these days, but I sure didn't feel like listening to her gush over the baby.

I walked back into the kitchen to get one of the anise cookies. "Wow, Cath. Are you wearing jeans?"

"Yup. I got them at Mitchell's." She stood up. "Do you think they fit right?"

"Perfect. And they look good with that sweater."

"Oh, look," Cathy said as she walked toward the living room. "I can't remember the last time I saw Ruff and Reddy." She sat on the edge of the couch where the cats were curled up together, sleeping. Now I knew I'd never get rid of her. My mom came in the back door with groceries and Jerry Michael came downstairs for a cigarette. "Hey R.A., can we put your little record player in the hall upstairs? I brought some albums to play. Oh, I didn't know you had company."

"It's just Cathy from next door. She brought scrapers over and some anise cookies."

"Well, hello there, Just Cathy. I believe we've met at one time or another. Did you say anise cookies?"

Cathy followed me upstairs while I moved my record player into the hall. She noticed the rolls of new wallpaper that were in my mom's room on the bed. "Oh this wallpaper is so cute," she said. "It will be fine for a boy or a girl."

"I like the old stuff. I guess a teen-age boy had this room. We never changed it 'cause Renee's usually at college or summer stock."

Cathy glanced at the wall in Renee's room that still had wallpaper on it. "You like that?"

"Yeah, I've always thought it was cool. Ever since we moved in."

I picked up a piece of the old wall paper from the floor. It had a black background with martini glasses and olives sprinkled on it.

"Well, not for a baby," Cathy said.

Jerry Michael came up the stairs with a pile of albums.

"I work better with music," he said as he leaned the records against the wall.

The album on top was *Blonde on Blonde.* The album they'd played at Hogan's basement, and Michael had spoken about with such reverence.

"My friend Michael loves this album," I said, picking it up and looking at the back of the cover.

"Really?" Jerry Michael asked. "How old is he?'

"My age. A friend from school, but I met him last summer when I was in the hospital."

"Hmm, that's rather impressive. A kid your age that appreciates *Blonde on Blonde.* But wait. Did you say you were in the hospital? I don't remember Renee telling me that."

I looked at Cathy. "That's no surprise. Right, Cath?"

Cathy looked confused, and then Renee came out of the bathroom.

"If you girls aren't going to help, then clear out of the way. We have a big job ahead of us."

"I can help," Cathy said. "I brought more scrapers."

"That's really nice of you, Cathy," Renee said. "Especially since my own sister didn't even offer. But I think it'd be too crowded."

I felt like knocking Cathy and Renee's heads together. Jerry Michael turned around with an album in his hand.

"I think we could all fit," he said. "But only if Ruth Ann's headache is better."

"Headache?" Renee asked. "Oh, I should have guessed she has a headache because there's work to be done. How convenient."

"We better have some aspirin," I said and stomped down the hall.

After we'd finished scraping the wallpaper, my mom talked all of us into coming downstairs for one of her favorite Saturday lunches. Steamed artichokes with lemon butter, and Italian bread with giardiniera.

"Where's Ray Charles?" Jerry Michael asked. "Last time I was here we listened to Ray while we ate artichokes. And wasn't Trudy here? I was hoping to see Trudy again."

"You'll be seeing her later," my mom said as she got up and put a Ray Charles album on the stereo. Jerry Michael stood up and started singing *I Can't Stop Loving You,* grabbed my mom and tried twirling her around. She laughed and pushed him away. "You're crazy, Jerry Michael."

"Come on Aunt Marla. When was the last time you cut a rug at lunch?"

Cathy reached for another piece of bread. "Probably never." We all burst out laughing because it was the first thing she'd said since she'd offered to help.

After lunch, Renee and Jerry Michael were going to hang the wallpaper, so Cathy left. I really hadn't minded being around her once my headache went away. My mom left to run more errands, so I called Maureen and filled her in on the escapades at Hogan's basement. She and

Johnny had gone to a movie and tonight he was going over to her house. It felt like way more than a week since we'd hung out together.

Larry brought pizzas for dinner from Cathy's uncle's place. My mom set a big salad bowl on the table.

"Where's Bruce and Trudy?" I asked him. "I thought they were coming with you."

"Picking up beer. They'll be here soon.

"Jerry will be happy to hear that."

"He's a beer drinker?"

"I don't know about that. But he wants to see the crazy Trudy. Last time he was here he only got to see the advising Trudy."

Larry nodded as though that made perfect sense. Trudy burst through the door just as we all sat down. She was wearing a sparkly gold jumper over a black turtle-neck and fluffy pink slippers. She went around the table hugging and kissing each of us. When she got to me, she said, "Ruthie's eyes are still green. That's a sign, you know."

"A sign about what?" I asked.

She shook her finger. "We don't know yet."

After we ate, my mom got out her Drambuie, and before long, Trudy and Jerry Michael were dancing to my mom's old records. Renee went to bed because she was so tired from wallpapering and being pregnant. They would finish the last wall tomorrow. When Larry brought out a deck of cards, Jerry Michael and I decided to see if we could find a good movie on

TV. I flipped through the TV guide while Jerry Michael turned the dial, checking all three stations.

"Nothing in here sounds good," I said, tossing the booklet aside.

Jerry left the dial on Saturday Night at The Movies, which was *Becket*, and it had been on for almost an hour. "Hey, there's a great horror flick coming out in a couple weeks," he said. *Night of The Living Dead*. It was made on a shoestring, but I guess it's over the top cool."

"Thanks. I'll be sure to check on that."

A year ago, that would have been a Tandem Riders event. I'd hardly seen Angela, Peg or Irene since the beginning of school. I felt a little twinge in my heart. I wasn't even sure they knew Renee was pregnant.

"Now, if you don't mind," Jerry Michael said. "Tell me about the hospital. Did you have a cyst on your ovary? That seems to run in the family."

"I wish it had been on my insides. It was for my psoriasis."

"No kidding? It must have been a lot worse then."

"They covered me with tar every day. It was like a horror movie."

"You poor thing! How long were you in there?"

"Ten days. It was supposed to be longer, but..."

"But that's where you met the cool boy who likes Dylan?"

"Oh, yeah. But we're just friends."

"The big question. Is he cute?"

"I think so. He wears glasses, but he has a great smile."

"Oh! Just my type. Whatever are you waiting for, dearie?"

I laughed. "You know something, Jerry? I can't understand how you and Renee are so tight. You're *so* different."

"Yeah, I really noticed today the way you two clash. Being pregnant has to be hard, you know. Especially in her situation."

"It is worse now, but we've always clashed. Believe me."

"You just wait, little cousin. That bundle of joy will change everything."

I fell asleep listening to side one of *Blonde on Blonde* and dreaming about my old Tiny Tears doll wrapped up in artichoke leaves.

Mrs. Abraham's massive collection of Hummel statues stared at me from the shelves above Maureen's TV. Mary Lou had called the night before to tell us that she and Vinnie had decided to be "just friends," so we'd all have to find different rides to school. Maureen's dad worked close to our school, so the plan was for my mom to drop me at her house and then get a ride from him.

"Well," Maureen said, looking over her shoulder, "No more butts on the way to school."

"We should quit anyway," I said. "I heard they might go up to fifty cents a pack by the time we graduate."

She laughed. "You are such an old lady sometimes."

We clammed up quick, as Mr. Abraham came bustling into the den with his briefcase. He was even shorter than my dad, with dark, curly hair. The other Tandem Riders hadn't believed me when I'd told them I'd seen him wearing a real nightcap with a matching nightshirt when I slept over.

"Ready, girls?"

I rode in the back seat of the navy blue Dart that we'd taken to Grand Haven last summer. I found myself looking for prostitutes as we drove down Division Avenue. That's what everybody did when they rode down Division. Even though I knew it was ridiculous at seven-thirty in the morning. Maureen and her dad were quiet in the front seat, and the radio was on a news station. I thought about Jerry Michael's boy advice. Tom was probably moving, and even if he wasn't, the baton-twirler was in the picture. If only my stomach would stop doing that grabby thing every time I thought about him. Michael was smart, funny, and so different than the other boys. He actually read books on his own that weren't assigned to him. I made a decision as we pulled up to a red light near school. I would flirt with him and see where it got me.

"Thanks for the ride," I said, as I closed the car door. Mr. Abraham lifted his hand and drove away.

I was surprised when I rounded the corner toward my locker, and saw Michael leaning on it. It seemed that my plan was taking form all on its own.

"Hey, Ruth Ann," he said. "I was hopin' you'd show up soon."

"Oh, hi," I said. "What're you doing here?"

"Well, I'm kinda on a mission."

"Really? What sort?" My heart sped up as I turned the combination on my lock. Maybe getting over Tom was going to be easier than I thought.

"Well, I'll get right to it. What do you think of Andy?"

"Andy? Schmidt?"

"Yeah, Schmidt. My best bud neighbor."

"He's nice. He's a really funny guy."

"Well, truth is. He's got it bad for you. As soon as he met you."

My head was swirling. This was the last thing I expected. I wasn't sure what to say.

"He's probably gonna call you tonight, if that's okay."

My mouth dropped open, because I wanted to say wait a minute. What about you? I want *you* to have it bad for me.

"So, is it okay?" he asked.

"Um, yeah. I guess so."

"Great. I'll tell him. See ya in history."

He turned away and walked down the hall.

At lunch, Denise sat next to me. "I heard the news about you and Andy."

"What news?"

"Oh, no," Denise said. "Here comes Julie. She's so pissed about Michael, and to be honest, I'm sick of hearing about it."

I wondered if she meant Michael talking to me in Hogan's basement.

Julie slammed her tray down and opened a carton of chocolate milk before I could ask Denise for any more information.

"Hi. Want a mint?"

I turned toward the voice, and there was Andy Schmidt holding out a roll of bright pink candy.

He sat down on the empty seat next to me. "Wintergreen. Want one?"

"Oh, no thanks."

I tried to smile, but I felt like running away. It was definitely another weird Monday, and I still had to get shots in my legs after school.

"I heard you girls got hold of some Sloe Gin on Friday," Andy said.

Just my luck. Word was probably out about my ashtray antics. I searched his face and decided he didn't know. It was bad enough that four girls knew about it. He tossed his silky platinum hair aside. It was interesting how the sunlight from the window shimmered through the strands.

"That stuff is rotgut. Did you keep it down?"

"Um, well. Not really."

"Hey, Fitzpatrick," he yelled to Michael who was walking in with Claudia Engles, a quiet girl from my Spanish class. He gave him a salute, and Michael beamed back at him with his flashy smile. I got the feeling he was showing off to him that he was sitting by me. I felt like a pie or a jar of jam at the fair. Or maybe even a prize pig.

Andy slapped the table. "Now if that isn't tits, I don't know what is."

"What are you talking about?" I asked him.

"Fitzie and that Engles girl."

Julie shoved her tray and stood up. "Oh my God. That does it!" She grabbed her purse and headed toward the girls' room.

"What's up with her?" Andy asked.

"Just a broken heart," Denise said. "You knew she was crazy about Michael, didn't you? But I really like Claudia, so I'm keeping *my* fat ass clear outa this." She brushed her skirt off and tightened her pony tail.

Andy tossed his lunch sack into the trash can by the wall.

"You didn't even eat that," I said.

"I had some fries. I throw those damn sandwiches away every day."

"Why do you make them?"

"My ol' lady makes 'em. I don't want *her* to get a broken heart like Julie."

"That's right. You live in East Grand Rapids."

"What's that supposed to mean?"

"Just what it sounds like," I said. East Grand Rapids was where the rich people lived. I dropped an apple core into my bag and stood up.

Andy stood up too. "Okay if I call you tonight?"

He called that night around eight o'clock. He strummed his guitar while he talked, and once again, he was really funny. His sense of humor reminded me of my dad's. A little on the crude side. And his stories were peppered with great details. We talked for close to an hour. It was way different than talking to Tom. His parents had never allowed him to use the phone for very long, so all he ever did was plan our next meeting place.

No Doubt in my Mind

When I got to my locker the next morning, Andy was waiting for me. He had a large red ring around his mouth.

"I know. I know," he said. "I look ridiculous."

"What the heck?" I asked.

"I still suck a pacifier." He burst out laughing at his own joke. "Band practice. I play the trombone. You knew that, right?"

"No, actually."

"I guess you didn't recognize me in my uniform. When I played at the game."

"I didn't watch the marching band. But I'll look for you next time."

He met me at my locker every morning for the rest of the week. Always with swollen lips and the big red ring around his mouth. On Friday he banged his head against the locker when he saw me.

"What's the matter?" I asked. "Did you forget something?"

"No! It's just that you're...." He banged his head "So." Banged his head. "Fucking." Banged his head again. "Beautiful."

I was so embarrassed that I didn't know where to look or what to say, so I punched him in the arm. "You're crazy. Cut that shit out."

"I can't wait to see you tonight at the dance," he said, rubbing his arm and grinning.

I had mixed-up feelings when I was getting ready for the dance. I kind of wanted to see Andy, but also kind of didn't want to. It felt good to be liked, but he seemed to have come out of nowhere.

"Ruth Ann, your ride's here," Renee called from downstairs. "Are you wearing eye shadow?" she asked as I brushed past her.

I sat next to Andy on the edge of the stage. He cracked me up, making comments about kids on the dance floor We slow danced twice, and then returned to our perch on the stage. Michael and Claudia stopped and chatted with us, holding hands the whole time. Our gym teacher, Miss DeHoop, frowned at them, from her post at the door.

"Hey Fitzie," Andy said to Michael. "Let's go out for an Old Gold." He zipped up his jacket. "We'll be right back."

Claudia and I were talking about Sister Consuela, the tiny nun we had for Spanish, when *Light My Fire*, came on.

"You can't say no. This is our song."

I turned my head. It was Tom. He took my hands and I jumped down from the stage without giving a second thought to Andy or the baton twirler. The grabby stomach feeling was back as soon as I was in his arms. I remembered him saying this would be our song, "forever 'til the end of time," and at that moment I knew it would be.

Chapter Twenty-One

As if shopping with my mom and Renee wasn't embarrassing enough, we were at Miracle Mart of all places. Renee was looking for cheap maternity stuff, and I needed underwear, so they made me go with them.

"You better pick up some knee socks too," my mom said after she tossed a box of Kotex into the cart. "Those shots have ruined quite a few pairs."

"Here?" I asked. "Underwear is one thing, but I'm not buying socks here. People *see* my socks."

I was saving up to buy Villager socks, but I didn't dare tell my mom or Renee.

"You're lucky Mom is even willing to buy you new socks," Renee said. "What a spoiled brat."

I felt like telling her that she was lucky Mom was willing to keep her around with another whole mouth to feed. Instead, I sucked in my cheeks and went off to look at records. As soon as I was flipping through albums, I felt a tap on my shoulder. It was Tom's next-door neighbor. I hadn't seen Marty since school started.

"Hi, Ruth Ann," he said.

"Oh. Hi, Marty."

"You hear about Tom?" he asked.

My fingers froze on the albums, and I shook my head.

"They're moving today. To Grand Haven."

I felt my heart sink. So it had finally happened. And he hadn't said a word about it while we were dancing.

"Well, I knew they were going to," I said. "I just didn't know when."

"Yeah, he says he'll be back a lot, but I don't know. Seems really weird, 'cause I've lived next door to him my whole life. And how 'bout Peg. You hear about her?"

"No. What about Peg?"

"She's going to St. Mary Magdalene starting Monday."

"Wow. I didn't hear anything about that. I wonder how Irene feels."

"Yeah, those two are always together," Marty said. "I guess Peg's parents think kids from Holy Rosary are too wild."

St. Mary Magdalene was the all-girls school. I wondered what her parents had been hearing. I had seen Peg at games and dances, but she hadn't been going to Hogan's basement with us. Maybe it was a good thing Renee was pregnant. My mom hadn't been hovering over me nearly as much.

"I'm here to buy that new song about Bobby Kennedy," Marty said. "You hear it yet?"

"Oh, yeah. You mean *Abraham, Martin and John*?" I'd almost cried the first time I heard it. Marty was a sweet kid. I couldn't imagine most boys buying that record.

"Well, I better go, Marty. Take it easy."

I circled the entire store before I found my mom and Renee. They were writing down prices in the baby department.

"How 'bout we stop at Kewpies for lunch?" my mom said after we put our packages into the car.

"I'd rather have tacos," Renee said. "Let's go to Fiesta."

"I'm not hungry," I said. "Can you just drop me at home first?"

"Are you feeling okay?" my mom asked.

"She's too good for Fiesta, just like she's too good for Miracle Mart," Renee said. "She'd probably be fine if we were going to Sayfee's or the Kent Room at Herpolsheimer's. Just drop her off."

"Renee's right," my mom said. "You have been acting like a spoiled brat. Ever since you started hanging around those kids from other parishes."

"That's not true," I said. "All my new friends are really nice. Denise has ten kids in her family. How can she be spoiled?"

They pulled up in front of the house and didn't even say goodbye. I got out and slammed the car door. It felt good to have the house to myself. I put on my old Rolling Stones album, *Between the Buttons,* and cranked the volume up as loud as it'd go. Then I flopped on the bed and tried to picture Tom in Grand Haven. First at the candy store, Fortino's, that Maureen and I had gone to, then the hot dog stand, and then at the beach. I pictured him walking along the water's edge with the wind blowing his hair. At least he wouldn't be with the baton twirler now. But Grand Haven probably had plenty more just like her. This all made me think about Maureen, so I decided to call her and tell her the news. She said Terry O'Malley had already told her. His mom had heard it from Marty's mom.

She also knew about Peg switching schools.

We decided to call the other Tandem Riders to see if they wanted to hang out with us at Wilcox Park and Hogan's basement. Peg and Irene were going to a movie, but Angela and Mary Lou said yes. I was glad I'd be seeing Maureen because we hadn't hung out in a couple of weeks.

Angela's dad gave us a ride to Denise's house, and we walked to the park from there.

"A bunch of the boys are coming later," Denise said. "They scored a whole case of beer. Michael asked me to get a hold of his new girlfriend, Claudia, to see if she could come out, but there was a big fight going on at her house when I called. I guess her family life is not the greatest."

I stayed quiet. My family life was not the greatest either, and I wondered if people talked about it when I wasn't around.

"Isn't it hard for you to be friendly with Claudia?" Mary Lou asked Denise. "I mean 'cause of Julie. She seems so pissed about Michael liking her."

"To be honest," Denise said. "I'm better friends with Michael than Julie. I've always had lots of guy friends. They never like me any other way, but I get it."

I wondered if Denise wished the boys would like her the "other way." Without thinking, I threw my arms around Denise. "You are my favorite new person of the year, Denise LaCroix!"

"Well, the hell with boyfriends, then," Denise said. "Who needs 'em?"

"Hell, yes," Angela said. "Who needs 'em?"

The five of us locked arms and hollered, "Hip Hip Hooray! Who needs 'em?" all the way down Denise's street.

"Katie and Frannie are already here" Denise pointed as we ran down the hill into the bowl of Wilcox Park. The two girls were sitting against a tree trunk, smoking. We all sat in a cluster waiting for it to get dark so we could drink the Boones Farm Frannie's sister had bought for us.

"The boys are over at Eddie's drinking that beer," Katie said. "His parents are gone. I think Andy's with them, Ruth Ann."

"Are you going with Andy?" Angela asked me. "I thought I heard that."

I really didn't know what to answer, because I wasn't sure myself.

"Think it's dark enough yet?" Frannie pulled the wine bottle out of her jacket.

"Not here!" Katie said. "We should go more into the woods."

We scooted a little ways down the embankment that led to the creek, and Frannie opened the bottle.

"I sure like this better than Sloe Gin," I said.

"So what about Andy, Ruth Ann?" Katie asked. "You never answered Angela."

"That's 'cause it's hard for me to answer. He's really funny, that's for sure."

"Her very first love just moved to Grand Haven, you guys," Maureen said before she took a swig.

"Yeah, but didn't you break up ages ago?" Katie asked.

"Hey, you guys," Denise said, "we were just singing about the hell with boyfriends. What happened?"

"Yeah, no shit," Mary Lou said. "Let's forget about 'em. I'd rather hear about your sister's baby anyway, Ruth Ann. Do you hope it's a boy or girl?"

As much as we wanted to forget about boys, I was relieved when they came trooping up behind us, because I didn't feel like talking about the baby. The boys were loud and kind of drunk, though they complained about a case not being enough for the seven of them. We all joked around while we finished the wine and then people started splitting off here and there. Andy and I walked back to the grassy bowl and sat looking at the stars. Somebody had their radio on, and the song, *Abraham, Martin and John,* was playing. It made me think of seeing Marty earlier, and hearing about Tom being gone. When Andy tried to kiss me, I let him. It seemed like a good enough distraction from all my feelings. It was a pretty good kiss, even though he tasted like beer, and I liked the way the moon was shining on his silvery blond hair. But there were no sparks like I had with Tom. We kissed a few more times before walking over to Hogan's basement. While we were walking, he stopped and lifted his leg on a fire hydrant.

"Holy cow, that's something my dad would do. You remind me of him so much," I said, "that it's hard to believe."

"I hope that's a compliment."

I wasn't sure that it was, but I laughed anyway.

"Hang on a minute," I said. "I love this song."

I set the hallway phone down, went into my room, and turned up the dial on my radio.

"Okay, I'm back."

"What song is it?" Andy asked.

"*I Heard It Through the Grapevine.*"

"No kidding? That surprises me."

"Why?"

"I don't know. I guess 'cause everybody likes it. Seems like the only music anyone at Holy Rosary likes is Motown. You just don't seem like a Top 40 kind of girl."

I wondered what Andy saw in me that made him say that. I wanted so badly to be like everybody else. That's what I'd been working toward ever since I could remember.

"Yeah, but sometimes everybody likes something 'cause it's so good. It's a great song. You can't argue with that."

"Yeah, I guess not," he said. "Hey, are you sure you can't get over to Hogan's basement on Friday?"

"I don't see how. By the time we get done with my sister's birthday dinner, it'll be too late. But maybe I can on Saturday."

Andy called every night now. We were considered a couple by everyone. Especially Michael. Sometimes Michael's enthusiasm about me and Andy was kind of annoying. He just seemed too happy about the whole thing. The two of them were such good friends, they'd even named their penises together. Michael's was Trigger. Andy's was Bullet. One of his favorite things to say to me while making out, was, "Steady, Bullet." He still waited at my locker every morning with the red ring around his mouth. Because he made me laugh, and called me beautiful all the time, I wasn't sick of the attention yet. It was a good way to keep my mind off Tom, my psoriasis, and Renee's growing belly.

Renee's birthday dinner was at Bruce and Trudy's house. Trudy told me I could bring Maureen, so that helped to make up for missing out on Hogan's basement.

Maureen and I planted ourselves on the couch as soon as we got there. Trudy flounced out of her kitchen in a hot-pink flowered dress with fluffy, purple slippers, and set a bowl of potato chips on the coffee table. "You girls want dip-it with those?"

"Dip-it?" I asked.

"Isn't that for cleaning your coffee pot?" Maureen asked.

Trudy threw her hands up and returned with a cigarette hanging out of her mouth and a carton of French Onion dip. "You like my music?" She pointed to the record player in her dining room. "These are records from my country. Just for a minute. Then I'll change it to Frank Sinatra. But you girls probably like the Presley. I don't have his records."

When she left the room, we heard her telling everyone in the kitchen we didn't like her music.

"They don't like Elvis either, Trudy." That was Larry. Good ol'
Larry, who had taken me to *A Hard Days Night,* when there was nobody
else to take me.

"Wow," Maureen said, as she stopped with a chip halfway to her
mouth. "Look at that foot stool. Is it inflatable?"

I walked over to a clear foot stool with a bouquet of plastic red roses
inside and picked it up. "I don't think you blow it up, but it does feel like a
beach ball."

I set it down and then noticed a wrought-iron magazine rack on the
other side of the chair. I squatted down and rifled through it.

"Anything good?" Maureen asked.

"Nah, they're all ancient."

Then I noticed the last magazine because it was larger than
the *Family Circles* and *Redbooks*. It was a *LIFE Magazine* from 1966. I
pulled it out and bent it backwards to straighten the crease.

"What's that?" Maureen asked with a mouthful of chips.

"It's old, but look, it's all about LSD."

I sat on the edge of the couch and read out loud from the cover. "One
dose of LSD is enough to set off a mental riot of vivid colors and insights
or of terror and convulsions."

"Oh my God," Maureen said. "That sounds terrifying!"

I leafed through it to find the article.

"Well, doesn't it?" she asked.

"Doesn't it what?"

"Sound terrifying?"

"It sounds kind of intriguing, if you ask me," I said. "And this reminds me of a *Time Magazine* Renee had once. It's probably still in our attic."

"You scare me sometimes, Ruth Ann. You would never take it, would you?"

I shrugged. "Probably not, I'm just curious. What about pot, Maur? Would you at least try that?"

"Maybe pot. I don't know. But listen here. You better not turn into a hippie on me."

My mother called us into the dining room for dinner, so I put the magazine back in the rack.

The next day when Renee and my mom left to run errands, I poked around in the attic. I found an old doll blanket and a couple of Golden Books that I had when I was little. I sat down and read, *Susie's New Stove*, which had been one of my all-time favorites. Then I ventured into Renee's corner. I found her old cheer-leader uniform wrapped in tissue with moth balls, her story-book dolls that I'd never been allowed to touch, and a box of letters.

I figured the old *Time* magazines had been thrown out, but a pile under a box caught my eye. The box held some dishes that I hadn't seen in years. I set the box aside, and there were the *Time* magazines that Renee had subscribed to for a college class. The LSD one was still there, and I remembered the cover because I'd read it back in sixth grade. I moved over by the window and re-read the article. When I heard my mom's car pull into the driveway, I shoved the magazine back into the pile and replaced the dishes on top.

I thought about the article while I cleaned my room and did my my homework. I wondered if LSD was only in places like California or New York. I asked myself if I had the chance, would I try it?

"In the meantime, I'll just have to settle for Boone's Farm," I said out loud to myself in the mirror, as I applied blush to the apples of my cheeks. I'd just learned the technique from Denise.

"Do you ever hear about anybody at Holy Rosary smoking pot?" I asked Michael later when we were sitting on the floor in Hogan's basement. I figured he'd be more apt to know than anybody else.

He didn't answer me right away and I noticed his forehead was wrinkled above his glasses. "I....don't think so. Why?"

"No reason," I answered. "Just curious, I guess. I heard my cousin, Jerry Michael, talking about it when he was here."

When Andy's game of Setback was over, he came over to sit by me and Michael. I was feeling bored and restless, so when Andy took my hand and led me to the space behind the furnace, I was more than willing. An old army blanket was on the floor which I figured had been put there on purpose.

After a few minutes of making out, Andy inched his hand under the bottom of my sweater. "Is this okay?" he asked.

"It's fine," and when he held me closely, I could tell that "Bullet," wasn't at all "steady." I thought about being in the tent with Tom and thinking that his was upside down and remembered him laughing about it. I wondered if any girls in Grand Haven made him laugh like that.

There was something way different about being like this with Andy. Something sad and far away. It wasn't Andy's fault. He was so nice to me. Even nice enough to ask if it was okay to be under my sweater. I loved the way he looked at me between kisses. His lips looked smudged and his eyes seemed filled with thoughts. It made me want to kiss and hug him more, but that's all that I really wanted.

Denise and I were in her bedroom looking at her earring collection that was dangling from five different earring trees. They were organized by color, shape and size. I was spending the night and going with her in the morning to help her babysit all day.

"So," Denise said. "How are you and Andy doing? I saw you made your way to the other side tonight."

Looking in the mirror, I picked up a multi-colored teardrop earring and held it to my ear. "The other side?"

"Other side of Hogan's basement. That's what the boys call it."

"Oh, yeah. We did."

"That's it? Oh, yeah? You know he's crazy about you."

"Oh, he's really nice. And so damn funny."

"Nice and funny, huh? That doesn't really translate into the romance of the century."

I shrugged and smiled at Denise in the mirror.

"Is it your old boyfriend? Do you still have feelings for him?"

"Well, funny you ask, 'cause I actually was thinking about him tonight." I thought about Tom saying, "forever, 'til the end of time," and a shiver ran up my spine. "It may end up being a curse, though."

Chapter Twenty-Two

"Uh-oh," Denise said. "Somebody needs their diaper changed." She picked up the baby boy and sniffed his bottom. "Well, it's not you. It must be your sister."

I followed her to the changing table and watched her wipe away poop, then clean and powder baby Marcy, while she went on talking to me about something that had happened in algebra class on Thursday.

"Wow," I said. "You're really good at that."

"But you babysit a lot too, right?"

"I do. But mostly for the boys across the street. They're seven and nine."

"Never for babies?"

"Well, I did, but then I got fired. I think I told you about that when I was in the hospital."

"Oh yeah," Denise said. "All those boys came over and got you in trouble. I remember now."

"I started watching Orna Lee right after she was born. And I really missed her after her jerk dad got mad at me. Even though she screamed bloody murder her first couple months."

"Well, it won't be too long before you'll be changing your niece or nephew. You better practice."

I felt like somebody had dumped cold water on my head. I walked over to the window and straightened the Raggedy Ann and Andy curtains.

"I can hardly believe there's gonna be a baby at my house. It feels like this has all been a dream and I should wake up now."

"So I take it you're not too fond of babies."

"They're okay. But right in the house? All the time?"

"Don't worry. You'll get attached really fast. They grow on you. Wait and see."

The phone started ringing in the other room. "Can you finish this up?" Denise asked. "I'll get the phone."

She ran out of the room and I snapped the baby's corduroy pants at the crotch and down the legs only to find they were all wrong and I had to start over. Then the baby started to fuss, probably because I wasn't Denise, who I could hear talking on the kitchen phone to the parents. "Everything's fine. The twins love my friend, Ruth Ann."

I picked up a plastic kitten and squeezed it, so it would squeak. Marcy stopped fussing, and grinned after three squeaks, and when I did it faster, she started laughing. Denise came in with baby Matthew on her hip.

"You goofball, that's the dog's toy."

"Oh, well," I laughed. "It worked. I think maybe she does like me."

"Let's take them for a walk. They'll sleep better."

I turned back to the changing table, and the baby girl was holding her arms out for me. I felt a little tug on my heart and picked her up right away.

"How old did you say they are?" I asked Denise.

"Eight months."

"I think that's pretty close to Orna Lee's age."

Maybe Denise was right. I had gotten attached to Orna Lee and her brother, Ralph. But I shook off the feeling. What business did Renee have being a mother? I pitied her poor child.

We put the babies down for a nap after lunch and both collapsed on the couch.

"Holy cow," Denise said. "I almost forgot. You have to see this book they keep in the husband's underwear drawer."

She returned from upstairs holding a worn out looking paperback.

"Let me find something good," she said, flipping through the pages.

The Rosy Crucifixion, I read aloud from the cover. "I heard my cousin talk about that book. It's banned. No wonder he hides it in his underwear."

We read out loud about a guy with a giant boner that wouldn't go away and laughed until our sides ached. When the doorbell rang, Denise screamed and threw the book in the air. "Shit, who's that I wonder?" She crammed the book under the couch cushion. It was a neighbor checking to see how we were doing with the twins. I couldn't stop laughing so I went into the kitchen and dried the dishes.

When I got home, Cathy and her mom were sitting at our dining room table with Renee. Cathy practically jumped out of her seat when I came in. "Oh hi, Ruth Ann. We're planning the baby shower. Wanna help?"

"No thanks. I've had enough babies today."

She followed me to the kitchen. "That's right. Your mom said you were sitting for twins. But I didn't know they were babies. Was it fun?"

"It was better than I thought it would be. Especially with Denise."

I took a bowl out of the cupboard and helped myself to some of the beef stew my mom had made for dinner.

"Want some?" I asked Cathy.

"No thanks. But you should read the food list they're making for the shower. And the decorations will be darling."

After they left, the phone rang. When I picked it up, someone was singing, *California Dreaming*.

"Hi Jerry Michael," I said.

"RA, I'm so touched that you recognized my voice right away."

"Who else would be singing the Mamas and Papas when I answer the phone?"

"I guess you're right. How's life, little cousin? Did you take up with the intellectual?"

"No. I took up with his best friend."

"You did not!"

"Yeah, I was too late. The intellectual already liked somebody else. And anyway, he was dying for me to be with his best friend."

"You can't give up that easy."

"It's okay. I've decided it's better not to go for the boy everyone likes. It's less complicated."

"Well, my oh my. Aren't we mature? How's your sister holding up?"

"Bitchy as hell, but okay, I guess. She's still working at Wurzburg's and knitting baby stuff all the time. Are you coming for a visit again soon?"

"I might just do that. And don't forget to go see *Night of The Living Dead*. Remember, I told you about that?"

"Okay, I'll check today's paper. Thanks, Jerry Michael."

"Thanks for what?"

"I don't know. Just thanks."

"Well, if you're much obliged, then I'm much obliged. Hey, if Renee's not soaking her feet or anything, call her to the phone, okay?"

After I handed the phone to Renee, I scooped Reddy into my arms, and took him upstairs to my room. Marianne Faithful was singing *As Tears Go By*, on the radio, a song that usually made me feel sad. This time it didn't. I knew Jerry Michael had called for Renee, but I had the feeling that he really liked talking to me now, too. I thought about his last visit and got up to look in Renee's room at the wallpaper they'd hung. When I switched on the light, the daisies came to life. I had to admit, it was better for the baby's room. The martini glasses weren't right for *any* bedroom. I guess I'd been acting like a brat about that. Next thing I knew, Renee was right behind me.

"What are you snooping around for?"

"I'm not snooping. I was just looking at the wallpaper."

"You don't care about the wallpaper. You were about to sneak out of here with something."

"I was not, damn it! Talking to Jerry Michael made me think of it."

"Oh, I bet! And you know what, Ruth Ann? Don't waste his time when he calls me. He has a very busy schedule. He doesn't need to hear your drivel."

I felt like slapping Renee. It took everything I had to keep my hand at my side. I turned around, stamped down the hall, and slammed my bedroom door as hard as I could. Aretha Franklin was singing, *Think*, on the radio. I cranked the song up as loud as it would go.

Renee and I barely spoke for the next few weeks. I stayed out of her way and she stayed out of mine. She was wearing only maternity clothes now because she looked so pregnant. I didn't remember her looking that pregnant the first time. Even at the end. Maureen told me that happened with second pregnancies.

It was almost dark when I came home on the Monday before Thanksgiving. Renee was sitting alone at the dining room table when I walked in the house.

"Where've you been?" she asked. "And why are you walking like that?"

"I'm walking like this because I had sixteen shots right in my psoriasis patches."

I peeled my navy blue socks down to show her the puffed up welts and dried blood on my legs. "And not that it's any of your business, but I went to the library to do some research."

I'd actually only spent about twenty minutes in the school library, helping Michael's girlfriend, Claudia, shelve some books. Most of my time was spent after the doctor appointment, smoking cigarettes in the lady's lounge at Herpolsheimer's. It had become quite a hangout lately.

When I looked in the kitchen, I only saw Ruff, munching on Purina Cat Chow. "Where's Mom?"

"She went bowling with some people from work."

"Bowling? What the heck is that about?"

"She's entitled to have fun once in a while."

"Well, I know that. But she's never gone bowling before."

"There's more of these in the kitchen. Help yourself. It's my second package."

Since we couldn't go to the Fiesta Cafe every day, Renee had started eating frozen cocktail tacos. By the dozens. I'd never tried them before, but since I was hungry, I took six off the cookie sheet, and put them on a plate with some chopped lettuce. I sat across from her at the table.

"Aren't they good?" she asked me.

"They're all right, I guess."

"You wouldn't believe what happened on *Dark Shadows* today."

I knew she was dying to tell me. I popped another tiny taco into my mouth, chewed slowly, then finished my entire glass of milk. Then I looked straight into her beautiful blue eyes that everybody always raved about. "So? Are you gonna tell me or not? What happened on *Dark Shadows*?"

Chapter Twenty-Three

"If you want a ride to Maureen's, you better get up right now, young lady."

"Mo-ommm, shut the door. Your hair spray's choking me to death!"

The room was filled with clouds of Aqua Net. I buried my head under the pillow and my mom marched in and yanked it off. "Did you think I was joking?" she said sharply. "Get up right now or I'll leave without you."

"She was on the phone with that boyfriend until ten o'clock," Renee said from down the hall. "I heard her say he has a phone right in his room. Of course, he does since he's from East Grand Rapids."

I wanted to kick the door shut, but when I stood up, my legs were so stiff from the shots I could barely walk. I slathered them with lotion before I put on my knee socks, then pulled the giant rollers out of my hair. Thankfully, Renee had already left by the time I got downstairs. I threw a sandwich together, grabbed an apple to eat in the car, and gathered my books.

"Did you have a good time bowling last night?" I asked my mom as we drove to Maureen's house.

"It was all right. Why?"

"No reason. I just wondered. I didn't even know you liked bowling."

"Well, I happen to be pretty good. In fact, they asked me to join the league"

There it was. I'd be stuck alone with Renee every Monday night. Then I remembered the baby I'd also be stuck with. As hard as I tried, I couldn't picture my life two months from now.

I let myself into Maureen's back door, as I now did every morning. My mom had to drop me off early so she could get to work by eight o'clock. Teeney only yapped twice since he was used to me. I could hear Maureen and her parents walking around upstairs. I didn't feel like checking my homework, like I usually did, so I looked around the room and thought about the party Maureen had last year at this time. Tom and I had slow danced and then ended up on the couch in the living room. I'd had psoriasis for just a few weeks and only Maureen and Cathy knew. That was right after my dad had come for a visit and brought me medicine. The heartbreak stuff that never really helped.

I couldn't remember if my dad had come to visit me since then. I'd gone to Saginaw in the spring and summer to visit *him*. Then, like a kick in the gut, I thought about my birthday last January. He was supposed to come and take me out for dinner. It was his birthday too, and we were going to celebrate together. But he said it was snowing too hard in Saginaw, so he didn't come.

"What's up with you?" Maureen asked as she practically bounced into the den.

I was staring at the ceiling.

"Why so deep in thought?"

I straightened up. "Oh, I'm just thinking about stuff."

Maureen put her coat on and applied lip gloss. "Are you okay?" Then she yelled over her shoulder. "We'll be out in the car, Dad."

Before we had a chance to talk, Mr. Abraham got in the car and said good morning to me as he backed the car out of their driveway. Maureen switched on the radio. The disc jockey was talking about the chance of snow on Thanksgiving and then the song, *It Was A Very Good Year,* by Frank Sinatra came on. My dad loved that song. Here I was just thinking about him five minutes before. I tried to swallow the lump in my throat because the last thing I needed to do was cry in Maureen's back seat. I probably didn't even have a damn Kleenex. Listening to the words, I wondered if my dad thought he was in the "autumn of his years." Maybe. Forty-seven was pretty old.

After Mr. Abraham pulled away, Maureen looked at me. "Don't tell me you're okay, 'cause clearly, you're not. I know you too well."

I closed my eyes and took a deep breath. "I'm fine. Nothing that a few puffs won't take care of. Let's hit the girls room."

Andy plopped down on the stool next to me at lunch. The smell of his greasy French Fries almost made me sick. He tossed his sack lunch toward the garbage can as he did every day but missed.

"Why don't you just save your mom the trouble and tell her you never eat those sandwiches?"

"Nah. The ol' lady thinks her ring bologna and mayo make my hair shiny. I don't wanna break her heart."

He smiled with all his teeth after cramming his mouth full of fries. His nostrils flared because he was holding back laughing at his own joke. I pictured his mom standing at the counter cutting ring bologna and it made me want to break up with him. But it would be too much trouble.

Rain pelted the window during history class. I looked at the dark sky and wondered if it was raining in Saginaw. I pictured all the cars on my dad's car lot. He and his friends were most likely playing cards inside the little office. I could just see my grandma looking out the window and saying, "Jiminy Christmas," with her Yiddish accent. Wilma and Aunt Dorothy were probably typing away at their secretary jobs in double-knit suits, and my dad's houseboat, The Whole Megillah, was probably rocking back and forth in the Saginaw River.

"I asked you a question, Miss Bloomfield."

Sister Mary Margaret had a round red spot on each of her cheeks.

"Yes, Sister. Sorry, Sister."

"I asked you who it was that created Cuneiform?"

I almost said the Phoenicians but caught myself just in time.

"The Sumerians?"

"You don't sound very sure of yourself, Missy. That's sixth-grade history. You were most likely staring out the window in sixth grade too."

I was probably staring at Gerard Waterman, since I had a big crush on him the whole year.

"Yes, Sister."

It had stopped raining by the time school was over. I walked downtown with Denise and Irene. They were telling me about the silly games they had to play at their family reunions every summer.

"Do you still see Peg all the time?" I asked Irene.

"Not that much. She got right on the student council at Magdalene's and has meetings all the time. It's so weird because I've always gone to school with her. My whole life."

"It is weird," I agreed. "Gee, it never crossed my mind last year that the Tandem Riders would change."

We heard some thunder in the distance.

"Oh no," Denise said. "Here it comes again. Let's run into Herp's."

After a quick look in the Junior Miss Department, we headed to the ladies' lounge. I made a mental note about a blue cable-knit sweater I liked. I was getting tired of rotating the same five crew necks with my uniform skirt.

We were standing in front of the sinks when Michael's girlfriend, Claudia, came out of a stall. I could tell she'd been crying.

"I thought it was you guys," she said.

"What's the matter, honey?" Denise put her arm around Claudia's shoulder.

She rolled up her sleeve and showed us a large bruise on her upper arm. Then she untucked her blouse and showed us another one on her ribs.

"What happened?" Irene asked.

"It's been at least six months since the last time he did this," she sniffed. "I thought maybe it was over."

Irene handed her some Kleenex, and we led her into the lounge area and all sat down.

"Maybe you should talk to somebody," Denise said. "One of your relatives, maybe?"

"I feel like running away," she said. "I promised Michael I wouldn't, but I'm scared to go home."

Denise looked at her watch. "I hate to leave now, Claudia, but I'm babysitting at six tonight, so I need to run."

"And I'm supposed to meet my dad at his office in ten minutes," Irene said.

"It's okay, you guys," Claudia said. "Just go. And thanks for listening."

Denise gave her a big hug, and then the two cousins left together.

Claudia looked at me and smiled.

"Thanks again for helping me at the library yesterday."

"Oh, I had to kill time anyway before my regular Monday doctor appointment."

"What's your regular Monday doctor appointment?"

I rolled down my olive green knee socks and showed her my swollen bumps and psoriasis. For the next half hour, I babbled on and on about everything from Wilma's martinis to Renee's upcoming baby shower. Claudia had even prettier eyes than Renee. Not only were they a startling blue, they were kind. I poured my heart out and so did she. Her life made mine feel almost normal.

"Have you ever thought about moving to your dad's?" she asked me.

"He used to ask me all the time, but I think it would break my mom's heart. I'd feel way too guilty. And besides I have so many friends here."

"I don't know," she said. "I sure wish I had somewhere else to go."

She looked at her watch. "I better go. My next bus is in eight minutes. You leaving?"

I glanced over at the pay phone in the corner. "No, you go ahead. I think I'm gonna make a collect call."

I gave the operator the phone number for Dixie Used Motor Sales. After ten rings and no answer, she told me to try my call again later. I blinked hard to keep from crying. I missed my dad so much. I picked up the receiver and dialed 0 again. This time I asked the operator to call my dad's apartment. Still no answer. I hung up and walked back to the chair that I'd left my books on. A plump black lady wearing a rain hat was holding a Kleenex up to a little boy's nose and telling him to blow. She glanced over to me.

"You okay, honey?"

I nodded and tried to smile. "I'm okay. Thanks."

"You sure now? You don't look so good."

"It's really nice of you to ask. Thank you."

I smiled at the little boy, then walked out of the lounge and back to the Junior Miss department. I felt better after I looked at the sweater again.

A delivery truck pulled into our driveway as I unlocked the side door. I stood waiting while the guy took a large box out of the back and set it on our front porch.

Renee had just been dropped off from work. "Oh, good. It's here," Renee said, walking up the front walk. "Help me bring it in."

"What is it?"

"The baby crib. It's my shower gift from Aunt Maxine since she won't be coming, of course."

When Renee and my mom talked about diapers and teething rings all during dinner, I realized there just wasn't room in this house for the three of us *and* a baby. I waited until they were busy watching *The Doris Day Show*, and dialed my dad's number. Claudia was right. I did have another choice. I'd meet new friends there. And after all, the Tandem Riders were falling apart. I'd miss Maureen and Denise, but I'd be back for visits. Visits to my house? That felt weird. Maybe this was a mistake. Too late.

"Hey Sport, I was planning on calling *you*," my dad said.

"Oh. You were? How come?"

"Just to see what's shakin'. So what's shakin'?"

"Oh, not much. I was kind of wondering about Thanksgiving."

"Thanksgiving?"

"Yeah, are you going over to Grandma and Dorothy's or what?"

"They're coming with us to Wilma's sister's house."

That was a surprise, since I'd never seen Wilma anywhere near my aunt or grandma.

"Going next door to the Eye-talians again this year?"

"No, Mom's cooking and we're having company. I was kind of thinking..."

"Well, Sport, here's the news. The reason I was planning to call you. Me and Wilma bought a house yesterday. A beautiful ranch off Gratiot Avenue and we're putting a pool in, come spring. You and Mimi can swim at midnight if you want. Right in the backyard. You're gonna love it, Sport. Maybe I'll get you to stay more than a week."

"Well, maybe. In fact..."

"Now you're talkin'! I gotta run, though. Dorothy's waiting on me to look at her carburetor. You behavin'?"

"Yes, but hey, Dad..."

"Good girl. I'll call you soon. And listen here. You picture yourself diving off the real diving board right out the back door. Hear me, Sport? Think summer. Bye."

I could just picture Wilma floating in the pool on a raft, in a gold lamé swimsuit with a pitcher of martinis. More than a week of that, and I knew I'd be flipping her raft over.

I shuffled back to my room and flopped on the bed. Maybe I didn't have another choice like Claudia said. Maybe I never did. I tried to think back to the last time my dad mentioned me living with him. Was it before he and Wilma got married? Maybe he only said it when they were "living in sin" because there was no way it could have happened then. But part of me felt relieved.

The next morning in homeroom I was scrambling to finish a Spanish assignment I'd forgotten to do. The girl behind me tapped me on the shoulder.

"There's someone in the window trying to get your attention," she whispered.

I looked up and saw Tom and another boy crouching down and peering through the window of my basement homeroom. Tom was waving at me. I was so shocked, I could barely think straight, and my heart started thumping as I lifted a hand. I glanced quickly to the front of the room where Mr. Shannon was rifling through papers as if he'd lost something. When I looked back to the window, Tom was pointing toward the street. I shrugged. Did he expect me to walk out? I looked at the clock. The bell would ring in about seven minutes. He pointed to the street and they took off. My next class was in the west building, and maybe he knew that.

I gathered my things and walked up to the teacher's desk, figuring I could get out if my plea was period-related.

"Mr. Shannon, may I please visit the rest room before the bell rings? My next class is in the west building, and I need to take care of something."

It worked. Mr. Shannon blushed and gave permission. I walked out the side door toward the street and glanced around. The housekeeper at the rectory was shaking a rug, but other than her, nobody else was in sight. I walked across the street toward the west building.

"Hey. Over here."

When I turned around, I saw Tom and his friend leaning against the side of the gym building, smoking. Tom jerked his head back and motioned for me to come over. I crossed back and looked both ways to be sure nobody was watching me, and hoped people weren't looking out of the west building windows.

"What are you doing here?" I asked as I got closer.

"Well, hi to you too," he said. "This is Vic. Vic, Ruth Ann."

Vic was tall, and had thick dirty, blond hair that hung over the whole side of his face. He didn't answer when I said hi, just nodded.

"Hey, wanna take off with us?"

"You mean skip school? That must be what you did. How'd you get here?"

"Vic got his ol' man's car. Come on."

"I can't do that. You know how strict attendance is. I'd get grounded for life."

"Oh yeah, then you'd miss out on seein' Andy boy, right?"

"You should talk. Where's your baton twirler? Is she absent today?"

Tom laughed. "I didn't want to see her. You're the one I think about all the time. Get lost for a while, huh Vic?"

Vic disappeared behind the building. Tom pulled me toward him by the sleeves of my pea coat and kissed me like he had last summer in the tent. He tasted the same and smelled faintly of Brut. I could have just died when I felt it in my stupid embroidered Wednesday underpants. How could this happen right before Spanish class, right on school grounds, right across from Holy Rosary Cathedral? The bell rang and kids came pouring out of both buildings and filled the street.

"I've gotta go," I said.

He brushed my lips ever so softly with his. A tantalizing opposite of the last kiss.

"Don't forget me, Ruth Ann," he whispered and nibbled my ear at the same time.

"I really have to go," I said. "Seriously."

"I'll be back," he hollered as I scooted across the street.

I walked into Spanish class, and it felt like everybody was looking at me. Was that possible? Did somebody see us and already spill the beans? I slid into my seat next to Teddy Zukowski.

"Hey, you see LaBelle hangin' around here this morning?"

I couldn't believe my ears. First of all, Teddy and I hadn't been friendly since our argument last summer over Zeke, the singing black kid in the park. I'd been avoiding him ever since school started, even though we'd been assigned seats next to each other.

"Yeah, I saw him. So?"

By lunch time it seemed like the whole school knew Tom had shown up. Maureen cornered me in the hall, Mary Lou in the girls' room, and Andy brought it up at lunch.

"So I hear your ex was around earlier today," he said. He smacked his sack of bologna sandwiches on the table three times, then rolled it up so hard I expected mayonnaise to squeeze out. I searched his face to try and figure out what he knew and decided to take my level of nonchalance up even higher than I had been all morning.

I shrugged and nodded at the same time, then took a bite of my cream cheese and olive on rye.

"So, did you see him?"

"Yeah."

"Talk to him?"

"For a minute. I had to get to Spanish."

He popped three wintergreen candies into his mouth and studied my face so closely that I was pretty sure that somebody had seen us making out, and that somebody had told him.

Chapter Twenty-Four

"Hey," I said, as I placed the cranberry sauce on the table. "Aren't we having pumpkin pie?"

"Trudy said not to bother," Larry called from the kitchen. "She's bringing dessert. Do you think this is enough salad?"

I walked back into the kitchen and helped myself to a cucumber slice.

My mom spooned corn relish into a glass dish and glanced at the salad Larry made.

"It's enough. There's plenty of other stuff."

As much as I usually hated holidays, I was relieved it was Thanksgiving. I needed four days away from school, and questions about Tom. And since we were having company, my mom and Renee would be less likely to pick on me.

"These cats are going crazy around this turkey," Larry said. "I haven't even seen them awake since last summer."

"Make yourself useful, Ruth Ann," Renee said. "Put them in your room."

"What's that supposed to mean, Renee? I've been useful."

"Why don't you do that?" my mom asked. "We don't want Renee to trip on them."

I picked up both cats just as Trudy burst into the front door holding a large plate with wax paper.

"Hellooo! Look what I'm bringing here. *Apfelstrudel* just for all of you. And the baby."

She kissed both of Renee's cheeks after she said baby.

"Ah, Ruthie green eyes. You're still not taller. Stopped growing I guess. You know what that means?"

I shook my head as I took note of Trudy's silver hair bow that I was pretty sure had come off a present.

"It means you are a full-blooded woman now."

I felt myself blush because it made me think about how Tom's kiss had made me feel. Did the entire world know?

Once we were all seated, Larry made a toast about the wonderful people around the table.

Trudy bowed her head. "*Vater segne diese speice.*"

"Amen to that," I said.

"Father, bless this meal is what she said," Bruce added.

Then he and Trudy kissed, and she brushed off his shoulder and straightened the bow on her head.

"Prayers sure sound better in other languages," I said.

"What do you mean?" Larry asked.

"You know, like when Mass used to be in Latin. I just liked it better then, I guess."

"As if you ever paid attention, anyway," Renee said. "All you do at Mass is look for your friends."

"I don't know about the rest of you," Larry said. "But this is the juiciest turkey I've ever eaten. Marla, you've outdone yourself."

"And I can't wait to try your strudel, Trudy," I said.

Trudy's eyes filled with tears. "It's my mama's recipe from the old country."

Bruce handed his hanky to her, and she dabbed her eyes.

"A toast to our host," Trudy said, raising her glass of beer.

I could tell she'd been practicing that one by the grin on her face.

"We have important news to announce," Bruce said. "We are all finished with apartment life."

Trudy stood up and her bow fell on her plate. "We bought a house!"

"You too?" I asked without thinking.

"Fantastic!" Larry said. "Where is it?"

Trudy laughed heartily. "It's on Hall Street and it has a down-the hill-yard."

"The back yard is terraced," Bruce added. "We closed the deal yesterday and we should be in by Christmas."

I buttered another roll as everyone talked at once about storage space, bathroom colors and cracked linoleum.

When it had quieted down, Renee piped up. "What in the world were *you* talking about, Ruth Ann?"

I tried to play dumb, but it didn't work.

"Who else is buying a house? You said, you too?"

I cleared my throat, trying to stall. "Oh. Dad."

"He's buying a house?" my mom asked. "How do *you* know?"

"He told me when I talked to him the other night."

"I didn't know you talked to him. Why didn't you mention it?"

"I guess I forgot. We only talked for a minute.
"What did he want?" Renee asked.

"Oh, just Happy Thanksgiving. That kind of thing."

My mom and Renee were both staring at me like they thought I was lying.

"I can't believe you didn't tell us that he's buying a house," Renee said.

"Well, sorry. I guess I forgot."

Renee set the gravy down and looked around the table. "Hmm, I guess he's got money for some things."

Thankfully, Trudy's beer spilled, so the questions stopped. The last thing they needed to hear about was the nice ranch house with a pool.

I babysat all day on Friday for David and Steven because their mom had to work. It was a nice enough day that they rode bikes and played catch. Cathy sat on the steps with me while I watched them.

"Can I ask you a personal question?" she asked me as she scraped a stick back and forth on the sidewalk.

"You can ask. I can't promise I'll answer."

"Do you get your period every month?"

"Unfortunately. Why?"

"Well today is the first time I've gotten it again since that first time. Remember?"

"That happens to everybody the first year, Cath. But Jeez Louise, that seems like ages ago."

I thought back to when Cathy hollered over from Frankie's window to tell me, and I felt like I was getting old. Then I thought about Renee and my mom treating me like a ten year old all the time, and I started laughing.

"What's so funny?" Cathy asked.

"I was thinking about that book we looked at last summer. Remember *teen-itis*? I was just thinking that I have it. I feel too old sometimes and then too young other times."

"Yeah, me too."

"I hear the phone ringing inside. Keep your eyes on the boys a minute, okay?"

It was Denise asking if I could help her babysit the twins on Saturday. I called my mom right away to see if she could drive me to Denise's the next morning.

"Guess what?" I asked Cathy when I came back out. "I'm babysitting all day again tomorrow with Denise. For those twins."

"Wow, that'll be great for Christmas presents," Cathy said.

"Yeah, I guess. I was thinking about a sweater I saw at Herp's. With both jobs, I could probably get the matching skirt."

"Maybe we could get together and make gifts this year," Cathy suggested.

"Like potholders?"

"Not potholders. Maybe mittens. My Aunt Mary is teaching me to knit. I could teach you."

"Cathy, Christmas is in less than a month. That's okay. But thanks. I'm gonna call the boys in now. It's time for them to watch *The Buck Barry Show*."

"Okay, see you Sunday at the shower."

I nodded, not wanting to think about it.

My mom dropped me off at ten the next morning so the twins' parents could go "Santa Claus shopping," and out for lunch by themselves.

"I'm so glad you could sit with me," Denise said as she wiped Marcy's face with a wet washcloth.

"Well, thanks for asking me. Two day-long jobs in a row is just what I need."

I noticed a look on Denise's face that made me realize she called me instead of other friends because she knew I needed the money. But I knew Katy did too.

"You could've asked Katy. She probably needs jobs really bad. Her mom doesn't even work, does she?"

"I give Katy lots of jobs, and anyway she's probably getting hired at Rax with Frannie."

"Wow. I need a real job. Maybe in January when I turn fifteen."

We took the babies out of their high chairs and let them crawl around in the living room. I had to admit, I was glad to see them again.

I ran the stick over the toy xylophone. "They're already bigger since the last time."

"Hey, just so you know," Denise said. "Word has travelled that you were making out with your old boyfriend at school on Wednesday."

"Oh no, are you kidding?"

Denise shook her head. "I talked to Michael and I guess Andy's pretty pissed. Have you heard from him?"

"No, but that's 'cause they went to Detroit for Thanksgiving."

"They didn't end up going. His sister got the flu."

My heart sunk. Since I hadn't heard anything, I thought the whole thing had just gone away.

"Does Michael hate me?"

"He'll get over it, don't worry. I just thought I should warn you."

"Oh, yeah. I appreciate it, really. What exactly did Michael say?"

"Oh, I don't know. Just somethin' like he was disappointed. I don't know. Don't worry about it, okay?"

Disappointed. That made my heart sink even lower. The last thing I wanted to do was disappoint probably the coolest boy I knew. I was so embarrassed that I almost felt sick.

"Maybe I'll call Claudia," I said. "Do you know her number off the top of your head?"

"No. I guess we could look it up. Why do you want to call her?"

"Maybe she could say something to Michael. It was an accident, Denise."

She was on all fours sniffing Matthew's butt. "An accident?"

"Yeah, it just kind of happened 'cause he took me by surprise. Showing up like that."

A make-out accident? Holy Cow. Was I turning into Renee? What was the next step? A sex accident?

"As soon as you finish those dishes, "my mom said, "you can come over and help with the decorations."

"I'm sure Cathy took care of those a week ago."

"I told Francesca we'd help her, so get a move on. Our present is already over there, but you need to sign the card. It's up on my dresser."

My mom had bought the playpen and some diapers, but thankfully, hadn't asked me to chip in. I trudged up the stairs and headed toward my mom's room but glanced into Renee's room first. There it was completely assembled. The baby crib from Aunt Maxine. I could hear Renee on the downstairs phone, so I tiptoed in. The mint green baby blanket that Renee made was folded over the edge. It had tiny flecks of other colors in it that I hadn't noticed when she was knitting it. It reminded me of mint ice cream. I rested my hands on the blanket, was surprised at the softness, and felt a tiny twinge in my heart.

"Come on, Ruth Ann," my mom hollered up the stairs. "Hurry up."

I scooted back to her room, signed the card, and glanced in her mirror. No reason to change. The outfit I'd worn to church was good enough. I dreaded going to this silly shower anyway.

When we got next door, Cathy was practically galloping between the kitchen and dining room. She was wearing the brown Poorboy top and print skirt I'd helped her to pick out last year right after Thanksgiving. Another ancient memory. Why was I having so many lately? Is this what happened once you hit a certain age?

"That looks good," I said, pointing to a giant platter of meats, cheeses, and olives.

"It's antipasto," Cathy said.

I didn't bother to remind her that I'd had it at her house more than a few times.

"Italians don't really believe in baby showers," she said. "They're superstitious about it. So this is very exciting for me."

"Same with Jewish people," I said. "My grandma wouldn't come. I was hoping my dad would bring my Aunt Dorothy, but I guess there's a bad weather forecast over there, too. Renee's college friends from Mt. Pleasant had to cancel too."

Cathy straightened a yellow bow on a gift. "Oh, that's too bad. I know you wanted to see your dad."

I decided not to say that I never expected him anyway.

Trudy arrived next, carrying a rocking horse and more *apfelstrudel*. I thought she was going to cry when she saw all the food, decorations and gifts. Within minutes, Renee's friends from work, the Wurzburgers showed up, and a few ladies from the neighborhood followed them. After a feast of antipasto, lasagna, salad, and bread, Renee opened gifts and we played a few ridiculous games. They made Renee carry balloons between her knees and try to drop them into a laundry basket. She was a better sport about it than I would have expected. We were all handed a little diaper that was pinned and cute, and whoever had a piece of candy bar in it was the winner. It was Cathy, and her face turned bright red. She won a manicure set in a shiny, gold pouch.

Along with the *apfelstrudel,* there was cannoli, anise cookies, and of course Cathy had made a cherry chip cake. I was in the kitchen refilling the coffee creamer, when Bonnie, one of the Wurzburgers, came over to the refrigerator and stood right next to me. Bonnie was my least favorite Wurzburger. I always got the feeling that she didn't like me.

"So," she said. "I hear you're being a brat about the baby."

"What?"

"You heard me. You need to pull it together, young lady. Your poor sister has been through hell, losing her husband and being left pregnant on her own. Where's your patriotism? That baby's father died for our country."

Trudy walked into the kitchen with an empty platter and glanced at us.

Bonnie lowered her voice. "So stop acting spoiled and grow up."

My blood was truly boiling. I wanted it to spew out of my nostrils directly into Bonnie's fat face.

Trudy set the platter down and walked toward us before I could even speak.

"Ruthie, is there problem here?"

She looked at Bonnie with such piercing eyes that Bonnie stepped back and walked out of the room.

"Good thing you came in here, Trudy. I was about to kick her ass."

Trudy punched her right fist into her left palm. "*Genou!* What did she say?"

"I'll tell you later. It's okay now."

Mrs. Cicerelli walked in. "Is anybody getting the cream?"

Trudy squeezed my shoulder. "Cream is coming, Francesca. You made a wonderful baby party for my good friends and I thank you for that."

The wind whipped at our faces as Cathy and I carried the presents back to our house. It was hard for me to put up with her chatter because I was so angry. I'd always thought Bonnie was a bitch, but I was furious about the fact Renee must have said rotten things about me. How else would Bonnie think I was a brat?

"Shouldn't we take the stuff upstairs?" Cathy asked after I set a pile on the dining room table. "I heard your mom say the crib's all set up. Can I see it?"

"Sure, go ahead. I'll go back and get the last of it."

When I got outside, it was snowing. The sky was dark gray. Just the way I felt inside. I picked up the pile of gifts from Cicerelli's living room floor. My mom, Renee, and Trudy were all helping in the kitchen, and I could hear them talking about the Wurzburgers. I wondered if Trudy would mention anything about the Bonnie incident.

No Doubt in my Mind

I stayed in my room, doing homework, and listened for the phone. I hadn't talked to Andy since lunch on Wednesday. I was beginning to miss him. He could usually get me to laugh, no matter what. There was no doubt in my mind that he was mad at me. Especially since he'd been in town all weekend, and not called. I'd never called him before, but I decided it would probably be smart if I did this time. Otherwise, it would be really awkward at school. The last thing I needed were a bunch of questions about why he wasn't sitting with me at lunch.

I opened my bedroom door to drag the hall phone in. Renee had just reached the top step. She looked more tired than I ever remembered.

"Thanks for bringing the gifts over," she said.

"It's fine. And you better stop talking to Bonnie about me."

"What's that supposed to mean?"

"She told me I was a spoiled brat, and un-patriotic."

"Un-patriotic?"

"Because your *soldier* husband died for our country."

Renee opened her mouth, but for once she seemed at a loss for words. I closed my door on the cord and dialed Andy's number. His father answered, which made me feel funny. I hated the idea that girls shouldn't call boys, but that's how most parents still felt. Mr. Schmidt didn't sound like he cared one way or another. He just called Andy to the phone.

"Hello?"

"Hi. It's me, Ruth Ann."

"Oh. What do you know? I didn't expect to hear from *you*."

"Well, Denise said you didn't leave town 'cause your sister was sick. I just wondered how you're doing."

"Okay, I guess. I had the radio on earlier and it made me think of you."

I felt a sliver a hope. Maybe *And I Love Her* or something like that had come on.

"How come?"

"*I Heard It Through the Grapevine* was on."

"Oh, that's right. You were surprised I like it because everybody else does."

"Yeah, well maybe *I* never liked it 'cause I knew the whole damn thing was gonna come true."

"What whole damn thing?"

"Think about it."

I ran the lyrics through my head. Oh shit.

"I'm confused," I said for lack of another response.

"Just think about it, okay?"

"I guess we should talk." I said

"We'll see. I gotta get back to geometry right now."

I knew this was a bad sign. Andy had never chosen homework over talking to me before. I thought about calling Maureen, since I could usually count on her for moral support. If anyone understood my dilemma, along with my strangeness, it was her. I dialed her number over and over, but the line was busy.

Chapter Twenty-Five

"Wake up, Ruth Ann."

"I'm not a brat. I'm not a brat."

"Stop muttering," my mom said. "It's after seven."

I rolled over and threw the covers back, actually relieved it was morning, so I could wake up from my dream. Bonnie, the bitch, had been chasing me around the tables in the school cafeteria. I kept passing Andy and Tom who were watching us as they shared a platter of antipasto. They ignored me when I pleaded with them. "You guys, tell her I have to get the cream for Mrs. Cicerelli."

"Don't talk to her. She's just a brat," Bonnie said over and over.

I shuffled in and out of the bathroom, trying to shake off the dream, and finally began to get dressed. I pulled my camel colored crew neck over my head. The gold circle pin was still pinned on it from the last time I'd worn it. Renee was sitting on the couch petting Ruff when I came down the stairs. She was wearing her coat that she could no longer button, and she looked puffy and tired.

"Why are you still here?" I asked her.

"I'm waiting for Bonnie. She's picking me up for the next couple of weeks, so I don't have to take the bus."

My mom walked into the room. "And it's out of her way. She's such a good friend. There's still enough turkey for a sandwich, Ruth Ann. Get out there and make yourself one. We're leaving in fifteen minutes."

I clamped my mouth shut and walked straight to the kitchen, to look for the cinnamon Pop-Tart I'd hidden. Larry had brought them for me on Thanksgiving. While it was toasting, I threw together a turkey sandwich, since that's all we had for lunch. The phone rang while I was screwing the lid back on the mayonnaise jar. Renee had just left, and I knew my mom was upstairs attacking her hair-do with a last cloud of Aqua-Net, so I made my way to the phone.

"*Monday, Monday, so good to me; Monday morning, it was all I hoped it would be.*"

"Hi, Jerry Michael."

"R.A., you did it again. I feel so loved."

On a different day, I would have laughed.

"Well, is it?"

"Is it what?" I asked.

"All you hoped it would be?"

I couldn't even answer him because it felt like I'd swallowed a pencil.

"R.A.? Are you still there?"

I cleared my throat. "Yeah, I'm still here."

"Oh, good. For a minute, I thought you'd hung up on me. I need to ask Renee a theater question for a paper I'm writing. Is she gone already?"

I wanted so badly to tell him that she'd been been picked up by the she-devil of Wurzburg's. But my mom came downstairs with a furious look on her face.

"Get off the phone right now. We have to leave!"

"It's Jerry Michael, Mom. He wanted to ask Renee something."

"Give me the phone and get your coat on."

I was hoping I'd have a chance to talk to Maureen about Andy. She always had good sense about these things. When I walked in her back door, she called me into the kitchen where she was peeling an orange.

"Oh good," I said. "I was hoping you'd be downstairs so we could talk a minute."

"Yeah," she said, "can you believe I got up on time for once, and it's a Monday."

She popped an orange segment into her mouth. "What's goin' on?"

"I'm not sure where to begin. But you know..."

The tea kettle began whistling and Mrs. Abraham came rushing into the kitchen in a hot pink robe with Teeney trotting beside her. "Well, good morning, Miss Ruth Ann," she said in her high pitched voice. My mom always said she sounded like the actress, Gracie Allen.

"How do you like this snow already?"

She opened a jar of Sanka and started talking to Maureen about all her plans for the day. Before I could say another word, Mr. Abraham was herding us to the car. I sat in the back seat and stared out the window, wishing I was back home with the covers over my head. Or maybe on the couch watching *Captain Kangaroo* with Ruff and Reddy. As soon as we got out of the car, three girls Maureen was friendly with came up and started talking to her.

No Doubt in my Mind

Maureen turned to me as I walked on, "Call me tonight, okay?"

I lifted a hand and tried to smile as I nodded. This day was already off to a bad start. When I got to my locker, there was no sign of Andy. It was the first time since Michael had told me he liked me back in September. *Monday, Monday, can't trust that day.*

Everybody groaned when our ancient English teacher, Sister Mary Ursula told us to take out *Great Expectations* once again, and to turn to page forty-one. Then she dropped the needle on the record for us to listen and follow along. Within five minutes, she was sound asleep, and Gerard Waterman opened the window next to him and lit a cigarette. Then the whole row of boys sitting behind him did the same thing. They all rested their elbows on the sill and hung the cigarettes out the windows. I wondered how it looked from the street below, and I smiled for the first time in days.

The doom and gloom feeling came back as soon as I headed to gym class. I hated almost everything about it, but the worst part was the blue cotton suits we had to wear which exposed my legs to everyone. Even after all these months, I still caught people staring.

Claudia was snapping up the front of her suit near my locker. "I sure hope we don't have volleyball again."

"Really? I hate it too. I thought I was the only one. They never make the boys play it. They always get basketball."

"I can't say I have cramps again," she said. "I used that excuse last week."

"I'll tell you what," I said. "If it's volleyball, let's beat it back down here when DeHoop isn't looking."

"Okay, just so nobody sees us. We could hide back there behind the showers."

We stomped up the stairs with the rest of the girls and took our assigned places for the warm-up routine. We could hear the boys through the wall, playing basketball. First Miss DeHoop took roll-call. As always, her hair was coiled up on top of her head like a small cake, encircled by a grosgrain ribbon. Today's ribbon was burnt orange. After roll-call we begged her to let Louise Shumway sing *People,* which we did at least once a week to waste time. Louise was Miss DeHoop's pet and occasionally she did let her sing.

"Not this morning, girls. We need to get through our routine, because we have volleyball again today."

Claudia and I exchanged glances as the music started. It was the same song every day that she used year after year, we'd been told. The theme to *Peter Gun.* We had to bend, stretch, roll, and kick to each beat of the music as Miss DeHoop watched and clapped along. When the song ended, she blew her whistle for the forty-five of us to group together. I inched backwards to the side door, and Claudia did the same. As soon as Miss DeHoop turned around to get the volleyballs, we hightailed it down the stairs to the locker room.

It was noisy enough above us that I didn't worry about anyone hearing us when I opened my locker to grab the Salems I'd snitched from my mom's pack. We hid behind the showers and sat on the floor, leaning against the wall.

"So," Claudia said, "how's life been treating *you*?"

"Like shit, as a matter of fact. But thanks for asking."

We both laughed.

"How was holiday time at your house?" I asked her.

"You really wanna know?"

Claudia put her cigarette between her teeth and unsnapped her gym suit. She slipped out of the sleeves and turned her back to me. There were two large bruises on her back.

"Oh, God. Your dad?"

She nodded and put her arms back in the sleeves. I put my hand on her shoulder. I was about to tell her how sorry I was, when we heard voices. We stubbed our cigarettes out on the floor and waved our hands around to try and get rid of the smoke. Somebody opened a locker.

"Julie told me," one of the voices said.

Claudia and I both shrugged. We couldn't identify who it was.

"It was pretty slutty of her if you ask me."

That was Louise Shumway. I'd know her voice anywhere.

"She doesn't deserve Andy Schmidt. That's for sure."

Oh Monday morning, you gave me no warning of what was to be.

"Thanks for the Tampax. I'll be right up."

We heard Louise go into the bathroom, and the sneakers of the unknown person going up the stairs. I put my face down and wrapped my arms around my knees. Claudia stroked my hair.

"They're bitches, Ruth Ann. You're one of the nicest girls I know. They don't even know you. Please don't let them get to you."

But whenever Monday comes, you can find me crying all of the time.

I lifted my head and could see true sympathy and understanding in Claudia's blue eyes.

"You're so nice to say that. But it's just one more damn thing. And I feel like hell complaining to you. None of it's as bad as what you have going on."

Claudia tucked a lock of hair behind my ear. "Hey, I get there's no bed of roses at your house, either."

There was no sign of Andy at lunch. I tried not to look around and was relieved when Denise sat next to me.

"Gee whiz," she said. "I think half the school's out with that cold. And guess what? The twins came down with it, so we're probably doomed."

"Oh, I guess I didn't notice," I said. "Who's all absent?"

"Tons of people," Julie said as she sat down across from us and opened her lunch bag. I could barely chew my sandwich. I was trying my best to look as normal as possible, even though I couldn't stop thinking about Louise Shumway referring to me as a slut. Nobody had asked about Andy. They probably assumed he was home with the cold. For all I knew, maybe he was. I could see Claudia and Michael at the next table. They seemed to be having a serious discussion. I wondered what they were talking about.

"So, are you?" Denise asked.

"Sorry," I said. "What'd you ask me?"

"Your outfit. That skirt and sweater. Are you buying those today?"

"Oh, yeah. My outfit. I think so. Maybe I'll just put it on lay-a-way, though. I might not get any more jobs before Christmas."

Denise opened her milk carton. "As a matter of fact, the Petersons want us both to babysit this Saturday for the twins and their friends' two toddlers. So they definitely need both of us."

"Okay, sure." I rolled my sandwich up in the wax paper and shoved it back in the bag.

"Hey, are you okay?" she asked. "Where's Andy, anyway? Is he sick?"

I shrugged and looked across the table to make sure Julie wasn't listening. She was busy explaining her eye make-up techniques to Katie and another girl.

"I don't know," I said. "I called him last night and he barely spoke to me. But, maybe he's absent. I just figured he was avoiding me."

Denise started to respond, but Katie interrupted. "Did anybody get that algebra homework? My brother had to help me."

"That reminds me," Julie said, looking at me. "Just so you know, Ruth Ann, I got my seat moved in algebra 'cause I can't stand watching you dig away at your scalp all the time. It's so gross and last week you made it bleed."

"Julie!" Denise snapped. "Shut the hell up. What are you thinking?" It felt like the two bites of turkey sandwich were going to hurl out of my stomach. I stood up. "Thanks, Denise," I said. "But never mind."

I walked out of the cafeteria, out of the west building, and crossed the street to get to my locker. There was no way I could face algebra, Julie, or anybody or anything. I put my algebra book back on the top shelf of my locker. I needed to hide out somewhere. I slammed the door and locked it. I had every right to leave for the day. My stomach was upset, and I was probably going to get a cold. Denise even said so. But I'd need my books for homework, so I unlocked the locker again, and took down the books. My head started to itch so badly, I felt like throwing the books against the wall. Damn that Julie. *She* deserved a bloody scalp. Her and her stupid hair-do and blue eye shadow. I threw the books back into the locker and left the building as fast as I could. I was halfway down the block when I heard someone call my name. Damn it all! I didn't think anybody had seen me.

"Ruth Ann, wait up."

I turned around and saw Claudia running toward me, breathing hard. "Denise just told me what that mean-ass Julie said to you. I can't believe what a rotten day you're having."

"Yeah, no shit," I said. "What next?"

"Where're you going?"

"I don't really know. Away from here. That's all I care about."

Claudia walked alongside of me. "Are you skipping class?"

"I can't stay here, Claudia. In the last twenty-four hours, I've been called a brat, a slut, and told that I'm gross. Can you blame me?"

"No, I really can't. But I'm coming with you, okay? Michael doesn't understand how hard it is at my house. I always just tell him my parents are strict, but I think Denise told him some other stuff. Just 'cause she cares, you know. But I'm really embarrassed. A guy like him should have a girlfriend from a normal family. So, it's really complicated now. He was asking me a million questions at lunch."

I couldn't think straight. Part of me wanted to be alone, so I could sort things out. I liked Claudia a lot, but those bruises on her back scared me. Plus, I didn't even know where I was going.

"I have thirty-five dollars," Claudia said. "Maybe we should run away."

It was such a good idea I wasn't sure why I hadn't thought of it myself. "Any idea where?" I asked.

"How 'bout Ann Arbor? My sister goes to U of M. She has an apartment there."

"Wouldn't she tell your parents?"

"She hates my dad. She'd be furious if she saw my bruises."

"I have all my babysitting money. Forty-two bucks and some change," I said. "We could take the Greyhound Bus."

"Do you know how?"

"Yeah, I take it to my dad's all the time. We just have to get ourselves to the station."

"Are you thinking of going to your dad's?"

"Kind of, but he hasn't even been to see me in over a year. I think he's forgotten I exist."

We reached the corner of Fulton and Division.

"I guess we should just walk to the station," I said. "Because I don't know which bus would take us there. It's at least a mile. What do you think?"

"Okay," Claudia said. "Let's walk there. As long as you know the way."

The snow had turned to slush and was slippery in spots. The sun had come out, and it was irritating to me, because it didn't match my mood.

"Aren't you worried about what your dad will do to you?" I asked.

"I am, but I also feel like he deserves this."

"He wouldn't take it out on your mom or the other kids, would he?"

"Depends on whether or not he gets drunk."

I felt like my mind and heart were filled way beyond capacity. Claudia's problems on top of mine were more than I could handle.

We walked into the Greyhound Station at 1:25. The bus for Ann Arbor was leaving at 1:45. That convinced me we were making the right choice. The next bus to Saginaw wasn't leaving for three more hours. Once we sat down in the smoky waiting-room, I realized my socks were wet inside my shoes. Looking down at my knee socks, I remembered it was Monday.

"Oh hell," I said. "I'll miss my appointment for shots today. Oh well. My scalp's already driving me nuts. I don't need more aggravation."

Before long we were seated on the soft blue seats of the bus headed to Ann Arbor in our Holy Rosary uniform skirts. I felt a mixture of fear and relief. I wanted Grand Rapids to be far behind me. Along with Bonnie, Andy, Tom, Julie, Louise Shumway, and especially Renee and her maternity tops, baby booties, fake wedding ring, and pregnant belly.

Chapter Twenty-Six

"I was here last August," I said to Claudia as we walked into the
Lansing bus station for a short lay-over. "Maureen and I were on our way
to stay at my dad's for a week. We had so much time to kill, we went to
the big department store down the street."

"Maureen Abraham?" Claudia asked. "You guys are pretty good
friends, right?"

"Oh, yeah. She's my best friend."

"Well, I guess she must be if she went with you to your dad's."

"We've done everything together this past year."

My heart felt heavy thinking about Maureen. Then I remembered I
was supposed to call her tonight. Now she'd think I forgot. Or maybe
she'd try calling me, and my mom would tell her that I never came home
from school. My heart got even heavier when I thought about my mom. I
pictured her pacing the floor, smoking Salems, while Renee wolfed down
boxes of tiny cocktail tacos.

We bought sacks of potato chips and used the rest room before
boarding the bus again. I kept thinking back to last summer and felt so
much older than I was in Saginaw. It never would have occurred to me
then that I'd be running away five months later.

"Are you sure your sister will be cool about this?" I asked.

"I told you, my sister hates my dad."

"Does she live alone?"

"No. Two other girls live there. One is her friend, Janice, from Holy Rosary, and she drives me nuts. But the other one is nice."

"Do you think there'll be enough room for us?"

"Oh, sure. It's a big place."

It was dark and windy when we got to Ann Arbor. When we got off the bus, we saw a guy with braids sitting on a bench playing a guitar and singing *Blowin' in the Wind.*

"Let's find the phone booth," Claudia said, as we walked past him, and entered the station, which was full of college students. Some of them were sitting on the floor, and a guy with a beard was playing bongos.

I looked around. "This sure is different than Grand Rapids."

"No kidding."

She stepped into the phone booth and dialed her sister's number. After letting it ring for a long time, she hung up. "I guess they're all out. Let's just sit here and try calling again in a while."

We sat on a bench and watched the commotion around us.

"Damn it all," I said. "We stick out like sore thumbs in these stupid uniform skirts. We might as well draw an arrow to ourselves that says runaways."

"You're right," Claudia said. "Maybe Patty can loan us some jeans. You're so short, though. But we'll see."

Claudia tried the number again, but still nobody answered. I was feeling tired and hungry, and starting to wonder if this whole idea had been a big mistake.

"I'm starving," I said. "Maybe we should check outside for someplace to eat."

"Okay. Let's go out and look around."

We stepped out and spotted a small cafe down the street. I was so hungry that I felt like kissing the checkered tablecloth when we sat down. We ordered cheeseburgers and Vernors Ginger Ale, and an order of french fries to share. While we waited for our food, Claudia tried her sister again on the cafe's pay phone.

"Well, I talked to Janice, unfortunately," she said when she returned to the table. "My sister's not there, but I guess the apartment's not far from here. So, I got directions and we'll just walk there."

After our food was gone, we stuck around watching people and drinking ice water. The waitress was giving us the eye, so we finally got up, and walked five blocks to her sister's place. Everywhere on the streets, there were college students who looked like pictures from Life Magazine. The only kids I'd seen like these were the guys from the beep-line last summer. A bunch of them were gathered on a corner, handing out papers.

Stop the War.
Come to the Quad at 4 P. M. on Saturday.
Draft Cards Will Burn!

We climbed up the back steps to her sister's second story apartment and knocked. A girl with curlers in her hair answered the door in a yellow quilted robe.

"Hi. You must be Patty's sister. I'm Helene. Janice said you were on your way. She's in her room writing a paper, so we have to be quiet. Patty's not back yet, but come on in. She didn't even tell us you were coming. Want some coffee? Here, sit down."

We sat down at the kitchen table while Helene smoked and continued chatting. I was relieved when the phone rang in the other room, and she excused herself.

"This place is kind of cute," Claudia said, looking around and fingering the orange striped curtains. "Don't you think? I wonder where we'll sleep. That must be a living room in there where she's talking on the phone."

"So, you've never been here before?"

Claudia shook her head. "No, Patty lived in the dorm last year, and I brought her back there once with my mom. But, I've never been to this place. Thankfully, Janice hasn't shown her face," she whispered.

"This kind of reminds me of being at my sister's apartment at Central," I said.

"Did she ever graduate?"

"No, almost. Who knows if she'll ever go back now?"

I looked up at the clock on the wall. We'd been waiting for close to an hour. Helene was still talking on the phone. Claudia got up and helped herself to a glass of water. "Want a drink?" She lifted a catalog from a pile on the counter. "Here's a roster of all the students. Holy cow. There must be a jillion."

"Let me see that," I said. "My cousin might be in there."

I flipped through until I came to the Ds. Sure enough, there was Jerry Michael.

"He is in here. Maybe I'll write his number down."

I took a pen out of my purse and found a receipt to write the number on.

"How well do you know him?"

"Really well. In fact, I talked to him this morning. He stays at our house pretty often."

We heard footsteps on the back stairs, and then a key in the door. A pretty girl who looked a lot like Claudia stepped inside with an armful of books. She was wearing a suede, fringed jacket. "Oh my God! Claudia? What the hell are you doing here?" Then she looked at me. "What's going on? Is Mom okay?"

Claudia stood up and walked toward her sister. "Calm down, Patty. Mom's fine."

"But what are you doing here?"

"This is my friend, Ruth Ann. We've both been kind of miserable for one reason or another. Actually, a few reasons, and we decided..."

"To run away?" Patty asked.

"Um, yeah, I guess."

Patty set her books on the counter and folded her arms across her chest.

"Tell me what's going on." She looked at me. "And sorry, nice to meet you, Ruth Ann."

"Same here," was all I could manage. I felt like running down the back steps and looking for the students who were protesting the war.

"First of all, how did you get here?"

"Bus," Claudia said.

"Is it Dad?" Patty asked.

Claudia looked at me. "Should I show her?"

I only shrugged because I felt so uncomfortable. I picked up my pen and started doodling while Claudia showed her bruises to Patty.

"That sonofabitch," Patty said. "When did he do this?"

"After you left on Saturday. He got really drunk, and then didn't come home until Sunday night."

"Did he hurt anybody else?"

"No, just me, as usual. He thinks I'm wild, and I hardly even leave the house."

"He'll kill me if I let you stay here, Claudia," Patty said. "You know that, right?"

Then she turned to me. "What are *you* running away from?"

"A bunch of stuff," I said. And then it all came tumbling out. "My older sister's pregnant, so things at my house are really awful. And I have some weird boyfriend stuff going on. But nothing as bad as Claudia."

"Oh, yes you do," Claudia said. "On top of everything else, your parents are divorced, and Patty, the poor girl has a terrible case of psoriasis. She gets around a hundred shots every week."

"Oh, it's way better," I said. "You should have..."

A studious looking girl in glasses practically stomped into the kitchen. "Excuse me, but could you all take this discussion up elsewhere? I can't concentrate, and I have work to do."

"We're sorry, Janice," Patty said. "We have a small problem here, and my sister and her friend will be spending the night. But I promise, we'll all be quiet."

"Spending the night? You'd actually consider harboring runaways, Patty?"

"It's not like that, Janice," Claudia said. "Don't worry, okay?"

"I don't even want to know. In the meantime, just keep it down."

She went back to her room and shut the door.

"Just for tonight, you guys," Patty said, as she hung her coat on a hook by the door. "Hear me? I'm calling Mom as soon as Dad leaves for work in the morning. I'd call this minute, but I don't know what he'd do. Then you're on the 11:15 bus back to GR. I mean it. I could get kicked out of school for this."

Claudia looked at me apologetically. "Okay."

"And you," Patty said looking at me, "you call your mother and at least tell her that you're okay. Otherwise, you'll have to go to the runaway shelter."

Chapter Twenty-Seven

I lay in the dark, trying to get comfortable on the cushions that Claudia's sister had given me to sleep on. Claudia was sound asleep on the couch. None of this was turning out right. Part of me wished with all my heart that I was back at home with Reddy snuggling under the covers of my bed, but I shuddered when I thought of all the stuff I'd been through the past week. I'd already felt like a reject in my family, and now I felt like one at school too. How could I go home and act like everything was okay?

My mom had been furious on the phone when I called to say I was all right. Especially when I didn't tell her where I was. There was no way I could go home to that anger. It seemed like the only answer was to live in Saginaw with my dad and Wilma. Even though it felt like my dad had lost interest in me lately.

I thought about how everybody used to think I was funny and smart. I'd tried hard to be, since I knew I'd never be beautiful like Renee. But once I started "developing," as my mom and Renee always called it, it felt like I irritated everybody all the time. I was in the way.

My eyes flew open when I realized that if I was out of the house, Renee could move into my room, and the daisy wallpaper room could be just for the baby. It was a clear decision. They needed me out of there, and I knew just what to do.

I threw back the blanket and felt around for my skirt and sweater. I remembered my purse was on the desk behind the couch. As quietly as possible, I unlocked the door and tiptoed down the back stairs. I walked to the corner, and stood looking both ways, trying to figure out which direction might have a phone booth. I went the opposite way of where we'd come from, because I didn't remember seeing one.

A few people were on this street, even though it was after one in the morning. A couple stood on a corner, making out passionately, and a distinguished looking man passed me, holding the leash that was attached to a dog with very short legs. After walking close to three blocks, I saw a phone booth in front of a gas station. I looked around carefully before crossing the street, to be sure nobody saw me. I was pretty sure I would never pass for a college student.

I dialed Jerry Michael's number and it rang about eight times before a sleepy sounding voice answered hello.

"Hi. Jerry Michael?"

"Nope. This is Barry. Hang on."

I heard a muffled conversation, and then Jerry Michael was on the phone.

"Hello?"

"Hi, this is Ruth Ann. You know, your cousin. I'm really sorry to wake you up, but I'm in Ann Arbor."

"Ruth Ann? You're in Ann Arbor? For what? A college tour? You're not stewed again, are you?"

"No, I'm not stewed, and I'm not on a college tour. I'm only a freshman. I'm here 'cause I sort of ran away. And I sort of wondered if you'd come and get me."

"Holy Mary, Mother of God. Please tell me this is a prank call, R. A."

"Sorry, it's not. I'm really here. I've made kind of a mess of things. But, I'll owe you for life and explain everything when you come."

"Do Aunt Marla and Renee know where you are?"

"Well, they know I'm alive. But not where I am."

"Okay, listen. just tell me where you are. I'll have to come on my bike."

"I'm at a gas station on Glen Avenue. A Standard Station."

"Okay. I think I know where you are. Is it by Catherine Street?"

"Yes. I was staying right by there on Ann Street."

"With who? Oh, God. Tell me later. I'll be there in just a few minutes. But I gotta tell you, little cousin. We have to call Aunt Marla. I'm already the family pariah. Harboring a runaway will put me over the top."

That was the same expression Janice had used. I figured it must be an Ann Arbor thing.

I waited in the phone booth for about fifteen minutes before Jerry Michael pulled up on his bicycle. I opened the phone booth door and threw my arms around his neck.

"Were you talking to your mother?"

"No, I was just pretending to talk, so I could stay in the booth and not look weird."

"Pretty smart, R. A. But I still can't believe you're standing in front of me at two in the morning on this side of the state. How the hell did you get here? Oh, never mind. Hop on the back, and we'll talk at my place."

I was relieved that his fender was flat so I could sit on it. I'd pictured myself on his handlebars. I put my arms around him and he pedaled many blocks before we got to his street. I couldn't believe it when he cut down Ann Street, right past Patty's apartment. Even though I was afraid they'd see me, I looked up to check for lights. Still dark, so I figured that nobody missed me yet. Before long, he pulled up to a house with a front porch, where he left the bike.

"You live on Division Street? In Grand Rapids, that's where the prostitutes stand on corners."

"Yeah, Renee told me."

"She did? Oh. I can't imagine her telling you that."

I followed Jerry Michael to the front door. His apartment was to the right when we stepped inside. We walked into a small living room with large posters on two walls.

"You get cozy, little cousin, and I'll make cocoa. Oh. The powder room is over there if you want to freshen up."

I sat on the edge of his couch and looked around. There was a fringed scarf draped over the top of the lamp, and pillows of all sizes on the floor and couch. It felt like the room was hugging me. Jerry Michael set two steaming mugs on something that looked like a kitchen table with sawed off legs. I picked up a book and flipped through it. Poetry.

"How do you say his name?" I asked.

"Ram-boh."

"Yeah, I thought it was French."

"That belongs to Barry. My roommate. He's from New York. Jewish. He thinks he's the next Allen Ginsberg."

I nodded, even though I didn't know who Allen Ginsberg was. Jerry Michael picked up the phone from the end table. "Please don't hate me, but I have to call your mother. I'll do all the talking, and I promise to keep it short and sweet. For now, anyway."

"All right, if you really think you have to."

"I have to." He dialed the number. "Aunt Marla? Hi. It's Jerry Michael over in Ann Arbor. I'm sorry it's so late, but I thought you'd like to know that Ruth Ann is here with me. She just got here and I had no idea she was coming. But she's safe. That's the main thing. I thought about waiting until morning to call, but...."

He listened and nodded a bunch of times, then started twirling the cord around his finger.

"I know. I know. No. I haven't even had a chance to talk with her yet. I know. Yes, of course. You try and get some sleep, Aunt Marla, and we will figure all that out in the morning. I will. Okay. I know. Yes, I know. Goodnight."

"Holiest of shits, R.A. You scared that poor woman to death. Maybe I should put you on a plane to Algeria. I think Thomas Wolfe was right."

I must have looked as confused as I felt.

"Never mind. Drink your cocoa. Then fill me in on what the hell this is all about. I don't know about you, but I am wide awake now!"

I told Jerry Michael all about kissing Tom at school, being called a brat by Bonnie at the baby shower, getting the cold shoulder from Andy, overhearing someone refer to me as a slut for kissing Tom at school, and then finally, being called gross for scratching my head and making it bleed in algebra.

"Everybody hates me, and I couldn't take any more. You can understand, right?"

"Well, if you ask me," Jerry Michael said, as he blew out a match, "if you'd just gone after the cute intellectual guy, you'd be way better off, and we might all be sleeping in our beds this very minute. But never mind that. Now, how in the world did you pick Ann Arbor and who the hell lives over on Ann Street?"

So then I told him all about Claudia, her drunk dad, her bruises, how we took the bus, her sister, her sister's roommates, and that she was Michael's girlfriend.

"Get out of town! The girl you ran away with is the person you relinquished the cute, intellectual to? Oh, never mind. What I need to know, dear heart, is if the ladies on Ann Street all know where you went."

"They were all sleeping. Even Claudia."

"So, even your friend doesn't know you left?"

"I would have told her, but she was sleeping. Plus, I didn't want to be put on the bus at 11:15. I just took off. I'd barely be gone for twenty-four hours if I took that bus."

"Okay, my head is spinning. You're even wilder than I was at your age. But I'm not knocking it. Barry would say you have chutzpah. You must know chutzpuh. Doesn't your grandma speak Yiddish? I wonder if Barry knows that. We better get some shut-eye. Hang on, I'll get you something to sleep in and some bedding for you."

He returned with a t-shirt, pillows, blankets, and a roll of Ritz Crackers dangling from his mouth. "Now, you just get comfy on the sectional, and here's a snack. Remember the powder room is right there. Anything else?"

"Yeah, who are those guys on the posters?"

"Che Guevara and Oscar Wilde. Aren't they gorgeous? I'll tell you all about them over breakfast."

"Okay, and who were those other guys? Thomas somebody and Allen Ginsberg?

"Wolfe. Thomas Wolfe. He wrote a book called *You Can't Go Home Again*, but I was just kidding. Of course, you can go home again."

"I don't even know how to thank you."

"It's a far, far, better thing I do than I have ever done. It's a far, far better rest I go to than I have ever known. Good night, little cousin."

"Good night, big cousin."

I pulled the blankets up to my chin after slipping out of my uniform skirt. I felt calm for the first time in days. Closing my eyes, I whispered to myself, "Maybe you can tell me all about Barry, too."

No Doubt in my Mind

I wasn't quite awake, but I realized I was chewing. I'd been dreaming about my dad's homemade french fries. He was sliding them from a spatula onto Wilma's lap, and she was yelling, "Stop it, Danny. I'm wearing shorts!" I was sitting between Tom and Andy, and Michael was taking pictures of us with my Polaroid Swinger camera. He said it was for evidence that I had kidnapped Claudia. "That's not true," I protested. "I didn't even want her to come with me."

I opened my eyes and turned over on the couch. One of the poster guys was staring straight at me. It was barely light in the cozy living room. I would have snuggled under the covers but my stomach was growling, and I wanted to get out of the dream. Something smelled delicious.

I thought about the dream. What if Claudia hadn't come with me? I would have gone to Saginaw, and I wouldn't be nestled in this comforting place that smelled so good. I couldn't quite see into the kitchen, but I slipped back into my uniform skirt and the camel colored crew neck with the circle pin that I had chosen yesterday morning. A lifetime ago. My legs felt sore and several of the patches were cracked. One of them had bled in the night. I checked the couch for blood and was relieved not to find any. My knee socks felt scratchy, but my legs looked so bad, I put them on anyway.

When I walked into the small kitchen, there was a short guy standing at the stove with his back to me.

"I'm Ruth Ann," I said. "I hope you already knew I was here."

He turned to me with a spatula.

"Hi there, Ruth Ann. Not only did I know you were here, this banana pecan pancake has your name on it. Maybe you didn't know *I* was here, though. You look kind of surprised."

"Oh, sorry. You're Barry, right? I knew you were here. It's just your spatula that threw me."

He turned the spatula upside down, looked at it, and shrugged.

"Did Jerry take it from your house or something?"
I laughed. "No. There was a spatula in the dream I just had."

"Really? That sounds like a poem waiting to be written, if you ask me."

"Oh, yeah. Jerry Michael said you liked poetry. Or write it, maybe? Is he still sleeping?"

"No, he's off to buy syrup and cigarettes. I bet you're starved, though, so pull up a chair." He set a bottle with a half-inch of syrup on the table and a plate with a golden-brown pancake in front of me.

Barry's dark hair was pulled back into a short pony-tail and he wore tiny glasses with no frames. I'd seen them once or twice in magazines lately. He was wearing a vest made of all different colored corduroy patches over a white shirt. His face was so kind that I wanted to lay my head on his shoulder.

"You must go to college here, too?" I asked.

"I'm in grad school."

"Have you guys been roommates long?"

"Just since June, but we've known each other for a couple of years.

We were stage hands for a play back in '66."

"Oh. What play?"

"Oh Dad, Poor Dad, Mama's Hung You in the Closet..."

"And I'm Feelin' So Sad," I finished.

"Ha, that's funny, you know it."

"My sister was in it in at Central, and me and my dad hated it."

"Oh, yeah," Barry said. "Jerry did mention Renee being in it."

"Have you met Renee?"

"No. I haven't had the pleasure."

I wanted to say that I couldn't imagine the word pleasure in the same sentence as Renee, but I kept my mouth shut. We heard the front door open and then the inside door to the apartment.

Jerry Michael was singing *Good Morning Starshine*, as he entered the kitchen with a girl with shiny cheeks and long blonde hair.

"Hey, little cousin. This is Brigida, one of Ann Arbor's finest folk singers. Brigida, this is Ruth Ann, one of the most adventurous high-school freshman in these United States."

She held her hand out to me. "Well, the pleasure is all mine. It's an honor to meet a woman of adventure."

Pleasure. There it was again, not three minutes later.

"I'm glad you've eaten, and your circle pin is back on, R. A. Brigida has offered a fair trade. She will loan us her car in exchange for Mr. Rubenstein's famous pancakes."

"Okay," I said, even though I wanted another pancake. "Where are we going?"

"We are heading over to Ann Street so you can tell your friends that you're not in jail or a shallow grave."

I made circles on the plate with my fork.

"Jerry, she's a growing girl," Barry said. "Let her have another pancake. It's not even eight-thirty."

I ate two more pancakes and even drank a cup of coffee with lots of milk in it, while the three of them talked about an upcoming poetry reading. But then it started to feel weird that nobody brought up why I was there. I was almost relieved to put my arms in my pea-coat.

As soon as Jerry Michael turned the key in Brigida's ignition, he looked at me. "After we get this over with, we have to figure out how to get you back. I wish you could stay all week, but we both know that's impossible."

"I'm not going home. At least not to *that* home. I want to live with my dad. I'm just gonna be in the way. With the baby and everything."

Jerry Michael turned the car off. "That's really it, isn't it? It's not boyfriends or any of that other stuff. I kind of figured it was the baby."

I started crying. Just like that. It was too hard to act cool and grown-up when I felt like a five-year-old. "I thought you understood the other stuff," I said. "You said you did. Last night, anyway."

"That other stuff is bad, R. A. And I do understand. But that stuff's like the tip of the iceberg. The baby's the real iceberg. Right?"

I nodded and started sobbing. He put his arms around me and I cried and sniffed on his shoulder. "I'm sorry. I didn't mean to do this."

"You needed to do this. A long time ago, little cousin. Let it out, already. It's way overdue."

I fished a Kleenex out of my purse and blew my nose. "I could really use a cigarette," I said.

Jerry Michael offered me a Kent from his pack.

"My dad smokes these," I laughed. "For the coupons."

"Me too. I got my dad a fishing rod for his birthday with the coupons."

"They really could use my room, you know."

"What?"

"I figured out that Renee could move into my room and the daisy room, you know, the one you wallpapered? That could be the baby's room. A real nursery."

"I can see how you came to that conclusion, R. A. But you've got it all wrong. They not only want you there, they're going to need you there. They probably don't even realize it yet."

"For what?"

He turned the car back on and started driving. "To babysit. Renee will probably have to work some and maybe take classes to finish her degree."

"Are you kidding? They would never trust me. I've only told you about one or two times I got in trouble. You don't even know the worst of it."

Jerry Michael started singing a song about trouble. My dad would probably call it crooning.

"I swear, you have a song for everything in life."

"That was the blues, little cousin. The blues *are* for everything in life. Way back since the cotton fields. Okay, now. Which house is it?"

I pointed to Patty's house. "That one. You have to go up the back steps."

Jerry Michael parked the car and we headed up the driveway toward the back of the house. I was about to put my foot on the bottom step when I heard someone shouting. "Stop it, Daddy, you're hurting her."

"I don't give a dilly damn if I'm hurting her. She's got it coming."

I turned and looked at Jerry Michael. My mouth was hanging open, but words wouldn't come out.

The back door opened, and Claudia burst out, crying. The man behind her gave her a shove and she almost lost her footing. Patty was behind him, sobbing. "Don't hurt her anymore, please!"

We stepped out of the way and when Claudia saw me, she started crying even harder. A trickle of blood was coming out of her nose. Her dad gave us a hateful look. "Mind your own god-damned business!"

Patty slammed the door shut. I wasn't sure she had seen us, but I wouldn't have known what to say or do anyway. We stood frozen in place until we heard them drive away.

"Holiest of shits, Ruth Ann. That girl should have gone to California."

Jerry Michael lit up a Kent when we got in the car and offered one to me.

"I could use some of your mother's Drambui with this," he said. "That guy was a beast."

My teeth were chattering, but not from the cold.

"I shouldn't be taking your butts. You're a poor college student. I have my own money to buy some."

"Heavens to Cousin Betsy, R. A. Just take one. Aunt Maxine sent me twenty bucks last week."

He took a long drag on the cigarette and pulled away from the curb. "She does that every now and then."

"She bought the baby's crib."

"Did she, now? Hey, do you think I should've punched your friend's ol' man?"

"No," I said. "He might've taken it out on her. And anyway, it all happened so fast. You didn't even have a chance. Poor Claudia. He's as bad as she said."

"I wonder if we should call the police."

"We didn't even see the car."

"True," Jerry Michael said. "I guess we should let her sister handle it. Now, about *you*."

"I'll call my dad at the car lot. He'll come and get me."

"You think so? It's about a ninety-minute drive from Saginaw. And we *have* to check in with your mom."

"I can call her at work."

"I don't know, R. A. You really want to start all over in a new school?

Sounds like you have such good friends there. You have that bike riding group and the cute, intellectual guy."

"You mean the Tandem Riders? We're not so close now that we're at Holy Rosary. One of them even went to the all-girls school. And, please drop the subject of Michael. He's Claudia's boyfriend. That's all there is to it."

It seemed like changing the subject would be a good idea. "Does anybody over twenty live in this town?"

"I know what you mean, but I'm pretty used to it."

Jerry Michael parked the car, and we walked up to the house.

"I have a class in a half-hour," he said as he unlocked his front door. "But let's quick make these calls."

Brigida was washing the dishes, and singing a song about flying away, when we came in.

There was no sign of Barry.

"Ruth Ann's mother called as soon as you left," she said, "and wasn't happy that you left without calling her. She wants to be called at work, immediately."

"There you have it, little cousin. Get thee to the telephone."

I dialed my mom at her office, hoping her boss was standing there, so she wouldn't yell at me. She answered after the first ring, and I could tell by her voice that she was gritting her teeth. That was a bad sign, but I dove right in anyway, telling her that I wanted to live with my dad.

"How dare you tell me you want to live with your father and that whore! You might as well have spit in my face! And anyway, your father's at the auction in Flint, so he can't even be reached."

"On Tuesday?" I asked. "But he always goes on Thursday."

"I guess you've forgotten that last Thursday was Thanksgiving. I'm coming to get you straight from work, and I don't want to hear another word about it. Put Jerry Michael on the phone this minute, you hear me?"

I'd been holding the phone so Jerry Michael could hear the conversation. When I held it out to him, he gave me a terrified look.

"Hi, Aunt Marla. You're right. I'm so sorry. Okay. Yes, I realize that. Of course."

When he started giving her directions to his house, I took a cigarette from his pack that was lying next to a book, *Howl and other poems*. It was by Allen Ginsberg, the guy that Jerry Michael had mentioned last night. I flipped it open from the back and read the last stanza of a poem called "Wild Orphan." The words could have been talking about my dad and me. Jerry Michael hung up the phone and I read it out loud to him.

> *And the father grieves*
> *in flophouse*
> *complexities of memory*
> *a thousand miles*
> *away, unknowing*
> *of the unexpected*
> *youthful stranger*
> *bumming toward his door.*

"Very profound, little cousin. But I have to get to class. Your mother will probably be here around eight. I'll be back before four, so just make yourself at home. Keep reading *Howl*, why dontcha? It'll expand your mind."

"Like LSD?"

"Stop that talk. You're in enough trouble. Hey, Brigida," he hollered. "How 'bout a lift to my class?"

Chapter Twenty-Eight

After they left, I paced around for over an hour, wishing I'd gotten a key, so I could take a walk. I ate an apple from the almost bare fridge, and two spoonfuls of peanut butter. My head felt like it was full of tangled webs. I was partly relieved that my dad wasn't coming but dreaded going back to the stuff I'd run away from. Plus, I'd probably be grounded for a year. I didn't think my mom had ever been this mad at me before.

My legs were even more sore than usual. It made me realize that the medicine and Saran Wrap at night did help with the pain, if nothing else. I found a bottle of hand lotion in the bathroom cupboard and put some of that on my legs. It was better than nothing.

Howl was a pretty good distraction. I really liked the poem, "Sunflower Sutra", even though I didn't understand it. Getting your mind to expand probably required some confusion, I figured. It was about a sunflower that forgot it was a flower and thought its skin looked like a dirty old locomotive. I rolled down my knee socks and blew on the sore, cracked patches. Between my skin and the despair I was feeling about my situation, I felt like a dirty old locomotive too.

All I could think about was calling Maureen. I decided that I'd try calling her at four-thirty, and just give Jerry Michael a few bucks to pay for the long distance call. I wished she was home already, so I could talk to her by myself. I wanted to tell her about Barry, along with all the other things that had happened.

I woke up to the sound of water running. At first, I had no idea where I was. When I remembered, I got a sick feeling in the pit of my stomach. This was the worst mess I'd ever been in. Why the hell did my dad go to Flint today of all days? Then I sat up on the couch. I could take a bus to Saginaw. My dad would be home by the time I got there. If only I'd thought of it sooner. Before somebody came home. I rolled my socks back up, embarrassed that whoever was in the kitchen had seen my messed up legs.

Barry was holding a match to a burner on the stove when I looked into the kitchen.

"Oh, hi, Ruth Ann. Sorry to wake you up."

"It's okay. I didn't mean to fall asleep."

"Well, you did have a late night. I'll have coffee ready in a minute."

"Thanks, but my head is so fuzzy, I think I need some fresh air."

He looked at me with a wrinkled brow. "Oh?"

"Yeah, I'm just gonna take a short walk."

Before Barry could object, I slipped on my coat, grabbed my purse and closed the door behind me. I felt guilty that I wasn't telling the real truth. But, at least I hadn't lied by saying I'd be right back.

I stood on the corner, trying to figure out which direction I should take to get to the bus station. Taking a wild guess, I went straight because I knew if I found the cafe where we'd eaten the night before, I'd have no problem. It had begun to snow, and the sky was getting dark. I tried to stand my coat collar up because the tips of my ears hurt from the cold.

I finally asked a lady at a bus stop for directions and had to back track several blocks. When I spotted the cafe, I thought about darting in to get warm, but decided against wasting the time. Snow was falling steadily when I finally reached the bus station. I hurried to the ticket window only to find out that the bus to Saginaw had left an hour earlier.

"Next one's at 5:45," the man at the window said. "You can purchase a ticket now for four dollars and twenty-five cents."

I glanced at the large clock on the wall. It would be over two hours before the next bus left.

"Okay, thanks," I told the guy. "I need to think about it."

I wandered over to the newsstand and picked up a *Journal* magazine. There was a black model on the cover and it said she made a thousand dollars a week. I spotted a *Seventeen* magazine and wanted to look at it because there was an article in it called, "How to Grow Away From Home," but there was a lady standing next to me, who kept looking up from her magazine and glancing sideways at me. I was worried that she knew I had run away, so I turned my back to her and kept reading the Journal. I got frustrated when she didn't leave, so I walked over to the candy bars, and bought a Payday to eat on the bus. When I looked back toward the magazines, the lady was staring at me like she was going to turn me in.

I slipped into a room with a lunch counter and took a stool with my back to the door, hoping she wouldn't see me. I ordered a bowl of chicken rice soup and ate it as slowly as possible to kill time. When I finished, the clock said it was four-thirty. I still wanted to call Maureen, but I'd have to get a lot of change for the long-distance call. I certainly had enough time, but I was afraid the lady might be lurking around. Maybe she'd called the police or the child welfare department or something.

At four-forty-five, I slipped off the stool and left the lunch room. The lady wasn't by the magazines, so I went back to check the article on "How to Grow Away From Home." The first paragraph said, "Some teenagers separate from their parents gingerly, as if inching into a cold swimming pool. Others take it like a high dive." I'd not only taken the high dive, I'd tied myself to an anchor. I put the magazine back and looked for the phone booth where Claudia had tried to call her sister last night.

I wondered how Claudia was doing and if she'd made it to school in the afternoon. I'd missed a day and a half now. I'd been getting pretty good grades. Now I'd be behind. Would my mom make me go back tomorrow already? But, wait. Wasn't I going to take the bus to Saginaw to start all over? Was I or wasn't I?

I stopped in the middle of the bus station and looked back and forth from the ticket booth to the telephone booth. I missed Maureen. That much I knew for sure. I headed back to the candy counter and got three dollars' worth of quarters for the phone. After I picked up the receiver and dialed the number, the operator came on and told me to insert three quarters. Mrs. Abraham picked up the phone after the second ring. I panicked and hung up.

No Doubt in my Mind

What was I thinking? Everybody must know by now that I'd run away. What was I going to say to Maureen's mom when she asked me where I was or what I was doing? The quarters didn't come back. Damn it all! Seventy-five cents gone forever. Over an hour of baby-sitting. I felt like crying.

I sat down on a bench and held my purse tightly against my side. There might not be any babysitting jobs in Saginaw, but maybe I wouldn't need any. My dad would probably give me a big allowance. But maybe Wilma wouldn't let him. Babysitting made me think of Denise. She was somebody else I'd like to talk to. Most likely, she'd just tell me to come home. And besides, Maureen was the friend I could really talk to about boy stuff. Denise was just a friend to boys. I felt really bad for thinking that. I got up and looked at the board with all the departures. Tulsa. Maybe I should just forget Saginaw and go to Tulsa. Cleveland? Detroit was close. That would be cheaper. An old man smelling of booze sat down next to me with a cigarette dangling from his mouth.

"You gotta light?" he slurred.

I shook my head and changed seats. It was five-fifteen. I needed to make up my mind. What if the bus sold out like the Beatles movies did back when I was a kid? I got up and walked up to the ticket booth. I was glad that a lady had taken the place of the ticket guy who'd been there before. He might have gotten suspicious of me. I looked over my shoulder to be sure the newsstand lady wasn't around.

"I'd like a ticket to Saginaw, please," I said.

319

"That'll be four dollars and twenty-five cents. You can board in fifteen minutes. Just listen for the announcement."

I felt antsy. Now that I'd made the decision, I wanted to get going. I went back to the newsstand and flipped through the *Journal* again. It was so unusual to see a black model. How cool that she made a thousand dollars a week, but I knew they only put that on there because she was black. I looked at advertisements for hair straightening products and glowing skin. My hair was a mess. No curlers or Dippity-Do for days now, and I knew the skin on my legs was cracked and bleeding under my knee socks. Maybe my dad could take me to see Wally the pharmacist tomorrow. Or would I be in some new school already? Maybe he'd put me in Mimi's school if he could pull some strings. Then I thought about her country-club friends who'd made fun of my psoriasis last summer.

Oh, no. What was I thinking? Maybe the slut thing at Holy Rosary wasn't going around. Maybe it was only between Louise Shumway and the other girl in the shower room. And who the hell was Louise Shumway anyway? Just a goodie-two-shoes that could sing one song. But that bitch Julie had embarrassed me about the psoriasis on my scalp.

Then I heard the announcement to board the Saginaw bus. Damn, damn, damn it all!

Why had I wasted the precious four dollars and twenty-five cents? This was the biggest mistake yet of this whole entire mess. Between the lost phone booth money and the ticket, it was a whole New Year's Eve worth of babysitting. And now I didn't even want to go to Saginaw. I couldn't be happy there *or* in Grand Rapids. Could I ever be happy anywhere? Had I ever been happy anywhere?

"You're my favorite teacher of my whole life, Mrs. Van Hoose. And I wanted to get Mrs. Tilley for fourth grade next year.

"I'm sorry you're moving, Ruth Ann, but I think you'll like Grand Rapids. My husband grew up there. He said it snowed there once in July!"

"In July? Oh no! Well, we just moved here last summer so my sister could go to college. It's my favorite town, and I don't want to move away."

"Doesn't your mother like it here? Is your sister staying for college?"

"My mom says there's no full time jobs here, so that's why we have to move. I think Renee's coming with us."

"Well, I want you to promise me that you'll stop in and say hi whenever you come back to Mt. Pleasant, you hear me?"

I was completely happy in Mt. Pleasant. Before I got jerked out of there when Renee was pregnant. *The first fucking time!* All of this was Renee's fault. Every solitary bit of this mess was Renee's fault. I should be in Mt. Pleasant cleaning Mrs. Van Hoose's chalkboards and volunteering in the Fancher School library. Not trying to figure out where the hell I was supposed to live and how the hell I was supposed to live with this hideous, horrid disease I was plagued with.

No Doubt in my Mind

I darted behind a spinner rack of comic books, set my purse on the floor, rolled down my knee socks, and scratched my psoriasis until blood rolled down my legs and into my loafers. I wanted to scream, "I hate Renee," at the top of my lungs, but instead, tears rolled down my cheeks. They announced the bus was leaving in five minutes. I wiped my eyes, pulled up my socks and cut to the front of the ticket booth line.

"Excuse me. Does the bus to Saginaw stop in Mt. Pleasant?"

"No, dear. Mt. Pleasant is north of Saginaw and a totally different route. Your bus is leaving. You better get on it so you don't miss it. Or do you need me to make a phone call?"

"No thanks. I was just curious."

That did it. There was no doubt in my mind that she was suspicious. I went out the door to where the busses were lined up. The Saginaw bus was practically full. I got on and found a seat in the second row next to a lady in a hat that looked like Larry Mondello's mother on *Leave It To Beaver*. She smiled and scooched over an inch to give me some room. My heart was racing, and I felt more mixed up than almost any time I could ever remember.

The bus driver tipped his hat to all of us, then closed the door and turned on the engine. Just as he began to back up, someone pounded on the door. I could see a flat palm smacking the glass. The driver pulled the handle back to open the door, and there was Jerry Michael standing with a terrified look on his face.

"Can I help you?" the driver asked.

"I need to get one of your passengers. Ruth Ann Bloomfield."
He came right up the steps and spotted me immediately.

"Ruth Ann. You have to come with me." He looked at the driver. "It's
a family emergency."

I stood up. "What happened? What are you talking about?"

"It's Renee. Your dad's on the way. You have to come with me."

"If you got time, Miss, go get yourself a refund," the bus driver said.

"Okay, thank you."

He closed the door as soon as I stepped on the ground.

"We don't have time for a refund," Jerry Michael said.

"Are you sure? It was over four bucks. What's going on, anyway? Is
she gonna have the baby?"

"Something happened at work, and they sent for an ambulance," he
said. She's in the hospital. Your mom said it was a bad headache and then
a seizure." He looked through the glass door. "Okay, there's no line. Go
ahead and get your four bucks."

It felt like I was dreaming as the lady counted the bills into my hand.
My head felt light and I got really hot. I grabbed the counter.

"You don't look so good, R. A.," Jerry Michael said. "Maybe you
better sit down. Here, take your coat off."

He led me to the nearest bench and we sat down.

I looked at Jerry Michael. "Is she gonna be okay?"

"I hope so."

"And the baby?" I felt my lower lip tremble.

He shrugged and handed me his hanky. "We just have to wait and see. I'm sure they're doing everything possible."

I dabbed my eyes. "Did you ride your bike here?"

"No, it's snowing too hard. Your dad's gonna have a helluva time getting here."

"My dad's really coming here?"

"Yeah, he's on his way. Your mom got a hold of him at the auction in Flint, 'cause she's at the hospital, of course."

"Holy shit, Jerry Michael. If you'd come two minutes later, this would have been a disaster. I was headed for Saginaw. My dad and I would have missed each other."

"Yeah, I figured that much."

"Is this the first place you looked for me?"

He nodded.

I held his hanky out to him. "I'm sorry I'm such a lousy cousin."

"What's that supposed to mean?"

"I've really put you out. And then I go and take off, like a spoiled brat. But, seriously. I just couldn't face my mom."

"Well, you would've been in a lot worse trouble if your mom had driven all the way here after work just to find out you'd taken off."

"You're right. I guess I'm not thinking straight. I'm really sorry."

"Stop apologizing. Are you feeling better? We should get going."

"I'm okay, I guess. Are we walking?"

"No. I've got Brigida's car."

I put my coat back on, and we walked outside. It was snowing hard and the wind was blowing. The car already had an inch of snow on it.

"Your friend bailed me out a couple times today," I said as I brushed snow off the windshield with my coat sleeve. "Letting us use her car."

He lifted the windshield wiper and scraped underneath it. "She doesn't mind. And, she's making spaghetti. I bet you're hungry, and there's no telling when we'll eat again."

"What do you mean, we?"

"Hospital food? No, thanks."

"Does that mean you're coming too?" I asked as we both got into the front seat.

"If your dad doesn't mind, I'd like to come. I wouldn't be able to concentrate here with all this going on. I can write my final papers in the waiting room."

"My dad won't care."

As soon as I said that, I had to wonder. I was pretty sure my dad didn't know about Jerry Michael being gay. What if he called him a fruit loop or something?

We could smell the spaghetti from the front porch. My stomach was growling, and that made me feel guilty. How could I think about food when I didn't even know if Renee might be dying? Or the baby. That made my heart leap into my throat. What the hell was going on? Did I all of a sudden care about the baby? If the baby died, everything could go back to the way it was. I thought about the little green blanket with the flecks of color that Renee knitted. I wondered if it was it still folded over the edge of the crib just like it had been.

Barry was sprinkling oil and vinegar onto a big salad when we walked into the kitchen. Brigida was taking garlic bread out of the oven.

Barry set the cruets down, wiped his hands, and put his arms around me. I started crying right on his toweled shoulder. He stroked my out-of-control hair. I couldn't believe nobody was yelling at me.

"You guys are all way too nice. I'm such a little bitch."

Barry stepped back and blotted my tears with the kitchen towel. "*You are not!* You're a teenager. A teenager with some fucked-up stuff going on."

Even my dad didn't say fuck around me and he swore every two minutes. I felt more grown-up than I ever had in my life.

I handed the towel back to him. "But aren't you all mad at me for running away from running away?"

Brigida threw her head back and laughed. "Now, there's some material for a new song. I'll be writing that one tonight."

"Hey, now," Barry said. "Let's all dig into this feast. Brigida makes *the* best spaghetti!"

We all sat down at the tiny table and began eating. I watched wax trickle from a candle that was stuck in a wine bottle and felt a pang of homesickness. We had a bottle at home just like it that we also used for a candle holder. I guessed it was a college thing because Renee started sticking candles in wine bottles right after her first semester at Central.

"Renee's not in a coma or anything, is she?" I asked.

"Oh, I don't think so, R. A.," Jerry Michael said. He helped himself to more garlic bread. "But your mom didn't say a whole lot on the phone. She's probably got an IV or two, but she's most likely conscious."

"Knowing Renee," I said, "she's most likely polishing the nightstand, and dusting the window sills. She did that last summer when I was in the hospital."

Jerry Michael grinned like he totally understood and then glanced at the clock on the wall. "I just hope your dads got his snow tires on."

For some reason, I started thinking about Trudy carrying the rocking horse into the baby shower and I felt sad. Sad and ashamed of myself. All this with Renee going on, and then me running away on top of it. Trudy would never look at me the same. Trudy, who would have kicked Bonnie's ass for me.

We all cleared the table and then I insisted on washing the dishes. Barry dried while Brigida played her guitar in the living room. Jerry Michael was in the bedroom off the kitchen packing his duffel bag. He stepped into the room in a thick cable-knit sweater that looked like oatmeal.

"Mind if I borrow this, Babs?" he asked Barry. "I hear it's like the North Pole over there in Grand Rapids. I've only been there in the summer."

"Go ahead. That thing's way too hot for me."

I looked sideways at Barry who was drying his wire-framed glasses on the towel. I'd figured he was gay, but *Babs*? That pretty much sealed the deal and it made me even more certain that he was Jerry Michael's boyfriend.

"Is it really like that?" Barry asked me.

"Is what like what?"

"Is Grand Rapids like the North Pole?"

"Oh. I don't know. I guess so. I heard it snowed in the summer there once, but it gets really hot in the summer just like the rest of Michigan.

"I'm sorry you're moving, Ruth Ann, but I think you'll like Grand Rapids. My husband grew up there. He said it snowed there once in July!"

There she was again. Mrs. Van Hoose. My favorite teacher of all times. I looked up at the bottle of Aunt Jemima syrup on the shelf above the sink. She was looking down at me. I pictured her sitting in the living room listening to Brigida play her guitar. I would lay my head in her lap, and she would stroke my hair, and hum. Then I pictured Trudy and Mrs. Van Hoose on each side putting their arms around me and telling me everything was all right and I didn't need to worry anymore.

Chapter Twenty-Nine

"For cryin' out loud," my dad grumbled. "At this rate we won't get there 'til five o'clock in the morning."

He shook his pack of Kents and took one out with his mouth, then reached over his shoulder to offer one to Jerry Michael in the back seat.

"Thanks, Uncle Danny. I smoke Kents myself."

My dad had showed up at Jerry Michael's apartment right after nine o'clock. I was glad that Brigida was still there so things didn't look suspiciously gay. She was on the couch taking notes in a spiral notebook with text-books spread around her, and Barry was sitting at the desk, typing. It was probably a poem about hoboes, alley cats or junkyards, but hopefully to my dad it looked like college stuff. Not a gay boyfriend to my gay cousin. I crossed my fingers that Jerry Michael didn't break into song or quote any lines from movies like *Carnival of Souls.*

"I don't ever remember snow like this in November," Jerry Michael commented.

"Yeah, and one damn shitty time for it to happen," my dad said.

"What all did Mom say about Renee?" I asked.

"She said things were pretty touch-and-go right now. They've got all kinds of doo-hickeys hooked up to her with tubes and stuff."

"Sounds like an episode on *Ben Casey,*" I said.

"Not a good comparison, Sport. *Ben Casey* doesn't always have happy endings."

If Renee had a choice of which drama to star in, her first choice would probably be *Dark Shadows*. *Ben Casey* would for sure be a close second.

"But, hey," my dad said. "Let's just hope for the best, hang tight, and we'll find out when we get there."

If we get there, I felt like saying. I'd never seen my dad drive with two hands on the wheel. He was never this cautious. His usual style was to turn the whole steering wheel with one finger. The snow was so blinding at times that we had to rely on the tail lights in front of us, just to know we were still on the highway.

"So, Jerry Michael, is your pop still keepin' the grocery store goin'?" my dad asked.

"Oh, yeah. He and his brothers will most likely be doing that until they're ninety."

Uncle Vernie Lee wiped my cheeks with the corner of his apron.

"Hey there, little one. You'll be goin' home in a day or two. Your mama and daddy just need some time apart. Hey, let me show you our new magic straws. You won't believe it."

He opened a box and took one out.

"See that brown stick inside the straw? Well, guess what? That's chocolate. You drink your regular milk with one of these and you got yourself chocolate milk. Presto! Just like that. And this whole box of straws is a present for you from Vernie Lee's Grocery Market. How do you like that?"

"Well, business must be good then, huh?"

"Better all the time," Jerry Michael answered. "They even hired a guy to make homemade sausage on Fridays. And how's your car lot doing?"

"Not bad. Not bad. Helluva lot better than the pawn shop."

"Glad to hear that. Hey, thanks a lot, Uncle Danny, for letting me hitch a ride with you. Renee and I've been real close the past few years. I wouldn't be able to keep my head on straight sitting around Ann Arbor, worrying about her, and the baby, of course."

I'd never heard anybody call my dad Uncle Danny before. I had dozens of cousins on my mom's side, but I only saw them with my mom and Renee. The two on my dad's side lived in Florida and I couldn't even remember them.

"Yeah," my dad said, glancing in the rearview mirror. "She has mentioned the two of you being buddy-buddy. I guess you're probably into all that theatre stuff too, huh?"

"Oh, some," Jerry Michael answered. "Not like Renee, though. She's got real talent. Acting *and* directing. I'm more of a playwright. I'm in graduate school for play *writing.*"

"Is that right? What kind? Funny ones? Whodunnits?" My dad chuckled and lit a cigar. "Boy, oh boy. She's made us sit through some doozies, huh, Sport?"

Jerry Michael laughed really hard. I was glad he wasn't insulted. I figured he was probably writing my dad into a play at this very minute. He *was* great material, that was for sure.

331

"I can't tell ya the last time I was in Ann Arbor," my dad said. "Looks like it's kinda overrun with beatnik types, huh?"

I looked sideways at my dad. Where was he going with this? Had he really looked at people walking around? In a blizzard? He must have noticed Barry's stubby ponytail. Or Brigida's guitar. Not to mention the posters of Che Guevarra and Oscar Wilde on the wall. Not that my dad would know who they were. But it sure didn't look like Renee's college apartment. Except for the candle in the wine bottle. Renee really only acted beatnik-ish around Jerry Michael.

"Mind if I turn the radio on?" I asked. "Maybe we can find a weather report."

Every station had reports of snow and high winds with many roads being closed.

By midnight, we were only as far as Battle Creek. My dad was glad he'd chosen the southern route because they said the worst weather was by Lansing.

"I'm gonna stop here for gas," my dad said. "Maybe they'll throw in some Corn Flakes or Rice Krispies since we're in cereal city. You two use the rest room. I'm gonna try callin' the hospital from that phone booth."

Jerry Michael and I watched the gas station attendant try to clean the windshield, but the fluid froze on the glass. He shrugged at us and gave up. My dad handed him some bills and got back in the car. He tossed each of us a Mars Bar and tore one open for himself. "Here, maybe this'll help keep us awake. Decided against Cokes, so we don't have to stop again."

"Good thinkin'," Jerry Michael said. "We should be about halfway by now."

"Well, I got hold of one the nurses and she says not much has changed. Your sister's asleep, so that's good, I guess."

It was after one in the morning when we got to Kalamazoo, which was only a half hour from Battle Creek. Once we headed north on U.S. 131, the roads were clear in no time at all. There was only a slight dusting of snow on the grass. Traffic was sparse, and my dad lit another cigar.

"Now we're talkin', huh, Sport? Find us some music so we stay alert here this next fifty miles."

I switched the radio back on and the Doors were singing, *Love Me Two Times.* My stomach did a slight churn because I could never hear the Doors without thinking of Tom. Who I had loved two times. And who had gotten me into a couple of messes at least two times.

As we approached downtown Grand Rapids, I could see the giant, neon green letters at least a mile before we reached it. Butterworth Hospital. Somewhere inside that tall building, Renee and the baby were hooked up to stuff that was keeping them alive. At least so far.

"Is this the same hospital you were in, R. A.?" Jerry Michael asked as we entered the lobby.

My dad stubbed the last of his cigar out in the ashcan and looked at me oddly. I wondered if he'd forgotten about me being in the hospital or maybe he was surprised that my cousin knew about it.

"No, I was in St. Anthony's, which I've tried to forget."

Jerry Michael put his arm around my shoulder and gave me a squeeze. "Sorry. I didn't mean to drag up bad memories."

I needed that squeeze. "It's okay. I'm just glad you're here."

We took the elevator up to the maternity ward on the seventh floor. We passed a long window full of babies in clear plastic boxes. Some sleeping, some screaming. Nurses were holding a couple of them. Renee's room was down one long hall and then another. Far from the roomful of babies. When we stopped at the nurse's station they told my dad he could go into Renee's room, but Jerry Michael and I would have to stay in the waiting room. We sat down on the hard vinyl chairs and both let out huge sighs at the same time. My mom came into the room and I was shocked at how much older she looked. Had I only been gone for three days? Jerry Michael stood up and hugged her immediately. She started crying on his shoulder, then stepped back and looked over at me. "I hope you realize what a loyal young man this cousin of yours is." She began crying again. "Do you?"

I nodded. "Of course, I do, Mom. That's why I called him."

"Don't even get me started on that, young lady. Your sister is one sick girl in there, and we have no idea if this baby will survive. The last thing I needed..."

Just then a man entered the room, loosening his necktie and lighting a cigarette at the same time. I could have kissed him because my mom stopped talking. You could tell by his pacing he was probably waiting for his wife to deliver a baby.

"Can we see her, Aunt Marla?" Jerry Michael asked.

"Maybe after her father." My mom glared at me.

I stood up. "Can somebody please tell us what's going on?"

My mom lowered her voice and glanced over to the man who was pouring himself a cup of coffee. "She's in a light coma. Her condition is called eclampsia and it can be very dangerous to her and the baby. They're hoping that she wakes up soon and they will probably have to do a caesarean section."

I could see tears in Jerry Michael's eyes. "Do the doctors think she'll be okay?"

"They're not saying much." My mom reached into her purse for a Salem, and Jerry Michael lit it for her. "It's a pretty common condition, and so they seem to know what they're doing. But it can be life threatening."

My heart was beating so fast I put my hand over it. This was my fault. If I hadn't run away, probably none of this would have happened. Renee and my mom would have watched TV and gone to bed just like any other Wednesday night. Now Renee and the baby's lives were hanging in the balance and if they died it would prove that Bonnie had had been right all along. I was a brat. Not just any brat. A selfish, mean, death-causing brat. I noticed my mom's pack of cigarettes sticking right out of the top of her purse next to a wad of tissue. Sniffing loudly, I grabbed a tissue, and a Salem at the same time while she continued to describe Renee's symptoms to Jerry Michael.

"I need the ladies room, "I said, turning to walk out the door.

Jerry Michael was pulling Barry's sweater over his head, when I came back from the bathroom. He threw it down, inside out.

"That thing was too hot," he said. "At least for here."

"No kidding. Grand Rapids is not the North Pole. Where's my mom?"

"Back with Renee. We can't see her yet because only parents are allowed in the room. At least for now. So, I guess we're bunking in here."

The orange vinyl furniture didn't look very comfortable, but I felt wide awake, anyway.

"How are we gonna sleep on this stuff?" I asked. "It looks like my neighbor Cathy's Barbie furniture."

"I know neighbor Cathy," Jerry Michael said. "And believe it or not, I know Barbie furniture."

I looked at the sunburst clock on the wall. It was just like the one at Ralph and Orna Lee's house, where I used to babysit. It was a quarter to three.

"They'll bring you pillows and blankets," the expectant father said, dropping his newspaper down from his face.

"Sounds like you've been here before," Jerry Michael said.

"This'll be number four. We're hoping for a boy this time. We've got three..."

He stopped when a nurse came through the door.

"Congratulations, Mr. Wondergem. It's a girl! And she's all ready to meet you."

The man shrugged at us with a grin, then stopped at the door, reached into his inside pocket and tossed a cigar to Jerry Michael, and a bubble-gum cigar to me.

"He may not have gotten his boy, but he sure is lucky everything went smoothly," Jerry Michael said after the man was gone.

"Yeah, caesarean sections are pretty dangerous, right?"

"I guess they can be at times. I'm also a little worried about the baby being early. But we need to stay optimistic, little cousin." Jerry Michael started jiggling his foot.

"Then stop that," I said pointing to his foot. "You're making me nervous."

A housekeeping lady brought us each a pillow and blanket, and Jerry Michael fell asleep right away. I woke up when I heard *The Today Show* playing on the TV. A different cleaning lady was running a feather duster over the TV screen with a hand on her hip. When a commercial came on, she turned around and noticed I was awake and Jerry Michael was groaning. She straightened the magazines on the coffee table and shuffled out of the room.

"What time is it?" Jerry Michael said with one eye open.

"Quarter after seven."

"Any news?"

"Not so far. I feel like peeking in to see, but I don't even know what room she's in."

Jerry Michael threw the blanket back and sat up. "I need coffee. Let's go find some."

I slipped my feet into my loafers and stood up, stretching. "I can't even imagine how bad my hair looks. Not to mention the lack of toothbrush."

"I have toothpaste. You can use your finger."

"Isn't there coffee over there?" I pointed to the metal container in the corner.

Jerry Michael walked over and lifted the handle. "Nada. What the H? There was plenty last night when Mr. Wondergem needed it."

I laughed. "I forgot she called him that. Do you think that was really his name?"

"Sure it was. Sounds Dutch. I heard there's a lot of Dutch people on this side of the state."

My dad came into the room shaking his head. "Sit down, you two. I've got some bad news."

We both sat down at exactly the same time. I heard the air compress in the vinyl cushions.

"Renee woke up, but she isn't seeing so good."

"What?" I asked. "What do you mean?"

Jerry Michael's hands flew over his mouth. "Holy Mary, Mother of God. Tell me she's not going blind."

My dad shook his head. "Let's hope not. But they said this kind of thing happens with whatever the hell this condition is. The good news is that it's almost always temporary."

"The poor thing must be terrified." Jerry Michael stood up and took the Kent cigarette my dad offered him.

"She's scared shitless," my dad said. "Helluva way to wake up, huh?"

"When can we see her?" Jerry Michael asked.

"Maybe after the doctors leave." My dad took a roll of money out of his pocket and peeled off a ten dollar bill. I noticed his hands were shaking. "Go see what you can find to eat around here. I might catch up with you in a while."

"Dad? Does she know we're here?'

"We've told her a few times, Sport. I think she knows. But, don't forget. They've got her pretty doped up."

I did my best to freshen up in the bathroom, but I was a sorry sight. Jerry Michael was leaning on the wall looking pale when I came out.

"You've got more than a goatee now, you know."

He rubbed his hands over his cheeks.

"Oh, well. This is no time for high fashion. Coffee will help everything. Let's go find some."

We headed down the same hall from the night before. A black couple were tapping the window that looked in on all the babies. The young woman was wearing a peach robe and a triangle scarf that looked very familiar. She turned to us, then back to the window, back to us again, and stared.

339

"Vivian?"

"Ruth Ann?"

"Yes. Oh my God! Denise told me you were...expecting."

"That's right, your friend. I did run into her."

I noticed that Jerry Michael's eyebrows were higher than usual.

"Oh, this is my cousin, Jerry Michael. Vivian and I met last summer when I was in the hospital. She worked there."

"Still do," Vivian said. I've been delivering trays there for a whole year. This is my husband, Maurice."

Jerry Michael put his hand out to Maurice and they shook hands.

Maurice was handsome and looked a couple of years older than Vivian. I turned toward the window. "So, show me your baby."

Vivian pointed to the plastic box right in front of the window that said Baby Girl. "There she is, right there."

My heart felt like it was melting on the spot. The tiny brown baby had chubby cheeks and a pouf of fuzzy hair. She was the cutest baby I'd ever seen.

"Oh, Vivian! I can't believe she's yours. Did you name her yet?"

"Lyla. After my granny."

"That's so pretty. She looks like a Lyla."

"What are *you* doing up here?" Vivian asked.

"My sister, who was due in about three weeks had a seizure at work yesterday. She has a serious condition. I forget the name of it."

"Eclampsia," Jerry Michael said.

"That's right. Anyway, they might have to do a caesarean section today. And things are getting more complicated."

I didn't mention the possible blindness because I didn't want to believe it.

"Don't you worry," Vivian said. "She's gonna be just fine. I can feel it in my bones. Her little baby'll be hangin' out with Lyla before you know it."

"Thanks, Vivian. I hope you're right."

We hugged and then Vivian backed up, keeping her hands on my shoulders. "You see what I got on my head?"

"Actually, the scarf caught my eye before I realized it was you."

Vivian turned to Jerry Michael. "Ruth Ann gave me two scarves like these. I never met such a nice patient before."

"Well, we both talked about our hair problems." I reached up. "Like I have right now, in fact."

"I was sorry when you left the hospital, but I hope you got better."

"Well, sort of. Off and on, I guess you could say. It's so great to see you. We better go get some coffee for my cousin here before he falls over. I'm sure we'll see you again."

"I'm in Room 720," Vivian called down the hall as we walked to the elevator.

After the elevator doors closed, Jerry Michael turned to me. "You never cease to amaze me, R.A."

"Hmm. Is that supposed to be a compliment?"

"As a matter of fact, yes, it is."

"Good ol' Vivian."

"I wouldn't call her *old* Vivian," Jerry Michael said. "*How old is she?*"

"She's at least a year older than me."

"You're not even fifteen yet!"

"Next month! Anyway, I sure love the name, Lyla. I wonder what name Renee will pick."

"She never told you?"

"Me? Are you kidding?" I asked. "Has she told you?"

Jerry Michael looked relieved when the elevator doors opened, and a bunch of nurses stepped in.

I tugged on his shirt. "Well, has she?"

He scrunched his eyebrows at me and didn't say anything. The doors opened on the first floor and everyone got off.

"Okay," he said, pointing to a sign, "It looks like the cafeteria is down this hall."

We followed the nurses into a room decorated with ivy wallpaper and plastic ivy hanging everywhere possible. The breakfast choices looked terrible, so I got a small box of Sugar Smacks and a carton of milk. Jerry Michael chose a plate of eggs and ham and two cups of coffee.

"Is that all you want?" he asked me. "That's not a very good breakfast, R.A."

"I know, but it's the only thing I can stomach right now."

We sat in a booth and I sliced the cereal box with a knife and poured the milk into it. I loved these boxes from the variety packs, but my mom never bought them.

"So," I said, "Are you gonna tell me the names she picked?"

"Gee, R.A., I don't know if I should. If she didn't tell you...."

"Like she ever tells me anything! They didn't even tell me about the first *baby* 'til the night before."

"First baby? What are you talking about?"

I stopped chewing and looked up. "Holy crap. I figured you knew."

My dad walked up to our booth. "Slide over, Sport."

He set down a tray with pancakes and sausage and looked over at Jerry Michael's eggs.

"You trust those are real? I figured they were fake, so I passed 'em up." He tucked his napkin into the collar of his Banlon shirt. "So, it looks like I'll be a *zaide* before the day's over."

"A what?" Jerry Michael asked.

"Grandpa," I said. "*Zaide* is Yiddish for grandpa."

"Well, well, well," my dad said. "I wouldn't have figured you knew that, Sport."

"I've spent enough time around Grandma Gertie to pick up a thing or two."

"Well, anyway," my dad said. "Your sister's in labor and they might not have to do a caesarean, after all. That's why I'm grabbing a bite now."

"Do they think that's okay?" Jerry Michael asked. "Is she strong enough to handle it? What if she's in labor for twenty-four hours? I've heard that can happen."

"Highly doubtful," my dad said. "Not with the second one."

His fork stopped halfway to his mouth. He looked at Jerry Michael first, and then me.

Jerry Michael coughed into his napkin.

"Jiminy Christmas. He didn't know, did he?"

I shook my head and started. "Dad, I..."

Jerry Michael reached across the table and put his hand on mine. "If there's something I'm not supposed to know about, I'm great at changing the subject, right R.A.?"

"Marla would send me to the moon for this," my dad said. "I guess I thought the two of you being so close. Shit. All I know is, I've got one helluva big mouth."

"It's okay, Dad. We can trust Jerry Michael." I looked straight into Jerry Michael's wide eyes. "Renee gave a baby up for adoption five years ago," I said.

"Heavens to Cousin Betsy," Jerry Michael said. "I wonder why she never told me. Let me think...five years ago I was in high school. I guess we weren't as close then, but still ...."

"Hardly anyone knows." I thought of last summer in Grand Haven when I told Maureen and felt a pang of guilt.

"Well, it doesn't even matter," Jerry Michael said, leaning back in the booth. "We need to stay focused on right now. Let's get back up there."

The three of us got on the elevator and went back to Renee's floor. My mom was in the waiting room smoking a cigarette and drinking coffee.

"The doctor was checking...things," she said. "So, I stepped out."

"Marla, get something to eat," my dad said.

"Not now." She stubbed out her cigarette and left the room.

We spent the next several hours watching quiz shows and soap operas and waiting for news. At one o'clock, I wandered down the hall to peek into Vivian's room. She was in bed, holding her baby and cooing to her. She spotted me standing in the doorway.

"Hey, Ruth Ann, come on in."

I looked down the hall both ways. "Is it allowed?"

Vivian glanced over at her roommate who was sound asleep. "Probably not, but we'll find out, won't we? If I remember correctly, you're kind of a rule-breaker."

I laughed. "Okay, but I don't want to get you in trouble." I walked toward the bed and lightly touched the baby's soft hair. "How do you do, Baby Lyla?"

"Do you want to hold her?" Vivian asked.

"Are you sure?"

Before I could refuse, Vivian pushed the tiny bundle toward me. I gathered her up in my arms and sat down on the hard, plastic visitor's chair. The baby was warm and making cute little movements with her mouth. I couldn't imagine Renee offering her baby to me.

"Does she cry much?" I asked.

"Not really. How's your sister doing?"

"Turns out, she's in labor. So, maybe no caesarean after all."

"Is she still having all the other problems?"

"I really don't know. I'm so tired, I can't think straight. I ran away on Monday. I'm only back here 'cause of all this."

"Ran away? Where'd you go? How come?"

"I meant to go to Saginaw to my dad's, but I wound up in Ann Arbor at my cousin's. The one you met. And there were lots of reasons, I guess."

"Partly due to your sister?" Vivian asked.

"Well, yeah, partly."

"Seems I remember some trouble between the two of you."

"That's for sure."

"I guess your hair's all curly 'cause you haven't been home," Vivian said.

I laughed. "Yeah, if I ever run away again, I'll bring a triangle scarf. I just walked out of school and got on a Greyhound bus. Didn't even know what the hell I was doing." I looked down. "Sorry, Lyla."

She gestured toward the nightstand. "There's a scarf in there. Go ahead and take it. In fact, it's the other one you gave me."

I held the baby a little more tightly. "This is the cutest baby I've ever seen. I mean it."

Vivian grinned. "Well, black babies are always the cutest."

"Too bad Renee's going to have a boring white one."

"Are you sure about that?"

"Holy Moly. That would really send my family over the top."

We burst out laughing.

A nurse stepped into the room. "Mrs. Streeter, visitors are not allowed when the babies are out. Oh, my stars. They are certainly not allowed to hold the babies. You'll have to leave right now, young lady."

I handed Lyla to Vivian.

"Go ahead, now," Vivian said. "Take that scarf."

"Are you sure, Viv?"

She gave me a look that made me laugh, so I grabbed the scarf out of the drawer. The nurse huffed over to Vivian's bed, took the baby from her, and looked at me. "You have to leave the floor immediately. Visiting hours are at three."

"Her sister's in labor and very sick," Vivian said in my defense.

The nurse gave me a stern look. "Then I suggest you get back to the waiting room."

Jerry Michael had his papers and text books spread all over the coffee table in the waiting room.

"Where'd my mom and dad go?" I asked him. It felt weird to say mom and dad in the same sentence and have them actually in the same place. My mind flashed to Renee's first pregnancy when my dad slept overnight in my mom's room and I thought they were getting back together. But that was before Wilma. And the ranch house with the built-in swimming pool.

"Aunt Marla's in with Renee, and your dad's looking for a phone booth. He needed to call the car lot and your Aunt Dorothy.

"Did my mom eat anything yet? She's gonna be really grouchy if she doesn't."

"Your dad said he was getting her a sandwich whether she liked it or not."

"Yeah, my dad's like a Jewish mother when it comes to food."

"I've really enjoyed him. He's a good guy."

"Yeah, and I bet you always heard otherwise. Renee pretty much hates him."

My mom came rushing in. "Her sight's getting better and labor's moving along, so they're pretty positive it'll be a regular delivery."

My dad walked in carrying a small cardboard box. "Okay, we got chicken salad, roast beef, tuna, and there's vegetable soup in those cups. You gotta eat, Marla. All of you, eat."

"Danny," my mom said. "Renee's doing much better."

My heart felt very full when my mom said Danny. I thought of the wedding picture I'd found in her drawer. He was in a soldier's uniform and she was wearing a suit. They'd been married in the priest's house. Grandma Gertie said it was a *shanda*.

"Am I the only one who doesn't know the names she picked?" I asked. Everybody stopped talking and looked at me.

My dad stopped unwrapping his sandwich. "What the hell? Why

can't we tell Sport?"

"We probably told her," my mom said. "And she just wasn't listening."

I raised my voice a little too loudly. "That's *not true*."

"Maybe we didn't think you even cared," she said. "But, it's Bobby if it's a boy, and Kerry if it's a girl."

"They're Kennedy names," Jerry Michael added with his hand over his heart.

I nodded. Of course, Kennedy names. I should have guessed.

"When can we see her?" Jerry Michael asked.

"Yeah, no kidding," my dad said. "These kids have waited long enough. C'mon, you two. Follow me."

"Listen, Danny," my mom said. "You can't just march in there like you own the place. They need permission first."

"Hold the phone, Marla. I think Renee would like to see her sister and cousin. And it's better to do it now. Before this labor deal turns into a scream-o-rama."

"Five minutes. Hear me?"

We followed my dad into Renee's room. She had two IVs running into her arm, and a screen above her head with zig-zag lines. I knew from *Ben Casey* that it was a heart monitor. Renee's face was even puffier than it had been when I last saw her Monday morning. She glanced at me but didn't smile until she looked up at Jerry Michael who was right behind me. Her smile even looked like it hurt.

"Hi," she said. "I'm in rough shape."

Jerry Michael leaned over and kissed her cheek. "You are going to be fine, dear cousin. This I know. And so will little Bobby or Kerry."

I grabbed hold of Renee's fingers and gave them a squeeze. "Watch out," I said, turning to Jerry Michael. "That sounded a lot like *Rosemary's Baby.*"

"What do you mean?" he asked.

"Rosemary always called the baby Andy or Jenny while she was pregnant."

"Oh, R.A. I'm so impressed. I do remember that," Jerry Michael said. "Don't worry, little Bobby or Kerry."

I chimed in with him. "We'll kill them before they can touch you."

"I don't appreciate the connection," Renee said.

Of course, Renee couldn't take a joke. She had to be critical, even when she was in labor. But I did feel sorry for her. She looked so weak and tired.

"Uh-oh," she said. "Here comes a contraction." My dad left the room.

Renee leaned on her elbows, pulled her legs up, and made a scrunched-up face that I could feel myself making. When I looked at Jerry Michael, he was making it too. She sounded like a whimpering puppy.

Jerry Michael looked at the ceiling. "If you were Rosemary, you'd say...never mind. Sorry"

Renee was squeezing my hand so hard, I thought she'd break my fingers. Then it stopped, and she let go.

"Enough, you two. No more Rosemary's Baby, understand?"

"This whole ordeal has been pure hell for you," Jerry Michael said.

"Oh damn it all, no Rosemary connection intended. Forget about hell. It's been a nightmare, how's that?"

My sister actually grinned and put her hands over her face. She didn't want to let on she was amused.

Jerry Michael placed his hand on her shoulder. "Just know it will all be over soon, and before you know it, you'll be onstage playing Titania or Regina or Nina."

Renee smiled and shook her head on the pillow. "You're such a character. You should be in Ann Arbor. You didn't need to come all the way here. Especially in a blizzard." Then she looked at me. "And you better straighten up and fly right. Our poor mother was out of her mind worrying about you. Don't pull another stunt like that. Oh, no. Here comes another one."

Just as she gripped the edges of the mattress, a nurse came in waving a thermometer around, and told us to leave. Jerry Michael blew Renee a kiss. I held up a hand and we walked out.

"Wow," I said. "No matter what's going on, she still has to ream me out."

"Don't give it a second thought," Jerry Michael said, draping his arm around my shoulder. "I've heard it said that women in labor will say all kinds of crazy things."

I gave him a shove. "That's baloney, and you know it. Like you would know anything at all about labor."

We walked into the waiting room, and somebody's arms were around me before I knew it. "There's my Ruthie. Safe and sound."

It was Trudy. She was wearing a powder blue coat, made of some kind of fur that, at first glance, looked like a robe. On her feet were rubber galoshes that I suspected belonged to Bruce.

"Trudy's here to pick you up," my mom said.

"Pick me up?"

"Yes," Trudy said. "You're coming to my house and I'll make you *kartoffelpuffers* and *weiner shnitzel*."

My head was spinning. I looked around for my dad, but he wasn't in the room. Jerry Michael was sitting on the vinyl couch with his mouth open and the best confused face I'd ever seen.

"But...wait," I sputtered. "I can't leave now."

"You are still in trouble, Missy," my mom said. "For your little escapade. I can't allow you to miss any more school. We'll call you at Trudy's after the baby's born. This could take all night."

My ears were so hot it felt like steam might come out of them. I looked at Jerry Michael who shrugged, then at Trudy who was lighting a cigarette, and then straight at my mom.

"I need to be here. I don't care about school. This is way too important and you can't make me leave. Don't worry, I'll make up the damn school work. You guys are always leaving me out of stuff. But I won't let you this time." I marched over to the vinyl couch and plopped down firmly next to Jerry Michael with my arms across my chest. The air in the cushion made a hissing sound just as my dad walked in.

"What the H is goin' on in here?"

Trudy turned toward my dad and then looked at my mom.

"This is my dear friend, Trudy," my mom said. "She's come to take Ruth Ann home, so she can get a decent night's rest and go to school tomorrow."

"There's no way I could sleep," I said. "I'm not going. I'm staying right here 'til Bobby or Kerry is born. And none of you can make me leave."

"For cryin' out loud, Marla. Let her stay if she wants to stay." He looked at Trudy. "Nice to meet you, Trudy. Ruth Ann thinks the world of you."

My dad knew the whole story about Trudy sneaking out of East Berlin, but I was glad he didn't let on. She smiled, and I could have kissed my dad for saying just the right thing. The last thing I wanted to do was hurt Trudy's feelings. I especially loved her for wanting to kick Bonnie's ass at the baby shower last Sunday that now seemed like a century ago.

"Listen here, Danny Bloomfield," my mom said. "Where do you get off acting fatherly? You've never had to make one decision concerning either one of my girls, so what makes you think you can start now?"

"*Your girls*? They're just as much my girls, for your information. And as far as decisions go, you're tryin' to make a bad one right now! That little girl wants to be by her sister, and I think that's damn sweet. If she wants to be here, she should be here." He put a cigar in the corner of his mouth and turned toward Trudy. "This is no offense to you, Trudy. It's nice as hell of you to offer to help. But why don't you just take off your pretty coat and keep us company."

By this time Jerry Michael had tucked his hands under his thighs and he looked like he wanted to run over and kiss my dad. I wasn't thrilled about him calling me a little girl, but I felt like kissing him too.

Trudy looked toward my mom who had turned her back. "Marla," she said. "What should I do? You want me to stay, to leave, to what?

My mom threw her hands up. "I don't know, Trudy. What do you want to do?" She rummaged in her purse for a cigarette. My dad walked over to her and lit it.

"I know!" Trudy exclaimed. "I'll go home and bring the *kartoffelpuffers* and *weiner shnitzel* up *here*. And I'll bring Bruce and even maybe Larry! The snowing is much better than it was before. What does everyone say? Okay?"

Chapter Thirty

I tucked the soft green blanket with tiny colored speckles around the baby and gently patted her back while she slept in the wicker bassinet from Aunt Maxine.

"Ruth Ann," my mom called to me as quietly as possible. "Maureen's here."

"Send her up," I called back. The baby stirred slightly and shuddered a sigh.

I could hear Maureen tip-toe up the steps and to the doorway of the green daisy room. She stood with her fuzzy mittens over her nose and mouth. "Oh, my God. She's so tiny."

"She's asleep," I said. "But you can see the side of her face."

Maureen moved toward the bassinet as if she was walking on hot coals. "Wow. One week old. I'm sure I've never seen a baby this young." She giggled. "She kind of looks like a loaf of bread in a basket."

"Touch her hair. It's like silk."

Maureen took off her mitten and ran her fingers across the baby's head. "You're right. It's so soft. Oh, Ruth Ann. Or I should say, Aunt Ruth Ann."

Our hug was the longest I'd ever had with a friend. When we finally stepped apart, there were tears shining in Maureen's eyes and I was blinking back my own.

"See," she said. "It turned out all right. Didn't it?"

"Well, yeah. Better than expected. That's for sure."

"I saw Renee talking on the phone before I came up," Maureen whispered. She looked back at the doorway. "Is she...any nicer?"

"She's really nice to the baby."

"Does she let you hold her and stuff?"

"Oh, yeah. Pretty much."

Maureen bent down to get a closer look at the baby. "Kerry, right?"

"Yup, which is after one of the Kennedys, and Ann, after me. Kerry Ann."

"Well, wadda ya know? There's hope for you and Renee, yet." She stretched her arms over her head. "So, ready to go? We're supposed to meet the girls at twelve."

"Just let me grab my shoes and coat."

We cut through the park and headed to Alger Heights. Mary Lou had called all the Tandem Riders to eat lunch and go shopping in Alger Heights. Part of me wondered if she was using it as an excuse to cross examine me about running away and all the stuff that led up to it. I decided to get it over with. My plan was to act as worldly as I felt. And it was good practice before going back to school.

"Thanks again," I said. "For bringing me all the homework."

"Did you get most of it done?"

"It was a ton of work."

"Well, yeah," Maureen said. "Two weeks worth."

"I've got a little more, but I think it'll be okay. I really felt better by Thursday, but we didn't want to take any chances."

"Oh, yeah. 'Cause of the baby, right?"

"Partly," I said. But also because people with psoriasis can get worse after strep throat."

"Did yours get worse?"

"It was already bad from not having all my ointment stuff when I took off."

"Promise me you won't do that again."

I smiled. "I had some badass adventures, Maur. I kept wishing you were with me."

"Like what?" She lit a Winston. "You haven't told me a damn thing!"

We walked slowly through the park, smoking and laughing as I filled Maureen in on Claudia's situation, Jerry Michael, Barry, Brigida, Vivian, and of course the birth of Kerry.

"So, you were at the hospital the whole time?"

"Yes, my mom wanted to send me off with her friend, Trudy, but I stuck to my guns and stayed."

"There is no doubt in my mind," Maureen said, "that this could be a book."

"Who knows? Maybe it will be someday."

It was just like old times eating at the Sundae Shoppe with Angela, Mary Lou, Irene, and even, Peg. When Peg told us what it was like going to the all-girls' school, it made Holy Rosary sound pretty good. Maureen winked at me as she squeezed ketchup onto the side of our fries. I knew she was relieved that none of them had brought up my running away. They asked all kinds of stuff about the baby, and I was completely okay with that.

Everybody scrambled to the juniors section at Mitchell's Young at Heart, but I hung out in the baby department, looking for a Christmas gift for Kerry Ann. I chose a Polly Flinders yellow dress with pink smocking. Mrs. Roshevsky smiled at me when I walked up to the counter with it. "I bet this is for one of the little ones you babysit for."

I was surprised at how excited I was to tell her it was for my new niece.

"Oh!' she said. "That's wonderful. *Mazel Tov*!" She leaned forward and whispered. "That's Jewish for congratulations."

"I know," I said. "My dad's Jewish."

"You don't say!" She studied me as she wrapped the dress in pink tissue paper. "What's your last name?"

"It's Bloomfield. But, he lives in Saginaw."

"Oh, I see."

I hated telling her I was from a broken home, but I'd always wanted to tell her that I was half Jewish because somebody had told me Mrs. Roshevsky was Jewish. I'd finally gotten the chance. And I was pretty sure *she* didn't think it was a *shanda*.

Chapter Thirty-One

Denise and I sat in a booth at Rax Roast Beef waiting for Katie and Franny to punch out. We'd been sipping our drinks for as long as we could, trying to avoid their boss's dirty looks.

"I sure am glad Claudia seemed okay to you," I said. "I've wanted to call her, but I'm terrified of her dad."

"Yeah, he's a doozy, all right," Denise said. "Sad thing is, she'll never get to leave the house again."

"Poor Michael. How are they ever gonna see each other?"

Denise shrugged.

Frannie and Katie walked toward us with their coats, and we headed around the corner to Hogan's basement.

We could hear the band playing outside the door. I stopped in my tracks, knowing that meant Andy would be there.

"Are you okay with this?" Denise asked. "You can change your mind."

"No, it's all right," I said. "I gotta face the music sometime."

"Ha ha," Katie said. "Seriously, though. He's my brother's closest buddy. You better be nice to him."

"What's that supposed to mean?" Frannie said. "You want her to drag him behind the furnace and have her way with him?"

We all burst out laughing before Katie pushed the door open, and the guys stopped playing when we walked down the stairs. Andy's hair shimmered in the light. He blew it off his forehead and avoided looking at me.

"Okay, guys," Dennis Hogan said. "Let's take five."

I watched Andy set his guitar down and light an Old Gold. I could tell he was nervous. Michael was sitting on the floor in the corner, smoking and thumbing through a music magazine. I sat in front of him and he looked up.

"Hey, stranger," he said. "Wow. It's good to see you."

"Good to see you too. How's Claudia?"

"What can I say? She's okay, I guess. She'll be happy to see you. You'll be in school on Monday, right?"

"Yes, unfortunately," I said. "I didn't come last week 'cause I was sick. I hope she's not pissed that I took off and went to my cousin's. Everything was so last-minute. We didn't even know we were running away until we got on the bus. When I heard her dad was coming in the morning, I decided to go to my cousin's. I just wasn't ready to go home yet."

I wondered if Michael knew anything about Claudia's dad hitting her and wasn't sure if I should mention it. There was an awkward moment before I noticed he was looking up. I turned around and saw Andy standing behind me. "Hi, Andy," I said.

He squatted down. "Hi. You feel like taking a walk?"

"Um, okay. Sure."

I turned around as I followed him up the stairs and shrugged to Denise who was staring at me as we went out the door.

He lit another Old Gold. "Hey, I hear there's a new addition at your house."

"That's right," I said. "I have a new niece. Kerry Ann."

"So you're Aunt Ruth Ann. That's pretty cool."

"It is, really. I wasn't sure I'd like it. But I do."

"So, It's good to see you. I still can't believe you took off."

"Yeah, it was kind of crazy. But I'm kind of glad it happened and I'm kind of glad I'm back."

We walked for half a block without talking. His chin was tucked inside his coat and his hands were deep in his pockets. I was relieved that he didn't ask for details or bring up Tom or anything that happened before I left.

"I wrote a song about you," he said.

"About me?"

"Yeah. How 'bout we go to my house and I'll play it for you?"

I wrapped my scarf around my neck. "Right now?"

"Why not?"

"Denise's brother, George is giving me a ride home at ten-thirty, and don't you live in East Grand Rapids?"

"It's only about nine blocks from here. Besides, it's not even eight o'clock. I'll get you back to Hogan's in plenty of time."

When I hesitated, he said, "Don't worry, you won't have to meet my parents. They're in Chicago for the weekend. And my sister's down at

Michael's house, hanging out with his sister, Anna Banana."

The air was crisp, but there wasn't any wind, so I decided a walk might be good.

"Well, okay. I guess there's time."

"That's cool. Hey, did you hear about the SoulBenders?"

"No, what?"

"They changed their name to the Phlegathon and they're playin' somewhere next weekend. You wanna go?"

"Probably, yeah."

I thought about seeing Tom last summer when the SoulBenders played at the park and I got a funny twinge in my stomach that lasted for two and a half blocks.

The kitchen light was already on when we came through the back door of Andy's house. It shined into the other rooms that Andy said we should keep dark in case the neighbors were watching. Even in the dark, I could tell their furniture and carpeting were expensive.

"This is really nice," I said. "Are Beaver and Wally gonna show up?"

Andy did his usual snorty laugh which made me remember I mostly liked him for being funny, like my dad. "What's that supposed to mean?"

"It's a compliment," I said. "I feel like I'm at the Cleavers'."

"Okay, you should know. You and your Beaver re-runs. Have a seat while I get my guitar."

I sank into a cushy sofa in front of a huge window. An afghan as soft as baby Kerry's blanket, was draped over the back. I couldn't tell what

362

any of the colors were in the room since it was only lit by the lights from outside and the moon.

Andy came back with a guitar and a package and sat down next to me.

"So," I said, "I guess you have two guitars since you left one at Hogan's basement."

"Well, yeah. I left my electric over there. This is my acoustic."

"I know it's acoustic."

"That's right. You said you took lessons. You should play *me* a song."

"That's okay. All I really learned was *When Irish Eyes Are Smiling*, for my mom's birthday. You play your song."

Just as he began strumming, we heard a key in the back door.

"Oh, shit," Andy said. "Must be my sister. Quick, jump back here. She'll tell my parents for sure."

We both leaped over the sofa and lay down on the floor. His sister began setting things down in the kitchen, opening the refrigerator, drawers and cupboards. She turned a radio on and started singing along to the song, *Time Has Come Today*. I thought back to the summer when Maureen and I had listened to the song on my dad's boat, trying to figure out what it meant. It made a little more sense to me now because I felt so much older. It was about the world needing to change and how we're responsible for the changes.

Lying there in the dark, I realized I wanted to be responsible. I wanted to know other people who wanted things to change. Bad stuff would just keep happening if we did nothing. Denise had told me that Frannie's mom was going to college, to protests, peace marches, and that she was really cool. Maybe there'd be time to ask Frannie about that when I got back to Hogan's.

The phone rang during a commercial for Burger Chef. Andy's sister turned off the radio and answered. "Okay, I'll be there in five minutes."

Andy swiped his forehead with the back of his hand to show relief. I stifled a giggle. He leaned over and brushed his lips with mine. Even though I wasn't sure where our relationship was going or even if I wanted one, the kiss felt nice. He tucked my hair behind my ear and kissed me again. The back door slammed. We peeked out the window and watched his sister walk down the street.

"Back to Anna's, huh?"

"Yeah, it's just three doors down from here. I guess their food wasn't good enough, so she came back here to eat. We do have some kick-ass ice cream if you want any. Now, where were we?"

He kissed me again, this time with his tongue. "Whoa, steady, Bullet," he said, and I couldn't help but snicker. When he slid his hand under the back of my sweater, and tried to unhook my bra, I broke off the kiss and pulled back before he succeeded.

"Sorry," he said. "I wasn't sure..."

"It's not you, Andy. It's me." I paused and looked out the window. "I'm feeling kind of weird about a whole bunch of stuff. I can't really explain it. Even to myself."

"Hey, don't worry about it," he said. "I get it. You've been through all kinds of shit lately. These things take time. I can wait 'til next weekend."

I smiled. "Weren't you gonna play me a song?"

"Oh, yeah."

He reached over the back of the couch and got his guitar. The cozy spot on the floor, in front of the window made me feel like a little kid. Way before I even wore a bra, much less had a boy fooling with it.

The song was slow in some places, then it would get very fast, and slow down again. He ended the song by placing his hand over the strings and looking up at me. "It's called *Ruth Ann: A Mystery*," he said.

"Hmm. So, I'm a mystery, huh? Okay, Ned."

"Ned? Did you call me *Ned*?"

"Nancy Drew's boyfriend. No, seriously, it's a good song, and especially the way you play it. You're so damn good. But, I guess I kinda thought there'd be lyrics."

"Really? Do you think it needs them?"

"Jeepers, Wally. It's really swell."

"You really mean it, Beaver? Gee, thanks."

What could I say? I didn't have the faintest idea why that song was about me. And as much as I liked Andy, I couldn't help but feel guilty for not liking him as much as he deserved. I felt like he needed a different girlfriend. Somebody way less complicated than me. Maybe he knew that already. *Ruth Ann: A Mystery.* The title of the song probably made sense, anyway.

And if it had words, he wouldn't be able to use it again. I'd heard that

Joanne Smitter had a giant crush on him. Maybe after me, it would be *Joanne: A Mystery.* Or better yet, *Joanne: Devoted to me.*

Denise was really understanding about my taking off from Hogan's basement and I knew it was partly because she hoped I was all patched up with Andy.

"So," she said in the back seat on the ride home. "Are you guys back together?"

"Gee, I don't know, Denise. He's a sweetheart, but I'm kind of a mixed-up mess."

"Oh, cut it out. What's in that bag?"

"He gave me an early Christmas present. It's *The Beatles White Album.*"

"No shit? Wow, a double album! That is so cool, Ruth Ann. He loves your ass. There is no doubt in my mind. You know that, right?"

"I don't know what I know, Denise."

We pulled up to my house and I thanked Denise's brother and his girlfriend and told them my mom would be forever indebted for not having to go out.

When I came in the front door, my mom, Renee, Larry, Bruce, and Trudy were all playing cards around the dining room table.

"Ruthie's home," Trudy shouted.

"Shh...the baby's sleeping," the rest of them said at the same time.

Trudy clamped her hand over her mouth. "Sorry, I can't be used to it yet."

I walked into the kitchen for a snack and noticed a plate of anise cookies on the counter. I grabbed one and stuck my head in the dining room. "Where'd these come from?"

"Cathy was here," my mom said. "She was hoping to see you but ended up rocking the baby to sleep for Renee."

Oh boy, I thought. How would I ever explain running away to her? I decided right then and there that I'd avoid her for the rest of my life.

I said goodnight and started for the stairs.

"Oh, I almost forgot," my mom said. "A package came for you. It's up on your bed."

Ruff and Reddy were sleeping together right in the middle of my bed and Ruff's butt was on the brown paper package. Even though I slid it out carefully, he turned around and meowed at me. I tore the end open and a book fell out. *Howl* by Allen Ginsberg. I opened the front cover and read the inscription.

Dear R. A.,

You may think at times that you're a "wild orphan," and I'm sure you'll continue to have "complexities of memories," but I want you to know that I loved having the "unexpected youthful stranger" at my door. Just remember you are anything but a stranger and you will always, always, always be welcome at our door. Much love, Jerry Michael and Barry

No Doubt in my Mind

P.S. We must see Rosemary's Baby together SOON !

I tucked the book under my pillow and turned on the radio. The song, *Love Is All Around,* was playing. I sat in front of the dressing table, looking in the mirror and singing along. A burst of laughter from downstairs made me smile. This had been a good day and an even better night. My cousin and his most likely boyfriend cared enough about me to send a cool as hell gift and a sweet note. The song was saying there are no beginnings. It also said there are no endings. After a pretty rotten year, I was ready for January, and to be fifteen. New beginnings, maybe. More endings, for sure. I switched off the radio because I heard Kerry Ann crying in the green daisy room. I walked down the hall and picked her up. She snuggled on my shoulder in the fuzzy green blanket and I bounced her a little bit. I heard my mom ask Renee if she should get the baby. I came down the stairs and when I got to the bottom everyone was looking at me from around the table.

Renee stood. "I can take her."

"I'm okay. I've got her."

"Oh. You want to give her a bottle?"

"Sure. We'll be over in the rocking chair."

The moon was shining on the baby's face as I rocked her. Renee smiled when she handed me the bottle. There was no doubt in my mind. This was a new beginning.

Author's Note

Once again, this book wouldn't exist without my daughter, Camille Shotwell Brown. She has my sensibilities, but I don't have her skills. I am so grateful that we make a magical team and continue to be kindred spirits in every way. Thanks to Chris Byron for all she has done to support me through the years, and in all her promotion of both books. Thanks to both Chris and Melissa Fox for helping to create the wonderful program for "Gone Before Spring" at the Grand Rapids Public Library. A special thanks to the library staff for all their support and promotion as well. Thanks to my husband, Gregg Shotwell for his Sherlock Holmes proofreading and ultra-sensitivity for the character Ruth Ann. Thanks to West Michigan Writers Workshop for seven years of learning how to be a better writer, week in and week out and for encouraging me to write this sequel. A special thanks to Nathan TerMolen for his insightful, magical suggestion that set the entire book on its course. Thanks to the workers at The Psoriasis and Eczema Treatment Center for allowing me to advertise my book in their facility, and to Dr. Marek Stawiski for his support. Thanks to Maureen Barringer and Teresa Thome for reading my first draft and for their support and enthusiasm. Thanks to Maureen, Mimi, Cathy, Denise, Vivian, and my sister Karen who were loosely depicted as themselves in this book. And especially to those who are in the book but no longer with us, my mother, father, and cousin, Jerry Michael. To all my readers, it is an honor beyond belief that you've read either or both books and I am filled with gratitude and wonder.

About the Author

 Sheila Solomon Shotwell is a writer and also an actor who has performed in children's television, commercials, on stage, and an improv troupe. Her favorite role was Mona in *Come Back to The Five and Dime, Jimmy Dean, Jimmy Dean*. She has worked in Jewish education as a religious school director and Bar/Bat Mitzvah tutor. She has also been a nursing assistant, bookseller, reading specialist, and outreach presenter for the Grand Rapids Children's Museum. She created Zip Zap Improv which was a program to teach kids life skills through theater games. She has been published in Lilith Magazine, Jewish Currents, Zeek, Advance, Display, Voices, and BUST. Her passions are music, particularly blues, reading, antiques and vintage clothes. She has five grandchildren and lives with her husband, Gregg, in Grand Rapids, Michigan. They also consider Clarksdale, Mississippi their second home. Her first novel was *Gone Before Spring*.

www.ingramcontent.com/pod-product-compliance
Lightning Source LLC
Chambersburg PA
CBHW051113120726
47905CB00005B/1255